ISBN: 979-8-9907413-2-4

Dedication

To my family, friends, and now fans, your support has been amazing. I love you all.

For this book, I wanted to give special thanks to and dedicate this book to my uncles. Their strength of character, love for our family, and their sense of humor, helped shape me into the man I am today.

To my Uncle Frank, you shall always be like a second father to me, always there whenever I needed you. Thank you for being there when my father could not. Your dedication to our family has always been an inspiration to me.

To my Uncle Larry, you pushed me to be my own man, you are greatly missed.

To my Uncle Jim, your commitment to family, many amazing stories, and sense of humor have been both great reminders of where we come from and the importance of doing the right thing. yet making sure you're laughing along the way while you do it.

Contents

Chapter 1 – Creation Points

So, my journey begins as pretty much all isekai stories do, I was pulled into another world, another dimension/reality, all the above. Apparently, my travel to another reality/dimension caused me to go through the space between all realities. This space is known as the Sea of Chaos. It contains or connects to everything that is or could be. Perhaps more the potential of those things, I had a significant amount of potential to absorb. At least that is how my guide described it. Sure, he went into a bunch of stuff about gifts from God, bloodlines, a unique connection to Omni-Magic and Creation. There was some talk about the Dark making a claim, I'm sure what he said was important, oh well. That part is all a bit fuzzy; I wasn't completely paying attention. Hey, you would be distracted too if you just ended up in another world. I'm still learning what this all means.

I mean I am literally in another world! My previous life is over! Now what? That is where my thoughts were so I kind of missed the introduction by my guide but I figure I am a quick learner so I will sort it all out one way or another.

Anyway, one thing my guide made a point to emphasize is that I will have a habit of not adhering to the exact laws of this new world. In other words, I should be mindful to understand this reality's natural laws which for me are more "guidelines". Oh, and this world is more like an anime from my world, as long as I don't get any stupid nose bleeds for no reason it should be fun. I always wanted to journey to other realities so why not here. As part of my journey to this world I gained these creation points, not exactly sure what they are, other than they grant me the ability to give myself features and powers. Apparently, I ended up with 39,000 points, 13,000 points for Mind, 13,000 points for Body, and 13,000 for Spirit which blew my guide away.

"There is power in that Trinity, every traveler gaining a certain amount for each area. That is orders of magnitude greater than any other traveler I have ever heard of. The total is what you should concern yourself with as you can technically use those points wherever you choose, 'guidelines' remember."

Shaking his head he continues, “In fact most powerful travelers maybe end up with 100 to 200 points maximum. Yet here you stand having absorbed so much. I’m surprised you did not explode.”

“EXPLODE?!”

‘Way to bury the punch line, so note to self, no traveling across the ‘Sea’ until I get a better handle on this stuff.’

“Give me a moment. After, I will discuss the Dark’s claim and explain your situation.”

I have to give it to my guide, after he got over his shock, he helped me understand the options and showed me a cool RPG or role-playing game like interface. My guide was adamant I use most of my points before stepping through the final threshold to this world. According to him most points are used on someone’s base ability stats and maybe one or two Magic types or unique skills. With so many points he did not want me leaving until I decided what to spend them on, or as gamers like to call it finish my build.

I had a lot of options I could use these creation points on and at first it was a bit overwhelming, but I eventually got the hang of it. The options reminded me of a lot of D&D and other types of RPG character building and broke down into the following groupings (perhaps my familiarity with RPGs is why they broke down this way, who knows, moving on. The following menu options were available:

Base Ability Stat Points (Strength, Intelligence, Wisdom, etc.)
Secondary Stats (Defense, Flexibility, Senses, Luck, etc.)
Knowledge & Special Abilities
Powers & Magic
Skills, Proficiencies, & Languages

Each one had a bare-bones definition or descriptor:

-**Base Ability Stat Points** (Strength, Dexterity, Constitution, Intelligence, Wisdom, Charisma are your general foundation that defines how easily you can perform various actions)
-**Secondary Stats** (Defense, Flexibility, Luck, Intuition, Creativity are focused more on specific reactions and how those actions interact with the larger world)

-**Knowledge & Special Abilities** (Unique abilities or knowledge that give bonuses towards certain actions or negate the requirements of other interactions)
-**Powers & Magic** (Grants access and/or mastery over a superpower or Magic type)
-**Skills, Proficiencies, & Languages** (Gain knowledge and mastery over tools, musical instruments, professions, etc.)

Well to start, I focused on my body and mind attributes. I brought each Base Ability Stat to 2,197 (13x13x13), did I not mention I kept seeing 13 everywhere for some reason. This system had 13 ranks which I thought was odd. It was like this place had a strong connection with the number 13, like super strong connection, but I digressed. After that I brought each of the Secondary stats to Rank 13 and a few a bit higher. It was always a good idea to invest in yourself. With my base and secondary stats taken care of I decided it was time to focus on the other options like magic!

Where I spent most of my time was going through all the possible special abilities, powers, and magics. This was where the spirit part of the trinity comes in. One's spirit fueled magic and powers in this world. Some spirit signatures were attuned or had specific affinities. Having vast potential meant max affinity across the board, which meant I could choose from any of the powers, nothing was greyed out to me. My inner gamer and love for magic translated into a bit of a shopping spree with these creation points.

What was most fascinating about powers and magics was some powers gave me inherent access to a spell without having to cast or memorize that spell. The best way I could describe it was like the difference between a sorcerer who has the power within them vs. a wizard that has to study and practice the spell in order to master it or commit it to memory. This meant I could gain all sorts of spells, instantly know them, and cast them without all the crazy chanting or outside requirements, effectively giving a magic noob a max level spell or my favorite, Fireball (it was the first one I picked just so I could say "I cast fireball").

I will say the Magic and powers section was pretty interesting. First off, according to my guide, certain Magic types were normally restricted or not available to people regardless of what they wanted but my experience was far different. Everything you could possibly imagine was open for selection, it was a bit overwhelming as I said but what really fascinated me was the system itself. If you wanted a particular spell or power, you had to first unlock that type or school but what was most interesting was how vast or narrow those options were. You could gain a pyromancer type of Magic or gain an elemental mastery type which of course Fire Magic was a part of.

The way my guide explained it to me was "Most people do not have unlimited affinities or an intuitive understanding of the universe to be able to grasp larger concepts that would grant them such options. Again, the laws are truly guidelines for one such as you."

Each of these types were also not created equal when it came to creation points. I first had to decide how much I wanted to invest into that school or area of magical expertise and understanding, the amount invested would help you have innate mastery of that type of magic. How much you invested would help unlock greater knowledge or more options of the spells available to learn.

Then I had to invest points in specific spells I wanted to know like the back of my hand.

What a weird saying, I mean how often do you really study the back of your hand? Anyway, I digressed, where was I? Oh yes, Magic!

The theory was the more I invested in overall mastery, the more I'd be able to later learn new spells of that school or create my own spells of that Magic type. If I was starting a new life where magic existed, I was going to learn everything I could about magic! Of course, instead of pyromancy, I took Elemental Mastery because of "Fireball!" But also, who doesn't want to sling Lightning bolts around like Zeus or Thor?!

As I was using creation points got me curious about creation itself, so when I saw that option, I also took Creation Magic. When I told my guide I took this magic, I thought his eyes were literally going to pop out of his head, apparently that type of Magic is reserved for, well let's just say its super restrictive. Though that wasn't at the top of the Magic types I invested the most in. I put most of my investment in Purity and Omni-Magic as apparently it lets you do all the types of magic but also lets you disrupt or transform Magic into whatever you want, you know the whole energy is not destroyed only transformed into another state, see I paid attention in physics class. Literally my guide fell over and had to take several dazed moments to collect himself. His only words being, "You will be unstoppable if you use that right. Could it be that there is more going on than even I am aware? God really does work in mysterious ways!"

Lastly, I spent a good amount of time acquiring various skills, techniques related to professions, random knowledge about the world and its people, and of course languages. This knowledge would round out both my body and mind capabilities. I had no idea what I was going to do when I got to this world but make no mistake I wanted to be prepared for as many situations as I could. Plus, I always enjoy crafting, it seems wrong if I didn't use some creation points to help me create future masterpieces. Combined with the purchase of knowledge of the various cultures and languages I might encounter; I was starting to feel as prepared as one could possibly be. You know the saying the battle is won or lost based on how much you prepare, and I was going to use these creation points to their maximum efficiency.

After consecutively shocking my guide from one unbelievable thing, after the next I decided to keep the rest to myself and just fell inward, searched, and selected what else I felt made the most sense. When I was done, I had spent almost all my creation points and told my guide I was ready to go.

"Excellent! Now that that is over, you should review your results before we get into picking your new life. You can pull up your Status sheet my thinking the word 'status'. In truth, you could associate any mental command, it is all about intent." My guide instructed.

I was just about to do just as instructed when my guide interrupted me. "Ah, one more very important thing. Not everyone sees the same thing when they open their status screen."

"Huh? What do you mean? How does that work?" I asked in confusion.

"It is simple. Everyone understands the universe in their own way. Your status screen is a combination of your understanding of the universe and a summary of what you want to see. I recommend when you get more familiar with the process you experiment with different ways to show your stats and summarize your information." My guide explained.

'That is a lot to take in. So, in other words, as I start to gain knowledge and learn more about myself, I can choose to see that reflected in my status screen, interesting. OK, well enough of all that deep self-analysis, let's give this a shot. Status!' I thought. Sure enough, just as my guide instructed a semi-transparent Status window popped up in my view.

Name: James Drake		Race: Dragon		Form: Human	
Stats					
Health Pool:	28,561	Mana Pool:	57,122	Stamina:	28,561
Health Regen.	1,300	Mana Regen.	13,000	Stam. Regen.	1,300
Strength:	2,197	Dexterity:	2,197	Constitution:	2,197
Intelligence:	2,197	Wisdom:	2,197	Charisma:	2,197
Abilities					
Proficiencies & Techniques (# of):			Magic & Powers (# of):		
Armor Types:		4	Magic Affinities		19
Weapons		13	Spells Known		128
Combat Mastery & Techniques		23	Spellcasting Modifications		5
Skills		48	Resiliencies & Immunities		24
Tools		36	Heightened Senses		6
Languages		34	Powers & Abilities		16

Ok there is being OP and then there is me! When I was picking everything, I did not realize how much everything added up. I mean now that I look at it from a summary level, this is the most ridiculous...wait, scratch that, redonkulous character sheet I have ever seen! No wonder this guide is so interested in me.

After that eye opener, I'm going to have to be cautious about learning how to tap into and self-regulate my power. With that consideration in mind, it was time to decide how I would start my new life.

Chapter 2 – Starting A New Life

My guide told me I had a few choices to choose from on where I could be placed. My options were as followed:
-Reborn as a child in a noble family
-Take over the body of someone who recently died at the exact point of death
-Lastly, Literary be dropped off in the woods, close enough to a settlement, and I could figure out a way from there.

Man, who would want to be dropped off in the middle of the woods to fend for themselves. Why would anyone choose that option. Though in all honesty the other options weren't that great either. I had zero interest going through puberty again, so the first option was out. I had invested a significant amount of points to dramatically increase my energy pool and both my health and energy regeneration rates so the idea of inhabiting someone else's body didn't appeal to me either. Plus, I added some cool dragon race aspects and other alterations to my body to make my form in top shape and arguably I looked much younger in appearance due to the overall health benefits I selected. One of the rules of life is to be yourself, unless you can be a dragon, then be a dragon! So, inhabiting someone else's body seemed like a really bad idea and a waste of creation points. Not really a fan of any of these options. Maybe I can negotiate a 4th option.

"Any chance I could go with a hybrid option?"

"I thought you might never ask!"

I groaned, "That doesn't sound good."

"Quite the contrary. Let me explain..."

After listening to my guide's proposal, I had much to think about. I was told about a prince that was sent away from the royal family due to failing health issues as a baby. A secret prophecy about their son only shared with the king and queen. The prophecy stated should the king and queen send their only son to this hidden valley isolated from everyone, that on his naming day he shall return stronger than ever and lead the kingdom into a golden age. So, with heavy hearts the king and queen sent their baby to an isolated estate in a hidden valley. The baby was to be cared for by their two most trusted servants, a husband-and-wife adventurer team who would give the child the parental love the king and queen could not.

The climate was mild in the small valley but the weather along the one pass to get out of the valley was very harsh and well hidden, as such left the valley tucked away completely isolated. Being the first born he should have a right to the throne, but the royal family was told the child must remain in complete isolation and only if he managed to survive to his naming day would the risk be averted, and the prophecy could be fulfilled. The loyal adventurer duo left in the darkness of night with the royal family's first-born son. They avoided all towns and people to ensure no one but the king, queen, and a handful of trusted allies knew the location of this isolated valley on the edge of their kingdom.

Sadly, the boy would not survive to see his naming day, as of this moment he was breathing his last breaths. Even more tragic, the husband-and-wife caretakers had just passed away, dying of old age. This did, however, also mean I can assume the prince's identity without having to take over his frail body and no one would be the wiser. I was skeptical but there was something about the story that touched me down to my core. These parents lost everything; they may not be my family, but I could honor their sacrifice.

The two servants sent to watch over the child were towards the end of their lives and died recently of old age. The frail prince was about to pass on as well. Leaving me the opportunity to not just step into the role as the prince but to honor these people. I spent some additional points to gain the knowledge of the prince and the sweet old couple who gave a child who was not their own a loving home. One, I figured the information would be useful but more importantly I felt like such honorable people should be remembered. I also spent some points on gaining the history of the kingdom and knowledge of the current geo-political information of the surrounding area.

What I learned made me giddy, the kingdom did not just have humans but also elves, dwarves, beast-kin, and a few other races! An honest to God fantasy-anime world! Most importantly I learned my soon-to-be family was respected and well regarded as an honorable family. The family had a history of treating all with respect and caring for all their citizens. Now that was a family, I could be proud to join. That was saying something because I loved the family I came from; they taught me so much that helped mold me into the man I am today. That will be the hardest of living in a new world, missing my loved ones. Perhaps, after I have mastered this world and my powers, I can eventually travel back to see them.

Well, that's enough time spent on things I can't change right now. Best to put my focus on where it will do the most good, on the path forward. Which brings me to another odd fact I learned, in my youthful form I looked uncanny like a younger version of the king. In fact, when I brought it up to my guide, he just had this big grin on his face. Like he knew I'd go for this option. It made me feel like I was being played in some way or some strings of fate were being pulled that I did not yet understand.

Now that I knew the family resemblance was so clear I better understood why my guide was adamant I would fit in. As I wasn't one that would delay once I made up my mind, I figured it was time to get a move on, I would learn nothing more here. I bid my guide a fond farewell and stepped through the portal to start my new life.

Guide's perspective

The guide watched his special charge step through the portal to start his new life. What he could not tell him was he knew why he had so many creation points and just how special he was. Hopefully it would be enough to overcome the difficulty that would arise from the change coming to that world. The Dark would claim that world.

"Perhaps he is the one that can shift the balance."

The guide had followed orders and seen to the delivery of that prophecy to that kingdom. They did not know all of what it fully meant but mortals rarely could comprehend such things. Free Will was important tenant to protect and it would be up to this unique man to choose.

"Yes, God truly works in mysterious ways."

Neither the Dark nor the Light could truly force anyone. As long as no one attempted to override Free Will, the other side could not act. Choice is what it will come down to, each side banking on what they believed was human nature to do their will.

"He is smart as he suspected that this path was already set for him. Be yourself, it is the only way to survive boy."

He was the first to spring forth. The Dark gets first shot at him. A man with royal blood and has been given great power and authority; such things have led to even greater corruption in the past. The Dark is betting on his fall, it is only a matter of time.

"He is now set on a path, but he will not be the last. Change is coming, prophecies will be fulfilled. Now to attend to the other matters."

James' Perspective

What felt like waking up from a dream, I found myself laying down on the floor. After standing up I realized I was in the prince's room, well I guess my room now. Luckily my guide said the prince's body would be completely vaporized leaving no trace of another person here. It makes a man wonder why the prince's body would be vaporized, what kind of illness would do such a thing. Things were not adding up and there was clearly more going on here than I was being told.

My attention might have been hijacked the moment I saw my reflection. I checked myself out in the giant mirror in the room, damn I am ripped! My oh my, investing creation points in one's body has its benefits. I also noticed my eye color had changed. My left eye had a purple iris, and my right eye had a green iris, it looked pretty cool if I do say so myself. I may have spent longer than normal admiring myself and how invigorated I felt.

After a moment of self-admiration, I decided no time like the present to get started in this new life. I turned around from the giant mirror and left the room, or at least I attempted to leave the room. One small problem... as I grabbed the door to open it, I happened to squeeze the door handle and rip the door off its hinges!

"Whoops! Guess I have to get used to my new stats. They really don't warn you about needing to moderate the amount of pressure you use when one's strength is off the charts. This will be interesting."

Putting the door back as best I could, I decided to explore the rest of this cottage home. Having learned my lesson with my door, I carefully applied the smallest amount of pressure as I opened each door I came across. I found the sweet old couple in their bed when I peered into the only other bedroom. They had died in their sleep holding hands, with the knowledge I possessed about their lives I knew it was a true blessing they both passed in their sleep together. I do not think either could have survived long after losing their other half. Finding such a lasting love was something to be treasured and remembered.

Using a reverse gravity spell, I lifted both their bodies in the air and wrapped them in their fine white sheets. I would find a place to bury them after I found the right place to do so. Bringing the bodies outside I placed them on the only cart I saw available at the estate. It was at that moment I turned and saw the rest of the valley.

The estate sat on a small plateau that allowed you to see across the whole valley as well as the pass leading out of the valley. It was breathtaking, the way the sun shined down on the small valley, the well-maintained garden on the side of the estate, the rolling hills with cattle, and a small forest of trees along one side. Truly a peaceful place to retire in, which in a way John and Susan (the old couple that passed) had been able to do, retire here in peace with their adoptive grandson.

It was at that moment I decided these two deserved to be buried here in this valley. After making that decision I found a nice plot of land not too far from the garden to bury them. I used Earth magic to move the ground and create a shared grave for the honored couple. I stood over the grave and said a silent prayer that they would finally be at peace.

Their spirits were long gone but after I buried them, I felt a light sense of peace. I realized this feeling was coming from a combination of my abilities with soul magic and a sixth-sense sensitivity to their spirits. This awareness let me know they let go of the small tether connecting their souls to their bodies. As they were moving on, they conveyed their appreciation of my sentiment.

With that done I returned to the house. The knowledge from the prince and old couple let me know exactly where everything was in the house. I planned to use that information to gather the items I wanted to take with me. From the memories I gained, John had been informed via raven that the king and queen dispatched the captain of the royal knights and a contingent of soldiers to escort the prince home to the capital. They were to arrive the day after the prince's birthday marking an end to his imposed exile. To my understanding that would place their arrival three days from now. Plenty of time to get a lay of the land, practice my powers and start an exercise routine.

First things first, I created some water in a bucket inside the estate, checked out the garden and the stored food in the cellar. Putting my new cooking skills to the test I prepared a gourmet meal of seasoned beef and vegetables paired with a nice wine that the couple had been saving for when the prince came of age.

"Hey, I am of age." I told myself. Seeing how I was the prince now I felt it was appropriate.

"Time to celebrate my new life!" I exclaimed as I took another bite of the rather amazing meal I prepared. I mean man this is delicious!

"Worth every point spent learning culinary arts skills!"

After my meal, I went outside for a combination of physical training and magic practice. The first thing I realized was how different I felt! Most of my life I had been pretty active but towards the last few years of constant lockdown and minimal activity I had the start of a dad bod. Feeling the rush of the wind on my face as I ran at speeds, I didn't even know was humanly possible was exhilarating! Then I realized something even cooler, I could fly!!!

I mean come on, of course flight was one of the first abilities I spent my creation points on. Taking to the skies was like a childhood dream fulfilled. Talk about sense of freedom, not to mention the view. I flew high enough to see beyond the valley and mountains. I could see the treacherous pass with its high winds and what seemed to be eternally cold weather. A forest butted up against the mountains on the other side. There wasn't another town for miles, and I can see why no one would even bother messing with these mountains based on how steep and unforgiving they looked. No wonder this valley remained so secluded.

Sightseeing over with I returned to the estate and decided to peruse both the library and my room. It was clear based on the state of my room how much the prince loved to read; never mind I already knew that from his memories. He read all sorts of subjects from magical theory to history, legends, and adventure stories. Not being able to go anywhere and trapped in one place can give one a bit of wanderlust or at least a growing interest in adventure.

I continued to get an understanding of the various books in the library. The selection was impressive, it was clear the king and queen wanted their son to be well informed and learn as much as he could. This works for me as many of the books were about magic which I can use to explain my proficiency in magical arts. I also found a map of the continent, which helped me wrap my head around the new world I lived in.

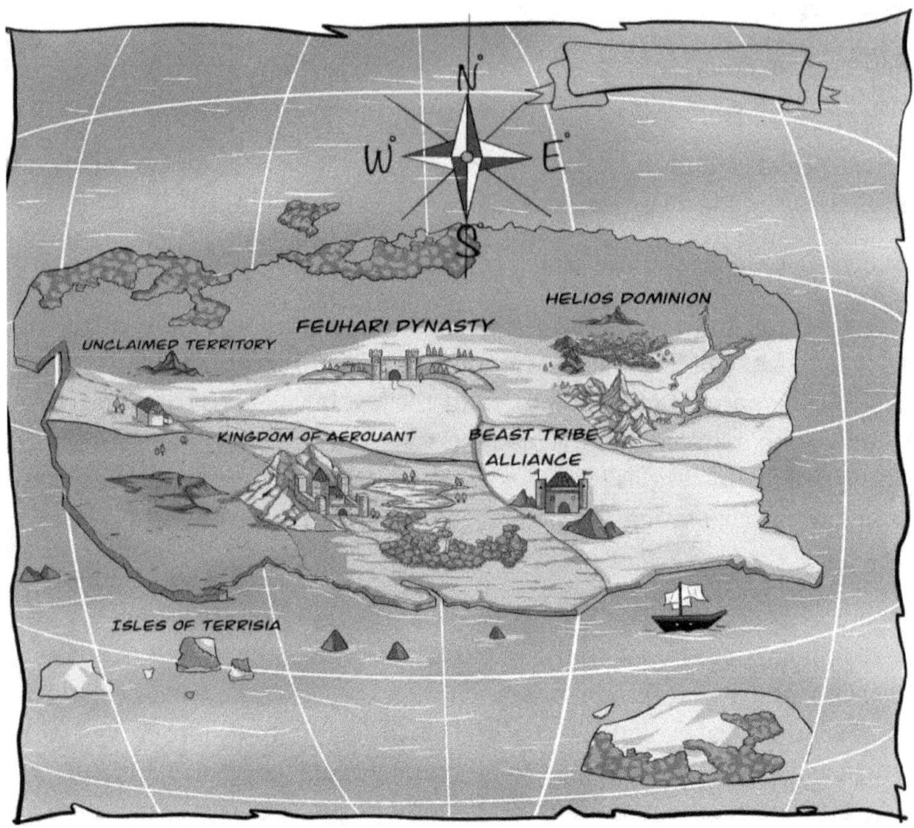

Over the next few days, I fell into a routine. I would cook, train/exercise, practice my magic, and then read, explore the valley while performing a combination of attack moves and spells, and at the end of the day read some more. I found with my increased mental and physical stats I not only recovered extremely quickly but also found it easy to speed read through the books. My eidetic memory allowed me to fully retain the knowledge and compare the information to what I already knew at record speeds. The three days passed by in the blink of an eye.

Today was supposed to be the day after my naming day. In this world, a person's naming day was society's acknowledgement of adulthood. It was at this point in their life that one could decide what they wanted to do with their life or name the direction their life would take. Some entered an academy, or joined a guild, or started an apprenticeship to learn a trade. It was at this point they could no longer blame their parents for the choices they made.

From my knowledge of the royal family, it was tradition to enroll at the Royal Academy. At the academy a person could learn magic, combat, and/or a wide range of curriculum from governance and economics to farming. It was all up to one's aptitude and interest. I was beginning to get excited about truly starting my new life. Time to see where these escorts are.

I decided to use a beast-bonding spell I learned with creation points. This spell allowed me to form a connection with several birds that could act as my eyes and ears. I set up a few sentry birds on patrol who kept an eye on both the forest on the other side of the mountain pass as well as the pass itself. It came in handy being able to see what they saw.

"Very convenient indeed! Man, I love Magic!" I couldn't help but say as I looked through each of their eyes. It was like watching multiple split screens on a tv. At first it was disorienting until I realized I could let the knowledge wash over me and my new avian friends would ping me if they caught something of interest. Obviously because of this, it was no surprise when I saw the knights and soldiers approaching well in advance. What did surprise me, however, was how many people there were. My birds spied several armored men on horseback and on foot marching, some with swords, some that looked like archers. The entourage seemed to be escorting a fancy passenger carriage.

"I'm guessing that's for me. Man, that thing is gaudy!" I commented to myself.

Towards the back of the knights and marching soldiers my birds also detected a few horse-drawn carts that looked to be carrying supplies for the convoy. All in all, I counted 30 knights, 30 hunters/archers, 50 soldiers and a bunch of non-combatants supporting everyone in the convoy. Man, the king and queen were taking no chances in my retrieval. The caravan seemed to be a bit tired, it was clear they had kept up an arduous pace to ensure they arrived on time.

It took them a significant amount of time; more than I think they were planning to get through the pass. The supply carts and fancy carriage had to be left behind, which from my bird's eye observations the captain was not happy about.

"Ugh, all these delays. I hope John and Susan can forgive our late arrival." My birds heard one of the knights say.

Meanwhile the knights and soldiers near the forest were catching their breath and observing their surroundings. One of the men attending to one of the carts turn to ask their comrade, "Hey this forest sure seems to have a decent number of ravens, it is kind of creepy. No wonder no one tries to venture here. I feel like they are staring at us."

"Quit your yapping, they are just birds. Do not be so paranoid. The journey here may have been a pain, but it was uneventful. Stop worrying so much."

Time to get ready. I have two separate dimensions, one was a true greater demiplane with a luxurious mansion filled with any comforts I may require with surrounding land that can generate creation points over time, the other dimension was my very own private storage space. The storage space was a citywide empty space that made New York look like a tiny suburb in comparison to the size of my personal inventory. I planned to use it to store anything and everything I need as I discovered it's better than a refrigerator when it comes to preserving food and had zero weight impact on me, talk about convenient, but than what self-respecting gamer didn't love an awesome inventory system. When I was back with my guide, I created my personal inventory, the visualization practice helped me in the design of my greater demiplane and mansion. I had big plans for me greater demiplane, so I wanted to make sure I got it right.

Now that I had an idea of how long it would take them to get through the pass, gave me plenty of time to prepare for their arrival. I took this time to store food, all the books in the house, and other supplies in my pocket dimension. I also took the time to get ready to travel, putting on a heavy winter cloak that I could remove after we get out of the pass. I could regulate my body temperature and am resilient against cold but no need for them to know that. I figured it would be best to gradually reveal my capabilities over time.

When the knights finally arrived at the estate, they looked a bit haggard, you could tell they were not looking forward to going back through the pass. However, in their eyes spoke of a dedication and determination to carry out their duty. They brought with them 3 horses without riders, I imagine for myself and my two caretakers.

I waited for them outside by the entrance to the estate. Once they all got close enough, they seemed a bit surprised to see me waiting for them, but they quickly hid that under a mask of practiced discipline. They dismounted and all kneeled before me. The captain of the royal knights, Sir Reginald Spears, introduced himself and the other knights.

“It is an honor to meet you, my prince. My name is Sir Reginald Spears, captain of the royal knights. The man next to me is my second in command on this journey, Knight-Lieutenant Simmons. We were not expecting you to greet us upon our arrival, you do us a great honor.”

“Arise noble knights. Captain Spears, I was informed of your upcoming arrival today. I am ready to go when you are.”

Captain Spears noticed I was alone and asked, “Where are your retainers my grace? I would think they would be by your side.”

“Sadly, they passed in their sleep a few days ago, shortly after we received the king’s raven informing us of your arrival. I buried them out by the garden.” I said as I pointed in the direction of the garden, “They so loved that spot, and I could not bear to leave them in their bed after they have done so much for me.”

The captain and his knights all held faces of shock and sorrow, with a hint of something else I could not place until the captain spoke up. “My prince, you should not have dirtied yourself to do such manual labor. Though, it does speak well of your character to do so for your retainers. It pains us all to know you suffered alone, if only we arrived sooner.”

The other knights all nodded their heads in agreement with the captain’s words.

“First off captain, I have learned and practiced many things living out here in the middle of nowhere. Secondly, though I do appreciate your sentiments, I did not exactly dirty myself, I used earth magic to make their graves, so worry not.”

In unison several knights blurted out before catching themselves, “You know earth magic?!”

The captain looked back with a stern look at his knights for speaking out of turn and not properly addressing their prince, but I could tell he too held a mixed look of being surprised and impressed.

"Of course, as I said earlier, I have learned many things out here, as there is not much to do other than learn and practice. Do not forget that John and Susan were S class adventurers and masters of the sword and magic."

"Of course. I am sure they taught you many amazing things." Captain Spears replied.

'Let them think that. Technically I do have their memories, but they were not the only ones I learned from. Best to not tell them that though.' I thought before I replied to the captain.

"If you and your men are ready captain I would like to get through the pass before it gets dark. The pass gets far worse after sunset."

That seemed to light a fire under them as they all quickly moved into action.

"Of course, my prince! Do you know how to ride? If not, you can ride with me."

I loved riding horses ever since I was a little kid, no way I was going to not ride myself. "I learned to ride on the old steed before they were put out to pasture." 'Never mind that was when I was a kid on my home world, but once again, they don't need to know that.'

Knight-Lieutenant Simmons brought one of the horses over to me. He offered to help me in the saddle, which I graciously accepted with a nod.

After I was firmly situated, I thanked the man for his help. "Thank you, Lieutenant."

The rest of the knights mounted up and without another word we headed for the pass.

As we made it to the other side of the pass, I erected a quick ward to prevent anyone from returning through the pass. I didn't want anyone disturbing John and Susan's final resting place. Plus, the place grew on me even though I was only there a few days. They were my first few days in this new world and so what if I wanted to preserve it.

After making it down to where the rest of the caravan and soldiers made camp, we dismounted and joined the other knights in a quick meal.

"I want everyone to eat up before be begin our long journey back to the capital." Captain Spears commented as he took some slices of meat for himself.

"Captain, I appreciate the dedication, but it is clear the men are tired. I would prefer we not rush but ensure our people have enough time to catch their breath."

Captain Spears nodded, "The men will appreciate that, very well."

Several relieved sighs could be heard across the camp. "Oh thank the light."

As we finished our simple meal, the captain insisted I get in the fancy carriage, but I flatly refused. "Captain, if we are attacked do you not think it best if we don't place a giant target on my back?"

Captain Spears seemed hesitant, "You do have a point sire, but it just seems wrong your grace."

All the other knights and several soldiers seemed very uncomfortable with this development as well.

I knew how to read the room, "How about a compromise Captain? I ride inconspicuously until we get close to the capital, then I'll use the carriage. Sound fair?"

That seemed to make everyone a bit more comfortable. The captain still did his best to follow proper etiquette. "More than fair. Thank you, your grace, for indulging our concerns."

I decided to help further ease his concerns on proper decorum.

"Lighten up Captain. Don't worry, I learned proper court etiquette, I know how to act when the time comes. Just try to remember I grew up on an estate in the middle of nowhere, we didn't stand much on formalities, and I won't stand on such formalities on our trip."

Chapter 3 – Heading Home

The captain continued to take the measure of this now young man before him. He did not know what to expect. The king and queen had cautioned him of the possibility the prince would be weak or frail as they did not know when during his exile the illness would leave his body. They also told the captain that their most trusted servants were previously very capable court magicians and would ensure the prince was trained in both Magic and court etiquette but again it would be unknown how much they could teach the prince with his illness. Recalling that conversation, and what he knew of some of the pampered nobles, he was not expecting this.

The prince carried himself with a sureness in his actions, an aura of authority, and his eyes held a deep intelligence that seemed far beyond his years. Prince James, the captain really did need to start using his name, seemed to just be genuine, he showed actual consideration for the position and responsibility placed on the captain. This young prince has just turned into a man yet has the forethought of possible risks they might encounter and ways to reduce risks. He also shows genuine concern for the men and their well-being. These ideas would help the captain ensure no harm would come to his charge. Yes, this was a man worthy of following.

Seeing Captain Reginald Spears lost in thought, James just chuckled and went to go check the horse and saddle. 'This was going to be a long ride and in my previous life I still remember the importance of checking on your horse and making sure they were well taken care of.'

James produced a carrot he had pulled from the garden and stored in his pocket storage dimension. To everyone else it just looked like he reached into his satchel and pulled out a carrot. He figured it best to keep a low profile with such things as a giant city sized storage space. After feeding the carrot to his horse James proceeded to talk to the animal in a kind and caring voice, cooing it while he checked the saddle straps.

LT Simmons walked over to the captain while they both were watching what Prince James was doing. LT Simmons said in a low voice, "Prince James seems to be a very capable young man, nothing like what I was expecting but in a really good way."

“I agree wholeheartedly with that statement Simmons. I feel sorry for any nobles that underestimate him.” Captain Spears answered.

LT Simmons replied, “I felt proud to be included in this mission but now I feel proud but also a feeling of greater weight of responsibility. The importance of this mission is clear. Prince James must be able to ascend the throne when the time comes.”

“I agree lieutenant.” Captain Spears confirmed.

LT Simmons continued, “You know some of the factions Captain, when they realize just how capable he is they won’t like it.”

The thought seemed to concern Captain Spears and decided to shift the subject, as he answered. “I am aware of that lieutenant. But that is a worry for another day. Let’s get packed up and get this escort on the road.”

‘This is a well-organized ...caravan? Convoy? Let’s go with convoy! Anyway, impressive how quickly everything was packed up and ready to go.’ James thought as he wore a hooded travel cloak and rode along with the rest of the knights.

James thought as he moved his horse to ride next to Captain Reginald Spears, ‘I wonder if he will let me call him Reggie?’

“Captain, any idea on how long we think this trip will take?” James already had an idea of the distance after based on reviewing the map of the kingdom at the valley estate and the knowledge he gained from John and Susan.

“To avoid unwanted attention, our plan is to navigate around the towns and cities as much as possible along the way. With that in mind, we estimate four days travel time my prince.”

“This convoy is not exactly small Captain. I think attention will be unavoidable.”

“Do not worry my prince, you travel with some of the most highly trained royal knights and soldiers in the kingdom.” LT Simmons said as his horse came up on the other side of James.

"Oh, I am not worried, LT Simmons. I have the utmost confidence in all of you. I merely am stating people are bound to take notice of such a large convoy."

LT Simmons replied, "Let them, Prince James you point out any that look at you wrongly and I will teach them how to act towards the heir to our kingdom!"

James laughed; he enjoyed Simmons' antics. "Hahaha. I will keep that in mind Lieutenant. I appreciate your attempt to lighten the mood."

Captain Spears chimed in, "That is our lieutenant, comic relief."

LT Simmons smiled and gave a slight nod, then he realized what his captain had said, speaking up in mock protest. "Hey now! I resemble that remark!"

The convoy seemed energized after their much-needed rest and having achieved their first objective of retrieving the prince. During their journey, the prince would make his rounds, taking time to chat with knights, soldiers, and the support personnel like cooks and hunters. He would talk to them about anything and everything. James was more focused on getting to know them and learning what interested them. This seemed to brighten the atmosphere as they marched on, leading to the convoy making good progress before making camp for the night.

Everyone began to set up tents, make firepits for the evening meal, and establish guard rotations. Cooks prepared food as several scouts and hunters returned for the evening meal. The forest provided plenty of food to hunt so no one in the convoy would go without tonight. As everyone began to gather to eat, a cook made a point to bring Prince James a plate overflowing with food. One of the men intercepted it and tasted it to ensure there was no risk of poison. After confirming the food was safe to eat, the man bowed and handed James his plate.

"The food is safe to eat your majesty."

James took the plate with gratitude as it smelled amazing, and he understood the fact that this man had risked his life to protect him. "Thank you... What is your name?"

"Sloane, your majesty."

"Well Sloane, I appreciate you risking your life to protect mine." Prince James commented.

"Sloane has very high poison detection and resistance skills. The risk is minimal, and it ensures he proves his loyalty." Captain Spears commented.

James could tell there was something there. It was clear Captain Spears did not completely trust Sloane.

"Nevertheless, thank you Sloane, I appreciate your service."

Sloane bowed again and seemed to give a smirk to Captain Spears before turning around and going towards his own spot on the outskirts of the camp.

"Sit Captain, you too Lieutenant, and join me."

"Of course, your majesty" Captain Spears replied as he took his seat.

"It would be my pleasure." LT Simmons answered before he took his seat.

James observed the knights while eating. They were attentive, ready to be of service but still focused on their food. Most of the convoy seemed to slowly become more relaxed around him. Seeing that most were focused on their food and talking with their comrades, James decided to ask his question.

"So, what was all that about with Sloane?"

"Nothing sire, he is known for having a 'colorful past' and has been known to associate with shadier individuals. As such, we like to keep an eye on him." Captain Spears answered as LT Simmons just nodded in agreement.

"Very well." James said, deciding to drop the issue for now.

As they ate in relative silence for a while, James thought back to his interactions throughout the day. He had made a point to talk with as many as he could along their journey that day. 'I think deep down they appreciated my interest and lack of concern regarding protocols. Hopefully this will help reduce the feeling they might have of me being an unknown quantity. I was determined to win them over.'

After finishing his meal James decided to see if he could further win over those here. "Captain Reginald Spears would you be willing to spar with me and teach me some of your fighting techniques? I hear from the men that you are a master swordsman."

"I will not turn away from someone interested in growing stronger. Are you sure Prince James? I will not go easy on you." Captain Spears replied.

I nodded and stood. We both walked over to a clearing towards the center of camp reserved for the men to practice. I drew my sword, and he did the same.

Several people noticed Prince James and Captain Spears enter the clearing. Several stood and walked over, but all paid attention as the rest of the camp immediately grew quiet.

Captain said, "Mastering the sword requires both finesse and a willingness to push yourself past your limits."

With that said Captain Spears kicked off the ground and rushed Prince James, attempting to use both speed and strength to overpower the prince. It was clear Captain Spears was far faster than any normal human. He either was using body enhancement magic or broke past the normal human boundaries. To be expected for a person who held such an important post. He wanted to show the prince and everyone here the power of the royal knights. At least that is what he attempted to do.

To Prince James, even with Captain Spears using body enhancement magic, the man still seemed to move in slow motion. 'It is like he is moving through molasses.' Prince James thought as he waited for the captain to arrive. Out of the corner of his eye, Prince James saw Sloane draw his own blade willing to interfere. 'Hmmm, he seems protective, that or he just does not like Reggie here.'

To everyone else, Captain Spears was still moving far faster that everyone around him as he seemed to blur like a flash towards the prince. Several were worried the captain might be going a bit overboard to prove the power of the royal knights. Prince James felt like he had all the time in the world, so much so that he looked right at Sloane and winked at him. To James at his speed, it was a simple matter to parry Captain Spears blow with his hand pushing against the flat of Captain Spear's blade while bringing his own blade up towards the captain at the same time. To the captain's credit or honed battle instincts he was already twisting his body to dodge under the swipe.

Captain Spears used the dodge to gain some distance from Prince James. "Impressive your majesty, but perhaps that is to be expected as one trained by the legendary adventurers John and Susan. Time to kick it up a notch."

Sloane sheathed his weapon before anyone noticed as he thought to himself, 'This prince is quite capable and cunning, far more than he lets on. Competency I can respect.'

The Captain and Prince exchanged rapid blows across the clearing, each exchange the captain seemed to grow faster and faster, almost like he was building up momentum. Constantly increasing until after 30 minutes he seemed to hit a peak. The fight was getting harder and harder for everyone to track, and the royal knights had to activate their own body enhancement magic just to keep up with their moves.

Prince James thought to himself, 'Had I not learned so many combat techniques and had stats so high I do not think I could've kept up with the ever-increasing speed and exchange of blows.'

As the fight went on practically the entire camp was focused on the fight. Everyone cheering. To the non-combatants and regular soldiers, they had never seen the Captain's Relentless Momentum skill, but all of them had heard it. Even the other royal knights who had already been at their captain's side in battle, this was still a rare treat to watch such a powerful skill without being in a life-or-death situation. Several cheered and let their feelings be known as they watched the fight unfold.

"This is why he is the captain of the royal knights!"

"Agreed, so amazing!"

"I have never witnessed such a fight, no one has ever lasted this long again such a skill!"

Then there was their prince who was a complete unknown. What they had witnessed in the span of a day was a kind and competent young man who showed genuine interest in their lives and getting to know everyone. The crowd couldn't decide who to root for, so everyone just decided to root for both and just enjoy the show.

"Our kingdom is twice blessed to have two such amazing individuals!"

"Yes, this is such a wonder!"

"How can they keep going like this?!"

After the latest heated exchange of blows Captain Spears was clearly showing signs of running out of stamina. He ducked under one of Prince James' swings, rolled away to gain some distance between them.

Heavily panting, Captain Spears called out, "You are... quite...good." Catching his breath he continued, "There are not many people in or outside our kingdom that can keep up with my family's enhanced speed and ability to ramp up our attacks the longer the fight goes on."

"Thank you for the compliment, Captain Reginald. I can say I have learned much from this spar. You truly are a master in battle. I truly appreciate this lesson." Prince James replied.

"Lesson?! Hahaha, I think I could learn a thing or two from you! The way you countered my backhand slash, I'm going to have to incorporate that move. Prince James, if I may be so bold, please call me Reggie." Captain Spears said.

"Only if you call me James, at least while we are on this journey." I replied.

Both men sheathed their sword and approached each other, grasped forearms, and gave slight nod towards each other. Then both started laughing as a simple way to relieve the pent-up battle stress as only two guys seem to be able to do after attempting to beat the crap out of each other.

"Hahaha, the nobles will not know what hit them! Come James, let us share a drink to ease the soreness!"

"Sure, soreness, I'll buy that Reggie." Prince James chuckled.

James' Perspective

Watch rotation was set, and we all turned in for the night. I set wards in my tent to prevent unwanted visitors and quickly let sleep take me. After coming to this new world, having a body with such high stats I found I didn't need much sleep, if any really but for some reason that night I slept well and deep.

The night was uneventful, and morning came quickly. I awoke just before sunrise and after handling my morning business I began my daily exercise routine. I started with some stretches and then moved to various exercises. I would then rotate to different moves and repeat the process in different order to create muscle confusion to ensure proper warm up and continued growth.

As soldiers and knights woke up, they noticed my routine. Several seasoned knights and soldiers recognized the difficulty of some of the exercises. They had been impressed by my fight with Captain Spears especially because as the battle ran on it was clear I was gaining more and more of the upper hand. To them Captain Spears was a pillar of the kingdom, someone who never lost a battle. As they watched my exercises, they thought just maybe the moves were clues to my strength or just a sign of my dedication to improvement. Either way it did not matter, my presence seemed to have an influence on them. Many silently joined in on my routine including the Captain and Lieutenant. By the end of the exercises, most of the camp was following along. Even the scouts and hunters did their best to attempt the same moves. The cooks and other support personnel remained focused on their duties and getting breakfast prepared.

When I stopped, I was a bit taken back, it was as if a spell had been broken as everyone blinked and went back to their morning duties.

LT Simmons seemed to have a voice that could carry as he spoke loud enough for the whole camp to hear him. “Thank you, your majesty. That exercise is just what these men needed to help whip them back into shape.”

Several groans could be heard across the camp at LT Simmons’ words.

“Ugh.”

“He’s a slave driver!”

“I am so sore.”

“I agree, we should not shirk our training even when on a mission.” Reggie affirmed LT Simmons’ sentiment and to cut off any further disagreement.

Several of the royal knights came up to me and bowed.

“Thank you, your grace, for showing us such effective training techniques.”

"Yes, thank you, your majesty."

'I do not think I will ever get used to all the bowing and use of honorifics.' I thought as the knights went back to their morning duties.

After our exercise routine everyone ate a quick meal, packed up camp and we started our second day of travel. I observed more of the comings and goings of the convoy. Scouts would ride ahead and circle around the convoy to keep an eye out for monsters or beasts. Then the scouts would return and request assistance if they found anything they could not handle on their own. Royal knights and soldiers who were dispatched to support the scouts did not encounter anything that posed a true threat. Most beasts steered clear of so many people marching together. Only a few monsters were dumb enough to attack us, they were weak and easily dealt with. Some were even tasty after a little seasoning was applied.

So, the day went on. I continued to mingle between the convoy, getting to know the soldiers, cooks, hunters, and knights. We talked about mundane things. I learned about their families, what led them to serving their country and other random interesting facts. In all honesty, it was just nice to get to know everyone. As the soon to be crown prince, these were my subjects, which meant I had a responsibility to them. I may not be able to get to know everyone in the kingdom, but I could learn about these men and women.

We once again made good progress according to Reggie as we set up camp. That evening was nice and peaceful. The atmosphere of convoy camp was light and jovial, everyone seemed in good spirits. Everyone seemed to be more comfortable being themselves with me around. Several knights and soldiers shared stories of past battles both in war and in love. It was a good night, and I went to sleep with a smile on my face.

The next morning, once again the knights, soldiers, hunters, and even some of the noncombatants joined in my morning exercise routine. After our impromptu training session, several people thanked me for taking the time to teach them. Reggie and LT Simmons approached me. LT Simmons asked a question. "Your grace, would you be open to showing the royal knights back at the capital this morning routine of yours?"

"Of course, Lieutenant. It would be my pleasure."

They both thanked me before turning back towards their men and ensuring the camp would be ready to depart after breakfast. I just chuckled to myself. If these people were representative of the kingdom, I shall enjoy my time here in this new life.

Our third day of traveling was much like the second, non-eventful and filled with good conversations. Many in the convoy seemed excited to be getting close to the capital. The convoy decided to set up camp near the edge of a forest.

"We are almost home, my prince. So close to the capital we should not have any problems the rest of the way." One of the cooks commented as they handed me a plate.

'Don't you know you never throw out death flags like that! Ugh, some people!'

Chapter 4 – Death Flags

Shortly after our early evening meal, one of the hunters stumbled into the camp panting and bloodied.

"Trolls... Un-undead...outnumbered..." She warned of trolls and undead before she collapsed.

That was all the warning we got before we heard the shuffling and groans of the undead.

An archer shot a magical flare into the air illuminating the area. In the trees hundreds of undead could be seen with large trolls smattered throughout their forces.

Seeing this LT Simmons yelled, "Defensive formations! Now!"

Swords were drawn, arrows were lit, and everyone seemed to immediately fall into formation.

Like a swarm of undead skeletons, zombies, and several trolls rushed us.

'When did trolls work with undead skeletons and zombies? Wait a minute, those trolls look weird.' I thought as I looked at the forces heading our way. Then it clicked, those trolls looked weird because they were undead!

Captain Spears came out of his tent and called out, "Protect the Prince! Don't let them get to the carriage!"

I had to give it to Reggie, he was quick under pressure. I was nowhere near the carriage. He immediately implemented our previous plan of using the carriage as a decoy. Meanwhile LT Simmons and several other knights seemed to form a protective detail around me but in such a natural way as it just looked like our fighting formation.

It looked like our plan worked as the undead seemed to surge towards the direction of the carriage. As the knights and soldiers were centered more around the carriage it meant the undead were bashing up again the main bulk of our defenses. Looking out at our attackers, they outnumbered us at least 5 to 1.

The undead savagely attacked the defensive line. The zombies attempted to scratch, claw, and bite. The skeletons swung swords and maces. Each doing everything they could to overwhelm our people. However, these were trained soldiers, and they held the enemy at bay long enough for the royal knights to arrive.

As the royal knights joined the fray, they laid waste to the undead, some crushing the heads of the skeletons with their bare hands. Each royal knight had some level of body enhancement magic to empower their attacks. It was clear the undead skeletons and zombies were no match for the knights. Our soldiers knew how to work with and take advantage of the openings the knights made in the enemy formations causing the initial undead surge to slow. These men and women were well coordinated, as the knights pushed into the undead forces, the soldiers would advance their line as one. This allowed the soldiers to re-enforce the knights' efforts and ensure only friendlies were at their backs.

Then the 8' trolls arrived. Their brute strength was too much for a regular soldier as several were knocked back and into the air from each swing of their clubs. As soldiers fell on the battlefield, the noncombatants would pick them up and carry them farther into the camp towards what looked like a makeshift medics' tent. Seeing that our soldiers were no match for the trolls, the knights stopped their advance. Once again, the royal knights proved to be seasoned warriors. Without any prompting from their captain the knights divided themselves up into small teams to intercept this new threat. Each troll required coordination between the knights to keep them countered until they could find a weakness to take them down.

I watched all of this occur, my guards on all sides. As all this unfolded, the enemy's focus remained getting to the carriage. To further our ruse, Reggie remained near the carriage to give the appearance he was guarding something precious inside. A troll got through the line and headed straight for the carriage. To Reggie's credit, where it took a team of royal knights to counter a troll, Reggie took on the monster without any assistance. It was an impressive feat to watch. More importantly, it gave me an idea.

Someone intelligent had to be nearby controlling these undead. I activated my **Truesight** ability which allowed me to see the true form of anything I saw. This ability also lets me see auras and magic in a more visible spectrum. Which is how I saw strands of purple black energy that reminded me of ominous puppet strings coming out of the heads of every undead, flying up into the air and off into a canopy of trees in the distance.

'Looks like I found the puppet master of this little raid.'

Leaning over to my small squad of guards, LT Simmons, Sergeant Callus Thorn, and Mira Nightshade, "I found the one controlling these undead." I pointed in the direction I saw the purple lines going off into the forest, "They are behind that canopy of trees."

Mira looked at me confused and just said, "How?" Before shaking her head and continuing, "Never mind the how, let's go kill that bastard!"

"Do not forget your duty, Mira! We must protect the prince!" Chastised Sergeant Callus Thorn.

Hearing the sergeant's words, I looked over and smiled at LT Simmons and prepared myself for action.

LT Simmons saw the determination in my eyes and said, "Looks like our prince has a plan. Don't think we are going to be able to change our Prince's mind either. He has the look of determination to do something reckless." Shaking his head in resignation he looked at Mira and Sergeant Thorn, "I'll take the flack. Follow the Prince!"

I nodded once in appreciation to LT Simmons and rushed forward. Before they realized, I was already in front of them moving quickly to the frontline.

Sergeant Callus swore, "How in the ..." as he realized I had gained such a distance so quickly and then chased after me.

As I headed towards the frontline, I quickly surveyed the battlefield. Our forces were doing well to hold the enemy at bay, but I could tell some were starting to get tired. It would be only a matter of time before mistakes would be made from exhaustion. Time to pick my target.

I made a beeline for a side section of the frontline starting to spread thin as two knights were struggling with what looked like a 15' tall undead ogre. This brute made his appearance after the royal knights had intercepted the trolls. Its size alone was intimidating but with each swing of the tree trunk it wielded like a club the knights would have to dodge and then attempt to re-engage. This was making a clear hole in the defensive line, if not for the ogre's swings being just as deadly to allies as enemies we would have been swarmed already. It had to be dealt with first.

As I approached the line, charging my spell as I yelled with all my authority, "Separate and GET DOWN!"

The knights and nearby soldiers instantly responded to my order by either falling way back or jumping a good distance away. Seeing them clear of the collateral damage I made my move.

I unleashed my "**Fireball**" as I continued to rush forward. The giant ball of flame rocketed straight into the undead ogre and the surrounding undead. The explosion incinerated the top 3/4ths of the ogre's body and all the skeletons in a 20' circle in the area.

I arrived at the aftermath, without slowing down, grabbed one of the ogre's remaining ankle bones, and leapt over the still smoldering remains right into the skeletons not blasted back. Shattering any skeletons that got in my way using their buddy's ankle bone as a giant club.

"Time to make a path!" I called out as I was oddly finding it very therapeutic smashing skulls.

The two knights who dived out of the way just looked at the remains then at me in shock. As Mira ran past them, they looked at her, she shrugged and said, "That's our Prince" and took off after me.

Sergeant Callus following right behind Mira and chastised the dumbstruck knights, "What do you think you are doing just staring?! That's our Prince! Get your ass moving and help provide escort! Now!"

That seemed to snap the knights out of their shock and got them to remember their duty as they immediately ran to help protect their prince.

Captain Spears' Perspective

Captain Spears was on the other side of the battlefield finishing off a troll, using that moment to glance over in the direction of his prince to make sure he was safe. That is when he saw the prince do the unthinkable and run straight into the danger right towards an undead ogre!

'What was LT Simmons thinking?! They were supposed to be protecting the prince, not allow him to run head long into battle. I will have to have words with the Lieutenant should we survive this!'

Then his prince did yet another unthinkable and cast battle magic, not just any simple spell but a devastating ball of flame that took out the ogre in one shot and all the skeletons in the immediate area! Then he just grabs the ogre's ankle bone and uses it like a giant club to smash his way through enemy lines!

"How...?"

As much as he didn't want to do it, he had to trust his prince. After their spar he respected the young man even more, then he goes and does that unbelievable display of battle magic, his prince must have a plan. He would help hold the line and do his part.

Like him, several knights and soldiers were stunned at what they just witnessed. Seeing this, he had to snap them out of it.

"Hey! Focus! You are royal knights and kingdom soldiers; you have seen magic before! Focus! We must trust the prince! He has a plan! We must do our part! PHALANX FORMATION NOW!!!"

Mira's Perspective

Mira heard her captain call for phalanx formation, which would make the kingdom soldiers link shields and the knights would cast what defensive magics they had to help tighten the frontline. She knew Captain Spears saw what Prince James did, how could anyone miss an explosion like that?! All with one spell! This prince was not only an amazing melee swordsman but clearly talented in magic as well. Usually, people excelled in one or two areas, but this man seemed to exude competence and skill at everything he did.

The prince was all man. Every female in the convoy would catch glances and stares as he did his morning routine shirtless. 'Talk about fit, not an ounce of fat on the man. Focus Mira, thinking about the prince now can be a distraction. His safety is what matters right now.'

As Mira ran for her life to catch up to her prince, her thoughts once again wandered, 'How is he this fast? Well at least I have a nice view of his butt. Wait, where did that come from? Focus Mira!'

Looking back to see Sergeant Callus following with a few men in tow, I called out to them. "Best pick up the pace sergeant!"

Clearly winded Sergeant Callus replied, "Doing everything I can Mira! How is the prince so fast especially after casting that fireball?!"

Chapter 5 – Ned & the Undead

I made it to the tree line in no time at all, leaving my escort in the dust. Not my fault they are so slow. It was clear the necromancy lines of magic were coming from inside the forest. 'Whomever it is must have some way to sense or see the battle. Wait a minute...'

I switched to my far sight awareness. This is what allowed me to see things through my ravens and the other animals I befriended. Looking at the sky, I saw what looked like a few undead vultures circling the battlefield.

"That jerk is using a bastardized version of my recon method, unacceptable!" I said out loud in frustration, knowing I should've thought about that possibility sooner.

'I look forward to meeting this necromancer. Time to take out the enemy reconnaissance.' I thought as I ordered my ravens to dive bomb the vultures. Each vulture was attacked by multiple ravens from above catching them completely off-guard and tearing them to pieces before they even knew what hit them.

Speaking about getting caught off guard, I made the mistake of losing sight of my surroundings when my ravens attacked. Two undead trolls decided to make their appearance at that time. One swung his club to smash me like a bug but luckily my instincts kicked in and I was able to partially dodge the attack. The key word was partially as I was sent flying back into a tree. The glancing blow didn't really hurt as much as the sudden impact made me struggle for a moment to catch my breath. As I staggered to my feet the two trolls rushed to finish the job.

It took me a moment to regain my bearing as I dodged behind that same tree I hit, only for it to be taken out by one of the trolls. Shaking off the knock back again from the tree shrapnel, good thing I had erected a magic shield on instinct. "OK, now I'm pissed."

It was like the world slowed down or I just sped up as I quickly picked up my makeshift club while both undead trolls were still in mid-swing. I smashed one troll to the side and bashed the other one away. The fight quickly went from them rushing me to me knocking them around like they were nothing.

‘Hahaha, this is kind of fun. Time to end it. I have bigger fish to fry.’ I thought as I hit one so hard the head and right part of its torso were turned to paste.

I cast a disintegration spell at the other one as it got to its feet, turning it to nothing but ash. Looking further into the forest I caught sight of my target. He was a shorter, slender man in a dark cloak, hood covering his face.

The hooded necromancer seemed completely shocked to see me show up out of nowhere in the small forest clearing he was launching his attack from.

‘I’m guessing he was figuring those two trolls would take care of me.’

My guard finally caught up. Sadly, they had to fight through several undead who had closed ranks after I made my path through them. Once the necromancer saw my guard following me in the distance, he snapped out of his shock.

“Whoever you are, your biggest mistake was not just rolling over and dying! Now, SUFFER!” The necromancer yelled, raising the gnarled wand in is hand, and immediately casting a spell through it, sending a dark purple bolt straight at me.

“Suffer? Really? That is what you go with? Get some better lines cartoon villain.” I taunted as I grabbed the remaining corpse of the undead troll and threw it to intercept the spell. When the magic hit the corpse, it shriveled and decayed further.

Seeing his first shot missed infuriated the necromancer as he screamed and cast another spell through his wand. “DIE!

I responded in a mock surprised tone as I knew it would send this guy over the edge. “Man, what did I ever do to you? OK, well I did kill a bunch of your minions but in all fairness, they were trying to kill me and my friends first.”

My aura gave me a 360 degree extra sensory perception which is how I knew Mira and the others were approaching right on my heals, I could not risk them being hit with the death magic from that wand. So, I knew I had one choice, to deflect it.

Part of the reason why I grabbed that ogre’s ankle bone in the first place was because the body had been infused with dark necrotic energy, specifically this necromancer’s magic, and I could use that to my advantage here. I cast a shield around my makeshift weapon and smacked it against the bolt like a baseball bat sending it right back to the jerk that started all this.

If the necromancer was shocked seeing me show up in the clearing, or surprised when I used the remains of one of his own minions to intercept his attack, he was completely stunned and was not expecting his own attack to be sent back at him. Like I was playing magic baseball, I used my makeshift club to smack his spell right back at the jerk. As such, he was completely unprepared and took the bolt in his chest, not only knocking him off his feet, but lifting him off the ground. Completely falling on his back and smacking the back of his head on the ground. It was clear this necromancer was having a very bad day, and I was determined to make it far worse!

'Aren't I a stinker? Hehehe!' I laughed internally, as I thought of the perfect way, I could make this guy's day go from bad to totally screwed.

Reaching my consciousness out to the life in the surrounding area, I quickly cast another spell, causing roots to shoot out from the ground and wrap around his legs, arms, and neck, binding him in place. Then I had the roots extend to wrap around the necromancer's mouth preventing him from using any spells requiring verbal components. Not wanting to give this jerk a moment to recover I used these bindings to give me time to get up close.

His hood had fallen back revealing a mid-twenties/early-thirties human man. He reminded me of a rat in human form, beady eyes, crooked nose, skinny, and sickly looking. His eyes burned with hate at my audacity to bind him.

I smirked and said, "You look pissed. If you think binding you is audacious, you haven't seen anything yet." I smiled wickedly, then I placed my hand on his forehead and used Mind Magic to invade his mind.

Seeing how this was my first mental battle, I was a bit cautious about what kind of resistance I would encounter. I have played lots of fantasy and anime RPGs, plus read plenty of stories. One of the biggest takeaways, ALWAYS learn resistances or have immunities to certain attacks. Of all the possible resistances to have, mental protection is at the top of the list, you never want your mind messed with or hijacked. So, you can understand why I invested some significant creation points into Mental Control and Defense capabilities. Telepathy and telekinesis will be fun to use in the future but those mean nothing if someone can invade your mind and crack it like an egg.

I spent many creation points on my mind and how to use it and protect it, after all a mind is a terrible thing to waste. The knowledge and instincts I gained prior to coming to this world helped me know exactly how to conduct a mental assault and defense. I immediately erected my mental constructs and defenses, creating layer and layer of protective barriers. Then I set up various mental distractions and random thoughts to throw off anyone who even attempted to get through my defenses would first have to figure out which maze of thoughts to follow.

Sadly, for this jerk, he clearly didn't get the memo on learning how to protect his fragile little mind. It was clear I was way overpowered when it came to mental attacks. I quickly found his pitiful mental defenses. With a minor thought I shattered them to pieces.

"Wow you suck at psychic combat. Wait... are you drooling?"

Before I shifted through his memories, I had to find his magic. My people were still in danger, and I had to change that.

'Time to sever this guy's connection to his magic. Nice I knew this combination of mind control and nullification abilities would be worth every creation point. That just might be my favorite saying.' Laughing inside my head, I refocused on the task at hand. Reaching into his very being I found his connection to his magic, and like giant mental scissors, cut the connection. I would be able to re-establish his connection if I so chose, but as for the necromancer, you could hear the mental cry of anguish having lost something so vital.

Looking through my ravens flying above the battlefield, I watched as I severed the necromancer's connection to his undead and all at once all the undead my soldiers were fighting collapsed like puppets with their strings cut. I watched as all his undead minions lost the necrotic power keeping them animated and simply collapsed. With my people now safe, I took the time to sift through his memories.

The necromancer was named Ned and it appeared he worked for some noble. I quickly sorted through the man's memories to gain the intel I required. The noble was smart, Ned only met an intermediary that had hired him. It was clear something much larger was going on but that was for a later time. After I took Ned's memories it was time to address my men. With a mental nudge, I paralyzed Ned, his body instantly stopped moving.

I had the roots currently binding Ned to move his hands behind his back and wrap around his feet preventing any chance of running away. Then I let the roots separate from the earth so they could further harden and make it easier for my men to haul 'better off Dead Ned' away.

'Yes, that is his new name LOL.'

Before stepping away from better off dead Ned, I put him in a magically induced coma with a specific switch I could turn on later should he need to be interrogated. With that done, I rose to my feet and ordered the knights to haul him away. LT Simmons had just arrived to find me standing over our assailant.

"LT Simmons, I have subdued our attacker and severed his connection animating the undead. He is in a magically induced coma, please pick him up so we all headed back to the rest of the convoy."

The look on the faces of LT Simmons, Mira, Sergeant Callus, and the other knights assigned to guard me during this skirmish was priceless.

It took LT Simmons a second or two before he replied, "YES MY PRINCE!"

Without another word he picked up the 150lb man like he was nothing and everyone followed me back to camp.

'I will need to talk with Reggie about what I learned from Better off Dead Ned when I get a chance to speak to him alone.' I could feel the eyes of the knights staring at me as we walked back. 'Perhaps I overdid it a bit back there, going to have to be more careful about revealing my abilities to quickly.'

While heading back we saw Captain Spears heading our way with several knights and soldiers in tow. "Prince James I was very worried when you took off as quickly as you did."

"James, Reggie. We are not in the capital yet and we agreed to address each other informally as possible until then. Men who have crossed blades have no need for formalities."

"My apologies James, it takes some time. Is this the person responsible for all our troubles? I feared for your safety, but it appears you, LT Simmons, Mira, Sergeant Callus, and our other knights were able to subdue this miscreant."

LT Simmons spoke up immediately and loudly to make sure his voice carried back to our camp, "It was not us Sir! IT WAS THE PRINCE! HE DEFEATED THIS BASTARD ALL BY HIMSELF!"

I could see the eyes of Reggie and the others around him widen in shock.

Rumblings and murmurs could be heard.

"He stopped the necromancer himself?"

"First he takes out an undead ogre and now single handedly takes out a necromancer?"

"Yes, our prince is a blessing to our kingdom!"

As they walked the rest of the way back to camp, Reggie spoke up. "Impressive as always James. You must be tired James, please go rest."

LT Simmons chose that moment to throw our captive down on the ground in front of two soldiers standing guard and started barking orders. "YOU TWO! YEA YOU! Take this scum and tie him up in one of the empty wagons and put guards on him! NOW SOLDIERS!"

I just chuckled inside. 'I think LT Simmons just tries to see how loud he can get when barking out orders.'

I could see Reggie wanting to dress down LT Simmons and the others for letting me take off and then letting me take on the necromancer on my own. I wanted to correct that misunderstanding quickly. Plus, now that we were back at the camp, I had more pressing concerns as I watched people running about.

Grabbing Reggie's attention, "He is a pawn, Reggie. There is more for us to discuss later. Before we have any further discussion, please do not punish LT Simmons or the others, they were following my orders. I was the one who led the charge to find the necromancer."

I could see Reggie thinking through what he witnessed during the battle, what he heard as well as what he has seen me do in the past. Those quick facial changes flashed and then he just nodded at me. "Understood James. I will refrain from being too harsh in their reminders of duty."

They all seemed to wilt slightly.

With a sigh I continued, "Now more importantly, any losses? Any dead? How many wounded?"

This question brought Captain Spears up short. 'Once again, he shows his deep concern for his subjects.' the captain thought but ever the professional he replied, "We have several wounded. Most of our wounded have minor injuries..." sorrow showed on Captain Spears' face as he continued, "a handful with broken or shattered bones...no dead...but four with critical wounds including the hunter who warned us of the attack... I do not think they will survive the night."

Clenching his fists Sergeant Callus Thorn spoke up, "This necromancer hit us right between shifts of scout patrols. It is my fault your majesty, I let our forces become 'laxed so close to the capital..."

I cut him off, "There is plenty of blame to go around Sergeant but there is no need, I'll explain later. Reggie, take me to the critically wounded at once."

"My prince I would spare you the pain of watching them inevitably die. You should get some rest." LT Simmons commented.

"I have no intention of resting when our people are wounded and suffering." I replied.

'He really does care about his people' several of the convoy who watched the exchange thought.

I was led to a larger triage tent where I could hear muffled cries and groans.

'These men and women are tough.'

What I saw upon entering the tent broke my heart. Several non-combatants were running around helping bandage wounds or set and brace bones. Some knights were there as well, ones with some healing affinity focused on the more severe cases, doing what they could fighting to keep them alive. It was a fight they were clearly losing.

I immediately approached the female hunter that looked at death's door.

“Please let...” I couldn’t quite get the words out.

The knight, Kira, attempting to heal her seemed to deflate, misinterpreting my incomplete statement thinking I was ordering her to accept her death and let them go and to go put her talents towards healing the other injured.

‘The same thing the others tried to tell me. She is my dearest friend. I just cannot let her go.’ Kira thought in despair.

Kira knew her friend could not be saved yet she said, “but...she is my friend. I can’t just...” Then her training and duty kicked in, she was a royal knight after all, and her prince just gave her an order. “As you command...”

Placing my hand on Kira’s shoulder, “You misunderstand me, Kira.” Yes, I remembered her name, I had made a point over these last few days to get to know everyone and I had seen her and the hunter sharing meals and laughing together. It was clear they were friends.

“I am not telling you to give up on your friend.” I finished saying.

“I do not understand your grace.” Kira replied in confusion, not sure what I was trying to tell her.

Without another word I moved closer to the hunter. ‘Rita was her name if I recall.’

I knelt and placed one hand on her head and the other on the wound. Initially I cast a diagnostic spell to determine exactly what was wrong. I severed her pain receptors at the same time I began to heal the rather large hole in her stomach. Golden light began to glow all around my hands and start to suffuse Rita, as her whole body began to glow and lift off the makeshift cot.

Everyone in the triage tent froze, even those with painful wounds, so lost in awe of what they were witnessing. Rita’s wounds instantly closed, her bruises disappeared as well, if not for the damage to her leather armor, there would be no sign of injury. As I finished my healing, I reattached her nerve endings now that I knew the pain from the healing has passed.

Rita blinked a few times as she regained consciousness. She turned to me with a look of confusion, “My-my prince?”

Seeing her friend wake up, Kira could not hold it in any longer, "You... you healed her..."

I stood to give the friends some time as I did so Kira rushed in to give Rita a big hug. "I thought I'd lost you, my friend!" She said as tears of joy ran down Lara's face.

"You still owe me money, no way I'm letting you off that easy Kira." Rita said in good jest to her friend.

As I shifted my attention from the two friends everyone was just staring at me. It was LT Simmons and Sergeant Callus who both broke the silence at the same time. "You are a healer too?!"

Captain Spears, however, recalled what the king and queen had revealed to him before he departed on his mission. They told him of the prophecy and the reason why they sent their son away. He had heard many rumors about the prince over the years. The prevailing theory was the prince was very frail and had to be sequestered to protect his weak constitution. This, however, meant that in the eyes of the kingdom and especially the nobility the royal family had cast aside their only son.

He did not expect to be told of a prophecy and Reggie had mulled over what he had heard the whole trip to pick up the prince. In some ways he dismissed it, that was until he met the young man and kept getting surprised by James again and again as he learned of his capabilities.

'He is our salvation!' Reggie thought to himself, even more convinced that this prophecy was indeed true.

I paid the looks and comments no mind, I just went to the next gravely wounded person and began the process again.

"My prince, are you sure you should continue? You just made a miracle happen." Mira commented out of concern to what she just witnessed.

Brushing Mira's comment aside, I waved my hand and replied. "Nonsense, I can still help, and our people are in pain."

On and on I went, first healing those most severe, then moving to heal the ones with broken bones. All the while hearing comments and murmuring from those in the tent that could not take their eyes away from what I was doing.

"How is he still going?"

"How does he have any energy left?!"

"He's even healing the ones with broken bones?!"

As I progressed, several of the wounded I approached tried to say they would endure and not to worry about them.

"Please my prince, do not strain yourself, I can endure."

"I heal quickly, do not worry yourself."

"You should rest your majesty."

'Honorable men and women indeed' I thought.

After healing all the ones with broken bones in the medic tent, I collapsed into a chair. I instantly had several people around me making sure I was ok.

"You push yourself too much my prince!" Reggie, Simmons, and Callus said in unison.

"Please call me James" I said with an exhausted sigh.

Mira was there with a goblet. "Here my prince, it is a healing tincture. It will aid in your recovery."

"Thank you, Mira." I said as I took the goblet and began to drink it. Surprisingly it was mild in taste but flavorful and not what I was expecting.

"Well done, Mira. We will make you a proper knight after I instill in you enough discipline not to let your charge get ahead of you." Sergeant Callus said.

Mira just snorted as LT Simmons said in good humor, "He got away from all of us Callus or did you forget?"

They both clapped each other on the shoulder and just started to laugh as they exited the tent to go find some ale. As they exited the tent, I could hear LT Simmons yell "You there! Bring us some ale! Our Prince has just performed a miracle! Not only did he defeat that necro-twit, but He also saved our dying and wounded!"

It appears that broke the tension everyone in the camp was holding inside from the battle. Like a dam that broke the stress and cheers went up.

"Hurrah!"

"Long live Prince James!"

"Huzzah!"

Yet ever the chance to raise his voice I heard LT Simmons roar, "HEY, what do you think you are doing?! GET BACK TO YOUR POST! YOU ARE ON GUARD DUTY MISTER! MOVE IT! MOVE IT!"

I just chuckled and said, "He's a damn fine Lieutenant though he has the vocal strength of a Drill Sergeant, I'll give him that."

"Indeed, he is James. At times I think he does it just to out sergeant royal knight sergeant Callus" Reggie replied.

Kira came over and said, "LT Simmons is not wrong your grace. What you accomplished here today is a miracle. We only have a few great healers in our kingdom that could've saved someone so gravely injured as Rita was. Yet you did that and more. You are a gift from the heavens your grace!"

"Please enough. I appreciate the kind words..." I was cut off by Mira of all people, "Allow her to thank you my prince, you did us all a great service this day!"

Sighing, "My apologies Kira, I am just a bit tired. It has been a very long day."

"Of course, your grace. After today, what you have accomplished, none of us even know how you are not unconscious from mana drain."

Kira seemed to consider something in that moment and then drew her sword, placing it in front of her facing down, and got down on one knee. "Please your grace, it would be my greatest honor to serve you as your personal royal knight. I swear to stand by your side to heal and protect you always!"

Several conversations stopped as they witnessed Kira's display. Mira's eyes went wide, and her face went through several facial expressions of her own as her hand went to her sword, 'Dammit! Why didn't I think of that?! That sneaky...Maybe it's not too late, I could...' but her thoughts were cutoff with Captain Spears sharp words.

"Kira...Mira, enough of that! Though I understand and agree with your sentiments, those type of decisions are made by the royal family. Kira, rise and go celebrate with your friend. I will make both of your wishes known to the king and queen when I deliver my report."

Kira got up, put her sword away, "Thank you Sir!" was all she said as she left the tent.

Mira seemed to relax too, she did not seem as pleased and just gave a nod at Reggie before she too walked out of the tent.

After everyone left the triage tent, Reggie spoke up, "You know James, after today you will have several royal knights and soldiers wanting to become part of your personal guard. We all have only known you for a few days but in that short time you have shown genuine concern and interest in all of us. You are humble yet even in your baring there is a sense of sureness and confidence that leaves no doubt you are regal."

Speaking more softly, Reggie continued, "You bested me in our sword duel," raising his hand to stop my comment, "Don't say it James, I know what I know. At the end, exhaustion was starting to set in. It was only a matter of time."

'It is probably not a good idea to tell him that I could have kept on going and even at his peak of movement it was like slow motion for me. Yea let's keep that fact to ourselves.' I randomly thought as I listened to Reggie.

Reggie sighed before resigning himself to say what he needed to say, "You make my job and the job of my men even more difficult; you lead from the front, and by lead from the front I mean punch a hole right through the enemy's line. You rush right in announcing yourself with some of the most impressive battle magic I've only seen court magicians be able to accomplish; you take out and bind a dark magic user by turning his own attack right back at him!"

By the end Reggie had worked up a lot of energy. "After all of that you heal my men! I think every person here would follow you wherever you go if you and the royal family allowed it. Just look at Kira and Mira's recent actions."

Breathing a heavy sigh, Reggie let the stress from his shoulders go to regain some of his composure. "I know about the prophecy. The king and queen told me before I left to retrieve you the real reason you had been so isolated. When news of this spreads and trust me the men and women out there," Reggie waved his arm to signify the whole convoy, "will make sure to spread the news of what has happened here!"

'I am getting worked up again. I just have never encountered his like.' Reggie thought.

He exhaled a big breath and continued his passionate speech. "Now that you are back the knowledge of the prophecy will become more widespread. Combine that with this battle, you will have quite a following before you know it."

Once again Reggie waved at the camp. "As people get to know you, they will naturally flock to you. Heck, I wanted to bend the knee just as Kira did. With that said, there are factions both within and outside the kingdom that are not going to be happy with the influence you gain. After you are re-united with the royal family, it would be wise to choose an honor guard sooner than later. The various factions cannot be trusted, and you must be careful James."

I cut him off, "I am glad you brought that up. Let me tell you what I learned from our prisoner."

Chapter 6 – War Stories

After explaining what I had learned from taking Better off Dead Ned, I almost laughed out loud at Reggie's first response, "You know Mind Magic too?!"

Reggie had to sit down when I told him about how I used Mind Magic to rip the information from the necromancer's mind, and I do mean rip as I was not gentle.

Reggie continued speaking after taking a moment to accept yet another rare ability Prince James possessed. "Mind magic is one of the rarer talents, even rarer than battle magic or healing affinities. For you to be able to break an enemy mage's mind so easily, speaks clearly on how skilled you are with such a magic. You keep surprising me with how capable you are with such a wide range of diverse talents. How many other tricks do you have hidden away?" Shaking his head and raising his hand, "Nope, do not tell me. I do not want to know. It is better you keep such things to yourself. It is clear you gained much from John and Susan."

"Indeed, I did, they were both very capable mages and fighters." I replied.

"Yes, their deaths are a great loss to our kingdom, your parents and others will be saddened when they hear of their passing. I fear it will only further embolden the other factions against your family."

"Really? Why is that?" I asked Reggie.

"Part of what caused some of these factions to grow in influence was your parents' ordering our two most prominent adventurers to discard everything to care for a sick child even the royal family abandoned." Reggie explained as he winced with his final words.

Trying to recover, Reggie continued, "Please do not take my words as my thoughts on this matter. I believed what your parents did was a sign of love, to send the best to look after their child, what parent would not do such a thing."

"I did not take offense Reggie. You are telling me why these factions grew in power. I need to know these things if I am to help my family and this kingdom. Go on, do not sugarcoat anything."

'Once again, he shows a level of maturity so rarely found in the nobles. If we are lucky, my father will appreciate that.' Reggie thought as he continued his explanation. "Many nobles and commoners saw what your parents did as foolish and selfish."

"How so?" I asked.

"Think about it from their perspective. The King and Queen exiled their only son because he was frail and sent our best and most powerful mages and fighters to care for the child. This left the kingdom vulnerable."

"Vulnerable?" I voiced in confusion.

"Yes, vulnerable. John and Susan were known throughout the continent. Other nations knew if they went to war with our kingdom, John and Susan would be there to help our people. It was a deterrent. When other nations heard of what had happened, several took it as a sign of weak leadership."

"Ah, they saw what parents did as a weakness and add in John and Susan being seen as the big guns used to defend the kingdom, they saw it as an opportunity to push their agendas."

"Big guns?" Reggie asked, not familiar with that phrase.

'Damn idioms!' I thought as I tried to figure out how best to get out of this one. "A phrase I learned. It just means they were seen as the big weapons our kingdom had to defend itself."

"Ah yes. That is true. My apologies James, I had never heard that term. You must have learned much indeed from John and Susan."

'Whew, he bought it.' I thought, doing my best to keep a straight face. "Yes, I did learn much from them. Now back to these kingdoms and factions. How bad is it?"

"Luckily for the kingdom, your parents and your uncle are smart and clever people." Reggie stated.

"OK that is good to know but please explain in a bit more detail." I said with a bit of frustration. 'Like, how am I supposed to know what the heck that means without more context.'

Reggie continued, "Ah, my apologies James. It is such common knowledge I forget you have no real knowledge of how your family is. Your Uncle Marcus is the General of our Kingdom's Army, he is an honorable and brilliant tactician. His skills have led our kingdom to several key victories in our past wars and border issues. Many in the army are extremely loyal to your uncle as it is clear he cares for those under his command."

"That is good to know he is so well liked and respected." I commented.

Nodding, Reggie went on, "Indeed. Your father, the king, negotiated several treaties and in his younger years won various victories in battle. Your father and uncle are as close as two brothers can be. Such a relationship shows others how family should treat each other."

'Sounds like there is something there in the way he said that about family. I wonder if things are not good with his own family?' I thought but did not want to pry so I kept quiet.

"That brings me to your mother, the Queen. She is a light in this world. Your mother is bright and very politically savvy. Her ability to shame the pompous female nobles to do the right thing without slander or tearing them down, it is masterful to watch. Queen Sophia cares deeply for the people of the kingdom and worked very closely with the Church of Light to help as they can."

"The Church of Light supports my family?" I asked.

Reggie's facial expression told me otherwise. "Not exactly. High Priest Cendrin is close friends with your mother and works closely with her on relief efforts, but the church is not exactly an ally. They do not exactly boast or speak well of the royal family. General Marcus has made his displeasure known at the church's lack of support for your family. The church of course maintains its separate autonomy and focus on the light."

"Interesting, sounds like the Church has much sway with the people." I stated.

"Very much so James. In fact, I would caution you as there are several in the royal knights and the kingdom's army that are devout believers. Though they took oaths of service, they have an out clause that allows them to leave their service if it conflicts with their service to the Light." Reggie explained.

"That is good to know Reggie, thank you for sharing your knowledge."

"I will freely give my knowledge any time you require it." Reggie answered giving me a slight bow of his head.

"Knowing now what you have shared, it seems unwise for the information I obtained from the necromancer to be shared with anyone but my family at this time." I shared my thoughts, bringing us back to what started this conversation in the first place.

"I agree James. Several of the factions would use it to point fingers and just create more division within the kingdom." Reggie shared his assessment of the situation if this information got out.

We agreed to keep what we had learned quiet for now, until we got back to the capital and could inform the king and queen. I had used Magic to keep our prisoner in a deep sleep/coma like state which made it easier to not worry about any nonsense from him. Plus, with his connection to his magic severed he wasn't exactly much of a physical threat to well-trained knights and soldiers.

We had used my royal carriage as it was shielded from surveillance magic. Leaving the carriage after our talk as we both agreed it would be good to celebrate our victory with the men. Speaking loud enough for all to hear I called out to LT Simmons and Sergeant Callus who were standing nearby as guards.

"Both Captain Spears and I agree, we should celebrate our victory here today! Lieutenant, Sergeant, please arrange for everything!"

LT Simmons was the first to speak up. "You heard Prince James, what are you doing just standing there! Crack open the caskets of ale and mead we have on hand and let us celebrate!"

"Right away Lieutenant!" Sergeant Callus answered as he took off with gusto to see his orders completed.

Cheers of appreciation could be heard across the camp at our exchange.

"Yes Sir!"

"Thank you, your majesty!"

"Our prince is a godsend!"

"Here, here!"

I made a point to do at least one round around the camp making sure to at least make my presence known and more importantly show my appreciation for everyone putting their life on the line for me. Of course, I got plenty of "thank you" and "Thank you for the mead, you are the best!" comments. I also received many offers from knights and soldiers to join my personal guard. It warmed my heart to be a part of a celebration and comradery that can only come after surviving a life-or-death battle together.

As I walked through the camp I came upon LT Simmons as he was recounting his rendition of the story of what he witnessed in the battle.

"Then after he tells us to follow him, he literally blows up a giant undead ogre and the surrounding undead with one fireball! I mean one fireball! I nearly lost my eyebrows I could feel the heat from where I was in the back trying to catch up to our Prince."

One of the royal knights in the crowd sitting there listening to his lieutenant tell his tale spoke up. "I was too close, and I did lose all my facial hair including my eyebrows! The healer had to help me grow my eyebrows back. Still worth it though, that undead ogre was a beast to fight."

Several of the people listening laughed good naturedly.

"Hahaha!"

"I do not think that helped your looks any!"

"You needed a shave anyway! Hahaha!"

LT Simmons chuckled a bit as he continued telling his story. "I am figuring he is checking out his handywork but no, Prince James stops off at what was left of the corpse just long enough to pick up what's left of the ogre's leg, and he uses said leg as a magical club to bash his way through the enemy ranks like they were nothing! He did this all the way to the enemy commander! We kept having to fight the undead that would swarm away from him and then move in behind him. Even undead morons knew not to mess with our prince!"

LT Simmons had gathered a good part of the camp at this point as people laughed or looked over at me with awe-struck eyes. It was clear the lieutenant loved an audience.

"We finally catch up to our prince after he wiped the floor with two undead trolls who dared to strike our beloved prince..."

The crowd booed at that part of the story.

"BOO!"

"How dare they strike our prince!"

"If they were still around, I would make them pay!"

Raising his hand to quiet down the crowd, LT Simmons continued his story. "I know, I know my friends. I too was furious when I saw our prince knocked into a tree. My heart fell at such a sight! I thought to myself, I have failed our kingdom but then..."

He paused for dramatic effect, "...Then Prince James just walks out of the man-sized dent in the tree shakes himself off a bit and smacking them around like they were ragdolls for daring to harm him!"

More cheering went up.

"Hurray!"

"That is our prince!"

"Light be praised!"

LT Simmons began again after the cheers died down. "Then as we arrive to help our prince, the necromancer sends his dark bolt at us, Prince James uses said makeshift club to literally hit the attack, sending the dark blot right back at him! You should've seen the look on that necro's face."

Laughing a bit at his own memory of that moment, "HAHAHA! The only words he got out was 'What the..."

The lieutenant made a face that was a mix of slacked jawed shock look combined with the lights on, but no one was home. "The dark bolt hits the idiot square in his chest knocking him on his back and smacking his head on the forest floor."

Wiping a tear from his eye while laughing as others joined in, "I tell you I laughed so hard I couldn't barely hold on to my war hammer! Out of nowhere roots shot out of the ground and bind the necro' before he even had a chance to clear the dazed look from his face. After that Prince James rushes over, taps the jerk on the head and all the undead just collapse like the lifeless corpses they should be!"

As the story went on, I could see the awe and admiration of people in the convoy grow. Sure, they were laughing and celebrating their victory, but they all knew the main cause of that victory against such an overwhelming force without casualties was due to my efforts in the battle. The royal knights and soldiers knew they could've overcome such a force on their own but not without casualties, perhaps even significant ones, when dealing with the larger undead ogres and trolls.

Of course, LT Simmons just kept going, "Our Prince then heads straight back to camp, stares back down at the captain, mind you this is as our captain is trying to stare him down for leaving."

Looking over to Captain Spears, LT Simmons says, "Sorry Captain, I mean no offense!" LT Simmons just puts up his hands and shrugs.

Reggie takes it in good stride and just replies, "No offense taken, our Prince has balls, like Adamantine ones for sure!" As Reggie just laughs, everyone else joins in, my face starting to turn a good shade of pink from embarrassment.

LT Simmons took Reggie's response as approval to continue, "Our Prince demands to see our wounded and heads straight for the triage tent. He takes one look at our people's suffering and just casually says he will heal everyone in the tent...EVERYONE! Can you believe it?!"

After giving another shocked look and murmurs from the crowd he went on. "I just about fell over, I think some of the healers thought Prince James must've hit his head or something, hahaha. Yet before our very eyes he brings people back from the brink of death! Of course, not to be out done and prove us all wrong, he proceeds to heal broken bones, and other wounded! Keep in mind this after using some impressive battle magic! Both Kira and Mira wanted to..."

Both Kira and Mira flashed daggers in their hands giving LT Simmons a warning look. LT Simmons caught the implied threat in an instant, "No worries, Mira I was just going to say show your appreciation and devotion to our prince."

Cracking a winning smile at her, "WE ALL DO! DON'T WE EVERYONE!? LETS HEAR IT FOR PRINCE JAMES! This kingdom could not have asked for a better prince!"

"Yea let's hear it for Prince James!"

"Light be praised!"

"Hurray!"

"Thank you for saving us Prince James!"

"Thank you for healing me!"

The cheers and appreciation all blended into a cacophony of sound and emotion. I just smiled and raised my arm and hand in appreciation for their kind words and replied, "We are in this together my people, never forget that!"

I heard some cheers after I made that statement. Afterwards I stood up, said my goodnights, and retired for the evening in my tent. I was exhausted, not physically, as my stats and abilities seemed to do wonders for my stamina and energy levels. The exhaustion felt more from the emotional experience and dealing with so many people's admiration. This is definitely not something I'm used to. I mean I know my charisma stat is through the roof but come on!

As this journey progressed, I could see their admiration grow, first in how I treated them and showed genuine interest in their lives as I got to know them. Then I beat Reggie in our sword match and Reggie made a point that everyone understood I won even though I felt it was more of a draw. After tonight though, and what I did in the battle and after, Reggie was right, these people seem to have rallied behind me. The admiration and awkward behavior just exploded like a mushroom cloud. I think I liked it when they were just respectful but cautious, not knowing what to expect, now the way some of them look at me is like hero worship. 'It's ONLY been 3 DAYS!'

Oh well, adapt and move forward James. Like grandpappy used to say, 'You either adapt or die, no point in fussing over it!' Though my other grandfather's advice seems to fit here too, 'Always look for the good in every situation! Even in tragedy there is good, you just have to look for it!'

Saying a silent prayer of appreciation, I embraced both men's words of wisdom. I plan on fully embracing this life. I'd rather them respect me for my deeds than anything else. Perhaps this will help combat the nonsense I might have to deal with when it comes to interacting with nobles and the various factions out there.

Chapter 7 – Capital of the Kingdom

The next morning as I exited my tent to start my morning routine, I found both Mira and Kira guarding the entrance to my tent. 'Did they stand guard all night?'

"Please tell me you two got some rest last night?" I asked in concern.

"We took shifts to ensure you were well protected your majesty." Mira answered.

'Man, they really want the job of being my personal royal knights.' I thought as I just shook my head before replying. "I will not tell you to do otherwise but please make sure you get enough rest. You cannot effectively be my shield if you are exhausted, remember that."

"We will your grace." Kira quickly replied.

At this point in time practically all the royal knights, soldiers, and archers/hunters were awake and ready to join in my morning exercise routine. Afterwards, we all ate a hardy breakfast, during which Reggie informed me we would finally be arriving in the capital city later that day. I agreed to finally use the fancy carriage today, to my clear comfortability at riding around in such grandeur and feeling like I had a giant target painted on my back. I knew it was proper etiquette and I had already agreed to the compromise earlier.

I thought of my grandfather and his sage advice in my previous life to help me feel more comfortable with the situation. 'Do what you say you're gonna do. A man always keeps his word!'

Once we were underway, I was absolutely bored out of my mind. The fancy carriage wasn't too bad, a bit boring as mentioned earlier, so I spent most of the time looking out the window while practicing my non-flashy spells. At times just focusing on images and my understanding of the various magic types I've seen. Who would know that creativity and imagination would be my most important skills in life! Thank you, family, for nurturing and encouraging such skills!

Once again, I said a little prayer to God for my appreciation of the life I had before, along with a prayer to continue to look after my friends and family. Man, my family and friends must be so worried for me disappearing like that. Lastly, I said thank you for this second chance at a new life. Number one rule in life, show appreciation and enthusiasm for life and those around you even when they are not there any longer.

We gained a glimpse of the capital long before we arrived. The city looked massive, at least the size of New York City! Huge walls encircling the entire city that looked to be easily 10 miles wide. Farmland miles wide seemed to cover part of the plains heading towards the city. The complexity of such an architectural undertaking was mindboggling!

A large mountain range was behind the city both providing defense and from the knowledge I gained it also provided ore from a mine contained within it. Not too far was the forest we were coming out of, but it was clear we easily had another 80-100 miles before we would reach the city gates. I can see why so many flock to such a place, the natural resources combined with defenses would provide a level of security not found in most places I imagine.

It was a peaceful and relatively smooth ride for the remainder of the trip to the gates. The road was well maintained and was heavily patrolled. The view of the farms with their crops and farm animals reminded me of driving in Northern California before bad politics destroyed the vast amount of farming and food production for not just the state, but the country too. It was clear that these farms provided not only most of the food for the massive city up ahead but also part of the kingdom. It would be wise for me to tour these farms in the future, ignoring the people who produce the food your people eat is always a bad idea. Another rule in life and society, always make sure your farmers and food production are as free from nonsense as possible, you never want someone messing with your food supply. Some of my ancestors were farmers and ranchers, their life was hard enough without bad politics, the least I can do is help make their lives easier.

Several knights on horseback rode on ahead as we got closer to the gates to announce our arrival. A path was made in the sea of carts and people coming and going through these gates, allowing us to not have to stop and ride right through. It was clear those knights who went on ahead had been busy. As we approached it was evident the way they made a hole in the sea of people was a row of guards on each side, spears and swords drawn, to allow our royal precession to pass. I could hear the glimpses of comments.

"Ugh, some spoiled noble mucking everything up preventing us from getting into the city."

"You fool that's the royal crest. That's royalty in there."

At that moment Reggie decided to amplify his voice. "Make way for his royal highness Prince James! Eldest child of our King and Queen! Heir to the throne! OUR PRINCE HAS RETURNED!"

I winced and thought, 'Ugh. Of course, you'd put me on blast. No chance of slipping in quietly. Alright, time to put my game face on.'

The murmurs only grew louder. A few louder than others.

"The prince?!"

"I thought he died years ago?"

"No, you fool. He was sent away and put in isolation due to him being in poor health. Don't you remember?"

"Don't call me a fool! I remember just fine. I just thought I heard a rumor he died years ago."

"Hopefully he's not as bad as some of these nobles and foreigners."

"Be quiet. Do you want to get in trouble?!"

It seemed like Reggie had slowed down the precession just enough to give everyone a good long look at the carriage.

'I have a feeling he did that just as much for my benefit as theirs.' I thought. 'It did give me a chance to hear the various comments and give them a chance to study the carriage and get curious.'

We continued our procession with a bunch of guards marching us towards the palace in the center of the city. From the knowledge I gained from the memories I obtained, plus the books and maps I read, the city is divided into five different sections; four quarters, a city center that housed the Royal Palace, Church, and the Royal Academy. Some might consider the Church, Royal Palace, and Royal Academy separate sections based on the layers of walls and guards between them.

The most popular section which we happened to be traveling through first was the Trade quarter. This quarter held a huge open Market, several general stores, produce stands, butcher shops, and some shipping/import/export facilities. Several merchant families lived above their stores with the wealthier ones owning separate estates in this quarter or others.

Next quarter we seemed to now be traveling through was the Artisan quarter. This quarter was far more affluent. Several people still lived above their shop or had a separate estate. The difference of this quarter was a focus on specialization. Sculptors, masons, architects, enchanters, scribes, some mundane healers, and herbalists to name a few of the professions that lived and worked in this quarter. Like when the procession passed through the Trade quarter people stopped, came out of their shops, and tried to observe what was going on.

'It looks as though we are headed to the Noble quarter next. Is Reggie touring each quarter on purpose to make sure everyone gets a chance to see what is going on? They want everyone to know I have returned! Free press as it were.'

As we approached the Noble quarter, we saw the library which was placed between the Artisan and Noble quarters and was clearly a dividing line. The library was a massive building filled with scrolls, books, and historical documents. I couldn't wait to get a chance to explore that building.

'OK note to self, I am checking out that library when I get a chance. I used to love to go to the library back home before the government shut them all down. I can only imagine what a library in a magical world would contain!' I thought as we marched on.

Of course, as we passed into the Noble quarter the level of opulence immediately went up several notches. The estates in this quarter were various sizes, but even the smallest was far bigger than the ones in the Artisan quarter, and ridiculously so compared to those in the Trade quarter. From my recollection, this is where many of the Nobles either lived, or kept a home here when visiting the capital from their own assigned territories. This quarter also housed a few locations for foreign embassies, dignitaries, ambassadors, and diplomats.

The final key population in the Noble quarter with homes and estates closer to the Smithing & Military quarter are the mages and a few upper echelons of military, several of whom came from noble families, but established either separate branch families, or stood out and became a noble on their own merits. There was a significant difference between nobles that possessed territory in the kingdom and those that did not. Nobles with land had more responsibility to the kingdom and therefor held more authority than nobles without land. Several of these non-land-owning nobles were many of the kingdom's most powerful healers and battle mages who lived in this quarter. It was clear much of the power in the city was in this very quarter and I noticed that our procession slowed down considerably, making me glance out the window.

'Did the procession get bigger? Ah, they want to put on a show of strength and give them plenty of time to notice. Well played Reggie. These are subtle and overt tactics I'm going to have to make a point to pay attention to if I hope to thrive in this environment. Man, I hate politics.'

The final quarter was the Smithing and Military quarter. The military barracks and training facilities were housed here along with some direct connections to the Royal Academy. I saw several soldiers all standing at attention as we passed.

This quarter housed much of the military, both in the barracks for the Rank and file as well as several homes and estates for higher ranking officers and generational military families. As we moved further in the quarter I noticed some pubs, but what stood out the most were the forges. You could smell the metal and see the heat coming out of some of these forges. I dipped my hand in forging and metalworking, something about creating something with your own two hands just felt so right. Combined with most of my family was either career military or they did their part to protect people's liberties and ways of life, I felt like I was coming home as I looked around this quarter and took it all in.

As we passed by, I noticed people still stopped but as I peered into some of the forges, I could see several dwarves continuing their backbreaking profession ignoring the procession all together. It was clear the smiths, at least when it came to the dwarves, may have respected the royal family, but something told me they wouldn't be won over with anything other than grit and a strong backbone.

Lastly, we entered the City Center or what was affectionately called the "Heart of the City" or "Royal Center". This part of the city included the palace, royal academy, and the Cathedral of Light where the church was based out of. There wasn't a set or official religion of the kingdom. From the knowledge I had gathered, the kingdom was adamant about protecting religious freedoms, which was very admirable of them. With that said, the Cathedral of Light had the predominant presence in the capital. Their teachings permeated many of the laws and ways of life of the kingdom. They were smart about their placement as the Cathedral of Light was closest to the Artisan and Trade quarters so they could be closer to the people.

The Church employed many healers and scholars both part time and full time as priests, friars, and monks. They also had their own paladins, which acted as both holy warriors and defenders of the faith. It was interesting, as based on the knowledge I obtained, it appeared as though the church would have paladins join the kingdom's military when various wars and battles were fought but they were never considered a standing part of our military but solely separate. Which in theory made sense, they defended their country, but their primary charge was protecting the faith. Now theory is very different than actual reality where lines blur, or people don't take well to split loyalties. This potential dynamic is something I will have to keep an eye on, as well as make a point to observe some individual interactions to ensure I understand the true situation.

After circling around the Cathedral of Light we did a march passed the Royal Academy. It was closest to the Noble and Military quarters and trained many of the kingdom's nobles, mages, and military officers. Our kingdom's current royal court magicians and sword saints all came from this prestigious academy. In fact, it was my understanding that all the people in key positions of power and authority at one time went through the academy, including my parents and uncle.

Besides the Library and checking out the forges, I was most excited about the Royal Academy. My understanding was that most noble and wealthy families hired private tutors for their children to be taught the sword, or the basics of how to control their magic prior to their enrollment to the academy. With that said, it was kingdom law that anyone can attend the academy as long as they pass the entrance exam, but for the less affluent they have a much larger learning curve to overcome.

One thing I know as a fact in life though, is no matter the challenges, talent and determination find a way. One of our most powerful royal court magician healers, Lady Rollara and her sister Prophet Lara both came from an extremely poor family but possessed a larger energy pool and a true talent for healing and water magic.

Once a person turned 17 in this kingdom, they were considered adults. As adults they could apply for the Royal Academy. The kingdom, through the royal family and nobles, would provide initial testing opportunities throughout the kingdom. The kingdom and the Church of Light would partner to send testers to travel at certain times to different parts of the kingdom including remote villages to ensure everyone had equal opportunity to be tested.

If the person passed the initial test, they would be allowed to take the entrance exam for the Royal Academy. Though costs were associated with such efforts several nobles sponsored those that showed promise or talent. These sponsored individuals would either end up working for that noble family or join the military to help pay back their sponsor. Some nobles would sponsor guards or their kids' friends for political gains, or control over minor noble families, or lastly, to ensure their children had retainer to see to their whims.

Attending this academy was something I truly looked forward to. As someone who now lived in the capital, I would be automatically allowed to take the entrance exam without having to wait for a tester to arrive at my location. It would be hard to contain my excitement with this whole concept.

I kept thinking to myself, 'Hello, I'm going to Magic School. Why yes, I am a Wizard! LOL!'

I was lost in fantasies of wizarding school when finally, we arrived at the Royal Palace. It was huge! Uh, who designs places like this?'

Reggie dismounted and came to open my door. He whispered ever so softly, "It is time Prince James. Please remember while we are in the capital, I must address you in a formal manner."

'I guess I must get used to calling him Captain Spears again, ugh. That makes me a little bit sad. Well guess it's time to meet my parents and little sister Aurora.' I thought as I replied, "Understood Captain Spears."

I schooled my face to ensure I had tight control on my facial expressions. After taking a few seconds to breath and ensure I wasn't showing any emotions, which was hard, as I was a complete bundle of nerves, I stepped out of the carriage. 'Maybe they will be just as nervous as I am.' I thought as I exited the carriage.

On the way here, one of the non-combatants that accompanied the royal guard here was a royal seamstress by the name of Mrs. Teege. She was a sweet slender lady who looked like she was in her early 60s. She kind of reminded me of my grandmother on my father's side. Sweet as can be but brokered no nonsense. Mrs. Teege had joined the convoy for the sole purpose of ensuring I was dressed properly when I arrived in the capital.

No joke, her words to me were, "I will not have a prince of our kingdom look like some ruffian or common adventurer! The shock of such embarrassment would kill me!"

She made it clear on the trip here that she absolutely adored my parents. So, she was so adamant that I 'look just right', her words. This translated to a few awkward moments of getting poked and prodded as I tried on a few outfit combinations until we both settled on what I was wearing now.

She had taken my measurements to ensure the outfit for this occasion was tailored to fit me "just right" to quote Mrs. Teege. I swear if I hear the words 'just right' one more time I might cast a fireball to burn something down out of pure frustration over how much that woman fusses over me and my outfit. The last part of the trip she was in the carriage to make sure I was properly prepared. Don't get me wrong, like my grandmother, I love the sweet lady, but I can dress myself thank you very much!

Luckily, I could pass off wearing 'travel clothes' so she kept it rather simple for what would be considered normal for my high station. Keep in mind that was after I may have 'accidently' burned the outfit she originally wanted me to wear that had so many frills I could have passed myself off as a flamboyant pirate who would rather have a tea party than be a swashbuckler.

'OK breathe James, just breath. That nightmare outfit is nothing but ash that has long been scattered by the wind spell I casted. It is not coming back!' I thought distractedly to shift my mind from my nervousness.

As I stepped out of the carriage, I wore high-end leather pants, purple silk undershirt with a red and gold tunic. Honestly the whole outfit was the most comfortable clothes I've ever worn in both of my lifetimes. 'I don't know how she did it but thank you Mrs. Teege, one you realized I was in her words my father's son you relented and made me something I felt most comfortable in, you are a master at your craft.'

All the royal knights and guards all bowed their heads as an acknowledgment of my station as prince of the kingdom. I was escorted through the gates and through the main courtyard to the royal palace's primary entrance. I didn't have to wait long to meet my new family as they waited at the top of the palace steps with an honor guard of their own.

Chapter 8 – Meeting the Family

As I already knew what my parents looked like it was nothing too unexpected except it was clear they were the definition of Royalty. My father King Gerard stood straight; with a commanding presence I could sense even from several hundred feet away. His stance was also one that was clear he was no stranger to battle.

Then there was my mother. If my father was the epitome of commanding presence, my mother, Queen Sophia, was the epitome of grace and feminine beauty. Even from here I could see an intelligence in her eyes and what I think is compassion or concern. It was clear why she was so well liked and respected among the people.

To her side was my 15-year-old sister Aurora. She too looked elegant in her fine dress; it was clear she would grow up to be a striking beauty like our mother. Looks like I'm going to have my work cut out for me making sure no wannabe suitor tries anything with my sister. I am the older brother after all, it is part of my duty to protect her. Never had a younger sister but I did have cousins I was protective of, and no one messes with my family!

I noticed a few other noteworthy people at the top of the stairs. First was a mountain of a man standing next to my father. It was clear he was General Marcus, leader of the kingdom's army and a known sword saint. His baring alone comes off as capable and dangerous. If what Reggie told me about him was true, the kingdom was lucky to have such a shrewd tactician. It warmed my heart to know my father and uncle were so close. It made me miss those I consider brothers and family, but I quickly buried that deep to keep the mask of no emotion on my face.

Next to my sister but a little behind her was a woman in elegant robes, my guess is this is the royal court magician and headmistress of the Royal Academy Lady Rollara. The woman clearly had a rather large mana pool as I could sense it from here. Turning my **Truesight** on and quickly off, in that glimpse, I saw the tell-tale signs of water and healing magics coursing through her.

Also next to my sister was a man clearly dressed in a priestly garb, I imagine this is the archbishop of the Church of Light, also known as High Priest

Cendrin. He had a warm smile on his face as he held his golden staff. Not sure how much I trusted the man, but it was clear that his eyes watched every move I made like a hawk.

As I began to climb the palace stairs my mother's face began to change from her mask of calm beauty to one of emotional impatience. Her hands twitched as though she was trying her hardest to hold herself back and maintain decorum. That restraint didn't last.

As I slowly climbed the stairs, still a bit nervous about this interaction, my mother bolted forward just as I past the three quarters mark. She slammed into me, completely taking me off guard & wrapped me up in a big bear hug. The woman clearly had some ability to infuse mana into her body cause it truly felt like I was being crushed by a bear!

"Uh...?" I stammered.

"My baby boy is finally come home! I have waited long enough to hold you in my arms, I will not be denied another second!" My mother blurted out.

"Can't breathe..." I wheezed. Truth be told, my stats were so high this was not a problem, but I thought it best to not let that be widely known.

My father just shook his head with a rueful smile on his face as he walked down the stairs to join mother and me. The others waiting followed suit.

"Honey let the boy breath, he's a man now. It does not do well for his mother to act in such a way." My father tried to appeal to my mother's sensibilities, but she was having none of it.

"No! I have waited too long to hold my child!" Was her only reply as she squeezed me tighter further burying my head into her chest as she was a few steps above me when she lunged for me.

"Mother... I... can't... breathe." I repeated louder this time in the hope she would get the hint.

That seemed to get her to release me. "Oh, my poor baby! Are you ok? How was your trip home? Where are John and Susan?"

My mother may have released her bear hug, but she still held me at arm's length refusing to let go of me as she pattered me with questions.

"Sadly, they passed a few days before Captain Spears and his men arrived to escort me to the capital. I buried them on the hill facing the garden they tended facing their favorite view." I answered.

"Oh, my baby was all alone, and you had to dig the graves of the people that cared for you in our absence! They were good people. You poor thing! We will make a point to honor their passing and celebrate their life." Was my mother's reply as I could just tell she wanted to give me another bear hug. Luckily father stepped in to rescue me.

"Sounds like you did the right thing and honored their memory, as to be expected of my son. Now let me get a look at you. How fared your health on the trip home?" the king asked.

"I appreciate your concern father, but I have fully recovered from my childhood illness and rather enjoyed the trip back to the capital. Captain Spears and his men provided great company and did a great job escorting me here. They even protected me from an undead army attack. They are to be commended for their bravery."

"An undead army attack?!" Everyone said at the same time.

"My poor baby!" My mom said before she pulled me into a bear hug. "Lady Rollara please check my baby the prince for any damage and heal him right away!"

"I will need you to release him my Queen if you wish me to examine him." Lady Rollara said matter-of-factly to my mother.

'Thank you, Lady Rollara! You are a lifesaver!' I thought in appreciation.

"Oh of course! Do whatever you have to do!" My mother said to Lady Rollara as she released me.

I mouthed to Lady Rollara 'Thank you' to which she just gave me a warm grandmotherly smile and said, "This will take but a moment your highness."

Placing her hand on my head. As her hand began to glow, I felt a tingle as I could tell some kind of magical scan was being performed. I could've blocked it but that seemed counterproductive so to everyone watching it looked like I just stood there. However, what I was doing was studying the magic she used until I realized what it was. The spell was an improved version of what I used to assess the injured after the battle with the undead. Even more importantly, I realized I could now copy it!

'Well, that will come in handy.' I thought to myself.

Everyone waited with bated breath to hear Lady Rollara's diagnosis. After a few moments she gasped.

My father was the first to respond. "Is he alright?! Death Magic can be very insidious; whatever you need to heal him you shall have it!"

Lady Rollara simply gave a little chuckle and replied, "My apologies for worrying everyone. The prince is just fine, better than fine even. My gasp was when I reached his energy, your son has an exceptionally large energy pool. In fact, it is the largest I have ever encountered!"

"Larger than even you Lady Rollara?!" The priestly looking guy who I was pretty sure was Cendrin said.

"Yes, High Priest Cendrin." Lady Rollara answered, clearly not very pleased with the man.

'Yep, bingo, there it is! I called that one.' I internally chuckled at my Charlie moment.

"Truly a blessing from the light! I must inform the clergy." High Priest Cendrin exclaimed.

Some murmuring between everyone there ensued for a short moment.

In that moment Lady Rollara leaned in and whispered to me, "I did not tell them how much bigger, but I will tell you so you understand child, I would be a drop of water in comparison to your ocean. I'd keep that quiet for now. We will talk later."

'I was really beginning to like this lady. She kind of looked like Maggie Smith and totally reminded me of my nana, total heart of gold, but... do-not-ever...under-any-circumstances... get on her bad side.

After that quick message she straightened and spoke louder, "If the royal family would indulge me, I would like to work with the prince to help prepare him before he enrolls in the Royal Academy."

Both my father, mother, and high priest nodded their heads and for some reason my sister's eyes brightened. 'Hmm, wonder what that's about?' I thought as she spoke for the first time, "My brother is going to get instruction just like me!"

'There it is!' I immediately had another Charlie moment.

Then my sister smiled for the first time. She practically radiated warmth with such a genuine smile that it instantly melted my heart and I vowed to protect her always.

I couldn't help but lean down to get to her eye level. "I will consider such a thing a great joy, especially if it means I can finally get to know my little sister." I said as I ruffled her hair.

"Do you mean it big brother? You want to spend time with me?"

Her adorableness once again melted my heart. At that moment I double swore I'd protect my little sister no matter what.

"Of course, I mean it little sister, we are family after all. I hope we can make up for lost time." I replied with a genuine smile of my own.

My sister Aurora jumped into my arms giving me a tight squeeze.

'Well at least it is clear this is a hugger family. Which works for me as that is how my family was.' I thought as I returned the hug as I told her, "Yep, anyone that hurts you is going to answer to me!"

My mother had moved over to my father. They both held each other and smiled watching the exchange. My mother was the first one who spoke, "Oh darling. Our family is finally reunited after all these years. I feared this day would never come."

My father replied, "It is good to see but I want to know more about this undead attack." He turned to the man next to him, "Don't you agree General Marcus?"

The man I now knew to be my uncle, General Marcus nodded and spoke up "Captain Spears report!!"

All eyes looked to Captain Spears. This entire time Captain Spears and the other royal knights that escorted me were on one knee bowing.

Captain Spears raised his head and replied, “Your Grace. We have the necromancer responsible for the attack in custody. The attack took place the last night before we arrived at the capital.”

General Marcus interrupted Captain Spears, “That close to the capital?! How many undead, Captain?”

The King replied before Captain Spears had a chance to speak. “You and your men may rise Captain. In our excitement to be reunited with our son we did not realize all of you were still bowing so long.”

Captain Spears and his men rose, “You are most gracious your highness. It is our duty to serve and do not mind such things.”

The King nodded in a show of acknowledgement of his dedication to service.

Captain Spears turned to General Marcus, “To answer your question General, there were roughly over 200 undead consisting of skeletons, zombies, undead trolls, and an undead Ogre.”

Both the King and General looked rather concerned. My mother, High Priest Cendrin, Lady Rollara, and my sister all had horrified looks on their faces.

General Marcus spoke up, “That many undead a day’s travel from the capital?! How did so many undead go unnoticed this close?!”

Captain Spears answered, “From what we discovered General, from our captive, was he entered the area with a smaller force of 50 under concealment magic at night. He then kept to the forest gathering undead from the local population of monsters there, converting them into undead skeletons and zombies. I was planning to provide a more detailed report later, General.”

“That is fine Captain. For now, answer the most important question, how many men did we lose to such a force?”

“None.” Captain Spears answered matter-of-factly.

Several people spoke up, one right after the other.

“None? How is that possible?” General Marcus asked.

“Well done, Captain! As to be expected of the royal knights and army!” High Priest Cendrin said.

"Thank you for protecting our son." My mother said clearly relieved yet seeming to want to put me in a bear hug again. Luckily, father held her close in his arms.

Captain Spears replied, "We owe that mostly to Prince James sir. He was the one who subdued the necromancer and then healed my men, saving several from death or debilitating injuries. He fought with honor and was a true hero."

The king elbowed General Marcus, "Ha! You hear that, Marcus?! Chip off the old block! Well done, James!"

General Marcus just looked at his king while rubbing his ribs before replying, "Indeed impressive your grace. If you'll excuse us my King."

General Marcus then looked at Captain Spears, "Come Captain, let us go talk. I want to know everything."

My father just chuckled before pulling me in for a side bear hug, "Hahaha. Do not worry, your uncle is always focused on protecting the kingdom, you will get more time with him later. Come son, let's get you settled, and you can tell me all about it."

My father kissed my mother and sister goodbye and practically dragged me into the palace. After we made it inside, he took me to a fancy parlor and shut the doors so we could chat in private. "OK son, tell me everything." He said with a smile, clearly excited to talk to his son the hero.

The conversation with my father had been illuminating.

First, I learned that my father, the king, was no stranger to battle, which I already knew from Reggie. He was impressed with my recounting of events and praised me just as much for healing my escort as he did for subduing rather than killing the necromancer.

Second, there was a growing noble faction in the kingdom that seemed to be influenced by foreign or some other subversive element. My father had no proof otherwise he would've acted on it. The frustrating part was the nobles in this growing faction were being shortsighted, focused on personal power rather than realizing we all are stronger together.

Thirdly, the necromancer's benefactor seemed to be an intermediary as he has no clear ties to a specific family. Ned the necro was told he was hired to kill a prince and stop a prophecy, so whomever it was knew about that at least. To my father this was the most concerning news, as they had only told so many people about the prophecy in the first place. That meant someone talked. My father suspected High Priest Cendrin but had no real proof to back up his hunch. We both agreed to keep our captive alive for now with the hope of using him in the future to draw our enemies out.

Lastly, I learned my family's position had weakened over the last decade due to the fact my parents refused to name an heir or have any more children. Aurora at a very young age made it very clear she had no interest in ruling. My parents would never force her and deep down they could not give up hope of my return. Their faith was impressive.

My father's words had touched my heart, "If we named an heir that wasn't you son, it would be like accepting we had lost you, and that was something your mother and I could never do."

With my return they could finally name an heir and regain some of those nobles who are on the fence about joining the royal faction. My father also told me of a growing third faction led by one of the dukes. The man split from the royal faction because he believed the actions of my father and mother to send John and Susan away and not name an heir was selfish and, to him, weak character. What I knew but my father told me was John and Susan wanted to retire and their biggest regret in life was not having children, they had jumped at the chance to raise me.

After our talk, the king told me how proud he was of what I had done and made a point to tell me, "It is clear you have a sharp mind to quickly see the challenges before our family. I can not tell you how happy I am to have you home son."

The words got me choked up a bit. I mean here I had only met this man moments ago and he was showing me such acceptance and love. It made me then and there re-affirm my commitment to helping this family and the kingdom thrive!

"I will do everything I can father to help our family and this kingdom."

"I know you will son. Now you must be tired from your travels. We have prepared you a wing of the palace. Come let me show you the way."

My family had indeed prepared a princely suite for me with a huge comfy bed. This thing was like laying on a puff of clouds, it was pure heaven, especially after such an emotional day. I had a new family now, which in and of itself was a bit of a rollercoaster for me, as I missed my family from Earth. After meeting them and seeing how genuinely they cared and were overjoyed with my return, I just said a silent prayer in my heart thanking God for this outcome. With thoughts of appreciation, I quickly drifted off to sleep.

Chapter 9 – Honor Guard

Despite my comfy bed, I woke up early in the morning. I liked my internal clock & ability to not only know the exact time, but wake up at a set time each day, it was beyond convenient. I did not need much sleep really, but it still felt nice to rest my eyes and mind. Other than breakfast with the family in a few hours, I was to work with my parents to select my honor guard.

According to what I learned; these would be the royal knights assigned to serve as my personal bodyguards. The way the process was explained it seemed overly formal and drawn out, but it was designed to make sure various considerations were accounted for. Most of those considerations I was not going to care much about as competence was one of the key things I was looking for.

I decided to start my day with my normal exercise and training routine. I kept it limited to what I could do in my giant princely suite. With my enchanted speed it did not take me long to finish my warmup. As I began my meditation some key questions popped into my head.

'Should I find a safer place to practice where I can go all out? How much do I let on about my capabilities?'

These two questions led me to rethink one of my own demiplanes, it was going to need an overhaul. Walking into my Demiplane I realized it was massive. I had combined it with a spell I created similar to a popular spell idea from past tabletop games I played. I called it Magnificent Domain. The spell used some of the creation points I slowly generated and fed them to allow me to make creations of my own within the demiplane. The initial layout I created had a giant fortress the size of a city, contained within the walls were a Druid's grove, training grounds, and a huge several story estate that sat on top of a decent sized hill overlooking the demiplane. Here I could go all out in my training without fear of being seen or caught. The other advantage I built into this demiplane was incorporating some impressive time Magic into the place.

Using the knowledge I gained, time moved at an exponentially faster rate in the demiplane than outside it. My mental calculations figured for every second that passed outside the demiplane a full 169 minutes passed inside, which was almost 3 hours, 2 hours and 49 minutes to be more accurate. With this time dilation I could train, practice magic, and experiment with potions, crafting, etc. Though I found a certain peace in training, I was most excited to craft and make creations of my own.

I headed towards the training area and practiced for a few hours. After practice, I decided to use the one feat and magic I gained that I was perhaps most excited about, Omniverse Points or (OPs). With this demiplane intrinsically tied to me, these OPs would slowly generate and be available for use. This magic allowed me to create pretty much anything I wanted within the demiplane. Anything I created took a certain amount of Omniverse Points.

'Maybe these Omniverse Points, are the key to become truly OP.' That random thought made me laugh as I truly was Over-Powered, and I was only getting started.

Anyway, back to the points. The costs varied and I could only use so many points per day, as I was literally warping reality & bringing something into existence. I could even use them to expand the size of the demiplane. Too much warping of the world around me and I risked shattering the reality of this demiplane and that just seemed like a bad idea. Slow and steady was the key to success.

In theory I could create life forms but figured I should wait until I felt comfortable with creation itself. So, to start with I created a few mountain ranges. Within each I created different veins of metal ores. Each mountain range contained specific metal veins.

When I was done, I had four mountain ranges, one covering each cardinal direction, one with silver veins, one with gold veins, one with mithril veins, and one with adamantine veins. Sadly, each ore took different amount of OPs, mithril and adamantine took so many it would take weeks of realm time to have significant veins of the stuff. My goal was to eventually mine the ores to use in my crafting experiments, plus I knew the value of such commodities, I had a feeling would come in handy in the future.

With my points used up for the day and training exercise completed, I went into my mansion estate. Once inside my estate I partook in one of my favorite features I designed, large, heated baths. I had a whole full on Japanese bathhouse setup. I planned to try everything here. First up was the mineral bath, a quick shower, and after just soaked in a huge bath that was more the size of a pool. One word to describe it all, 'heaven!'

After my relaxing bathing session, I returned to reality. Walking through the portal back into my suite. I got dressed and with so little time passing in reality when I returned, I had plenty of time, so I decided to explore the palace.

When I exited my room, I found Captain Spears and a few royal knights waiting for me.

"Captain? What are you doing here?" I asked a bit surprised.

'I must get better at keeping my aura senses active all the time. I cannot let my guard down even in the palace.' I thought as I schooled my face.

"My apologies, sire, but as you have not yet chosen your personal royal knights and guards, I felt it was my duty to see to your protection." Captain Spears replied.

"Did my father or mother put you up to this?" I asked.

"Not at all, sire. I was the one who suggested it to his majesty. He of course approved and thanked me for my initiative." Captain Spears replied.

Letting out a sigh, I replied, "Of course he did. I was just about to explore the palace, having a guide would be appreciated captain."

"Let me show you the highlights, my prince." Captain Spears said before his men fell in behind us and we started the tour.

To say the palace was huge would be an understatement. A few hours had passed, and we weren't even halfway through the tour. Of course, part of that was due to Reggie giving me a combination of a history lesson and his best tour guide impression. There were giant ballrooms, grand halls, a few gardens, a private training arena, and my favorite, a combination library/map room.

The library was rather large and according to Reggie there were copies of books that could be found in the city library along with some tomes and other family documents not available in the city library. Of course, Reggie made a point to call out the fact that the city library did have a restricted section that held various books and tomes not even available here. In other words, I was going to have to spend a good amount of time here and in the city library eventually.

As excited as I was to read and learn, I found myself most excited for the various maps. There were detailed maps of the kingdom, including some that depicted key trade routes and where certain natural resources existed across the land. I found several maps of neighboring kingdoms across the continent, and a larger map of the known world. The continent we were on was the largest by far but there were still several continents and large island chains scattered across the planet. It was a treasure trove of knowledge that reminded me of how much I still had to learn. It was hard to tear myself away, but I was getting rather hungry, and I think Reggie was getting a bit antsy wanting to show me the rest of the palace.

Ever since coming to this world, to say I had a very healthy appetite for a growing boy was an understatement. I found I could use Magic to create food and water that did a great job of sustaining and strengthening my body, but I could not deny how much I craved meat, must be a dragon thing. I had one thing on my mind once my stomach started growling, 'Where is the MEAT!'.

"Captain, perhaps we can continue the palace tour another time. Can you please escort me to the royal dining room so I may join my family to break our fast." My stomach growled loudly right after I spoke.

"Oh! Of course, right this way my prince. I should have anticipated your need for food before we trekked all over the palace." Reggie replied after hearing my stomach.

"Non-sense. You were indulging me in my eagerness to explore. Let's get our grub on!"

"Grub... my prince? You want bugs? Was there not much to eat in the hidden valley?" Reggie asked in confusion.

"What? No! It is an expression as in let us go eat a bunch of stuff. Besides the hidden valley had a great ranch." I commented.

"I do not recall seeing a ranch, just the cottage and some cattle. I guess you could consider that a small ranch." Reggie thoughtfully considered.

I laughed at my internal joke, “HAHAHA! No, it was an inside joke, sorry Reggie, don’t worry about it. How much farther?” I asked as we walked more briskly through the palace.

“Not very far at all, my prince. It is right through these double doors.” Reggie answered.

———— - - - - - - - - - - - ————

When we arrived at the dining room my father and mother were already in the room and about to take their seats. My mother was of course the first one to respond. She bolted from her seat and wrapped me up in a hug again.

“Good morning my baby boy! You’re up early, just in time to break our fast together!”

Muffled, I do my best to respond. “...Good...morn...ing... Mother... Can... you... please.... release me?”

Luckily my father came to my rescue. “Darling, you’re suffocating him. He is not going anywhere. Let the poor boy take his seat and eat.”

“What? Oh, sorry honey. It’s just... every time I see you, I think about how long we have been separated. It’s hard not to want to hold on tight and not let go.” My mother said as she released me from her bear hug.

‘I felt for the woman. She was denied seeing her child growing up, so I cannot be too upset.’ I thought.

Collecting myself I replied, “I understand mother. I have been without you, father, and sister my whole life in this world. I too am happy for us to be reunited.”

“My baby, come sit with us. Captain Spears why don’t you join us too.” My mother said while practically dragging me by my arm to sit next to them.

“Yes Captain, join us. We can discuss the royal knight candidates while we eat. Besides I have other matters to discuss that could use your input. We are just waiting for Marcus. Ah there he is.” My father said as General Marcus was escorted into the private royal dining room.

“Thank you, the royal family is too kind to this humble servant.” Captain Spears replied as he took a nearby seat at the table.

"Good morning, Marcus, come take a seat." My father gestured.

"Yes, sit-down Marcus." My mother said.

General Marcus took a seat and looked over at Captain Spears. The general saw this as a perfect opportunity to get the captain to corroborate the reports he received from his men who helped escort the prince back to the capital. "Captain, it is good to see you, and I see Prince James is already awake. I am not surprised from the reports I received about you from the soldiers on the convoy."

"Reports?" My father, mother, and I said practically at the same time.

Turning to his brother and sister-in-law, General Marcus answered. "Yes. According to my men, Prince James here, would wake up early every morning and do a series of morning exercises and training. Over the few days it took, most of the soldiers participated in these morning activities and attested they noticed some gains as a result."

"Yes, I can vouch for that General. Every one of my knights felt subtle improvements in their movements and endurance at the end of our journey." Captain Spears provided.

One thing I had learned about the power structure of the royal faction was that Captain Spears reported directly to the king and queen as did the royal knights, however the various armies of the military reported to my uncle General Marcus. Of course, General Marcus reported directly to the king, and they were as close as any brothers could be. Growing up, even as kids, they fought side by side in several battles when my father was still a crown-prince defending the kingdom. In General Marcus was not only the General of the army but also a loving uncle who adored my sister Aurora. One thing I truly admired about this family was how much they loved their family and the people of this kingdom.

During joint efforts between the royal knights and the military, the knights lead the military. Only General Marcus and of course the royal family outranked the royal knights in combat.

General Marcus stroked his chin. "Interesting. Perhaps we could incorporate these exercises into the training regimen for the military. Where did you pick up these routines Prince James?"

“During my time of isolation, there was not much to do other than study and very slowly develop routines to grow stronger. I am more than willing to help the military however I can. If my routines will make our soldiers and royal knights stronger, then of course it is my duty and pleasure to train them.” I replied.

My father slapped the table and laughed. “Hahaha! You hear that, Marcus?!” With a huge smile on his face, my father continued. “My son’s sense of commitment to the betterment of our kingdom. He takes to it just as we did when we were his age.” My father proudly stated to his longtime friend and brother.

“Indeed. After you have selected your personal royal knight guards, I can arrange for you to train several of our colonels, majors, and some lieutenants.” General Marcus stated.

That gave me an idea, “Captain, if you are open to adding the training to the royal knights, we could start that training tomorrow morning. The officers won’t know me but to my understanding they respect the royal knights, seeing them going through the same training could help with their acceptance.”

“Of course, Prince James. News of your exploits has already spread to all the royal knights. None would deny a chance to grow stronger, let alone learn from you, my prince.” Captain Spears replied.

“Genius! I was just going to make it clear to learn or suffer my wrath. Ha, he’s just as shrewd as you were back in our younger campaign days, perhaps even more.” General Marcus boasted to his brother.

“See how much he takes after me!” My father exclaimed, clearly beaming with pride.

“Of course, I take after both you and mother.” I said.

“Awe! My baby is so sweet!” My mother said as she looked like she wanted to wrap me up in another hug. ‘Man, I was hoping to reduce her clinginess not add to it. I wonder if my extremely high Charisma is helping me say all the right things or if it is affecting them, heck probably both.’ I thought for a moment.

“See very shrewd. He knows exactly what to say.” General Marcus joked.

We talked briefly of what to expect later today. Captain Spears mentioned how adamant Mira, Kira, and several other knights that escorted me home expressed their interest, including LT. Simmons. General Marcus mentioned how Rita, the scout I saved, as well as others, offered to join my extended guard on travels and diplomatic missions in the future.

As we talked my sister finally had woken up and sleepily walked into the dining room. Her hair was a mess, and she was still in her pajamas. It was clear my sister was not a morning person.

“Good morning sister.” I greeted her happily. I thought she was adorable and knew I already liked having a little sister. It did make a part of me miss my brother and cousins, who were more like siblings to me, but I shifted my focus back to the here and now.

“Good morning, Princess Aurora.” Captain Spears said.

“Good morning, my little Aurora.” General Marcus said.

“Good morning, Uncle Marcus.” Aurora said.

It was at that point my sister was finally awake enough to realize she was not just with her parents and our uncle, General Marcus.

“Eek! Big brother! Captain Spears!” Was all she got out before ducking back into the hallway that led back to her room.

A few moments later she returned, hair combed and no longer in her pajamas.

“Good morning mother, father, Uncle Marcus, Captain Spears, big brother.” My sister acted like she wasn’t embarrassed even though her cheeks were a nice rose color.

“What did I miss?” My sister asked.

“Not much, sister. Just conversation on the royal knight selection process and talk of training. How did you sleep?”

“I slept quite well big brother. Thank you for asking.” My sister replied. It was clear she was trying to recover from her earlier embarrassment.

"I'm still trying to figure my way around the palace. After the knight selection, would my little sister like to show her big brother around the palace?" I asked Aurora.

Her eyes lit up as big as saucers. "Big brother needs help from me?! Of course, I will gladly help my big brother! I will show you everything, including when to get the best sweets from the kitchen!" Aurora replied excitedly.

'She is absolutely adorable! Such a sweetheart! No one is allowed to harm her ever.' I thought as Aurora seemed to beam with the idea that she would not only get time with her big brother but also that she could help me get more of my bearings in the palace. It was rather cute.

———-----------------———

After breakfast, we all moved to a meeting room. I was required to review the record of various members of the royal knights. Some came from minor noble houses. All of them had once attended the royal academy so information was provided on their known capabilities, skills, and specialties.

With my vastly increased Intelligence and Wisdom attributes, not to mention my eidetic memory ability, it did not take long to read all the information, collate, and identify possible candidates. Thinking about what I was learning of this world and of this kingdom, I needed a wide range of skills for the various ideas I wanted to achieve in the future. Considering the typical roles in an RPG party, I saw the benefit of having someone for each area; a tank/defender, healer, close quarters combat, vs magical or ranged combat. With that in mind I would have to speak to Captain Spears and General Marcus to carry out my plans.

After my review was done, I noticed that my uncle and Reggie were facilitating most of the conversation while my mother and father sat there quietly listening and drinking tea. I decided to ask Captain Spears and General Marcus my questions. "Captain Spears, what does it take to become a royal knight?"

"Good question your highness. Normally, we look for candidates that are strong in a particular area, whether it be physical enhancement magic, or offensive Magic, healing, stealth, it really just comes down to finding the best of the best that wish to serve on the front lines to protect the royal family and this kingdom. Obviously, there are specific skill sets we tend to focus on but as you can see in the information packets, there is a wide range of other capabilities." Reggie replied.

I asked my next question, "What about royal court magicians?"

General Marcus replied to this question, "Royal court magicians must possess even greater magical capabilities. Typically, they come from some noble family. That is not a requirement, but rather most nobles possess some magical aptitude, in some ways it's how their families became nobles in the first place. They protected their people and the kingdom. Royal court magicians also directly serve the royal family but are not on the front lines. Think of them more as deterrents or helping to tip the scale in major conflicts. Whether it's healing as is the case with Lady Rollara, or bolstering defenses, or bringing greater offenses to battles. Each royal court magician excels in their field of magic."

"Interesting. Can a member of the military become a royal knight?" I asked.

Captain Spears answered, "Of course they can, several current members of the royal knights started out in the military and distinguished themselves enough to become a royal knight."

I looked at both men and said, "Good, because I want Rita to become a royal knight and be one of my personal protectors."

Reggie was the first one to chime in, "Your highness, though Rita is an exceptional scout, hunter, and archer, I do not think that qualifies her to be a royal knight. We usually look for additional skills."

General Marcus smiled knowingly and chimed in. "Don't you see what Prince James is doing Captain?"

"Huh? I'm not following General." Captain Spears replied to the General's question.

General Marcus continued, "It has been some time since we had someone from the military that wasn't some minor noble and strong in combat magics elevated to a royal knight. By making Rita a royal knight it shows the rest of the military they can rise regardless of social rank. She does have some exceptional archery and tracking related magical skills plus she did risk her life and darn near killed herself just to warn the convoy of incoming danger."

Captain Spears replied, "She did, and her early warning saved many lives. I see what you're saying General. She has no political ties and comes from a very rural area of the kingdom. But is that why you want her as one of your personal royal knights Prince James? I would much rather prefer someone with more capabilities to protect you."

I answered honestly. "That is only a part of my reasoning for choosing Rita. Such magical skills are well received in the military for their application, but I see no indication of such appreciation in the royal knights. My understanding is she is the best archer in the military, perhaps in the kingdom. She will be perfect when combined with other capabilities."

My father was intently watching the conversation and finally spoke up, "Other capabilities?"

"Yes father. I had time to study various tactics both in warfare and adventuring." I replied.

"Adventuring?" My mother asked with a hint of nervousness.

"Yes. Our fight in the woods was not against other human soldiers, it was against undead monsters. From what I've read there have been battles and conflicts over the years against high level monsters. We should incorporate some successful adventuring tactics into our training approach."

My uncle interrupted, "Ha! He is just like we were when we were young, always wanting to go on an adventure."

My mother frowned and spoke up. "Yes, let us not forget the dangers involved in adventuring. Our son is a prince and has other duties to attend to."

"Quite right my dear. Though, can we expect any different from someone raised by our top adventuring duo. I am sure he was raised on their wonderous stories." My father commented.

"That is exactly what I am afraid of." My other answered.

"Fear not mother. Though I want to be an adventurer, I was more focused on the lessons from adventuring we could incorporate. Things like assigning roles to a group or creating smaller squads with multiple skill sets to handle specific situations." I stated, trying to calm my mother's fears.

"Hear the boy out Sophia." My father replied.

My mother gave a frown to my father and just nodded to me as a sign to continue. "Therefore, I have made my selection based on these principles. I will have Rita fill the roles of ranged damage, tracking, and scouting. I have selected Kira to be a healer and Melee defender. Mira is perfect for stealth and dealing melee damage. Finally, LT. Simmons will fill the role of primary defender and party leader to take charge should I be incapacitated. I will be seeking out good, ranged magic casters but for now this is my selection. I would like to form more than one guard unit, but for now this group will make up the core leadership of my personal royal knights. Father and Mother do you approve?"

Aurora sat there watching the exchange. At first, she was rather bored. Sure, she cared very much about who was going to protect her brother, but beyond knowing the names and faces she wasn't really that interested. Afterall, what did she know about such things, she was still learning her magic basics. That was until her big brother shocked the whole room into silence. His explanation was amazing. 'Man, my big brother is so awesome! Finally, I do not have to feel guilty for turning down the throne. My brother will be a great leader.'

Witnessing her brother's clear intelligence and well thought out tactics, Aurora doubled down on her commitment to study hard and do what she could to help her family and the kingdom. 'Maybe big brother will be willing to teach me what he learned?'

General Marcus spoke up first, "Absolute genius! We should consider how to incorporate some of these tactics into the military. Our forces would become far more effective protecting our citizens from monster attacks. Perhaps we could even recruit some adventurers who are interested."

My father came around and gave me a side hug, "See Marcus, we have a genius on our hands! The prophecy is proving truer and truer every day! Well done son! I agree with your logic and selection!" My father turned to my mother and asked, "Darling are you supportive as well?"

"Yes of course! Well done son! I am a bit concerned you do not have enough magical support, but you already recognize that deficiency and hopefully we can fill that gap soon. In the meantime, you should spend time training with Lady Rollara to help you offset this area. Plus, it would be good for you to learn from such a wise woman." My mother replied.

Ever since meeting my mother I saw intelligence in her eyes, so I was not surprised by her well thought out recommendation to study with Lady Rollara. I was just surprised and proud of her for not rushing me in another bear hug. I did see her hands and arms twitch some, so she was considering it.

'Good job mom on not suffocating me. Keep it up.' I thought.

"Well said my dear. Captain Spears and Marcus make it happen." My father replied.

General Marcus came up and shook my hand, "Thank you my boy for continually thinking of my people and on how to better integrate the royal knights."

"Thank you, General Marcus." I replied.

"Please my boy, call me Uncle Marcus, your sister already does, even during formal events. Your father and I put our familial ties as brothers before formality. Family first, our father used to say. Besides, I'm the only one that can tell him when he's being a fool. It's the best part of my job!"

"Hey! I heard that!" My father jokingly replied as he brought General Marcus into a side hug with his other arm.

Chapter 10 – Royal Knights & My CWs

The royal family assembled in the throne room along with Captain Spears, General Marcus, many of the royal knights, several of the high-ranking military officers, and royal advisors. As this was a royal family matter, the other military personnel present in the throne room were not required but were invited to help further solidify the partnership between the royal knights and military.

The royal advisors, military officers, and royal knights were all kneeling while I sat in one of four throne chairs, myself to the left of king, my sister Aurora to the right of the queen. General Marcus stood next to me, and Captain Spears stood next to Aurora.

My father spoke, his voice carrying across the entire massive throne room. "Rise. We are here to formally acknowledge the appointment of royal knights who will be the personal guards to our son Prince James."

Once everyone rose to their feet my father continued. "Normally we do not include so many to bear witness in such matters, all will understand shortly why we have made this exception for this event. The appointment of personal royal knight guards is a decision reserved solely for the king and queen. After much discussion, both the queen and I have agreed to grant our son Prince James not only the authority to select his own personal royal knight guards but also the authority to appoint future royal knights."

There were several gasps and shocked expressions. Prince James' exceptional hearing allowed him to pick up a few whispers.

"The king and queen are abdicating their authority to their son?"

"Why would they do this?"

The royal chamberlain slammed his staff on the throne room floor. "SILENCE! YOU ARE BEFORE THE ROYAL FAMILY!"

Once the chamber fell silent my father finished his statement. "Prince James is also granted the authority to work directly with General Marcus, Captain

Spears, and the Adventuring Guild in the formation of special joint teams to address threats to the kingdom."

More whispers erupted and it took the royal chamberlain to use his staff again to get the audience to quiet down.

The last part of my father's statement granting me the authority to appoint royal knights and form special teams my father, Uncle Marcus, and Reggie were all adamant about. They were convinced my ideas regarding incorporating adventuring team tactics could both save lives and increase the unity of the royal faction. They believed I had learned invaluable knowledge from John and Susan and all of them wanted to see their knowledge put to good use.

'I think they just wanted to pass on some of their burdens to me. Ugh.' I thought.

It was time for my part. "It took some deep deliberation and consideration in the selection of my personal royal knight guards. To start, I have selected LT Simmons to act as primary frontline defender and lead my personal royal knights. His physical enhancement magic and current rank make him perfect for the two roles. Come forward Lieutenant."

Lieutenant Simmons smiles as he steps forward then kneels in from of me. "It is my greatest honor to fulfill this duty. Thank you, your highness!"

"Next, I select Mira to act as melee attacker and in various stealth roles. Her skills and physical enhancement magic make her perfect for these roles. Mira, please step forward."

Looking at Mira, I could see her practically beaming. She seems far happier than she should be. 'Did I really make that big an impression?'

My thoughts were answered as she too knelt in front of me and spoke, "I thought joining the royal knights was my greatest honor but serving you in every way you required with be my greatest joy and honor your majesty!"

'Geesh, why did you have to put it that way?! Dial it down a bit Mira.'

"Next, I have chosen Kira to act as defender and healer. I personally witnessed her tireless efforts to heal the wounded and defend the camp while we were surrounded by the undead. She has more than proven capable. Kira, please move forward."

If I thought Mira was excited, Kira seemed a close tie. She bowed before me. "I pledge my life, mind, body, and soul to serve and protect you, seeing to your every desire and whim."

'Even more awkward! I got this, breathe James, breathe man. Just got to get through this last part.'

"For now, I will lastly call Rita please step forward."

Again, there were shocked murmurs from the crowd.

"How?"

"She isn't a knight."

I stood, which grabbed everyone's attention and quieted the crowd. Speaking quickly before their confusion grew worse. "Rita, your selfless act of risking your own life to give us precious warning of the incoming attack, saved my life and the lives of many others. You possess incredible skill and magic for archery and tracking far beyond any other in this kingdom. I hear by raise you to the status of royal knight and select you as my final personal royal knight. The synergy of your skills will work well with the rest of the team. Now, take a knee."

It took a moment for Rita to move as she was still in shock as to what was happening. Her friend Kira's soft words snapped her out of her stupor. "You got this, Rita."

Rita stepped forward and kneeled in front of me. I drew the sword at my waste and spoke while moving the sword over her head to lightly tap each shoulder. "For demonstrating unwavering loyalty to the crown, the knights, and military of this kingdom, I appoint you to the rank of royal knight. As your first assignment as a knight, you shall join my personal royal knights in the role as ranged attacker and scout."

I could see the pleased looks on both the knights and military officers. This person saved several of the knights' lives and the military officers saw her as a chance to rise even further.

"Thank you all for coming to witness this event. Please spread the word. Let all know how much we value the commitment and duty of the royal knights, military, and adventurers who put their lives on the line to protect our kingdom."

The official ceremony was over, the royal chamberlain excused the assembled audience. The man bowed and left the throne room to attend to other matters.

General Marcus excused himself to talk with his officers. Captain Spears welcomed Rita before excusing himself as well. "Congratulations Rita, both on being elevated to the rank of royal knight and for your appointment to Prince James personal guard. Now if you excuse me, I have duties to attend to. Lieutenant, I formally pass on the duty of protection of the prince to you."

LT. Simmons bowed his head and replied. "I formally take up the duty to protect our prince."

My father left to meet with the royal advisors. It was clear on several of their faces they wanted to know more about what my additional authority meant. 'Father, good luck dealing with those jackals.'

Mother and Aurora left with Lady Rollara. My assumption was to continue her training and education. 'Man, I got to get in on that training like my mother suggested. Lady Rollara seems like a shrewd fox, and she knows the real size of my core.'

Enough mental distractions, time to meet with my new team. I turned to the knights gathered around me. "Now that all that ceremony is over and done with let us adjourn to my suite. There is much to discuss." I noticed the girls blushing some. 'Why are they blushing? Geez, this high Charisma is going to get me in trouble.'

Mira spoke up first with a mischievous smile on her face, "Is the prince inviting us into his room?"

'That's not what I meant!' I could feel my cheeks heating up.

"I was referring to my private conference room within my suite. Very funny Mira."

Mira, Kira, and Rita all started to laugh, even Lieutenant Simmons chimed in with a chuckle. "You walked right into that one your highness."

Shaking my head. "Fair enough. Come, let's talk. I want you all aware of my immediate plans."

LT Simmons took the lead and the other three surrounded me, Mira to my left, Kira to my right, and Rita behind me.

Once we arrived in the suite, both Mira and LT Simmons broke off to do a quick scan of the various rooms in my suite. 'Man, they don't joke around. What they are doing is pretty much unnecessary, I warded my room before leaving it, but they don't know that. Granted the wards were somewhat limited. This overzealous effort might be a bit annoying in the future.'

They returned quickly and we entered my private conference room. I took a seat and asked them to do the same. "Please be seated. It is time for us to talk. Let me explain some of my plans over the next few weeks."

"As you wish your majesty." Rita said as she took her seat.

"Please, call me James when it is just the five of us." I replied.

"My Prince, I simply cannot." Rita replied.

Giving a devious grin I asked, "Are you refusing a direct order from your prince?"

"Uh..." Rita stammered, looking to the others for assistance.

"Quit teasing the poor girl your highness. She just became a knight; she has no concept of what is and is not acceptable." LT Simmons countered.

Turning to Rita, LT Simmons explained, "It is not uncommon for one of the royal family to be more informal in private. It is a part of their trust in us to watch their back and not abuse the privilege. Did you not see how Captain Spears and Prince James were so informal on the journey here?

"Yes Sir." Rita answered.

"It's similar." LT Simmons stated.

"Oh, my apologies Prince James. I am still learning." Rita replied.

Kira stepped in to help her friend and show her appreciation. "Thank you, James, for your trust in our capabilities. We will do our best to live up to this honor."

They all nodded. Feeling it best to get things back on track. "I truly do appreciate the sentiment Kira and I meant what I said when I selected each of you. Everyone one of you brings a specific set of skills, and I've fought alongside some of you. I can't think of anyone else besides Reggie that I'd want watching my back."

After they nodded again, I started to bring them up to speed on my plans. "Eventually we will find other members to add to our party."

"Party sire?" Mira asked.

"Yes. All of you heard the authority I was granted to form special teams to deal with threats to the kingdom?"

After they nodded, I continued. "I plan to recruit from the Adventurers' Guild. They primarily are independent, but they have skill sets and techniques I'd like other teams to learn. On our trip back we dealt with a monster army. For some that was the first time dealing with such things. My understanding is we tend to engage the guild to help when it comes to monster extermination."

"What skills are you referring to my prince?" Mira asked.

"Team coordination when dealing with monsters versus others. The approach you use to fight monsters is far different than armies. My father, Uncle Marcus, and Reggie have all asked I take on this task and I've gladly accepted. However, the adventurers' guild won't just go along with this. First, their independent charter helps provide some protection from political maneuverings, but the people that make up the guild are still our citizens and my understanding still care about this kingdom."

"It is true my prince, before I joined the army I scouted with several adventurers. They all loved the kingdom they grew up in just didn't want to get stuck serving some lord or noble just to advance or make a life." Rita chimed in.

"Thank you, Rita, for the input. To help gain influence with the guild, the five of us will be forming an adventuring party. My mother wasn't exactly thrilled with this idea, but she understands the need."

"Sire, that seems rather risky. I have never heard of a royal knight doing such a thing, let alone one from the royal family." LT Simmons chimed in.

"That is precisely why we are going to do it. We will start at the bottom and work our way up. I have agreed to keep the jobs we take as low risk as possible, at least for now. Mother was very adamant I enroll in the royal academy to learn to defend myself and master magics."

"Uh, you're kidding right? You took out an undead ogre and used his leg as a club! What more do you need to learn? I mean come on!" LT Simmons said.

Laughing I replied, "True enough Lieutenant, but mothers worry about their children no matter what you say and there is plenty I can still learn from the academy, especially about magic. I will attend the academy and we will do various quests from the guild during my off time. This is part of a long-term plan, but I want everyone to be aware of it. Any questions?"

Mira jokingly raised her hand. "Yes Mira?

"Do we get to beat the crap out of any adventurer who is an idiot and bad mouths you before they realize who you are?"

'Wow is that foreshadowing or what?' I think but I laugh and respond, "Yes you have my permission to punch them as hard as you can in the face."

"Oh, that's not a good idea, Mira can hit pretty hard. I speak from experience." LT Simmons replied chuckling.

"Regardless, she still has permission to do so. Now, some other things to make you all aware of..."

Making sure I had everyone's attention I continued. "First thing tomorrow morning, I will be training royal knights and some military officers in the morning exercise routines and condition training I performed during our travels. Second, I will begin joining my sister's tutoring sessions with Lady Rollara to prepare myself for life at the royal academy. At some point I'd really like to visit the city library and tour the city. Which leads me to the last item. My parents will not let me explore the city until after the royal ball."

"Royal ball?" Rita asked in confusion.

Her friend Kira, who came from a noble family explained. "The prince must be introduced to high society. This gives the nobles in each faction a chance to size him up and get his bearing. I am not surprised they want to make sure the nobles meet you before the rest of the city does. Other wealthy merchant and artisan families will also be in attendance. This is also an opportunity for potential marital candidates to meet you, my prince. After all, with your return you are now the most eligible bachelor in the kingdom."

"Ugh, don't remind me. I had to listen to mother go on and on about it, in excruciating detail." I lamented.

"Ha, now that's a problem I wouldn't mind having!" LT Simmons joked.

"There will most likely be some foreign dignitaries as well, so possible suitresses could be from outside the kingdom too. Keep in mind your highness, it is not unheard of for one of your peers to have multiple wives. Your parents are a bit of the minority when it comes to royal and noble families on the continent." Kira commented with an unhappy look.

I noticed Mira's and Kira's faces seemed to sour with all this talk of potential match making.

"Enough talk about such things. It's bad enough I hear this stuff from my mother. The ball will be in a few days. After the ball, we will register with the Adventurers' Guild and take a tour of the city. In a couple weeks I will take the Royal Academy entrance exam and hopefully start classes. It's been a long day. I'll leave it to all of you to figure out a watch schedule. I'm going to get some rest."

I chose to go to bed early not because I was tired but because I wanted to spend some time in my Demiplane.

After entering my Demiplane, I of course enjoyed another long soak in the Japanese style Bathhouse. As I was relaxing, I started to think through my plans. I considered what issues I knew of and what issues were unknown. I decided to use my Mental Visualization ability.

Mental Visualization:
Description: Create images and text with a mere thought. Turn these visuals on and off at will. Classification is also possible if partnered with Partitioned Mind ability.

Partitioned Mind:
Description: You have learned how to lock away a part or parts of your very consciousness to protect your mind and sanity. Possibilities are endless.

I created a mental list using my Mental Visualization and Partitioned Mind abilities:

Known/Unknown Problems/Concerns:
-Foreign influences trying to undermine the kingdom (Unknown) -People not wanting me to fulfill the prophecy (Unknown) -Which nobles can be trusted (Unknown) -Kingdom's economic state (unknown) -Magical knowledge (Inherited, need to know this world's understanding) -Building a force to deal with Kingdom level threats (Starting, need resources) -Figure out why my guide was rambling about the Dark (Eventually figure it out)

In looking at my mental list I realized a few things. First, I have limited information. I will need to come up with a plan to create an information network, not easy but doable with resources and the right personnel I can trust. Attending the Royal Academy will help me begin to meet other members of society and learn what magical and technological knowledge this world possesses. This led to the second realization, I need resources and personnel. This too will take time, but I have some ideas I can use.

Having already created various veins of ore in the mountains of my demiplane, I used some OPs to set each of those veins to grow over time. I could turn it off at some point but did not think I would be doing that anytime soon. After purchasing the self-growth option, I decided to create mine entrances into each mountain.

With the mines established, I added some additional ores to provide materials needed to support what I planned. Looking at my work I started to ponder what to do next.

I said out loud to myself, "The problem I see now is a lack of workers to mine those materials. Well, if you don't have what you need create it."

Mind made up; I began the process to create what I required using the magic I was most excited about. I decided to start to use some of my creation magic. Of all the magic I absorbed and gained knowledge of, this magic had me most excited with the unlimited range of possibilities. Now to start to make some of those possibilities happen.

Two fundamental aspects of magic I gained were magic in all the various forms came down to your intent and strength of will to make things happen. With a high enough intelligence, you could learn to bring miracles about, knowledge truly was power in this world. Spells were ways to programmatically focus your will and intent into reality. Thinking of it as a language or code, you just had to learn the various components of the spell and that is when it clicked for me, spells are called spells because they are spelling out what you desire. Why did I never think of it like that before?

Some spells required words, some required specific hand movements, and others used material components as magical focuses or to put it in ways I could better understand, it is like a fuse in completing a circuit. All of that said, it came down to ways for the energy within and surrounding you to remain focused in a way to bring your intent and mind in sync to ignore all the distractions and make it happen. Eventually do a spell enough times, with a high enough intelligence and energy pool, you create a new pattern or habit that you can draw on.

But here is the kicker, all of it didn't really matter. Words, gestures, and magical materials are just crutches, a way to focus or draw more power, I do not require such things. As my guide told me, the rules of this world would just be guidelines to me. With my knowledge of how Magic inherently worked I just needed a strong image, enough will, and to let my natural intuition do the rest. My **Mental Visualization** and **Partitioned Mind** were the perfect abilities to help me achieve what I wanted.

"Don't worry about the how, just the result." No truer words were ever said.

What I needed now was workers to mine and perform other gathering tasks. I had knowledge of **Unseen Servant,** but they don't have enough strength. I could **Summon Elementals**, but that too was limited. Perhaps a mix or both with a bit of a twist. With the image clear in my mind I activated the necessary magics and clamped down hard with my will using Creation Magic to bind it all together. A golden glow surrounded the area and as the light dissipated for the first time, I beheld my new worker creation.

The worker was about a meter tall and looked like a hybrid of an earth elemental with crystals in key parts. These crystals could harden and become tougher than diamonds and morph into different tools. This would allow my crystal workers or CWs to provide a wide range of services.

"Ha, in my old life we called our temporary workers contingent workers or CWs. Heck I was a CW before I got a permanent job. My mind must've made some kind of subconscious connection there. Ha, it still works." I chuckled to myself.

My CWs have enough intelligence to follow multiple instructions and I instinctually knew they would remain roughly about a week. With the time dilation of my Demiplane, I would have to re-summon all the CWs every few mornings when I returned to the Demiplane. Not perfect but with my high energy regeneration I could recover quickly. After using this creation magic to give new form, I wanted something temporary in nature but if these little guys worked out well enough, I was confident I could make them permanent.

I summoned several dozen CWs and put them to work mining the various precious minerals within the mountains. I created a vast storage facility where they would deposit all the raw ore into it. Eventually I would need to build a forge and smithy here but wanted the ore to pile up a bit. Plus, I was low on OPs for now. Luckily, I created this place to help me generate a small amount of points over time.

As I watched my new creations work, I mentally added a note to my growing list. Each day I would use a certain amount of Omniverse Points to increase the growth rate of the various veins of ore so my CWs would never run out of something to mine.

I decided to supervise my workers for a few hours. My CWs seemed to enjoy working with their hands and being productive. While I watched I noticed I regained enough Omniverse Points to create a forge attached to a smithy, and some molds for creating metal bars. Nice thing about using OPs is the forge and smithy came fully stocked with tools and supplies needed for the smelting process.

"Man, it pays to have clear mental visualization!" I commented.

I dabbled in blacksmithing and leatherworking back in my old life. My Uncle used to do leatherworking and he instilled in me the importance of knowing basic skills that most people had forgotten. I always respected my uncle for that. I wouldn't have known as much as I did back in my old life if not for him. After gaining so many skills and professional knowledge my intuition used that knowledge to create more than just a building.

Looking at the size of the building I couldn't help but comment. "That thing is massive. There must be enough here for several blacksmiths and smelters to work simultaneously. This must be a dwarf's wet dream, heck I'm excited to use it in the future."

Then I realized one very important thing, "Why wait when you can do it now?"

I summoned a CW to bring the ore from the storage facility to the forge. With my smithing knowledge, I started two different processes, one to smelt the gold and one to smelt the platinum ores. The focus of each process was to smelt them down, remove the impurities, and pour the liquid metal into the casts. The advantage of having CWs is they had very high tolerance for extreme pressure and heat making them perfect miners and smithing assistants.

While my CW assistants held the super-heated ore, I used ice magic to cool the metals. After the metals cooled, I checked out my handy work. Having the CWs open the cast and drop the bars onto a sturdy table.

"There be gooolldd in them there hills!" I said in my best impression of a California 49er voice because of course the first thing I'm going to make are gold bars, and you have to sound like an old miner when you do it. I mean duh!

The idea of being able to mine and forge precious metals I could turn into resources and currency was cool but conceptually thinking about it vs. making it happen, let's just say I was a bit giddy. I made this happen, hard to compare it to anything. With enough time I could make anything, how cool is that?

Talk about grueling yet satisfying work, smithing and metallurgy was pretty freaking awesome! After several repeats of the various processes, I ended up with 100 gold bars and 100 platinum bars!

"I need to create a giant Scrooge McDuck vault and fill it with gold coins I can go swimming it." I said in excitement. Of course, I would not be doing that as it would be a sure-fire way of getting trapped, but I could dream.

"Hmm, I wonder if this is a result of choosing dragon as my race. I have a sudden urge to make a hoard and fill it with shinny things? Oh well, problem for a later day." I dismissed the random thought and got back to making things happen.

This was day one of me starting to accumulate the wealth I would need to enact my plans. So glad I invested in learning everything I could about smithing. So many skills I made a point to learn but the combination of magic and smithing was awesome.

My CWs were turning out to be invaluable too. They learned quickly, I could give instructions via telepathy or voice commands. They could even learn by watching, which made things even easier. I instructed a few of the CWs that were assisting me to take over the processes I performed to create the bars. As they didn't have ice magic, I showed them how to cool the metals. Observing the CWs for a while to ensure they followed the instructions to the letter. After feeling sufficiently satisfied that they had this well in hand, I stored the bars in my massive city sized pocket dimension and left.

For the second time this visit, I headed to the bathhouse to clean up. All the soot and grime I seemed to have accumulated and a nice soak just sounded like heaven. I removed my clothes and used one of my favorite spells, **Prestidigitation**, to clean my clothes. Sure, I also used it to clean myself and not just my clothes while traveling, but I am not traveling at the moment, and that was before I had this perfectly good luxury bathhouse. I cannot let this place go to waste. Where is the fun in that?

"God, thank you for this new amazing life." I said after enjoying another amazing bathing experience.

All the knowledge I gained about this world, the kingdom, the royal family, and the various threats here, I knew I had my work cut out for me but here in this moment, I'm good.

Taking a few more moments to enjoy this experience, I thought, 'Man who would've ever thought I'd be such a bath person. The Japanese know their stuff!'

As I left the bathhouse fully dressed and clean once again, I ordered a few CWs to move the bars of gold and platinum to the storage facility. I would retrieve them each time I visited. Sure, I could leave it all here, but this place worked differently than my personal pocket dimension. Once I put an item in my pocket dimension I could recall it with a thought, add in the fact that nothing ages, it's the perfect storage. I heard some lucky people had bags of holding; those things are a joke compared to my personal storage.

Just looking at all the activity of my CWs I was feeling a bit like a lazy bum, so I decided to get back to training and practicing my magic. I had designed an area where I could practice some of my magic. I say some as my demiplane was still not strong enough to withstand some of my more powerful attack spells. Eventually, this place would be fortified enough, both in realm stability and protection circles, to withstand my Grand Scale magic spells.

Chapter 11 – Starting a New Routine

When I finally walked out of my realm, several days of demiplane time had passed, yet only the evening had passed in this world. The time differential was a bit disorienting and if I didn't have my **Absolute Timing** ability, I would not be able to track time duration between the two places without losing my mind trying to keep it all straight in my head. It was barely about to be morning in this world. Here I just spent time to rest, train, practice my magic, try my hand at smelting some metals, and even minor crafting. Man, I loved having my own realm!

'Time to see what my knights are up to.' I thought as I exited my bedroom.

Mira immediately bolted upright and stood at attention.

"At ease Mira. Seriously, you do not need to be so stiff. Where is everyone else?"

Mira seemed to relax slightly and replied, "Simmons is getting some shuteye. Kira and Rita are just outside the suite on guard. We figured one of us should rest, two should guard the suite, and one should guard your door should you require anything."

"And you drew the short straw?"

She looked at me perplexed. Seeing her face, "Sorry, bad joke. I am concerned about all of you running ragged. Perhaps I'll need to select some additional knights to help sooner than originally planned."

"Do not worry about us my prince. This is our duty. We are proud to be your personal royal knights." Mira replied.

Seeing how earnest Mira seemed, I replied. "I'll drop it for now. Let's get some breakfast and head to the royal knight training arena. The military officers should be arriving early, and I'd like to assess the royal knights first."

Mira had a bit more fun than I would've thought waking up LT Simmons by sneaking into one of the guest bedrooms and yelling in his face to wake up.

"WAKE UP LIEUTENANT! OUR PRINCE NEEDS YOU!!"

"OH, Dear Go... Who? WHAT?" LT. Simmons quickly replied as he bolted upright from a dead snore.

I could tell she really gave it her all as LT Simmons was still shaking his head periodically to help clear the ringing out of his ear.

Rita and Kira both entered the suite when they heard the commotion from Mira's little prank as just chuckled at LT Simmons putting his finger in his ear and shaking it while trying to get his ears to pop.

Breakfast was quick as I wanted to get to the training arena early. When we arrived, there were already several royal knights and more flowing in as the time passed. I covered the basics with my team first, so they knew what to expect. 'Time to get this party started.' I thought.

"LT Simmons, if you would please rally the troops and get them into formation." I ordered.

LT Simmons smiled wide and approached his orders with gusto. Getting yelled at to wake up this morning I think gave him more incentive to yell at others. I almost felt bad for the other royal knights as he got them organized in what I assume was record time. A few of his comments towards the slower nights could be heard clearly across the training arena.

"GET YOUR REAR MOVING!"

"WHAT ARE YOU SMILING AT?!"

"Thank you, LT Simmons." I nodded before turning my attention to the knights in front of me. "As you may all have been informed, the king and queen have abdicated their authority over the assigning and training of the royal knights to me. In addition, I have worked with my Uncle Marcus, to invite several military officers to participate in this new program."

Paying close attention to their expressions before I moved forward. Noticing only looks of determination I continued. "Now that everyone is in formation, we will start with some light stretching to make sure you're limbered up before getting into the training routine. Any questions? No? Good, let's get started."

We spent a good 20 minutes on stretching. As we were wrapping up the stretching, the military officers showed up. Seeing the tired looks in some of their eyes and that a few seemed to be dragging their feet, I decided to get their attention.

"If you're going to come here to learn, make sure to come early. General Marcus made it very clear you are to learn and to not go easy on you. LT Simmons, get this new group into formation."

If I thought LT Simmons was happy before, he almost had a manic smile on his face now. He immediately started yelling and getting up into the officers' faces.

"What do you think you are doing solider?!"

"What are you snickering at? Do you want me to make you run laps?"

"Do not waste our prince's valuable time!"

SMACK

I could hear the hit as he knocked an officer to the ground by hitting him once upside the head.

"That is what you get for laughing at your friend's misfortune! Now give me twenty reps while you are down there! NOW!"

'Man, he really does love to yell at people. He missed his calling as a drill sergeant.'

Seeing everyone in proper formation, and sufficiently cowed by LT Simmons, it was time to begin. "All let us begin. First, I'm going to show you some endurance moves. They may seem pointless but in fact they will strengthen your attacks and streamline your movement in combat. Watch me closely."

So, it went on for a few hours. My team followed along, acting as drill instructors, getting after anyone who started to fall behind. It seemed almost like a game between the girls and LT. Simmons to see who could get to the person and yell at them before anyone else. LT. Simmons and Mira seemed to clearly be the most zealous. Sadly, for the royal knights and military officers that meant no one was spared or had a moment's rest during training.

"Good. You may all rest now." I ordered.

Several people collapsed on the ground panting, several more had their hands on their knees trying to catch their breath.

"UGH!"

"He is a demon!"

"I... have... never... trained... so hard... in my life."

"Remember, a big part of this training is building up your endurance." I commented.

LT Simmons spoke up. "My prince, if they have energy to complain, then perhaps they should be worked harder next time?"

"Good point Lieutenant. Perhaps we should." I smiled back at him evilly.

All the complaints stopped immediately. LT Simmons said into the silence. "That is much better."

One of the lower ranking military officers who was panting on the ground spoke up. "How are you not winded your highness? I know the King and General Marcus are warriors, but I thought you were on Death's door."

"I was. I'm better now." 'That was one of my favorite lines from an older tv show I loved back in my old life.' I continued, "I have spent time strengthening my body, mind, and spirit. What you are learning are the exercises I've found to be most useful. We will grow stronger together so all of us may be better prepared to protect this kingdom and our family and friends!"

One thing I always respected about soldiers was their commitment to something bigger than themselves. It is important to acknowledge their sacrifices and efforts for the ones they care about. Looking around at their tired faces, they all seemed to appreciate my interest in helping to make them stronger. "That is all for today. I will see you all back tomorrow morning so we can continue to show you other training techniques."

I could tell several of the military officers wanted to introduce themselves to me, but I wasn't ready for that yet. I wanted to get a better feel for each of them before I decided who I was interested in talking to. One thing I will give my personal knights, they paid attention to me and seemed to tell I was not ready to mingle with our men yet. My knights surrounded me and escorted me from the training arena. It was time to join my sister's magical tutoring session with Lady Rollara.

'Time to learn more about magic!' I thought gleefully as we walked to the special facility.

Lady Rollara had one of the larger ballrooms converted into an area for Magic tutoring. When we arrived, it was clear for me to see that Lady Rollara thought of everything when setting this place up. The walls were clearly re-enforced, some looked to be enchanted to withstand magical attacks. Various training dummies and targets made from different materials were placed in different sections, these dummies clearly also enchanted to resist magical attacks. As I continued to survey the room, I noticed different materials such as dirt, stone, water barrels, lit torches, and other random sections set up for use. However, the coolest thing seemed to be an obstacle course setup to change and shift as you moved through it.

'Ooo, that looks fun.' I thought as I watched the obstacle course constantly shift.

My sister was practicing a spell. When she noticed me, her concentration was broken and causing the spell to fizzle out. Lady Rollara chided my sister for losing concentration. It was evident Lady Rollara wasn't overly harsh with my sister. The way Lady Rollara looked at Aurora it was clear she was soft on her. "Now you know better my dear. No matter what, you must always maintain your concentration."

Aurora ignored the reprimand and called out to me. "Big brother! Over here! Did you come to train with your sister?!"

"Of course, sister. I said I would come and how could I let down someone so adorable."

Aurora blushed but her smile grew even bigger. "Awe, big brother is so sweet."

Lady Rollara spoke up. "Good timing Prince James. I was just reminding Princess Aurora of the importance of repeatedly practicing the basics so much you do not lose your concentration mid-cast."

"Starting with the basics is probably best for me, my lady." I said.

Mira and Kira both smirked at my comment which garnered a raised eyebrow from Lady Rollara, but she said nothing.

Aurora was the first to speak up, not picking up on the underlying message and taking my words literally. "I can show you the basics, big brother! I've gotten pretty good. This is the first time I've lost concentration in a long while."

"I would not consider two weeks a long time Princess." Lady Aurora commented.

My sister scowled at her but just kept on going. Nothing was going to bring her down or stop her from helping her big brother. "First Big Brother, you think about the spell as you tap into your energy and will it to respond, then speak the words while you do the hand motions. That is the hardest part, doing all of those together. It took me awhile to be able to keep all those things straight in my head."

Aurora went through the process of casting a spell and the result was a small fire bolt that shot out and hit the target. She seemed so proud. "Oh, yea and don't forget to aim too." Aurora said.

I ruffled her hair as I acknowledged her success. "Great job, little sister."

"Well done, Princess. Let us see if the prince can copy your results after only hearing it one time." Lady Rollara said.

"It's ok Big Brother if you don't get it. That's really hard to do. I think Lady Rollara is being a bit mean to ask something like that of you." My sister said as she scowled at Lady Rollara again.

Saying nothing, I looked at the target, raised my hand and then turned to look directly at Lady Rollara. I cast my spell, with no words or hand jesters, just did what I have always done since I learned magic, tapped into my energy, and willed it to happen. It was fast but the fireball I launched was far bigger than the tiny fire bolt my sister cast. My result was far more devastating as I ended up blowing the target to smithereens.

BOOM!!!

My sister just stared at the nonexistent target, then looked back at me slack jawed.

“Woops. Sorry about that, I was trying to hold back.”

Out of nowhere Lady Rollara started to laugh, and I mean a deep belly laugh.

“Hahaha.”

Wiping a tear from her eye she collected herself enough to clap her hands together and say, “Well done Prince James, well done indeed! From the information I collected about your battle with the undead army I suspected you had chantless magic, but it appears to be even more intuitive for you. It appears my sister was correct.”

“Your sister?” I replied confused.

“Yes, my sister. She passed away several years back but before she died, she took me into her confidence. Most did not know she was a Seer, a very powerful one. My sister is the one who had the prophecy regarding the young prince. Didn’t know that did you?” Lady Rollara said, still smiling.

—— Lady Rollara Flashback ——

“I remember it like it was yesterday. She was on her deathbed. The sickness she had was fatal and uncurable, no matter what was tried. It was just her and I and she pulled me in close.

“Sister, before I go, I must tell you of the strongest vision I had in my life. Only the king, queen, and their two most loyal servants know of this prophecy. You will know when you can share this with others.” Lady Lara told me.

“Is this why the sickly prince with those eyes was sent away?” I asked.

“Yes. He was born with one purple left eye and one green right eye. His father has green eyes, and his mother has purple, a mix of the two is possible but this goes beyond that. Each color represents powerful symbols. Purple for strength and fortitude of the mind and green for depth of soul and connection to our people.” Lady Lara stated.

"The Mind and Soul of the people. Just like our mother told us growing up. 'One would come to heal the soul and mind of the people." I said in reverence.

"Yes sister, just as mother said. If he can reach the age of maturity, then his gifts can blossom in all our hearts and minds. This kingdom will prosper and bring about a new age for us all." My sister explained.

"Then why send him away sister? Should he not be protected? Should we not guard him and hold him close to ensure no harm comes to him?!" I inquired.

My sister further explained. "No! I have seen it. Should the prince be surrounded and nurtured here then the sickness will grow and consume that which would blossom. But if he is isolated and cut off from everyone, save for the two that will teach him, then the man that comes from the hidden valley shall grow and the sickness will die on the vine."

Lara broke out in a bout of coughing. I helped her drink some water.

"Careful sister. Do not rush. I am here." I comforted.

After she recovered from her coughing fit, Lara continued, "In isolation he with read and study all manner of things, as such he will have time to understand the world in ways others cannot. Magic will speak to him; he will understand it like no other and do things with it no one has ever dreamed of. His energy pool will be massive and make yours look like a drop in the ocean."

"That seems highly unlikely sister. My energy pool is greater than any in our family's history. Such a person would be very dangerous if not taught control." I said incredulously.

Grabbing my hand, my sister spoke even more seriously. "You will meet him, teach him control... Lara squeezed my hand tighter. "This is most important, do not attempt to control him or force him to learn how we were taught. He will understand Magic and our world in ways that should not be stifled. The Dark shall surely claim him if any attempt to do so! Promise me, sister you will help him!"

"I promise!" I earnestly replied.

She died in my arms with a smile on her face after that. I will never forget the look of peace on her face or my promise to the person I cared about most in this world.

Hearing Lady Rollara's story had everyone present stunned. Kira knew the bare bones of the prophecy from the high priest.

'I will need to share this additional information with the High Priest. Any additional context from the person who gave the prophecy would help the Church of Light navigate properly.' Kira thought.

Lady Rollara could see everyone lost in thought. She remembered locking herself away after her sister passed to both mourn for her sister and to consider what she was told. 'They will require some additional guidance it seems to help them fully understand.' She thought.

Clapping her hands together to bring everyone out of their thoughts, Lady Rollara waited until she saw all eyes on her before speaking up. "Now all of you know the truth as I do."

Turning to Prince James, Lady Rollara continued. "When I checked you for any necrotic damage, I took the time to check your core for any damage. In my many years at court, I have had plenty of practice concealing my thoughts and feelings. All of that was put to the test to hide my shock at what I learned when barely touching your energy core."

"Is there something wrong with my core?" I asked in concern. 'Man, I really should've paid more attention to my guide when they were talking.'

Lady Rollara laughed heartily. "Is there something wrong with your core? HA, HA, HA! That is rich my boy. I needed that laugh." After collecting herself she continued. "No, your core, or what some call our pool of mana, is greater than any being I know of in our history and that includes dragons. Not even Demon Lords possess such a core."

"Dragons! My brother has an energy pool greater than dragons?! How is that possible?!" My sister exclaimed, looking at me with even more wonder.

'Maybe that has something to do with me being a dragon? Not going to tell my adorable sister that fact though. Why is she looking at me that way?' I thought as I heard my sister's comment.

"Lady Rollara, our captain said Prince James was special in ways he was not at liberty to discuss. Did he know about this prophecy?" Mira asked.

"Of course, my dear. The king and queen made a point to tell the captain, so he knew the risks and importance of bringing the prince home." Lady Rollara replied.

"That would explain why Captain Spears was so nervous and quiet on the trip there." LT Simmons commented.

"General Marcus had come to talk to the soldiers. He was adamant we do everything we can to bring Prince James home. I just thought he wanted his nephew brought back safe." Rita stated.

"His eyes were a dead giveaway." Mira spoke up.

Lady Rollara looked at Mira and asked. "What do you know of his eyes? Most would think it was just a fluke of him getting one eye from each of his parents. The fact that it is a part of the prophecy is even less known."

"No offense intended Lady Rollara, but I come from the Nightshade family. My mother was close to your sister Lady Lara before she passed. Our family specializes in learning things others try to keep hidden." Mira stated.

"I am very familiar with your family line my dear, but my sister was very careful who she told." Lady Rollara commented.

"My mother told me that she visited Lady Lara a few days before she passed beyond the veil." Mira replied.

"I never knew. Of course, I knew Minerva was close to my sister, but I did not realize she visited her or that my sister would reveal such things." Lady Rollara said almost more to herself than anyone else.

"Mother said Lady Lara was partially delirious with fever and my mother had to use some ice magic to help bring the fever down. It was a temporary reprieve according to mother, but Lady Lara told her out of appreciation of her kindness." Mira explained.

"Please convey my thanks to your mother for her help in easing my sister's suffering towards the end." Lady Rollara said in appreciation.

Mira bowed before continuing. "Mother had found another prophecy that referenced a man with special eyes, one purple and one green. She drew the connection between the two."

"Other prophecy, about the prince? I have never heard of a different prophecy. Would you tell me about it?" Lady Rollara inquired.

Mira's face blushed for some reason, and she bowed. "You will have to discuss that with my mother. I should not have mentioned it just now, it slipped out when I thought of Prince James' unique eyes."

"Can we please not talk about me like I'm not here?" I said, getting a bit uncomfortable with all this talk. 'Sure, I thought it was cool having purple and green eyes, now I know the significance, well part of it anyway. Would've been nice to have been told that. Wait, maybe I was told that? Geez, I really should've paid attention when my guide was talking.'

Lady Rollara spoke up. "My apologies, Prince James. It just brings joy to my heart to have my sister proven true. Many in court thought the king and queen's decision to send their only son away was odd and foolish, including many of the high nobles. Bits and pieces of the prophecy got out; other seers had fractured visions but none as clear as my sister's vision. There is more but that shall be saved for another day. It is clear I will need to speak with Lady Nightshade too."

As if she was distracted and then came back to her senses, Lady Rollara waved her had at the spot where the training dummy used to exist. "Seeing this little display of yours, it is very clear I must teach you control and to hide your strength. Sadly, you will not be able to hide your innate talent in magic, as silent casting is exceptionally rare, but they need not know your full capacity."

"How do you envision we do that Lady Rollara? My understanding is everyone is tested as part of joining the Royal Academy. One of those tests is magical capacity and magical intensity." I asked, with genuine concern on my face. 'The one thing I did pay attention to was to be cautious on revealing everything I was capable of. Being tested in front of the whole school seemed like a bad idea.'

"Do not worry my Prince, there are perks to being a royal and for knowing one of the teachers at the academy. In the past, members of the royal family have taken their testing here in the palace." Lady Rollara said as she waved to the training area. “That is why I set this training area up. Yes, this helps your sister in her learning, but it can also be used for testing.”

“You mean I can take my entrance exam here in the royal palace? When?” I asked in hopeful relief.

“I can coordinate for a few of the teachers to test you here in this tutoring area. As for your magical capacity and intensity that can be administered directly by me. Two are usually required to test magical intensity for safety and awareness purposes, but I can bypass that safety guideline. The main reason to understand magical intensity is if we get a student with high intensity, more classes regarding control are required to ensure they don’t accidentally hurt someone.” Lady Rollara stated while pointing to the destroyed target.

I shrugged as stated. “That’s fair, and point taken.”

“This has been done in the past to protect the royal family and not give upstart nobles or foreign nations an idea of the true strength of the royal family. Remember we sometimes allow foreign dignitaries stationed in the capital the approval to send their children to the royal academy as it is one of the best schools on the continent.” Kira stated as she nodded her head following along with where Lady Rollara was going with her plan.

‘I keep forgetting that Kira comes from a high noble family. I need to poke her for information.’ After that thought a random thought popped in my head about ‘poking’ Kira. ‘Damn this young body. Ugh, focus.’

“I meant no embarrassment or insult my prince. I merely think Lady Rollara’s suggestion is prudent.” Kira said misunderstanding the nature of the redness in my checks.

“It’s fine Kira. Lady Rollara, when can we get this test administered? I’m anxious to know if I will be accepted into the Royal Academy.” I said quickly, trying to change the subject from the redness of my cheeks.

Lady Rollara’s laugh was pure and full of mirth. “Ha, ha, ha, ha! Oh, you were serious my prince?” Noticing my confused look. “You have nothing to worry about Prince James. That little display alone would have several instructors competing to have you in their class. No, this process is mere formality for you and to test your other aptitudes and affinities.”

“Other aptitudes and Affinities?” Aurora asked confused.

Lady Rollara looked at Aurora, “Yes, my dear. You see your mother, Queen Sophia, has made a point for you to focus on your magic and healing skills. As you have been told, your affinities to water and healing are much stronger than your fire affinity and you have zero dark magic affinity. We test all the range of magic types to see what you’re strong in.”

“Oh. Is that why my fire spells are harder for me to cast?” Aurora asked.

“Yes, my dear. However, with your brother’s little display, it is clear he has a very strong affinity for fire magic which is perfect for a battle mage. We also know he did some healing which shows an affinity to life or light magic, but we must test the other magic types.”

“Could he have other affinities? I thought more than one affinity was rare.” Aurora asked.

“Yes and no. Affinities are a spectrum. Having high affinities in multiple magic types is what is rare, but that does not mean you cannot use a particular magic, your fire bolt spell is an example my dear.” Lady Rollara explained.

She continued to explain the testing. “Now we test more than just magic types. We want to understand a person’s aptitudes and training or interests. Of course, I am referring to various combat methods like swords, knives, or bows, but we can also check for crafting and other aptitudes. Those are usually done through demonstration and are graded by experts in those fields.”

‘Man, she has a great way of explaining things. No wonder my parents have her teaching my sister.’ I thought as I listened.

Lady Rollara continued her explanation. “Now to answer the prince’s question on when. I would say tomorrow or the day after at the latest. All the instructors live within the city and are already here getting prepared for the general testing. It will not be difficult to get them here.”

Aurora looked at me, “Wow big brother you’re going to be very busy soon. Are you going to have any time for me?”

My heart melted again looking at her puppy dog eyes looking up at me. “Of course, sister. In fact, would you like to go for a ride on big brother’s back?”

Her eyes widened, "Really? Yes, yes, yes!" She said jumping up and down all excited.

I bent down on one knee and let my sister jump on my back. As I stood up my sister commented. "Wow big brother, you are tall! I can see so much more from up here."

'Heart melting further, resistance not yet futile. Adorableness increasing.' I joked with myself.

Once I had my sister in a piggyback carry, I turned my attention to the rest of the room. "Lady Rollara, I hope you don't mind if we adjourn for the day. I can show you one other bit of magic as I leave with Aurora."

Curious, Lady Rollara replied. "Of course, Prince James, we have already been practicing for some time now. What other display of magic did you have in mind? I would be cautious with Princess Aurora on your back."

"Yes, please be careful with Princess Aurora. I am sworn to protect her Prince James." Aurora's personal royal knight stated.

I leaned my head closer and whispered to my sister. "Tell big brother, have you ever wanted to fly?"

Aurora's eyes turned into giant saucers as we lifted off the ground and took off down the hall. I could only make out a comment by the royal knights and Lady Rollara. "He knows flight magic?!" As the knights bolted after us, doing their best and failing to keep up.

As we sped through the halls weaving in and out, avoiding staff and guards, I could hear my sister giggling and screaming "WEEEE!!!!"

Chapter 12 – Pre-Exam Nerves

We sped past mother and father as my sister said, “Hi MOM & Dad! BYE Mom and Dad!” As she continued to giggle.

I couldn’t help it, I laughed along with my sister as we saw the expressions on their faces. It felt good to be able to brighten my sister’s day.

“He can fly?!” Both mother and father said in surprise.

It took a moment for my mother to collect herself and yell out a voice of concern. “Be careful!”

Ever my father, “Have fun kids!”

“It warms my heart to hear laughter in these halls again.” My mother commented as my parents took a moment to embrace.

Our personal royal knights ran after us, slowing just enough so they could bow as they passed by the king and queen. “Your majesties.”

“They get hurt, it’s your heads.” My father laughingly called out to the passing knights.

“I’m going to lose my job.” Aurora’s personal knight lamented as they were running to catch up.

“Don’t worry about it. The king was laughing, and it is not like any of us knew he could fly.” Mira stated.

“Yes, Prince James continues to surprise us.” Kira commented.

“Just roll with it. A royal knight must always adapt to any situation. Maybe you should join the morning training Daria. It would do you good.” LT Simmons huffed out.

“Who is the one breathing hard?” Mira teased.

“Hey, I am just fine without my body strengthening magic. You are the one cheating.” LT Simmons replied.

“I do not know what you are talking about. Besides, I agree Daria should join the morning exercises.” Mira answered.

“Uh-huh. Go ahead and ignore the fact that I can detect your use of magic.” LT Simmons deadpanned.

The knights finally caught up to us as we lay on the ground in the garden laughing.

“Again! I want to ride big brother again.” Aurora said.

“Phrasing.” I said out of pure reflex.

Aurora looked at me confused, clearly not understanding my Archer moment.

Laughing, “I mean, careful sister how you say that. We will find time to do that again for sure.”

“Prince James, I must plead with you to never do that again.” Aurora’s knight who I found out was named Daria. ‘What is with all these names that end in ‘A’, must be a cultural thing.’

“Daria, you heard my big brother. We absolutely plan to do that again.” Aurora replied, crossing her arms, and giving her best ‘don’t you ruin my fun’ look at her personal knight.

“Do not worry Daria, no harm will come to my sister in my presence. I am very protective of the people I care about.” I replied in the hopes of easing Daria’s concerns.

Daria looked to LT. Simmons, who was the highest-ranking knight present, for help. Simmons just smiled back at her and spoke up. “My prince, I was just saying how Daria would benefit from joining the early morning training exercises, what do you think?”

“Is that so? What do you think Mira?” I asked, knowing what Mira’s stance would be.

Mira smiled with a wicked grin. “It is one of the times I think LT. Simmons was thinking clearly. I completely agree.”

“Then I expect to see you join the morning routines.”

Thinking to herself 'That man is a demon in disguise! Betrayed by my own comrades!'

Realizing she had no way of preventing this, Daria answered, "Understood your majesty."

"Could've told us you could fly lad, nice thing to know you know." LT Simmons stated.

"Got to keep you on your toes from time to time. Plus, the surprise on everyone's faces was priceless." I said before looking at my sister and continuing. "But the joyous laughter of my sister made it all worth it."

"Awe, big brother!" Aurora said before giving me a big ole hug.

I pulled her to arms-length and asked, "Want to show me where to get the best treats? I do believe you promised me."

I chuckled a little as my sister's eyes lit up. She took my hand and started to pull me along. "This way, big brother, you're going to love the sweetbreads and other treats. I know right where they stash them!"

Everyone seemed to get caught up in my little sister's antics, laughing as Aurora pulled me along towards the palace kitchens.

While our knights were being sufficiently scolded and shewed away by the kitchen staff, my sister used the distraction to grab a few treats for us all. We ducked out of the kitchens and rejoined our knights before the staff realized what happened.

"Princess, I really wish you wouldn't do that. The head cook really gets upset at me for barging in and disrupting the 'sanctity of the kitchen' as she calls it." Daria complained to Aurora.

Of course, Aurora had a great reply, she simply handed the lady one of the sweetbreads and while smiling said, "But then we wouldn't get to enjoy these all the time."

She passed the other sweetbreads to the rest of us, "Enjoy! Tell me what you think Big Brother!"

Biting into the bread, I could taste honey and other sweet flavors, it was divine, perhaps a bit rich for me but so satisfying.

"Very yummy sis, great job." I say while patting her head.

Aurora just beams up at me while devouring her sweetbread, this kid just kept getting more adorable every minute. We had found our way back to the gardens and just sat there for a while, enjoying the tasty treat and the peaceful atmosphere. I once again said a silent prayer thanking God for this new life I now had. I may not know which side my guide was on, but that did not change my thoughts of appreciation at being given this second chance.

We stayed that way for a time, all of us lost in thought, until one of the palace staff came to get us for dinner. Tonight, I was to have dinner with my sister and parents. I instructed the sweet lady, who reminded me of the real-life Mrs. Buttersworth, to escort us to the royal family's private dining room. After thanking her, she excused herself as I held out my sister's chair before taking my own seat.

My parents had an odd look for a moment while I was helping my sister with her chair but then smiled after. "You know son, we have people for that." My father commented.

Aurora chimed in, "Daddy, I like when Big Brother does that, it makes me feel special."

"Of course, you are special, you are a princess and more importantly daddy's little girl." My father said smiling back to my sister.

My mother decided to give her perspective, "Though it warms our heart to see you two getting along so well, I would ask you both to be mindful of your station around others."

Seeing my sister's smile start to fall our mother continued, "But seeing how it is just us right now, it is completely fine." Seeing my mother wink at my sister and smile as Aurora's face brightened once again.

'Man, this kid truly is a national treasure.' I thought.

We ate an amazing meal. The food and spices of this world were impressive, but I guess that comes with living in a palace. I ate a rather large meal, noticing my appetite seems to have increased.

As we were finishing up, my mother spoke up, "Lady Rollara informed us that you are aware we intend to have your Royal Academy admissions testing conducted here in the palace."

"Yes mother, she mentioned it." I noticed she held back an urge to get up and rush me in another bear hug. 'She is definitely getting better about that.'

My father spoke up, "The testing will occur tomorrow at midday. We selected this time so you would be able to finish your training exercises with the royal knights and military officers, while also allowing time for you to recover your energy usage before the testing."

"That is appreciated father." I answered.

My father nodded his head and continued his explanation. "It would be best to know your ranking and have you enrolled prior to your ball, which will be in a few days. Your mother and I will of course be in attendance for your academy testing, along with Marcus and Captain Spears. Any questions?"

"No father, my understanding is that I will be tested in various ways so the Royal Academy will have an idea of where to focus my studies."

"Yes, your mother is an excellent healer and water mage, where I excel in fire Magic, physical enhancement magic, and various combat techniques. Having multiple aptitudes is not uncommon, however having strong affinities in multiple is rare, though I am sure you have been told that already. However, you come from strong family lines on both my side and your mother's." My father explained.

My mother put her hand on my father's before speaking up. "Do not worry my baby, your father and I will be proud of you no matter what happens tomorrow." It was clear she was making sure I felt accepted regardless. It was appreciated even though I knew I had nothing to be concerned about.

"I understand that mother but still let me say thank you for saying so." I answered. I could tell my father held her hand firmly. 'Thank you, father.'

"May I change subjects and ask a different question?" I inquired.

"Of course, baby, you do not need to ask permission. You can ask your family anything." My mother replied while holding on to the table, looking like she was trying not to bolt from her chair to 'take care of her baby'.

"This ball. What is the expectation? To my understanding, there are multiple factions in the kingdom, and they will be present, including some foreign dignitaries. Anything I should be prepared for?" I asked.

"Hahaha! Our son has a sharp mind honey! He is asking the right questions." My father boasted.

"Yes dear, he takes after both of us." My mother replied.

My father smiled at my mother's response. "Indeed, my love, I wouldn't have it any other way." He turned to me and replied. "As to your questions, I would prefer to discuss them after your academy testing tomorrow. Your Uncle Marcus, Captain Spears, and Lady Rollara will be present, and it would be good for all of us to discuss what to expect. Plus, I want you focused for tomorrow, this is an important step for you in getting the right instruction. I will not have my son missing out because he was too distracted with other matters."

"I understand father. If it is alright with everyone I would like to adjourn to my suite and attempt to get some rest." I replied, using this as a perfect opportunity to do my own training for tomorrow.

"Of course, honey. Let us know if you need anything." My mother said.

"Thank you, mother, I will." Was my reply as I gave my sister a head pat and then made a point to hug my mother good night; it took her awhile to be ok with letting me go from her bear hug, but I figured it best to show her I was here to stay. Deep down I appreciated her concern and love even if it was borderline smothering.

I had no plan on resting but rather returning to my Demiplane. I have OPs to spend and plans to further advance.

————- - - - - - - - - - - - - - - - - - ————

Walking out of the portal from my Demiplane back into my bedroom, I felt refreshed. Once again, I spent several days there, yet hardly any time passed here. The speed at which I could see results from my plans was very satisfying. There was also something almost intangible, a sense of peace while within the place I created. It was mine on a level I could not fully express.

The time dilation was a true blessing. I could rest several times over and have days to recover and still only a few hours pass here. It has allowed me to have the time to experiment in so many areas, especially my magic and crafting as of late. Sure, I practiced my various combat forms, but I just loved creating things and using magic, I mean come on, it's 'Magic!'

Well time to start the day. I want to be done working with the knights and officers early just in case I need to allow additional time for Energy Regeneration to top off my reserves.

Walking out of my bedroom, this time I found Kira waiting for me. "Kira, please inform the cooks to send breakfast early. Let's eat in the suite. I want to get to the training arena early today."

"Understood your highness. I'll have one of the others send for the food. Someone should be always at your side." Kira stated as she went to the door to talk to one of my other personal knights on the other side of the door.

It didn't take the kitchen staff long to bring us food. I secretly cast purify food and water. It had become a habit of mine. It's not that I was worried about poison as I was immune to pretty much all of them. No, it was more a habit as I shared my meals with my knights and would like them to remain healthy.

"Come, let us all eat quickly and get to the training arena." I said after the food was laid out on the table.

"You do not have to tell me twice your highness." LT Simmons said as he piled food onto his plate.

Breakfast was relatively quiet and over quickly. I could sense the unease and nerves from my knights. It seemed none of them wanted to distract me or discuss anything. 'They seem more nervous for my testing than I am.'

We walked to the training arena in silence, my mind focused on the various projects I was working on in my demiplane. As we arrived, I noticed both Uncle Marcus and Reggie present along with the royal knights and military officers ready to begin training.

"LT Simmons please get them started on warmups." I told LT Simmons as I approached General Marcus and Captain Spears. "Uncle Marcus and Reggie, what are you two doing here?"

Uncle Marcus spoke up first. "Ah my boy, it is good to see you. Do not worry, we both came to watch the training. We may have also ensured everyone was ready earlier than usual this morning. I want to make sure my nephew can finish early and have enough recovery time before your testing."

"That is very kind of you both. I appreciate your consideration and concern." I replied.

We watched LT Simmons and Mira get everyone warmed up. It was clear they both had more to say on the matter of my upcoming testing. Reggie was the first to speak. He told me with a concerned look on his face, "The testing is designed to be hard, however due to the fact that the instructors will be coming here, let's just say the difficulty level will be greatly increased."

"Why greatly increased? Are the instructors upset about private testing?" I asked.

"No, not at all, your highness. It is Royal Academy policy to be more rigorous on private testing than the public ones. This is a well-known fact across the kingdom. The benefit of this has been very useful for past royal family members and other high nobles. If someone passes during a private event it earns that family some clout and usually places the student in higher and more desirable classes." Uncle Marcus stated matter-of-factly.

"Of course, your family has kept this tradition and both General Marcus and I benefited in taking private testing. Though my contacts have told me the Royal Academy faculty is planning on being even more intense. As you know the royal faction has been in decline over the last 10 plus years, the hope is if you can do well in any one area it will send a message to all the factions that the royal faction is regaining its former power and growing stronger than ever." Reggie stated.

"How interesting. You both have given me much to consider. I do appreciate the warnings. If you'll excuse me gentlemen, I have some training to do." I said as I took my place at the front and took over the morning training.

---Sidebar Conversation---

After Prince James walked away to lead the morning training, General Marcus quietly spoke to Captain Spears, "You didn't tell him."

"Neither did you. My father will not go easy on him. If he passes my father's test, the nobles will hear about it." Captain Spears replied.

“Your father trained both the King and I when we were younger. I still have a few scars to prove it. One of the few sword saints we have in this kingdom. He is the founding pillar for one of the noble factions. I worry for my nephew; your father has been very vocal on the responsibilities of royalty and the duty of nobles should royalty not do their part.” General Marcus said.

“My father believes with his whole being those in leadership positions have a duty to be strong and decisive. He respects the King from his younger exploits but does not support the royal family’s decisions regarding waiting to name an heir or being more neutral with some of our aggressive neighbors. He sees such thing as weakness and opening the kingdom to attack.” Captain Spears explained.

“A kingdom must remain strong and ever vigilant if they wish to have peace. Your neighbors may not think as you do and will pounce on you the first sign of weakness they find.” I remember his lessons well, captain.” General Marcus recited.

“He loves this kingdom General. My father is exercising his right as a sword saint and member of the Royal Academy Advisory Board. As a duke of this kingdom, it is better he be on the board than others. My father may not be an ally, but he is fair and holds the Royal Academy to the highest standards.” Captain Spears stated.

“Aye, I agree with you there. I would rather have an honorable adversary than a backstabbing ally. Another one of your father’s lessons I still remember very vividly.” General Marcus commented.

“My father still thinks I should step down as Captain of the Royal Knights. He finds little honor in serving a weak family, his words, not mine.” Captain Spears said the last bit out of concern.

“Oh, I know all too well captain. Your father is one of the few that can get away with such words, he has the strength to back it up.” General Marcus waved off the captain’s concerns.

“My father will not override my decision to serve this kingdom how I see fit. It has been our point of contention for many years. He does not see what I have, your family loves this kingdom with all their being.” Captain Spears pointed to Prince James. “Your nephew is no exception. He will be ready, and I would rather not worry our prince.”

“Very well Captain, I will not say anything. However, be warned now, if any harm comes to my nephew, the duke will get a reminder of how decisive I can be. The King may be constrained not to attack a duke, but I will not hesitate, protocols be damned!” General Marcus said very pointedly.

“That is one of the reasons my father likes you General.” Captain Spears said with a smile.

———-----------————

Chapter 13 – Fighting a Sword Saint

After training, I once again excused myself and headed back to my room. I told my knights that I would get in a quick power nap. They looked at me curiously, not understanding what a "power" nap was.

"Is it some form of meditation, your highness? I have heard doing something similar can help recharge your energy pool faster." Kira said.

"So can sex Kira, but that's far more fun." Mira said laughing at everyone's dumbfounded expressions.

"Regardless, please do not disturb me. I will be done in time for us to walk over to the testing area." I said quickly to bring the conversation back on topic.

Of course, I was more interested in entering my Greater Demiplane, but they didn't need to know that. Sure, the time dilation will help speed up my recovery, though in reality my regeneration was high enough that I wasn't worried about being at 100 percent by the time noon rolled around. No, the real reason I wanted to return was I discovered another way to use OPs and that was to help in providing macro-enchantments on crafted larger items like carriages and structures.

I was in the middle of a few projects and wanted to continue my progress. Truth be told, I loved crafting. Deep down, if I could do nothing but create and craft, I would spend my whole life doing so.

After spending a good amount of time on my new macro projects, I of course had time to enjoy a nice relaxing bath. Besides crafting, this was becoming my other favorite past time.

"Ahh, this is heaven. I should build some communal versions of these baths if I ever decide to bring others here. What I have been able to do to the forge I have to say even I am impressed with my work. Hopefully I can get a chance to check out a few of the dwarven forges before I finalize all the runes."

After a good long soak, I figured it was time to check in on my CWs. The big lugs seemed happy as can be to just go on about their lives working. I could sense from them a feeling of being fulfilled, they knew their purpose and it brought them peace to be doing it. I made a point to remind myself of this fact and why purpose was so important for a person's well-being. "Perhaps crafting is part of mine. Well regardless, time to head back and get this testing over with."

Exiting my demiplane I felt refreshed and ready to take on these tests. I decided to change my clothes and put on a comfortable set of traveling leathers that gave me greater range of motion. I wasn't as concerned about the magic portion of the exam as I just spent several days practicing my magic. What concerned me most was the combat and swordsmanship part of the test. 'I really should've asked Reggie to spar with me for better practice. Oh well. Hopefully they don't have someone that grades very hard when it comes to combat techniques.'

Leaving my room, I found all my personal royal knights standing awkwardly by. I could literally feel the turmoil of their emotions. I wanted to cheer them up somehow but figured it would be best to give them a glimpse of what I am capable of when the time comes, the old adage 'actions speak louder than words.'

Rather than delay things further I said, "Let's head over."

"You look very well rested your highness. That 'power' nap seems to have done wonders. Perhaps you can show us sometime how best to achieve such refreshing results?" Kira asked.

Chuckling in my head I just remembered my brother's words 'Power naps are awesome!' To Kira I said, "Perhaps, power naps are pretty awesome." I couldn't help but laugh a bit at my inside joke.

I missed my family, but as long as I share their funny sayings and wisdom in this new world it is like they are still with me. In a way, perhaps they are. Some of the best words of wisdom I received after losing someone I loved was the simple fact that person is always with you. They have forever influenced who you are. As such a part of them will be forever with you, we just have to accept the good in what they gave you. Such thoughts helped me realize that no matter what I was never alone.

As we arrived at the magical training area, the first thing I noticed was how many people were here. Several people in various forms of dress littered the large, converted ballroom. Some men and women wore robes, some in full sets of armor, and others in leathers. I was not expecting this many people just for my entrance exam.

After I got over the shock of how many people were here, I noticed multiple areas set up clearly for conducting various tests, along with an elevated area for observation. I saw several chairs in the observation area and found two more regal chairs that stood out among the rest, my guess was those seats were reserved for my parents.

It wasn't even a minute before we were approached by a gray haired, tall man in shiny, light armor. It was clear the armor was a good combination of unrestricted movement and defense. I realized that I knew that fact from the blacksmithing and combat knowledge I had obtained. This gray-haired man was followed by Lady Rollara and a few other robed individuals.

"Let's get this over with boy. Time to take your measure." The gray-haired man said bluntly.

"Duke Spears, you know we cannot begin until the King and Queen arrive. You also know that you can only initiate the testing if the headmaster is not present. Seeing how 'I am' present, I will decide when we begin." Lady Rollara emphasized the last few words to show she would not backdown to the blunt man.

'Duke Spears huh? Oh yea, I can see the resemblance with Reggie.' I thought as I watched the byplay between Lady Rollara and Duke Spears.

Duke Spears turned to Lady Rollara with a frown and practically growled out, "Do not play games with me headmaster. Will you wait until the end of the exam for me to test his sword skills? Afraid he won't be able to continue after going up against a sword saint? Think he might fail the rest of his tests?"

A bit shocked to find out this guy was the sword saint I read about. His book was among John and Susan's belongings and made me realize this man was the same person who wrote the Art of Combat.

'I was just thinking earlier how I needed to practice my swordsmanship. Fighting this guy would be a good gauge of my skills.'

The fact Lady Rollara is the headmaster of the Royal Academy, was a bit of a surprise too but I recovered quickly. Deciding it best for me to chimed in, “Lady Rollara, if I may? I too would prefer to be tested by Duke Spears first. Even in defeat I can learn much from a fight with a sword saint.”

Everyone looked at me with surprise and shock.

Of course, the Duke spoke up first, “Hmph, at least the kid has some courage, or it could just be ignorance, we shall see which. If it is flattery, you will find that means nothing to me.”

Before anyone else could say anything else a grand chamberlain announced the arrival of my parents by slamming his staff on the ground making the room fall silent and all eyes turning to the man. “Attention everyone! Bow your heads! Our majesties King Gerald and Queen Sophia have arrived!”

My parents took their seats and my mother spoke up first, “Headmaster Lady Rollara, are we ready to begin?”

One thing I noticed was how differently my mother acted. She was poised and reserved, clearly, she was demonstrating the importance of proper decorum. I was used to seeing her as the overprotective mother who would smother me in bear hugs and be all emotional about her son, but this showed me a different side to her. It made me respect her even further and helped me understand how regal she truly was. ‘Now if I can just get her to keep working on the vice-grip bear hugs, I’ll be great.’ I laughed internally at my own random sense of humor.

Lady Rollara bowed and replied, “Yes, your majesty! We will begin with testing Prince James’ sword skills.”

Turning to me Lady Rollara said, “Prince James, let me explain what is about to happen for your Royal Academy entrance exam. As you and the duke have already agreed, you will undergo a series of practical testing of both your physical and combat capabilities. After this part of the exam, we shall test your mental and arithmetic skills, and various crafting and magic related professions such as alchemy. Once all these tests are completed, we will read your magical affinities, capacity, and intensity. Do you have any questions before we begin?”

“No Headmaster. Thank you for the explanation. I am ready to begin.” I politely replied.

"Very well. Please enter the sword arena. Duke Spears will explain the rules for this test." Lady Rollara said in an almost resigned way.

After both Duke Spears and I entered the arena area he started his explanation, "Alright brat, normally a timer is set, and you must survive until the timer runs out. However," the duke paused for effect, "as is my right, I'm changing the success criteria. In order to succeed in this test, you must defeat me! If you last long enough, I may give you a pass out of pity, but I wouldn't count on it. Oh and no using magic! I'll allow body enhancement magic but that's it! Got it brat?!"

I could hear several gasps and see out of the corner of my eye my father and Uncle Marcus both grasped their armrests hard, anger clear on their faces. I also saw Captain Spears grip his sword tight.

Lady Rollara shook her head and "Tsk, tsk. This will not prevent him from entering the academy, Reginald."

Duke Spears ignored it all and just smiled. "Any questions? No? Good! Alright, let's begin." He immediately rushed me. Having encountered this with his son I was expecting it and parried the initial set of blows.

"You survived my first round of attacks. Not many can. Let us increase the intensity a bit." Duke Spears smiled as I felt, and saw with my True Sight ability, magic begins to infuse his body and sword.

We danced around the arena, with me only deflecting the duke's attacks. It was clear where Reggie learned his fighting style and how it earned him his place as Captain of the Royal Knights. The duke was super quick and would use the energy from a counterattack to turn that energy against his opponent. If I attacked too heavily or didn't mind my balance, the duke would use that momentum to throw me off and then strike with a counterattack. Luckily, I didn't overcommit as I was mostly on the defensive at the moment.

As I studied the duke, it was clear even though he said he would increase the intensity, the man was not giving me his all. I was beneath him in his eyes and he was having fun humiliating an unworthy prince, or at least that is what I surmised. I may be quick to act but that did not mean I did not leverage my extremely high Intelligence stat.

Lady Rollara had ordered a series of timers to track the duration even though the duke had said time would not be a factor. It was clear she wanted everyone to see how long I could last against a sword saint. I could see why such a thing mattered as only a minute had passed and it was clear the duke was strong too, he hit like a truck.

All eyes were on our fight. I could hear random comments.

"The prince has lasted a minute against a sword saint!"

"Such a thing should not be possible!"

"I am glad the duke tested his combat and sword techniques as I would not want to be the one to do it."

"I agree, I do not think I would last a minute, the duke is terrifying!"

"What an accomplishment!"

The duke kept ratcheting up his speed and strength behind his attacks "I'm surprised you've lasted over a minute brat." He said after we broke apart after his last charge at me.

"Underestimating your opponent is never wise. You put that in your book. I read it while in exile." I commented.

"You read my book? How interesting. I do hope you are not trying to flatter me; it will not work." Duke Spears replied.

"You are a sword saint, I will not underestimate you Duke, nor will I attempt to flatter you." I retorted.

The duke rushed me again, adding a burst of speed with body enhancement magic. I saw the move coming and quickly side-stepped as I used my hand to push the flat of his blade off course before I used the momentum to gain some distance once again.

"Your son is Captain of the Royal Knights, and more importantly, in the short time I have gotten to know him, it is clear he is an honorable man. I'm guessing he learned that from his family." I said.

"Do not speak of my son or my family if you know what is good for you boy. I have no problem cutting a bad vine from the root!" Duke Spears snarled.

I must've hit a nerve. I saw both my father and Uncle rise from their seats; fury written on their faces at the outright threat. The only thing holding them both back was the knowledge that if they interfered it would invalidate my entire exam, which might have been the duke's plan all along.

"Cleaver duke. I like that you think on your feet, but so do I." I said as I beckoned the man to attack.

After another minute and intense clashing, I continued, "Let's make a wager Duke. If I last 10 minutes you begrudgingly acknowledge my skill with a blade. If I happen to beat you, then you join my faction, as such an act should be sufficient proof of strength. How about it?"

A few gasps came from some of the spectators at my boldness.

"Did he just dare to ask that?"

"The duke is going to wipe the floor with him."

"Lasting a few minutes is nowhere near lasting ten minutes."

"What nerve!"

Duke Spears laughed. "Hahaha! You've got some serious stones kid. It has barely been a few minutes. What do I get if I beat you before the 10-minute mark?" The duke asked with some genuine intrigue, it was clear he was enjoying himself.

In truth, I was enjoying myself too. Reggie was an awesome opponent and fighting him helped me become more comfortable with my new body and stats. Yet fighting the duke was on a whole other level of challenge.

"If I don't make the 10 minutes, I'll deny my right to be heir, and return to exile. If I fail to beat you after the 10 minutes, I'll join your faction." I said confidently.

My father spoke up, "No! I cannot allow this! I will go to war over this!"

My mother was even more frantic, "I will not lose my son again! I'll destroy you myself Duke!"

My Uncle Marcus roared, "No one is taking my nephew from us! I will kill you myself!"

'Awe. I internally made a heart symbol for these people. My family is pretty darn special. Thank you, God, for these people.' I thought as I made a point to appreciate this moment and those in my life.

My family's words seemed to catch the duke off guard, he wasn't expecting such vehemence. I heard him mutter to himself, "Perhaps they do have a spine after all."

I smiled back at the duke. "Well? Don't tell me the man who wrote Art of Combat is having second thoughts? What was it you said in your book? Oh yes, once you commit yourself do not waste precious time and energy on second guessing. Such acts lead to failure and reduce one's resolve. Retreating from an overwhelming force is acceptable but retreating because of doubt is foolish and without honor!"

"Deal!" Was all he said before he re-engaged, and the intensity of his attacks increased.

The duke kept going all out yet I kept him at bay. I did a few counter attacks, instead focusing more on defense and looking for opportunities to strike, which when you fight a sword saint are pretty much nonexistent. My goal was to run out the clock. I knew the man had to have high Stamina and his body enhancement magic would be top notch.

Despite all of the constant barrage of attacks I kept going, careful in how I engaged the sword saint. There were several moments of intense back and forth clashes before we would distance ourselves and reassess. For me I was achieving my goal and time passed.

After the 9-minute mark the duke was almost gleeful as he found new strength to lay into me. "You have surprised me, perhaps you bring out the best in the royal family."

Breathing heavily, I replied, "Just the royal family? When...was...the last time...you got this kind of workout?"

The duke laughed. "Ha, ha! I have not been challenged like this in decades. Perhaps you bring out the best in others period. End this now boy, I can see your exhaustion. I will not hold you to the bet."

"Why not? I plan to hold you to it!" I replied.

“Very well, time to end this!” Duke Spears said as he channeled large amounts of mana into his sword, as he rushed me once again.

The man hit like a semi-truck and if I had not infused mana into my own blade, it would’ve been sliced in half, me along with it. We exchanged several blows that began to leave impact marks on the ground from the intensity of the swipes. Both of us looked at each other and smiled, we both were having fun and each of us knew it.

Just at that moment we crossed the 10-minute mark and the duke started to laugh, “Looks like you get to keep your crown, Prince James! Haha it will be good to have you part of my faction!”

I winked at the man. “Or maybe you should join my faction.”

As if on cue, I shifted stances and started to go on the offensive. It was time to test out my new strength and reflexes. I increased my speed and hitting power, showing the duke what I was truly capable of.

I started to push the duke back. Every time he thought I overextended my swing based on the power behind my attack he would find me perfectly balanced. Several times I countered and found openings in his defenses.

‘Oh yea, this is why I learned martial arts, combat mastery, and weapons mastery!’ I thought with glee.

This is exactly what I needed to test myself. I was just stalling, buying time, one to avoid causing too much of a stir and two allowing both the duke and I to take true measure of each other. A sword saint was someone you never underestimated.

Plus, I needed the get the man off-balance to see if he would agree to my bet. There was no way I was going to pass up an opportunity to take out or reduce one of the noble factions that had pitted themselves against my family.

‘And here I thought I was just going to be taking a test. Got to love these anime tropes. Time to end this!’

I finally decided to use all my strength and speed in my attacks.

The sword saint rushed me once again. I easily batted away the duke’s sword attack with the back of my hand to the flat of his blade. Catching him off guard with how fast and easily I deflected such a powerful strike, I grabbed the man. Not giving him a chance to react, I flipped him over on to his back. Putting my foot on the flat of his blade and my sword at his neck, all in one fluid motion.

“Do you yield?!” I roared, the adrenaline still pumping through my veins.

The entire magically training area fell silent. No one even dared breathe. Then the duke spoke words no one in the entire kingdom ever expected the duke to say, “I yield!”

I reached down and grasped wrists with the duke and lifted him up as the whole area erupted in cheers.

“It’s a miracle!”

“Did you see that last move?!”

“Yea it was so fast I could barely keep track. One minute they were fighting and the next, the duke was on his back with a sword to his throat!”

“The prince actually defeated a sword saint!”

“I still can’t believe my eyes!”

“You are telling me! I thought the prince was done for when the duke said he would be the one to test him!”

Then the area fell silent once again when the duke got down on one knee, lowered his head, with his sword tip in the ground in front of Prince James.

My parents and Uncle were in mid-walk over to congratulate me when they too stopped dead in their tracks watching what was happening.

Duke Spears put power into his words so all in the hall could hear them. “I Duke Reginald Spears, the first of his name, do hereby pledge my sword, family, and house in the service of his majesty Prince James! I swear complete loyalty to one who has proven a capable warrior and decisive ruler!”

As if on instinct I replied. “I receive your pledge with the same respect and gravity it was given. Rise Duke Spears! It is a pleasure to know you!”

We once again grasped wrists and I helped him to his feet.

Once standing, Duke Spears continued to speak so all in the area could hear, "Let it be known that Duke Spears has joined Prince James' faction and will only recognize his majesty Prince James as heir to the throne! My faction is no more! There is only Prince James' faction!"

'Well, that should be interesting.' I thought as my parents and uncle approached.

My parents and Uncle Marcus arrived. My mother immediately locked me in a bear hug while General Marcus gave Duke Spears a side hug.

"You had me worried! Don't you ever talk about exile ever again! Do you hear me son?! I couldn't bare it; you almost broke you mother's heart!" My mother said while my father, Uncle Marcus, and even Duke Spears laughed.

Captain Spears wasn't too far behind and when he arrived Duke Spears embraced his son. "It appears you were right junior!"

"Dad, I hate when you call me that!" Captain Spears said but it was halfhearted as he had a smile on his face bigger than I have ever seen on the man. It was rare for him to get this kind of unrestrained affection from his father, and he made a point to engrain the memory forever into his brain.

I laughed inwardly at the unintended Indiana Jones reference. 'Man, what a life. I wonder how the rest of the entrance exam will go?'

———-------------———

Chapter 14 – Finishing the Entrance Exam

Lady Rollara got us all back on task with a magically enforced clap. "Prince James, your achievement is impressive to say the least. Reginald, I take it you are satisfied with the prince's combat techniques?"

"Absolutely! He passes with full marks. Though I might have to become his swordsmanship instructor. I am not sure anyone else would do." Duke Spears answered.

"You would come out of retirement?! Are you willing to train more than just the young prince?" Lady Rollara asked.

"As long as I can keep my seat on the Royal Academy council, I am willing to help train another generation of warriors. Though, I will still want to ensure that my prince gets private tutoring." Duke Spears replied.

"That would be a great boon to our newer generation." Uncle Marcus stated.

"No way I'm going to pass that up!" I chimed in.

"Very well. I will support your bid to retain your seat on the Royal Academy Advisory council. We can discuss later the details of your instructor duties."

Duke Spears just gave a slight head nod to Lady Rollara in acknowledgment.

Turning back to me, Lady Rollara said, "Sadly, as Headmaster I must insist, we continue your testing my prince. Are you ready to continue? I know you have just spent a great deal of mana and have been through much but once we start this exam, we must finish it."

I freed myself from my mother's death grip and replied. "Of course, headmaster. What is next?"

"After proving your expertise in the sword to such an extent, we can forgo any other Melee testing. Let us move on to ranged attacks with archery. Please head to the archery area." Lady Rollara said while pointing towards an area that clearly looked like an archery range.

A slender man in leathers with a bow and quiver strapped to his back was waiting by the range. I introduced myself, "Hello. I'm Prince James."

"I'm Illyrian and I will be testing your skills with a bow."

I realized the man was an elf when I saw his pointy ears. 'My first elf! Cool!'

"First test will be to hit the varying distance and size targets. After that, you will be expected to hit moving targets. We will switch-off between archery and axe throwing. Any questions?" Illyrian explained the fundamentals of the archery test.

"No, sir." I answered as the test seemed straightforward enough.

The archery and axe throwing test was a rather non-event after my duel with Duke Spears. I was able to hit every target, no matter the size, or distance, or how fast they moved. I expected as much as I wasn't about to pass up picking up archery and axe throwing skills when I first came to this world. I mean who doesn't get a kick out of throwing an axe?

Illyrian seemed thoroughly impressed, but I just thanked him for the test and returned to Lady Rollara.

"Headmaster where to next?"

"We shall now test your crafting skills. Please first head over to the alchemy station over there." Lady Rollara answered as she pointed towards a table with several beakers and tubes. The station looked to be something out of a medieval science lab.

The alchemy station was manned by a very short lady in purple robes standing on top of a large stool. Her eyes looked a bit larger than normal. She had purple hair to match her robes.

'Is she a gnome or some kind of halfling?' I thought as I approached.

The gnomish lady introduced herself after she made a slight bow. "It is a pleasure to meet you, Prince James. I am Saffron and I am the head alchemy instructor at the academy."

Her accent sounded French to me and almost melodic if a bit high pitched.

“For this test, I want you to make a minor health potion using the instructions from this book.” Saffron pointed to the open book on the table. “And use these ingredients. Any questions?”

“No ma’am.”” I said before turning to read the instructions.

The process was pretty simple in making a minor healing potion, I would distill the essences from the provided ingredients in cucurbits, collect the essences in an alembic, and finally pour them into a cauldron while infusing the mixture with mana. I was very careful to infuse the tiniest trickly of mana I could before handing the resulting health potion to Saffron.

“I hope you will find this acceptable professor.”

Saffron looked surprised when she took the vial. “That is far faster than should be expected. Let me see how potent it is. Appraise Item!”

A glow surrounded the vial and Saffron’s eyes grew a bit glassy and unfocused. Typical look of someone looking at a screen or information window. Her eyes grew wide. “You... you made... a Moderate Healing Potion instead! Such a thing is very rare an outcome but not unheard-of with the ingredients provided.”

“Is that good?” I asked.

Saffron turned away from her staring at the vial. “Is that good he asks. Of course, it is good my prince. It is beyond the requirements of the test. You could be a fine alchemist one day!”

“Thank you, Professor Saffron. If you will excuse me, I have a few more tests to complete.”

“Of course, of course. Go, go! I hope you will end up in my class this semester.” Saffron replied.

Turning back to Lady Rollara, she just pointed to a makeshift forge in the corner. “Your blacksmithing test will be to see if you can infuse your magic into an ingot without blowing it up.” Giving me a stern look, “You know like when you used too much magic on the training dummy.”

“Understood, headmaster.” I replied before heading over to the small forge.

The makeshift forge was manned by a short, stout man with a long reddish-orange beard. He was muscular and wearing a traditional blacksmithing apron made from tough, thick leather.

'OH sweet, my first dwarf!' I thought as I approached.

"Me name is Krag. It is time to further test your magical capabilities when it comes to craftin'. Before we start the real work, I want to finish out your physical tests."

Krag pointed to a station right next to the forge with several targets made of wood or simple stone. "We shall have you test your physical enhancement when not fightin'. Attempt to destroy those blocks and wood targets with your hands and feet."

I obliterated each target I struck.

Once again, I seemed to impress the burly dwarf test administrator. "Ye be hitting harder than me worst hangover lad. Ye got a real skill in physical enhancement. Now, that was just to make sure yer body can withstand the strain of smelting and infusing your mana into the metal." Krag said as he guided me back to the forge.

"Do you know anything about melting metal? You use your mana to help remove impurities. Not all the impurities can be removed but this test is to see how well you can do. The skilled can infuse the ore with mana to create magesteel?" Krag explained.

"I am familiar with the process if you will allow me to try." I answered.

The only reply I got from Krag was a hand gesture to begin.

I walked over and put on a blacksmithing apron and special gloves that were set off to the side of the forge. Checking the temperature of the fire, I added some fuel and once it was hot enough, I added the ore into the crucible. It did not take long to melt the ore down. Using my True Sight, I could reach out with my mana and separate the impurities.

After separating the impurities, I decided to go for extra credit. Slowly and as subtly as I could I began to push mana into the liquid metal. With my True Sight on I could see the point at which the metal could take on no more mana. At this point I poured the liquid into the cast and began the process of cooling the metal.

Using my tongs, I opened the cast and withdrew the partially glowing metal bar. Krag rushed over and got super close to the metal bar. I knew it was cooled but that did not mean it wasn't hot to the touch, but the dwarf ignored the heat as he exclaimed. "This is a bar of magesteel! As far as I can see, this is the purest bar I have ever seen!"

Krag stopped staring at the bar and turned to me. "This is impressive even for a dwarf. If ye were good at crafting', I might think ye got dwarf in ya."

"I have done some crafting and rather enjoy it." I replied. Krag's eyes bulged a bit, "Come by me smithy and I'll show ye some real craftin."

I chuckled, "As soon as I can, I would love to swing by and have you show me some crafting. I find crafting to help center me in a way I have a hard time describing."

"Aye lad. It sounds like crafting be in yer soul. I would welcome a chance to talk further." Krag said as we shook hands, and I turned back to Lady Rollara.

'I wonder what he means my crafting is in my soul. Oh well, yet another thing to figure out later.' I thought as I turned my attention back to the headmaster.

Lady Rollara directed me to my next test. "We will now test your magical affinities, capacity, and intensity."

She led me to an area with three pedestals, each with an orb on top of it. My parents, Uncle Marcus, Duke Spears, and Captain Spears all made a point of crowding around this new testing area.

"I cannot wait to see what our son's affinities are. I know he is strong in fire like his dad and uncle." My father boasted in anticipation.

Lady Rollara ignored my father's comment and continued to explain the next phase of tests. "It is simple, start with the orb on the left. Place your hands on it and attempt to push your energy into the orb. The orb will assess the intensity and density of your energy. This allows us to understand how well you can empower your spells and body with mana."

I placed my hands on the orb and attempted to push my energy in. The orb started to glow brighter and brighter, and brighter, several people had to avert their eyes from the intensity of the light. It continued to grow brighter as it emitted a humming sound, until the orb exploded. Luckily, I raised a magical shield as it grew brighter & started to hum.

Lady Rollara rushed forward, “My Prince are you ok?! Let me heal you!”

“My baby!!!” I heard my mother scream, and I was hit with a bear hug and a rush of healing magic. “Do not move my baby, mommy will heal you up!”

I waved my hands, tapping my mother to get her to release me. “I’m fine. No need to worry. I raised a shield as it started to hum.”

My mother reluctantly released me. “Quick, thinking my son. Barrier magic is one of your mother’s specialties too.” The last part she said with a smile, seeing that my barrier affinity must’ve been strong enough to handle that magical explosion.

Turning to the Lady Rollara who was doing her own magical investigation of my status I said, “I’m sorry, but I broke your orb Headmaster.”

“You overloaded the orb my prince. It would seem your magic intensity is higher than the orb can read. Most Impressive.” Lady Rollara stated.

“As to be expected from My Prince! Yet further proof of his strength and why I follow him!” Duke Spears said almost boasting. His son just shook his head at his father’s shameless antics.

Lady Rollara clapped her hands once and spoke up to get things back on track, “If you are ready my prince to continue. The next orb will measure your magic capacity. With this orb you just touch the orb as you open your energy pathways, no need to push the energy into the orb. This allows the orb to measure how much mana you have within your core without having to absorb it. In other words, less chance of this one blowing up.”

She then leaned in so only I could hear her whisper. “Do not worry, I felt your core before, this process will not be as explosive.”

Rather than delay things further I approached and touched the second orb. I did as I was instructed, and opened up my energy pathways, I could feel a subtle energy draw, more like something invasive was lightly touching the mana as it flowed through my energy pathways.

We waited awhile, after 15 minutes the duke spoke up, “Is the thing broken too Lady Rollara?”

“No, it is still calculating.” She replied without looking at the duke, her eyes fixed on the orb.

Another 15 minutes passed and one of the instructors spoke up. “Are we sure it is not defective or that the pool is too small for detection?”

“No, I can sense the magic, the orb is still reading his energy pathways.” Lady Rollara stated.

“Has it ever taken this long with anyone?” Captain Spears asked.

His father was the one to answer. “In all my time as both an instructor and on the advisory council, I have never heard of this taking longer than 5 to 10 minutes, 15 max and that was Lady Rollara’s test if I recall. I agree with Lady Rollara, the orb is working it is taking a long time to measure to reduce the chance it too explodes and can properly calculate everything.”

That seemed to quiet everyone down for a while as everyone settled in and waited.

After an hour it finished and Lady Rollara read the results out loud in complete shock, “A energy pool of 130,000?!! How?! I knew it was large, but this is even more massive that I thought!”

“Lady Rollara are you sure?! Dragons do not even possess such a capacity!” Uncle Marcus asked.

‘Technically that is not true Uncle as I am a dragon.’ Thought as I listened to the various exclamations.

“Headmaster, are you sure it’s not broken too?” A different robed man asked.

I replied in the hopes to cut off any further comments, “If what I’m seeing on the readout then Lady Rollara’s calculations are correct.”

“You know advanced computations Prince James?” Lady Rollara asked.

“Of course, it’s simple math, Lady Rollara.” I said.

“Simple? How are six digits simple calculations? I would say the computation tests are no longer required for you as this can count as your test.”

Turning to the rest of the audience that had gathered around the orbs, Lady Rollara spoke. "Yes, the calculations are correct. The prince has an energy pool beyond any being on record ever in our history, even dragons do not possess such an energy pool! If this does not prove the prophecy, I do not know what would!" Lady Rollara said the last part with firm conviction.

"Haha! That's my son!" My father joyfully stated as he gave his brother an elbow to the side.

Some present mumbled, "Prophecy? What prophecy?"

Lady Rollara raised her hand, making the room fall silent once more. "With these two tests alone, we have much to consider. Still there is one last test. Touch the final orb and open your energy pathways again and it will scan what magic types you have an affinity for and how close to 100 percent it is."

All eyes moved to the orb in rapt attention to see what affinities I possessed.

I touched the final orb and felt the now familiar feeling of something probing my pathways. Rather than resisting I let it happen. The readout on the pedestal started to populate. Luckily, for Lady Rollara and I there was enough of a distance from the orb and us from the rest of the people that we could whisper to one another.

Lady Rollara leaned in and spoke quietly in a voice only I could hear. "You can see it right, the readings?"

I whispered back, "Yes, I can read what the orb is saying."

Lady Rollara cast a Zone of Silence to prevent anyone but her and I from overhearing what she said next. "There are magic types I have never even heard of before! That alone is an astonishing discovery! Let us also not ignore the fact that every type of magic I have heard of happens to also be showing up on the display! All of them at 100% affinity!! My prince, I would say we keep most of these a secret and we can discuss them later. I cannot keep this Zone of Silence up much longer without drawing suspicion."

I quickly replied knowing she had to take down the spell soon. "I agree. I would rather not anyone know but you and I for now."

She nodded and said, “I cannot hide your affinity in all schools of magic, it will come out either way, and we must design a curriculum around your magic types. I can however keep secret these magic types I have never seen before; those we agree must remain secret.”

I nodded to Lady Rollara, and she dropped her spell.

Lady Rollara spoke loudly for everyone to hear. “It would appear Prince James has once again proven to be exceptional. The prince has 100% affinity!”

One of the robbed figures asked, “In what school of magic should I record the 100% affinity?”

“All of them!” Lady Rollara yelled.

The area fell silent once again.

The same robbed man raised his hand and asked when Lady Rollara nodded at him. “Um... Excuse me Lady Rollara, did I hear you correctly? Prince James has 100% affinity in all the schools of magic?!”

“Yes, Roger you heard correctly.” Lady Rollora said plainly.

“Is that even possible?!” Another robbed figure asked.

“I’ve only ever heard of one or two affinities at 100% for one person, some may have other affinities but rarely such a high percentage!” General Marcus stated.

Lady Rollara once again raised her hand and spoke clearly, her voice carrying across the whole testing area. “General Marcus is correct. We have never before seen someone with more than two affinities at 100%. Individuals can of course have access to multiple schools of magic, but those always vary in terms of affinity percentage. Once again, let me say this has never happened in our recorded history!”

She turned to Roger. “Make note of this unprecedented event, Roger.”

Lady Rollara turned to my parents. “Your majesties, I highly recommend we keep this as quiet as we can for now. There is no way we can keep this a secret for long but for the kingdom and the Royal Academy I implore you to agree with me on this matter.”

Both my parents took each other in their arms, looked at my uncle, Duke Spears, and Captain Spears, then LT Simmons and my personal royal knights, before turning back to Lady Rollara and nodding.

Lady Rollara nodded back. "All of you are bound by an oath of secrecy on what you have witnessed here today. This is just as much for your protection as the kingdom. Our prince is young and though he shows amazing potential, he is untrained in magic. We must help him learn as quickly as possible how to master his magic before the world learns what he could be capable of. Such knowledge discovered too early could lead to war or assassination to prevent our kingdom from gaining such a powerhouse."

Making a point of looking at everyone to ensure they acknowledged the risks before Lady Rollara brought the entrance exam to a close. "Let all here be witness, Prince James has received the highest possible score in all tests, exceeding expectations with a perfect score! It is my pleasure, as Headmaster, to accept Prince James into the Royal Academy!"

Lady Rollara then turned to the King and Queen, yet she spoke loud enough once again for all to hear. "My King and Queen, based on these results, I think it best the kingdom learns about the prophecy my sister gave all those years ago!"

My father looked at my mother, then at Uncle Marcus, and Captain Spears. They all nodded. My father clearly decided based on their input. "Very well. We agree with Lady Rollara's recommendation. Spread the word through the church and town criers. Let all know why we exiled our son, and his return has begun to prove the prophecy true!"

Lady Rollara smiled, and it was easy to see she had a look of vindication, not for herself but for her sister. 'Finally, my sister's gift to the world shall be known.' She bowed to my parents, "Thank you your majesties!"

————-------------——————

Chapter 15 – Getting Ready for the Ball

I joined my parents, sister, Lady Rollara, Uncle Marcus, Reggie, and his father the duke for a celebratory dinner. Of course, the duke crashed the dinner, my parents did invite him to join us, but he was already butting in and walking with us towards the private dining hall.

The duke had his arm around my father talking with him as we walked to the private dining room, "You know you should have told me about the prophecy. We could have avoided so many misunderstandings and disagreements over the years."

My father looked sideways at the duke and said, "It would not change anything. Unless you met him and took his measure, you never would support our decision."

The duke laughed, "Hahaha, you're probably right! However, there is no denying it after fighting him and seeing the results of his other tests My Prince is a genius in combat and magic."

The duke looked over to Lady Rollara, "Perhaps we should consider implementing a plan similar with the young nobles, take them away from their families and have them focused on learning such skills."

My mother's comment shut down that thought. "Taking away a child from his family is never the answer Duke. We sent our son with our most trusted servants who were a loving couple. A child grows strong in a loving home where they are required to do their part and help as part of a family. In this way they learn how they can contribute to society and find their own purpose. We need healthy and whole families not less. The environment we provided for my son was one where he had to work smart and find balance, that is what is missing from some of the nobles approaches to raising their children."

'Well said mother.'

Apparently, the duke agreed, "Well said your grace. Some of us have forgotten the sacred duty we have to our people and the kingdom. I had thought you and King lost sight of that, but it is clear that is not the case. Please forgive this stubborn old man."

"There is nothing to forgive. You have embraced our son, your prince, as the heir to the throne. Just put as much effort in supporting him as you did to rally your own faction and the scales will be balanced." My mother said.

"Of course, your grace! You are a wise a forgiving queen."

Dinner was pleasant. The food was balanced and very flavorful. To my surprise, the Duke, Uncle Marcus, Reggie, my father, and mother all talked about their own experiences of testing and their fond memories while attending the Royal Academy.

I learned that my father excelled at both body-strengthening magic and battle magic with an emphasis in fire magic. 'No wonder he seemed so pleased with the recounting of my battle with the undead army.' My mother, on the other hand, excelled at healing and support magic with strong affinities to light, water, and life magics. Each a formidable force to be reckoned with but together they were even greater than apart.

I also learned why my parents were so adamant on my attendance to the Royal Academy. Apparently, my parents fell in love at the academy, even though they had met several times prior at various events and balls, it wasn't until they worked as a team, that it became clear how much better they were together. They had hoped I could find such a partnership for myself there. My sister loved hearing that part of the stories being shared, and I too enjoyed understanding everyone just a bit more. Including the Duke, who seemed to make Reggie sigh at his father's antics, which I found hilarious.

Towards the end of the evening, we discussed the Coming-of-Age Ball my parents were planning in my honor. This is where nobles, magicians, wealthy merchants, and artisans would meet me and where my parents would announce me as the official heir to the throne. They also intended to let slip the fact that I got the highest score on my entrance tests, I think my parents and Duke Spears want to gloat.

My mother also made it very clear I would be introduced to the various eligible ladies at the ball. I inwardly groaned once again at my mother's antics. It was bad enough she would look for any excuse to hold on to me so tight and not let go, just as she finally was getting better at that, now she is trying to marry me off.

'Heck my own mother from my old world didn't have this much in my life, and she was Italian!'

I couldn't help but shake my head at how my new mother went from not letting go to swinging the pendulum the other way to trying to marry me off.

'I may inwardly groan but truth of the matter is they both have been amazing parents to me since my arrival. Then there is my sister who is adorable beyond words. Yes, I will protect this family.'

After dinner, we all were calling a night. The duke said his goodbyes and made it very clear that everyone in his previous faction would know to join mine. True to his word, the moment the duke returned to his estate, he wasted no time and dispatched messages to be sent to everyone in his faction. The messages were very clear, it told them to join my faction or be ostracized by the duke. He also told them that during the ball he would officially announce his support of my claim to the throne and that he was part of the prince's faction. There was no doubt in my mind that the duke meant what he said and wanted the whole kingdom to know it.

Having the Duke as an ally was a great boon for my family. Sure, I appreciated having someone so straightforward be part of my faction, but what truly warmed my heart was to see the duke joining my faction also seemed to help the relationship between a man and his son. Reggie may have groaned out loud at his father's antics, but I could sense the joy and feeling of peace at finally resolving the conflict between them. Such things were far more important to me than one additional person on my side.

As we said our goodbyes, Reggie and Uncle Marcus decided to escort me back to my suite. The conversation that occurred on the walk back surprised me.

"Thank you, Prince James." Uncle Marcus said.

"Huh? Thank you for what?"

"For proving the King and Queen right in their decision. It has been hard on them over the past several years. First, to be without their child and then to lose ground with the nobles as the people began to question the future of the kingdom. You are turning into the glue that is bringing this family and our kingdom back together."

"You are too kind Uncle. I love our family and glad I can do right by them; it is the least I can do for the love and acceptance they have shown me." I replied.

My uncle smiled wide and gave me a side bear hug. "I am proud of you boy! You may not realize yet how big a boon having one of the dukes so passionately voice their support, especially Duke Spears. Many of the nobles that used to be in the royal faction went to Duke Spears' faction out of loyalty to the kingdom and their fear of its survival. Gaining those people back will help your parents, but the duke is also, as you witnessed, an amazing fighter and tactician. There is more going on both foreign and domestic than I can share at this moment. In time we will discuss."

Uncle Marcus excused himself once we reached my suite and went on his way. After he left, Reggie asked to speak with me in private, so I asked my knights to wait outside. After giving my knights a nod and letting them know I wished to speak with Reggie alone, we entered my private conference room.

Once we closed the door Reggie spoke up. "I too should thank you, James. The rift between my father and I was growing worse and worse as time went on. Each of us understood in principle the other's positions but could not agree on a common path forward. You have created that path and I thank you."

Reggie got on his knees and bowed low. "I give my vow to you Prince James Drake; I am your man from now until death!"

'Well, this is not what I expected. Their rift must have weighed heavier on his heart than he cared to admit.' I thought before replying.

"I accept your fealty Captain Reggie Spears with the same gravity in which it was given." I said as I helped him up and onto a chair at the table.

"You are too kind Reggie. It is clear your father is a good man, and though we are heavily influenced by our upbringing, we are still our own people making our own decisions. I am proud to call you a friend Reggie, the first one I made and perhaps my only one in this world." I replied, memories flashed in my head of friends and family I left behind in my old world.

Reggie thought, 'Seeing the look on Prince James' face it is clear he is remembering something. The way James carries himself and that look of loss on his face, it is clear the prince is wise beyond his years. He sometimes even talks like a wise old man.'

After a moment of thought, Reggie decided to speak up. "Prince James, I am honored you consider me a friend. I do not think I am the only friend you have though my prince."

"Oh?" I replied.

"You seem to inspire loyalty." Reggie said.

That statement made me think, 'I wonder if that is a result of the Loyalty Magic I learned. Am I giving off some aura or doing something unconsciously? One more thing to add to the list of things to figure out. Man, this list is getting long. My buddy would be proud, he loved making lists. Wow random thought, bury emotion and get back to paying attention.'

"... I cannot believe you do not see it. Your personal royal knights have told me how grateful they are to be assigned to protect you. The more and more time they spend by your side the surer they are of how proud they are to stand with you."

'Yep! I definitely have to be doing something. I wonder what it could...'

My thoughts were interrupted by Reggie continuing his impromptu speech. "You have been isolated but you are home now, and you will find many wanting to be your friend and/or join your faction. Give it time and choose wisely."

"I appreciate the encouragement. I am fine. I do consider my knights friends and in some ways family. They are good people and I trust them but that does not change the fact that you are my very first friend Reggie." I stated.

Reggie gave a slight head nod of acknowledgement. "Point taken James. I consider it an honor my friend."

Giving Reggie a head nod of my own, I decided to shift the conversation in another direction. "Not to change the subject but I'm sure the leader of my knights LT. Simmons spoke to you?" I said.

"He did. He requested an additional 4 knights minimum be selected to ensure adequate protection for his majesty and proper rotation to ensure all his men be well rested enough to remain alert. Apparently, to quote the lieutenant, 'Sir, the ladies refuse to leave his side. At times I have to threaten them to get them to rest.' Still think you do not inspire loyalty?"

"Loyalty or something else I'm afraid." I answered.

"You are the most eligible bachelor." Reggie replied.

"Don't remind me. My mother is far too eager to get me married." I groaned.

Reggie chuckled and seeing my face, wisely got back on topic. "Ha, yes... well, back to LT. Simmons' request. I have brought the matter up with the King and Queen, they are quite supportive, though your father said something to the effect of 'that's my boy!' and your mother thought maybe all your knights should be women to ensure you are always protected."

I laughed at my parents' antics. "Haha, that sounds like both of them. I guess I hadn't noticed since three out of the four knights are women. Well, we should plan on selecting a minimum of another four knights before the ball."

"I'll arrange it for tomorrow. Have a good evening, James." Reggie answered.

"You too Reggie. I'll see you tomorrow after training." I replied.

Reggie left as Mira and Kira entered the suite. "Ladies. I'm going to get some rest. I hope you do the same." I said as I walked into my bedroom.

"We will do our duty and stand guard." Mira said.

"If there is anything you need do not hesitate to call upon us your majesty." Kira said.

'Geez LT Simmons is right. They need a break. I appreciate the loyalty but man I can see bags under their eyes.'

"Good night, ladies." I said, shaking my head as I closed my door.

I did my nightly ritual of putting up my wards before entering my Greater Demiplane. 'Time for a combination of intense work and enjoyable relaxation.' I thought as I walked into my realm.

——————-----------------——————-

The next morning, Reggie joined me in my room where we, along with my knights, had breakfast. During breakfast Reggie asked if Mira, Kira, and Rita would conduct the training in my absence this morning. The girls looked very uncomfortable with the idea.

"Why Reggie?" I asked even though I already had an idea of where Reggie was going with his question.

Reggie smiled at me as he replied. "It is simple your majesty. It is best we start right away with the selection process. Seeing how LT Simmons is the leader of your personal royal knights, I would like him to sit in on the selection process."

"Makes sense to me." Turning to Mira, Kira, and Rita I continued. "Girls, my apologies, but please facilitate the training and exercise session this morning. Captain Spears and LT Simmons will both be here to protect me should anything arise."

The three ladies looked crestfallen as they realized they could not disobey a direct order.

Rita was the first one to speak up. "As you command my Prince."

Kira was a few moments after with a sad look on her face. "If that is what you require of us, we will of course do whatever you require, your highness."

Mira looked like she was clearly not happy but too complied. "We will complete this task and return quickly my Prince." Under her breath I heard her say, "and those soldiers will finish quickly or suffer my wrath for being away from my Prince."

'Is she turning into a yandere?' I shuddered involuntarily at the thought.

See my shiver, Kira asked, "Are you cold my prince? Shall I fetch you a blanket?"

Realizing I let my emotions get the better of me, I quickly changed subjects. "No, I am fine, just a chill. Let us finish breakfast so we can get our tasks accomplished."

After the girls left, Reggie had one of the servants bring in a cart. On the cart were several stacks of papers with weights on them to prevent them from flying off while in transit. It seemed like Reggie put in a great deal of effort to pull the information I would need to make informed decisions.

"I have organized the candidates into different categories. Each stack is one of those categories." Reggie said.

Realizing my parents were not going to join us I asked what was on my mind. "Shouldn't the King and Queen be involved in this process? They were last time."

"Good question your majesty. That was the appointment of your first personal royal knight, LT. Simmons. The king and queen wanted to make it clear to the royal knights and the military how important you were to the kingdom. With your parents giving you authority over the royal knights, the decisions are yours, that is the burden of command." Reggie replied.

"Ah because I was in isolated exile, they needed to make sure our forces knew not only that I had returned, but more importantly the King and Queen's expectations on the priority of my safety. As to be expected of my parents." I replied, before sighing as I realized the other part of my parents' expectations. 'I asked for authority of the knights and now must prove to them and others of what I can accomplish.

After my brief moment of self-reflection, I looked at Reggie. "Alright, I interrupted you, Reggie. Please continue."

Reggie smiled as he saw my thoughtful expression. "Not a problem at all your highness. It is clear you are beginning to realize the scope of your responsibility. This is a good thing my friend."

"Thank you, my friend." I said as I gave a slight nod to Reggie.

"As for the candidates, the categories are as follows: exceptional melee, healing, battle magic, and utility/support. The last category has a wide range of different skill sets." Reggie stated.

"Hmmm." LT Simmons said while stroking his chin.

"More Melee fighters would be good, but we should look at some additional magic capabilities. Some support options might work well to fill in any gaps. How many more personal knights do you want my Prince?" LT Simmons chimed in and asked.

"Good question lieutenant. For now, I was thinking a minimum of four but a maximum of 9." I answered.

"Thirteen personal royal knights would ensure plenty of overlap in coverage and leave some room to send some on specific missions. It is a good number, your highness. I'm surprised you would go so high, you seemed rather reluctant of the whole personal guard situation." LT Simmons replied.

"Not opposed to it, more a matter of not used to it. Having all of you by my side brings me comfort to know someone has my back in a fight. Plus, I will need to rally the nobles and people of this kingdom, signs of strength are good for that." I answered.

"Very well let's get started. I would prefer we get as far as we can before the ladies return." LT Simmons said under his breath.

"Reggie, if my other personal knights return before we have finished our selection process, please inform them we are not to be disturbed." I said before turning to LT Simmons, "Better?"

"Thank you, my prince. I have no problem giving them orders and there is not question that they are loyal, it is just..." LT Simmons replied as he looked for the right wording.

Reggie chimed in. "Overly zealous when it comes to being in our prince's presence?"

"Yes, you took the words right out of my mouth. Thank you, captain." LT Simmons replied.

"Must be my exceptionally high Charisma. Man, what was I thinking?" I commented to myself.

"What was that? Did not quite understand what you said James." Reggie asked.

"Oh, it's nothing my friend. Just realizing some of the additional challenges in living around so many people now." I answered.

LT Simmons laughed a big hearty belly-laugh as he slammed his hand down on the desk. "HA, HA, HA! The interest of so many beautiful women is a challenge many of us would gladly take on! You are young my prince and the most eligible bachelor in the kingdom, heck the continent! Enjoy it! Stop fretting so much."

"HA! The lieutenant is right! Besides from what I hear, the queen has every intention of getting you engaged as soon as possible." Reggie laughed.

"Don't remind me." I groaned.

"It is the way of things my friend. Heck now that my father and I have reconciled, my own mother is making efforts to get grandchildren." Reggie commented.

"That is all well and good captain, but I was just trying to encourage him to have some fun! Ha, ha, ha!" LT Simmons replied.

Shaking my head at their good-natured jabs. 'This makes me miss my friends and our joking around but blessed to have friends here.'

I gestured to all the documents in front of us on the table. "Shall we get to reviewing all these files?"

We reviewed every file and that was no small amount. 'Reggie was very comprehensive in his preparation. I think the only royal knights that are not in this report are the ones already assigned to my family or the ones still going through their training and apprenticeship.'

After reviewing over 200 royal knight profiles, I now have a greater understanding of what the royal knights are capable of. 'I could accomplish much. Thankfully Reggie separated them into piles by skill set was most helpful.'

The piles were not evenly distributed. Exceptional melee tended to be the more numerous stack due to the nature of the royal knights. All royal knights had the ability to strengthen their bodies with physical enhancement magic but many also possessed exceptional weapon skills or some additional talent. The girls were a perfect example of this.

Mira was an example of an exceptional melee fighter. Her short-sword and dagger capabilities tied to her faster than normal agility is very impressive. I have seen her take down knights larger than her without breaking a sweat.

Kira was the example of a healer, her natural talent in healing runs through her family. Several of her family are in the church due to their natural healing abilities, which explains why her faith is so strong. She still had excellent fighting skills with the staff and proves even a healer can be a great fighter.

Rita was an example of support. Her talents with the bow are unmatched. I have seen her infuse mana into her shots making them able to accomplish some amazing things. Rita was by far the deadliest ranged fighter the kingdom has ever seen. Including her hunting and tracking abilities and she became very handy on longer expeditions.

The biggest hole I saw in my personal knights was having no one well versed in battle magic. This was not to a surprise, as the most talented magic casters tended to be royal court magicians. In addition to our lack of battle magic prowess we needed to have more than one knight of each skill set category. With these gaps in mind, we reviewed the various piles.

After much consideration I selected the following to add to my personal royal knights:

-Sergeant Callus Thorn as 2nd in command behind LT Simmons. He is also a formidable melee fighter with strong defense capabilities.
-Muro, a giant of a man and an exceptional tank with some earth mage capabilities to strengthen his body and protect his friends.
-Anara Rane the frost battle mage. She is cold as ice and a deadly damage dealer.
-Aeria Chemos, a wind mage to fill the role of support with her speed and area of effect spells.
-Taka Anella, a female knight who according to LT Simmons was a giant of a woman, she excelled in melee combat.
-Sloane, a knight who possessed rogue-like abilities and some access to shadow magic.
-Leonard Phillips, a knight with some minor healing capabilities as well as a diverse range of skills making him a good fit for a general support role.
-Cooper Cavaliere, a knight who came from a long line of knights famous for their mounted combat skills among other fighting abilities.

"Prince James... are you sure about some of these choices? LT Simmons asked hesitantly.

"Speak your mind, Lieutenant!" Reggie said on my behalf, knowing I would prefer to cut to the chase.

"Of course, sir. It's just that Sloane and Leonard are...not ideal." He said hesitantly again before continuing after seeing Reggie's annoyed face. "Sloane has..." LT Simmons paused as he seemed to be looking for the right words. "Sloane has 'difficultly' getting along with some of the other knights, I think it has something to do with the dark/shadow magic he has access to. As for Leonard, he is a good man and loyal, but for a knight his skills are average."

Realizing where the Lieutenant was coming from, I stated my reasons. "Let's address Leonard first. Yes, for a knight most of his skills are quite average but the point is that the skills he possesses are quite numerous making him a good utility player. The term I like to use is Jack-of-All-Trades."

They both looked at me confused so I tried to explain. "In other words, Leonard can fill multiple roles which can be invaluable to our small team. Having someone that can fill in anywhere we are weak or round out any team is a rare find indeed."

It seemed like the light bulbs went on over their heads because they seemed to understand now why I picked Leonard.

"I have a new appreciation for Leonard now. But what about Sloane? He cannot be trusted!" LT Simmons expressed his concern.

"Ah, Sloane is better at stealth and assassination, making him the perfect spy for covert missions. Such skills can also come in handy when trying to detect other users of dark/shadow magics. Mira is good at such things but according to your notes Captain, Sloane is the best you have in such skills."

"That is true...." Reggie hesitated before continuing. "It's just Sloane has been known to associate with many of our less than upstanding citizens."

"Exactly! I am counting on those connections." I replied.

Both men looked confused at my reply.

Seeing their confusion, I decided to explain further. "Gentlemen, sometimes we do what we must for the good of the kingdom and sometimes that means dealing with less than reputable characters if we need to deal with other shady individuals. Having Sloane on our team will help make those connections and possibly get answers from different channels not normally open to us."

"It does make sense, my prince." LT Simmons sighed, "It is ultimately your decision, your highness. I will trust in your judgment." LT Simmons said.

I turned to Reggie. "Captain, please make the necessary announcements. I would like to meet with my whole team later today. My mother told me that Mrs. Teege will be by later this morning to have me try on various outfits for the ball. I would like to meet with my team after all that nonsense is concluded."

"Hahaha, she's gonna turn you into a pincushion." LT Simmons laughed.

"I don't know why you're laughing Lieutenant. Mrs. Teege will be taking your measurements as well. In fact, all of Prince James' knights must be measured so she can create a matching honor guard uniform for the ball and other special occasions. This is a direct order from the queen." Reggie deadpanned.

"Can't I just wear my armor? I hate getting all gussied up. My duty is to protect my prince, not look all fancy." LT Simmons groaned.

"I'll pretend I didn't hear that, Lieutenant. As royal knights our appearance is a reflection on the royal family. In such events it is our duty to look our best." Captain Spears scolded him.

"Yes sir! My apologies Captain, our prince is so laxed on such formalities, I forgot myself for a moment." LT Simmons replied.

As LT Simmons put his head down after his apology, Reggie smiled at me. I could tell he was enjoying this chance to polish some of LT Simmons' gruff nature.

From what Reggie told me, LT. Simmons came from a small noble family from the same territory Rita was from. In fact, his family sponsored Rita's enrollment into the military. Some of the nobles had looked down on the Lieutenant when he first arrived in the capital due to his speech patterns. His family was one of the rare nobles who worked alongside the people they were responsible for. LT Simmons had picked up some of their more colorful ways of speaking. He of course polished his manner of speaking, at least for the most part, and was able to rise quickly with his talent with a mace and body enhancement magic.

In front of nobles, he knows how to act the part but around his men he is more himself. This was one of the reasons I chose LT Simmons to be my head personal knight, I could tell we were kindred spirits. The man would understand better than most my need to drop all the prim-and-proper speech and protocols to just be myself.

“Well if you excuse me my prince, I will take my leave and see your will done.” Reggie said as he exited the suite with a smile on his face.

——————- - - - - - - - - - - - - - —————

Chapter 16 – Well, That Was Interesting

Reggie left LT Simmons and I in my suite. I turned to LT Simmons and asked, "Hey Lieutenant, what's your first name?"

LT Simmons looked at me with a mix of shock and a purely dumbfounded expression. 'Have I really never told him my first name?'

"My apologies your majesty. I did not realize I never told you my first name. My full name is Sir Lexington Arthur Simmons, second son to Lord Simmons Count of Leffingwell. My mother calls me Arthur, but my friends call me Lex. It would do me an honor, if your majesty would also call me Lex.... or Simmons is of course fine. I mean.... I would never presume to tell your majesty..."

I raised my hand to cut off his rambling. This was so unlike him. "Why are you rambling? I've never seen you act like this."

LT Simmons took a deep breath and then replied, "My apologies your highness. I just realized that I never formally introduced myself to you. In court such an act is considered extremely disrespectful. I just never realized... you just always accepted me and frankly my father was always frustrated with my lack of decorum. That is part of the reason I joined the Royal Knights...I..."

I raised my hand again. "Seriously man! For the love of all that is holy calm down! I am not upset."

LT Simmons seemed to visibly relax some at my words.

I continued, "Look I asked because I realized I didn't know your first name and didn't quite feel right calling you Lieutenant all the time. It felt too impersonal. I don't take offense. Frankly we met out on the road, there has always been something happening and frankly I can't stand all the uptight nonsense anyway. Now I don't know that I'll call you Lex, reminds me of a villain from a story I read, but give it time Simmons. I expect you to be my right hand, especially when we start adventuring. I just have to get through this stupid royal ball, and we can actually go out and explore. I've been locked away long enough."

"I think I understand your majesty. Though I don't know what story you're referring to." Simmons replied.

"Please stop calling me 'your majesty' when it's just us. Call me James or if that won't work Prince if you must. Now why don't you tell me about the county you are from." I stated.

So, we sat there talking. Simmons told me about the county he grew up in and his family. It was clear he was a big teddy bear who deeply loved his mother and the people from where he grew up in. The county was one of the more remote counties of the kingdom but no less full of people. It was rather enjoyable and helped to pass the time. The girls were the first to return but they didn't get too far into the suite when Reggie came bursting in.

"Are you guys done already?" Mira asked.

"Can we see the list?" Kira asked.

"My apologies for the intrusion your majesty." Reggie said as he burst into the room. Trailing behind him were a small group of people I assumed were the new members of my personal royal knights. They all bowed, including Reggie.

"If it pleases your majesty, I would like to introduce you to your new personal royal knights and have them give their pledge of loyalty." Reggie said while kneeling and his head down.

"Get up Captain. For heaven's sake, all of you get up. I would rather stare into everyone's eyes when they give me their oath." I said, frustrated at all this formality. I wouldn't diminish their commitment or honor, but I wanted to look each of them in the face to make sure we both understood the gravity of it.

'I think Reggie did this just to mess with me or to get me to accept this part of my position.'

I looked at those assembled and spoke. "I have chosen each of you to serve as my personal royal knights. Each of you brings specific skills or traits to the table that this team will need. With that said our team is more than the sum of its parts."

I paused to make sure they were all understanding what I was saying. "I have been far removed from court and our kingdom's affairs for far too long. There is much I wish to accomplish and little time to do it in."

Noticing some of the looks towards Sloane as my eyes swept the room, I took everyone's measure before I continued. "Some of you wonder why you were chosen, and I can see in some of your eyes you wonder why others here have been chosen. Trust in me as your prince, I see much in each of you. If you wish to be part of my honor guard step forward and give your oath."

One by one, they all bent their knee to me and gave their oath.

"I shall be your honor guard, your shield against shield, arms against arms, your eyes and ears. This I give for the end of my days or until the prince releases us!"

Each one I accepted. After that impromptu ceremony was done, I turned to Reggie.

"Thank you, Captain, for once again helping me achieve my goals so expeditiously."

Reggie bowed his head and said, "It is my duty, but in this case, it is also an honor to serve your majesty. I will take my leave and return to my other duties."

After acknowledging Reggie, he left the suite. I turned to Simmons and the rest of my honor guards. "All of you already know Lieutenant Simmons. He is the leader of my personal royal knights and your commanding officer. You will work with him on any issues that may arise, and he will give you the schedule. With that said, know that I am still adjusting to a life at court so bear with my informality. Also feel free to come to me with any questions etc. Lastly, before I turn it over to LT. Simmons, I expect each of you to speak your mind when it is just us, I will not have lives risked because you were scared to speak your mind to me."

I turned to Simmons, "Lieutenant, they are all yours."

LT Simmons smiled, "Alright you bunch of pansies! Listen up! I'll say this once. It is an honor to be selected as a personal royal knight! As such, do not, I repeat do not, dishonor your post by bringing any shame to our prince!"

I just internally groaned. 'Simmons loves to read them the riot act. He really should be a Drill-Sergeant.'

Simmons continued, "Mira will be promoted to the rank of Sergeant and lead the first squad in my absence."

I smiled; Mira looked stunned as people congratulated her. Reggie, Simmons, and I had discussed this promotion as part of our selection process. Having a clear chain of command for each squad was important.

Simmons continued, "Kira shall also be promoted to the rank of Sergeant and lead her own squad."

Several people congratulated Kira as she too was stunned.

Simmons did not stop there. "Sergeant Callus Thorn shall be given lead of the second squad when I am not present. When on mission or in combat each of you will be responsible for a specific squad."

Simmons paused to make sure everyone was paying attention, so they clearly understood their chain of command. "Mira will lead the Stalkers. This squad will focus on scouting, information gathering, and quick strike missions. The team will include herself, Sloane, Leonard Phillips, and Rita."

Mira seemed a bit surprised to have Sloane on her team.

"Callus Thorn will lead the Bulwark Defenders. Their focus will be primarily on defense and breaking enemy lines. In other words, they bring the pain to our enemies. This team will include Callus, Cooper Cavaliere, Taka Anella, and Muro."

A few nods and smiles could be seen on the squad team members. It was clear they were thrilled to be assigned that role.

LT Simmons looked at me, after giving him a head nod, he continued. "Last but not least, is our Tempest Squad lead by Kira. This team will focus on magic and support. They shall include Kira, Anara Rane the frost battle mage, Aeria Chemos the wind mage, with Rita joining depending on mission.

"I will work with each of you on a rotation for ensuring Prince James' protection. I expect a member from each squad to be present at all times. We should have enough coverage to protect his majesty and make sure people get plenty of rest. Each of you get with your squad leader. Mira and Kira please coordinate with each other regarding Rita's schedule. Dismissed!"

With those last words each squad huddled together in some part of my giant conference room. I pulled Simmons to me with a wave. Simmons spoke softly to keep the conversation between us. "Yes, your majesty?"

I gave him a look.

"I mean Prince James."

I shook my head and focused on the reason I grabbed his attention. "Make sure Mira understands my expectations regarding both Sloane and Leonard. In fact, make a point to pull her aside and explain some of what we discussed."

"As you command my prince."

Sure, I could give the orders directly, and having a personal guard allowed for some flexibility in command structure, but a clear chain of command was critical. My plan was to leverage my knights to help lead in future battles and special missions. They would not be as successful if they lacked the discipline now, at least that was what my gut was telling me, and I always trust my gut!

Simmons walked over to Mira's squad and pulled her aside. After watching for a while, I called Mira's squad. "Stalker squad! Please approach!"

Rita looked over as she was in conversation with Tempest squad. I waved to her to stay there. Mira remained with LT Simmons as we already discussed the conversation, I wanted to have with the two remaining members of her squad. 'Sure, chain of command is important, but I have specific plans for Sloane. After they moved to where I was standing in the conference room they saluted and spoke up.

“Yes, your Majesty! How may we serve?!” Both Sloane and Leonard said in unison as they saluted fists to their hearts.

“I appreciate the zeal but it’s all good guys, at ease.” I looked at Sloane and continued, “Sloane, it is my understanding that you have some contacts in the seedier parts of society or shall we just say less than reputable.”

“Yes, your majesty.” Sloane replied with a bit of concern in his voice. He was used to being looked down on for having such connections.

“Good.” I said which caused the man to have a look of surprise.

“Good, your majesty?” Sloane asked a bit confused.

Ignoring his confusion, I explained my request. “I need you to reach out to those contacts and put feelers out. As you were there, you know we were attacked on the way back to the capital. Someone must know something, even if but a whisper. After that is done, bring Mira in to the continue the investigation. It is time we quietly started to make our own inquiries. Understood?”

The two Stalkers answered as one, “Yes your majesty!”

Looking at Sloane, “Oh, and Sloane, I want a private discussion with you later. Others may have concerns about your loyalties based on your associations, but I see them as a boon. We will talk later.”

Turning to Leonard Phillips, “Now Leonard, my understanding is you are just about average in everything.”

Leonard looked downtrodden. It was clear the man was used to being put down for his average abilities.

I spoke up loudly so that not only Sloane, but others could hear what I was about to say. “I think your talents are remarkable!”

“Remarkable, your grace?” Leonard asked in confusion.

“Yes Remarkable! You are average in every skill! Others may have focused on the first part of that statement your whole life, but I see the later half! To be able to perform each skill no matter if it be healing or stealth makes you the most well rounded and useful for any situation that may arise! You worked hard to become a royal knight and I know you will work even harder as one of my personal royal knights!” I continued to project my voice across the conference room. 'Chain of command is important but so is a bit of morale boost.'

"Oh yes, your grace! I will serve you most loyally! Thank you for recognizing my skillset! I will help wherever you need me!" Leonard replied as he bowed deeply to me.

"I know you will Leonard." I answered before turning to the rest of my knights.

That little show caught all their attention. "Sadly, before any of you leave, we all must be fitted for dress uniforms for the ball by Mrs. Teege. I apologize ahead of time for that upcoming joy." I groaned.

Some chuckles were heard across the conference room. Most of the knights knew such things were expected of them and appreciated my lack of joy in such formalities.

Shortly after my statement Mrs. Teege and a few of her seamstress apprentices seemed to manifest out of nowhere as if called into being.

Everyone saw the seamstress, and a few joined me in groans, others seemed delightedly be getting dressed up for the ball by Mrs. Teege.

"I will hear none of those groans! You are representing the royal family and as such, you will dress accordingly! If I hear another groan, I will see to it you my needle just might slip a few... or several times." Mrs. Teege said with a smile.

'Man, that woman is scary, she is deadly with that needle and her stealth skill has to be pretty high to appear so quietly.'

Apparently, Mrs. Teege was known for her tailoring skill and was highly sought after by nobles and rich merchants. I decided to put a smile on my face and consider myself blessed to have someone so talented in her craft helping me and my people. I would just hide my inner groan at being poked and prodded, especially after that threat.

———— - - - - - - - - - - - - - - ————-

It took her a few hours, but the woman and her staff were efficient. I only got poked like twelve times, I am pretty sure one for each groan she heard that I just couldn't hold in.

“Thank you, Mrs. Teege, for once again helping make this happen. Your skill is unmatched.” I said after her and her people were done taking everyone’s measurements.

“Of course, dearie, of course. Think nothing of it. I am glad to help the royal family. All of you have been through so much having to be separated for so long.” Mrs. Teege replied in a motherly tone.

“You are too kind and are the sweetest lady I know.” I replied.

Mrs. Teege blushed and waved my words off as she shoo’d away her apprentices. “You almost make me feel bad poking you, almost. It is good for a prince to represent our kingdom in the proper attire.”

“I understand, be patient with me, my lady. I am still learning.” I answered.

Mrs. Teege smiled. “Of course, your majesty, of course. Now on to important matters, your outfits! I already had designs in mind after I witnessed your exploits on our expedition to bring you home. Luckily, I was present and inspired by your deeds, so much is already prepared. I will have everything sent over tomorrow.” She said right before leaving the suite.

‘I don’t know how that woman does it. Magic must be involved. She means well and kind of reminds me of my grandmother. Short, sweet, but she would broker no talk back from anyone.’ I thought fondly as she left.

Shifting gears, it was time to put other plans in motion. “Stalker squad please approach.”

It didn’t take long for Mira and team to get closer. “Mira, now that all of that is done, your squad has orders. Make it happen...” I turned to look at Sloane, “and Sloane I’m counting on you.”

Mira’s squad put fists over their heart, bowed their heads, and replied in unison, “Yes, your majesty!” Before they too turned on their heels and left the suite.

Turning to Simmons I said, “Lieutenant, it’s been a long and eventful day. I’m going to retire for the evening while you finish working through the duty schedule.”

“As you wish Prince James.” Simmons replied.

Turning to the remaining knights, "Again welcome to my personal royal knights. I'm glad all of you are part of the team and thank you for accepting this post."

Seeing their positive reactions, I left the conference room and entered my private bedchamber. I could hear LT Simmons' voice carrying from the conference room. "The prince is never to be disturbed when he is in his private bedchamber. I have sensed powerful wards protecting him so do not get any ideas of sneaking in!"

'Interesting they can sense my wards. Good to know. Thank you, Simmons, for keeping the newbies away.' I thought as I locked the door and put up the very wards he mentioned. That done, I wasted no time and entered my Demiplane.

As tired as I might be, spending time in my demiplane was a godsend. The time dilation was becoming more and more of a boon, allowing me to do far more than I normally would, all while devoid of prying eyes and ears.

Once inside my fortress, one of my creations brought me some of the fruit from the various trees and plants within the demiplane. Some came from seeds I had saved from the food I'd received, some from the garden in the valley, lastly a few were from plants I created using my allotted points as they recharged. The time dilation allowed for these trees to grow and blossom in record time.

I sampled the various fruits etc. while watching my creations go about their tasks. As I sampled the food items, I found they all came out quite good. I marveled, thinking of my past life and how I literally had the opposite of a green thumb. 'So glad I picked up some druid and nature magic skills.'

As I walked, I came upon my rather large storehouse. It was coming along; I could clearly see various ores and bars stacked within. Several of my minions... "Man they do remind me of minions as they go about their assigned tasks. Huh? Well, 'back to work.' 'Alright then.' 'ZugZug' hahaha." I laughed at my internal blizzard game reference.

'Man, I have got to get some friends I can share these awesome references. I miss my friends.' I thought before lightly slapping my cheeks to bring me out of my brief melancholy. "Nothing that can be helped yet, focus on what is in front of you."

Turning back to watch, my minions were busy delivering ore from the mines, or coming and taking ore to the forge, or bringing back bars of metal. They had an efficient system going.

"Huh? I hadn't told them to smelt the tougher and far more rare ore such as platinum, mithril, adamantine, or oricalcum. However, seeing those bars of iron, steel, copper, silver, and gold is making my inner Scrooge scream for joy! Maybe I should have them try their hand at smelting the platinum?" I said out loud in thought.

I turned to them and said out loud, "Good job everyone! Keep up the good work!"

They seemed to groan in response, but they slightly picked up speed and I got a wave of joy coming off them.

"Never is a bad idea to express your appreciation to those that help you." I said to myself as I looked at the growing pile. There was much I could do with these resources when the time came.

After inspecting the storehouse and forge I made my way to the training area. As tired mentally as I might feel, I could not be lax in my own training. Once again, I did what I could to push my body and mind before calling it a night.

———— - - - - - - - - - - - - ————

Chapter 17 - Ice Queen

“Kira, do you know what Prince James has planned for us?” Aeria asked.

“From everything I have seen Prince James is a genius. He is clearly talented in swordsmanship based on his spar with the captain. Add in his ability to use battle magic and healing, I do not know of anyone in history skilled in all those areas. In the battle against the necromancer, it was at first total chaos. Yet our prince seemed to hone right in on where the necromancer was located, and from what I’ve been told, took him out singlehandedly.”

“I heard those stories too.” Anara commented.

“I answered your question Aeria with this so you can gain some idea of what he is capable of. Prince James seems to think several steps ahead. Whatever he has planned I feel it will take us some time to fully comprehend.” Kira replied.

“Having a battle mage squad is not unheard-of.” Aeria stated.

“That is true Aeria. But having one that is part of a personal squad is.” Kira answered.

“Having battle mages who can hold their own or tip the scales of a fight only makes sense. I can see why my old teacher Lady Rollara praises him so. I can see cold calculations in his eyes.” Anara said.

“I see glimpses of that, but I believe he is more driven by instinct or his gut. There is compassion in those eyes too, you can’t be such an effective healer without it.” Kira stated.

“Yes, I saw the warmth in his eyes but hopefully that doesn’t interfere with doing whatever is required in the middle of battle.” Anara said.

Shaking her head Kira replied, “Always the heart of ice Anara.”

“But of course! I do have some winter fey in my bloodline if my grandmother is to be believed.” Anara stated.

“One day I hope someone can melt that cold shell Anara.” Shaking her head again at how calculating her friend is, Kira turned her attention to her duties. “There is much to discuss my old friends.”

“Yes, let us discuss. This will be the first time since the Royal Academy where we will be able to team up again. My support Magic, Anara’s ice damage, and your amazing heals we were unstoppable.” Aeria said happily.

“I agree. It will be nice to team up again.” Kira said.

“Yes, it will be good to stand side by side in battle.” Anara stated.

Simmons approached nodding to the Tempest squad, “Ladies.”

“Lieutenant.” The three ladies replied in unison.

“Sergeant Kira, have you determined who will be covering what shift?” Simmons asked.

“We have not yet decided Lieutenant. However, Anara can cover the first shift. It would do her good to get to know the prince’s routine. As we are light on those with healing abilities I will coordinate with Mira on Leonard’s availability.” Kira said.

“How sensible of you.” LT Simmons said as he thought to himself, ‘I’m surprised, her and Mira seem obsessed with him, though Rita is not much different.’

Coming out of his thoughts, “Very well Kira, we can sort out the details later. It might be best to change the rotations up for a bit to help everyone get used to working together. I have already instructed Sergeant Thorn to assign his people and pick rooms.” LT Simmons stated as he pointed in the direction of another set of doors.

“Rooms lieutenant?” Aeria asked.

“Yes. I think there are enough rooms in the prince’s wing of the palace for each squad to pick a bedroom to use when off duty. I already reserved the one closest to his majesty for your Tempest squad. You’re welcome.” Simmons said as he watched the expressions on their faces light up.

‘Oh, the shenanigans I can see coming. The prince has no idea what he has gotten into. It is only a matter of time.’ Simmons thought.

“Good night.” Simmons said before turning around and heading to his room to get some shuteye.

“Just like Simmons, blunt, to the point, and no broker for an argument.” Anara said.

“It has served him well.” Kira commented.

“Nice backside too.” Aeria replied as she looked at the door LT Simmons entered.

“Aeria!” Kira admonished.

“What? I can look.” Aeria answered.

“You never change Aeria. You move like a breeze from one interest to the next.” Anara commented.

“Blame it on my element. I let the wind carry me to my next destination. Ha, ha, ha.” Aeria giggled.

‘I better chime in before they get into another element debate.’ Kira thought before speaking up. “Alright you two, let us discuss how we want to do our shifts.”

— -

Morning came quickly for Anara. She could not understand why she felt nervous. ‘Perhaps all the stories I’ve heard about the prince make him an interesting mystery? What is he planning? Why a focus on mages known for battle magic?’ Anara thought while she waited for Prince James to awaken and come out for breakfast.

The food had just been delivered by one of the servants.

‘According to Kira, Prince James is usually an early riser.’ Anara thought.

During her musing she looked at the other knights on duty with her, Sergeant Callus Thorn and Leonard Phillips. Callus, ever the professional, was standing at attention guarding Prince James’s bedroom door. Leonard Phillips was standing by the suite entrance and looked nervous as hell.

‘I don’t think anyone expected Leonard of all people to become a personal royal knight, least of all Leonard himself. The man is hapless as ever.’ Anara chuckled internally to herself.

Just then Prince James' bedroom door opened as Prince James walked out of his room shirtless. Missing shirt in his hand.

Anara's mouth opened and blatantly stared at Prince James' half naked figure.

'How is he so ripped?!' Was the only thing Anara's brain could think of for a moment. Once her brain finally caught up, she realized the prince had said something to her. Closing her mouth and wiping the partial drool she replied, "I'm sorry your highness, what was that?"

"I said, all of you please sit and join me for breakfast." Prince James stated again.

"That would not be proper, your grace." Sergeant Callus replied.

"Nonsense! You are my personal royal knights and as you can see there is more than enough food, Sergeant. I make sure the maids know to bring enough." Prince James said before smiling as he continued, "You wouldn't be disobeying an order now would you Sergeant?" Prince James asked.

Sergeant Callus quickly replied and took a seat. "No, your majesty! Thank you for thinking of us."

'He really needs to put a shirt on! This is super distracting.' Anara thought before she too took a seat.

Leonard timidly took a seat as well, looking completely lost in what he should be doing in this situation.

"Anara, right?" Prince James asked.

"Yes, your majesty!" Anara said while staring at his chest and abs.

"Is something the matter Anara? You seem rather distracted. Did you not get enough rest?" Prince James asked.

Blushing Anara replied, "My apologies your majesty. I'm just deep in thought."

"Ah. I can understand that. I too can get lost in my own thoughts." Prince James said.

"Was the Prince in mid-process of putting his shirt on?" Sergeant Callus said, realizing what was really distracting Anara.

“Ah yes. Thank you, Sergeant. It appears I too got distracted.” Prince James replied while putting his shirt on.

After he adjusted his shirt, Prince James turned to the sergeant “May I call you Callus?”

“Your Grace can do whatever he likes! It would honor me to be called so informally by your highness.” Callus replied.

“Excellent. Now let’s eat. Don’t be shy Leonard. You look nervous as hell.” Prince James said as he turned his attention to Leonard.

“Uh, yes... as you command, your highness!” Leonard awkwardly answered.

“Calm yourself man. Right now, just consider this situation as four people sharing a meal together. Drop all the pretense and stop worrying, you already got the job.” Prince James stated in the hopes to help the man start to relax.

‘He concerns himself of others. Kira was right, he is compassionate. Normally that would turn me off from someone. Getting lost in emotions is too dangerous in battle. Yet I find his concern endearing.’ Anara thought as she watched Prince James.

“Anara please eat, it is important you remain in good health.” Prince James said as he winked at her.

‘What is this heat in my heart? I feel the ice around it melting. What is happening to me?!’ Anara thought to herself as her cheeks reddened again for the second time.

“You look a little flushed Anara, are you feeling well? Do you require healing?” Prince James asked her.

Leonard, realizing he could be of use, began to rise from his seat. “I can help heal you if you require it Lady Anara.”

“I’m fine my Prince.” Anara said before giving a cold look at Leonard. “I do not require healing Leonard. Sit back down.”

Turning back to Prince James, “I think you are right your majesty; I should eat something.” Anara said as she grabbed food and started to eat.

"I am always right, Ha, ha, ha." Prince James said laughing to himself as if that was some inside joke.

After breakfast they all proceeded to the military training grounds to observe the officers and the other soldiers as they performed various exercises and battle routines.

'I still cannot believe Prince James' morning exercise routine is what they spend time practicing now. Where did he learn such effective routines.' Anara thought while watching the soldiers' exercises.

"Your Grace, may I ask you where you learned these morning routines?" Sergeant Callus asked.

'So, I'm not the only one thinking about his impressive feats.' Anara thought when she heard Callus' question.

"I learned most of it from John and Susan." Prince James replied as he thought, 'Granted I learned it through gaining their memories and knowledge. Those two really did love the prince and their people. What is the old saying? Oh yes, they are never truly gone. They live on in us, in what they taught us and how they made us feel.'

Turning back to Callus after his quick moment of deep emotion and appreciation once again for everything he gained from the two elders.

"The famous adventurer duo that retired to help raise you?" Callus followed up after noticing Prince James seemed lost in thought.

"Yes, their knowledge was quite extensive." Prince James replied.

"I would think so, they were some of the best this kingdom had to offer before they retired as a personal favor to the King and Queen. John the Lionheart was one of the most unstoppable fighters across the continent. He's a legend and one of the reasons I wanted to become a royal knight." Leonard said. Blushing once he realized the Prince, Callus, and Anara were staring at him.

"He speaks." Callus joked.

"Of...course...I speak." Leonard finally said after a moment.

"He's joking with you Leonard. That is the clearest you've spoken all morning. You are quite timid you know, don't be. I chose you for a reason so stop questioning why you are here." Prince James said.

"Why did you choose him my prince?" Anara asked.

"What?" Prince James asked absently while watching the morning routine.

"Why did you choose Leonard? My understanding is he is quite average all around, barely eligible to be a knight." Anara pressed wanting to know why the prince would choose such an inferior person to protect him.

This seemed to draw Prince James's full attention. "Ah but that is what everyone is missing. He is average in Everything. Literally a jack-of-all-trades. Such a person is a perfect member to fill so many roles when needed."

Seeing the three knights were all focused on him, Leonard included, Prince James continued. "People do not quickly see the value of Leonard because they only measure him by one skill in isolation compared to others who possess that one skill. Yet they are not seeing the entire capability of having a person be able to fill any gap or join any team." Prince James said, getting more passionate about his stance as he talked.

'Such passion, why do I want him to say such things about me in a passionate way.' Anara thought but she managed to school her face and replied, "Fascinating. I had not considered it from such a perspective. You have given me something to consider in future battle tactics. Thank you, your majesty."

"Thank you, your grace. No one has ever seen my skills in such a way or spoken so highly of me." Leonard said while bowing to Prince James.

"You have sold yourself short Leonard. I will have you filling various roles in future missions. Be proud of your wide range of skills. Your potential is endless, and I intend to tap that keg." Prince James told Leonard.

A moment later Prince James said more to himself than anyone else, "Phrasing! Got to watch how I say stuff with my high Charisma."

"Come. Let us join the morning exercises. I feel like working off some of this energy." Prince James said while walking onto the training field.

'I could think of how I'd like you to use some that energy.' Anara thought before rushing to follow.

Prince James observed his new personal royal knights as they trained as he considered what he had learned. It was clear his first impression of Callus Thorn was spot on. He was the personification of a loyal military officer and honorable knight. From the selection process he had learned that Callus was a former trainer which would serve his future plans quite nicely. Clearly a good addition to the team.

Leonard Phillips reminded Prince James of a typical nerdy and insecure guy who had no clue of his value or strengths. The moment Prince James realized he possessed so many skills it was clear Leonard had a hidden talent. This talent will be perfect to fill the gaps as needed. Hopefully the mini pep talk Prince James gave Leonard would help him begin to understand his value.

That left Anara. The woman many people called the Ice Queen due to her mastery of ice magic and her supposedly cold, calm, and calculating nature. However, Prince James didn't see it. Sure, she was calculating and perhaps a bit abrasive but calm or cold? No, that was not the impression Prince James received. She seemed very passionate deep down. If he could tap into that passion to strengthen her capabilities, he would help her.

'Though she did give off a bit of a yandere vibe, not complete psycho, but still something was there. I'm going to have to tread carefully with her and Mira.' Prince James thought.

Chapter 18 - Meeting with the High Priest

After the morning workout and training Prince James returned to his wing of the palace. Today he is meeting with High Priest Cendrin to discuss any last-minute details for the church's involvement in the official acknowledgment of Prince James as heir to the throne during the ball. Kira wanted to make sure she was present, so they decided to change his guards early to give Kira time to answer any questions.

Anara did not seem too thrilled to end the shift early, but she did not protest as she bowed to Prince James before making her way to her room.

Sergeant Callus, ever the professional followed protocol before he too retired to his room. "Sergeant Kira, I officially turn over protection of his majesty Prince James to you and your watch."

"Thank you, Sergeant Callus, I take up this charge with honor and shall not fail in my duty." Kira replied.

The new royal guard rotation consisted of Kira, Rita, and Cooper Cavaliere. Prince James sat in his conference room and turned his attention to Kira who looked nervous for some reason.

"Kira, what can you tell me about Cendrin? Please sit and tell me what you can." Prince James asked.

"My family has an affinity for Light magic and healing. Ever since I was a young girl, I spent time learning both magical and mundane healing arts. As a healer I spent much time with the church. High Priest Cendrin is a good man. He cares for the people of this kingdom and has spearheaded different efforts to help the less fortunate. His affinity for light magic is quite strong, which makes him a great healer and many in and outside of the church look up to him, me included. What else would you like to know your majesty?" Kira said.

'It is clear Kira is a follower of the light. I'm not sure I can get a straight answer from her. Guess I'll have to figure it out myself.' Prince James thought but said, “What can I expect from this visit and this official acknowledgment? Also, what role does the church play in all of this?”

“Ah, High Priest Cendrin’s role is to show support from the church. Though this kingdom is very adamant about the separation of church and state, that is more to protect the church than the state. The royal family and the church are both pillars to the people of this kingdom. The royal family sees to the prosperity and protection of its citizens. The church sees to the soul of the people. When people see both in alignment and agreement it helps ease their minds. The purpose of this visit will be to determine if you are like your parents. The king and queen genuinely care for the people and have done much to help our people flourish. Trust me you of all people have nothing to worry about from this visit your majesty.” Kira replied.

‘I wish I could believe that. My initial impression of the High Priest was favorable, but I must be cautious. Too many stories of people in power abusing their roles and pointing the finger at others when in truth they were doing the very thing they accused others of.’ Prince James thought.

Shortly after Kira’s conversation a knock was made at the front door and Cooper escorted the High Priest to our conference room table. “Your majesty, High Priest Cendrin is here to see you.”

Prince James rose to shake High Priest Cendrin’s hand, greeting him before gesturing for Cendrin to take a seat. “It is a pleasure to see you again High Priest Cendrin.” Prince James said.

“Please call me Cendrin, Prince James.”

“Only if you call me James in private.” Prince James replied.

“Very well James.” Cendrin replied while slightly bowing his head in acknowledgment.

“It is good to see you too Kira. We miss your help at the church. Your healing abilities were always so very appreciated.” Cendrin said while looking at Kira.

“My apologies High Priest Cendrin. My new role as one of Prince James’s personal royal knights limits my availability.” Kira replied without a hint of remorse.

‘Careful Kira, I don’t want him to think I’m taking you away from the church or are some kind of slave driver.’ Prince James thought.

“Of course, of course, I understand your duties, Kira. Any time you can spare is appreciated. There are so many in need.” Cendrin said before turning his whole attention to Prince James and said, “Shall we discuss why I am here James?”

“I would appreciate it Cendrin.” Prince James replied.

“As I’m sure Kira has already explained, the royal family and the Church of Light are two pillars that hold up this kingdom. The Royal family governs the land and its people. It is the church’s obligation to ensure the people have salvation in the afterlife. It is the Royal family’s right to determine succession. It is the church’s right to speak out against tyranny and oppression. It has become tradition that the church shows our support when the successor to the throne is publicly announced.” Cendrin explained.

“To show the people and the nobles that the Royal family and the Church of Light are united in the direction the kingdom is headed.” Prince James interjected.

Cendrin smiled at Prince James’ response. “Exactly my prince. Now normally the Church of Light has plenty of time to observe the candidate to the throne to determine whether there are any concerns and, where possible, help guide them should they start to go astray or allow power to corrupt them.”

“But since I was raised in seclusion by famous battle-hardened adventurers, one known as the ‘Butcher of the Plains’ there is warranted concern.” Prince James interrupted again.

“My prince has got it in one! You are correct these are valid concerns. Especially as rumors spread among the peerage of your exploits so far both on your journey home and since your return...” Cendrin replied.

Prince James once again interrupted. “Then there is the matter of the prophecy that was divined by your very own prophets. One who was the sister to the Headmaster of the Royal Academy. That is something you cannot ignore.”

"You are well informed James. I am guessing you have been talking with Lady Rollara." Cendrin replied.

"Among others. My sources have told me that some of the Church of Light priests have begun spreading the prophecy to the masses. Which I find very interesting if the Church's official stance has yet to be made." Prince James answered.

Cendrin's eyes widened for the briefest of moments before returning to a calm mask of civility. "The prince is very well informed indeed. Especially so, for being confined to the palace and military training area. It is clear I underestimated the fierce intelligence in those eyes of yours and your resourcefulness." Cendrin said as he looked into Prince James' eyes as he continued. "Yes, your suspicion is correct, I have discreetly shared the prophecy with my people. I have instructed them to share this prophecy and your deeds so far since your return."

It was Prince James's turn to be surprised Cendrin so easily admitted what he subtly had implied. He had but one question, "Why?"

"It is quite simple James, and something tells me you have already deduced the answer. There are many believers in the Light across all walks of life. As it appears you have deduced, I have faithful spies in the palace." Cendrin replied matter-of-factly.

Cooper and Kira seemed shocked. Cooper spoke up, "I never would've expected the Church of Light to resort to spying on the Royal family!"

"It's not just the Royal family. It's the nobles and even some prominent artisans and merchants." Prince James had replied to everyone's shock.

In fact, Prince James had received this interesting news from Sloane. What no one knew except Prince James and Sloane was Prince James formed a mental link with Sloane the day prior. Prince James did this so Sloane could act as his very own personal spymaster and keep him informed of any pressing information. Sloane had been impressed by the prince's capabilities and how the prince treated him with respect. This was the first time in Sloane's life that someone saw real potential in him and understood why Sloane kept such shady company.

Sloane loved his kingdom and fought hard to get where he was. He had long since learned about what the church had been doing and readily shared it with his new liege. They both agreed to keep what they learned and their mental link a secret so the spymaster could better serve in the shadows. Sloane, as a very cunning individual, had discovered this information but never shared it for fear of repercussions should the wrong person hear this. Yet now, Sloane held no such reservations as he trusted his prince wholeheartedly.

Of course, Prince James was not going to tell the high priest that or how Sloane has already started to recruit some of those in the criminal underbelly as spies and informants.

"Very informed indeed." Cendrin replied contemplating how much the prince knew.

Turning to Kira and the other knights in the room, Cendrin continued. "Prince James is correct. We have eyes and ears everywhere but do not mistake things. These are people of faith who share what they know out of an obligation to protect the realm and do what is right."

"How is spying on our royal family somehow doing what's right for this kingdom? It is the Royal family!" Cooper said clearly upset.

"Corruption rarely shows its face so openly. This allows the Church of Light to keep an eye on those in power and subtly influence where they can. It is this network I wish to tap into Cendrin." Prince James answered Cooper's question for Cendrin. This caused everyone to look at the prince in shock.

"You are ok with this your majesty?" Cooper asked.

"Ok? No, but I understand the why and think my spymaster can make even better use of them than the church can." Prince James said.

"Spymaster?" Both Cooper and Cendrin said in surprise.

"Sloane. It has to be." Kira said, finally rejoining the conversation after getting over one shock after the other as she listened to the conversation. This is not how she thought this meeting would go.

"Yes, Sloane." Prince James replied to Kira.

"You see Cendrin, my parents risked their only son and this Kingdom on a prophecy. They love both their family and this kingdom very much, you know that better than anyone, I suspect. I may lead with my heart but that does not mean I do not take precautions and steps to protect those I care about. I am a realist after all. Of course, I would be cautious of a person and organization who encouraged my parents to send their only son away, Cendrin is one of my mother's closest advisors, he had to have a hand in it, of that, I am sure." Prince James said.

After a few moments of silence with the Prince and High Priest staring at each other, Cendrin finally broke the silence with a sigh. As if a part of him deflated thinking about some past memory he replied to Prince James. "Humph. It appears not even I fully believed it, but I am beginning to truly believe. Yes, Prince James you suspected correctly. When I was informed of the prophecy, I encouraged your parents to send you away."

Kira in shock interrupted, "Why would you do that High Priest? Wait, Prince James how did you know he had a hand in it?"

Kira turned her head back and forth not sure who she wanted answers from.

Cendrin replied first. "My child, there is much you do not yet know even though you follow the Light. The day I was given the news about the prophecy... I had a faith defining moment."

Taking a pause before continuing as if reliving such an impactful moment in his life. "I was in morning prayers as I normally do and there was this light that shown brighter than the sun all of a sudden coming from my window and then nothing."

"Nothing?" Kira asked.

"I had a complete lapse in memory. The only thing I remember was my aide shaking me saying he found me staring up from my knees. He brought me the news that the King and Queen were given a prophecy."

Cendrin breathed out, almost getting lost in that memory again before he continued. "The moment my aide relayed the words of the prophecy to me I just knew. It was like a strong phantom memory just out of reach was telling me this must come to pass... that our lives depended on it."

Cendrin looked at both Prince James and Kira and continued his story. "So yes, I immediately went to the King and Queen offering my council. They confided in me what they were told. I told them they had to do it. I pushed as best I could, even so much as helping them convince the kingdom's two most powerful adventurers at the time to give up their lives and help raise you. I'm sorry my boy."

He paused, searching my eyes and as if finding something there decided to keep going. "As the years passed, doubt began to creep in, for all of us I think that was the case. Every time your parents would ask me if they did the right thing my answer was always emphatically 'Yes!' Even though in my heart I doubted it every time. Faith can be funny that way."

Cendrin seemed to get lost in self-reflection for a moment before regaining his focus. It was as if each time he was grasping at memories, and they were so impactful he would get lost in those moments. As if finally regaining control of himself, Cendrin shook his head and continued. "Here I am rambling. It is clear, Your Highness, that I have underestimated your capabilities. I came here today to take your measure, see if what I gambled on all those years ago was true.

"You have only been back for a short time, yet you are moving pieces into play and seeing things others are blind to. Thank you for helping an old man."

"Helping how?" Kira said confused.

Prince James was the one to reply. "To rekindle his faith. My ability to quickly intuit the truth. It's a line from the prophecy 'even though others will hide and distract, he shall be like the arrow to know the truth and bring that to the people."

Though Prince James thought, 'I wonder if it's just my high Intuition, Intelligence and Wisdom scores or my high Charisma that helps rally people to my side. Though his gap in memory is interesting. It sounds like some outside force influenced him. Now whether that was Light or Dark remains to be seen. Man, I should've paid attention to my guide.'

"You do seem to know and plan for things even before we realize it." Kira commented almost offhandedly. She had only heard mention the gist of the prophecy. This was the first time she heard an actual line from it.

'What else does the prophecy say?' Kira thought.

"As I said, it is clear you are far more capable than we have given you credit. It is clear I chose correctly." Cendrin said.

Looking like he was making his mind up about something, Cendrin stuck his hand out and spoke. “If you will have our faction, the Church of Light shall pledge our full support to your cause.”

Prince James immediately took his hand and spoke. “That is a given High Priest Cendrin. Can I call you Cendrin when we are among others?” He said this last part with a mischievous smile on his face.

“Of course, your majesty. Send your spymaster to me and I shall see them connected with our network.” Cendrin replied.

“Good. With that done, let us plan to meet periodically. We can let others think it is to help provide guidance in the Light. We can use the time to collaborate and make things happen. Plus, you can tell me more of what your scholars have uncovered over the years. If possible, I would also like to learn more about healing magic. For the most part what the outside world would be told is true, you would be providing guidance, just not exactly in the way they think.” Prince James answered with another mischievous smile on his face.

“Underestimated you indeed. Ha, ha, ha.” Cendrin chuckled as he excused himself, bringing the impromptu assessment to a close.

Chapter 19 – Another Visitor Today

After High Priest Cendrin left, it took Kira about 1.2 seconds to completely lose her composure. "How the...? When did...? No, no, better yet, what just happened, my Prince? I have never in all my years of service ever, and I do mean EVER, seen the High Priest act that way. For a minute I questioned if it was really him!"

"You and me both." Cooper replied just as confused before he continued. "I have never seen anyone talk to him in such a manner either."

"Indeed." Kira agreed before continuing. "Can you please explain, your Majesty?" Even in all her exasperation, her upbringing did not allow her to push too hard for answers.

"Hahaha! The looks on your two faces...Priceless." Prince James laughed.

The looks on Cooper and Kira, it was clear they did not see what was so funny.

"Alright, alright. Let me explain what just happened. Kira you were correct, High Priest Cendrin did come here to assess me" Prince James said the last words while using his hands to make quotations mark motion. This further confused them.

"What are you doing with your hands, your Majesty? Does that motion have some significance?" Cooper asked.

Trying not to laugh again, Prince James replied. "Yes, it does but it doesn't matter right now. Back to your questions. Cendrin was expecting a sheltered Prince, one who has been locked away, perhaps easy to guide" Prince James used the hand motion for quotation marks when saying the word guide.

"There is that hand motion again. What does that mean?" Cooper looked even more perplexed.

'Has he taken one too many blows to the head?' Prince James thought.

"He was expecting someone much like my sister, bless her heart. I was raised in isolation after all. What he found was something he hoped for, something that sparked a renewal of his faith. With me, he encountered the unexpected. He came here expecting to control the conversation so he could get the easy answers he wanted. What he found was zero control over the conversation but the answers he needed not wanted. Do you understand?" Prince James explained.

"Uh, not really sir." Cooper replied clearly confused.

"You showed him a glimpse of what the rest of us that follow you have seen. You are doing what we could only hope for. You gave the High Priest hope. Somehow what you said triggered a memory, a pivotal moment in his faith. All of us that follow the Light have had such a moment. Get it now Cooper?" Kira said.

"I think I do my Lady Kira." Cooper replied.

"I made it clear I knew things that most nobles who have lived their whole lives at court never figured out. Sloane has done a great job in keeping me informed since I appointed them to be my Head Spymaster."

"But that's the part I don't understand Sire. When did you have time? I have not seen Sloane constantly coming and going. How are they keeping you so informed?" Kira said.

'I made a point to get detailed status reports on the prince's activities, just as Mira did. It's so I can better serve, that's all...I swear.' Kira thought even as she said such words to herself, she knew they were hollow.

"Simple, Mind Magic." Prince James said.

'Wait did he say mind Magic? Can he read my mind? Is he reading it right now? By the Light what has he heard me say?' Kira thought with a growing worry showing up on her face.

"Do not worry Kira. I do not actively read thoughts." Prince James said.

'Though I have heard some of yours as they are pretty damn loud.' Prince James thought before continuing. "I tend to favor Soul magic over Mind magic, but this ability is very useful. It is a unique Mind magic called **Party Link**. Once the link is willingly established on both sides those involved in the party link can send mental messages back and forth over long distances.

As people get used to the link, they can send images and eventually it's like carrying on a conversation in person but in your head. Sloane has been constantly sending me mental communications."

'I never thought there would be an added benefit of learning to partition my mind. The help with multitasking is amazing.' Prince James thought as he let his words sink in.

"That gives an amazing advantage to your Majesty. Think of what could be accomplished in battle. Our enemies would never know what to expect. Do you plan to form this bond with the rest of us in your personal royal knights?" Kira asked almost hopefully, her previous trepidation vanished with the thought of forming any type of bond with Prince James.

"Eventually yes Kira but not yet. I'm still getting used to the ability. Plus, it would be good to discuss this with Simmons and the other Sergeants before we proceed." Prince James said.

Looking off to the side, Prince James smiled as he said, "Now that's over, I think it's time to talk with my uncle, General Marcus. He is here if you want to let him in."

"General Marcus? How did you…? Why is he here? Never mind, I'm learning you are clearly several steps ahead of the rest of us." Kira said in a resigned exasperation as she got up to escort the general into the conference room.

Prince James stood and shook his uncle's hand before gesturing for General Marcus to take a seat.

"It's good to see you Uncle. Funny to find you here in my wing of the palace." Prince James said even though Sloane had already informed him that the General got wind of his meeting with the High Priest.

'It's clear my uncle is curious to find out how that meeting went.'

"Yes, I thought I'd stop by and spend some time with my nephew." General Marcus said nonchalantly.

"You mean you didn't come to find out how my meeting with the High Priest went?" Prince James asked in a tone that clearly expressed 'I see right through you'.

"Oh? Did you meet with the High Priest today? Really?" General Marcus asked, feigning exaggerated ignorance.

Shaking his head at his uncle's antics. "Come Uncle, let's have lunch together and I'll fill you in." Prince James said before walking back into his suite and sitting at his dining room table where the maids were setting out lunch.

After they took their seats, Prince James figured he would get right to what Uncle Marcus wanted to know. "Cendrin has pledged his full support to the royal faction."

Uncle Marcus was just taking a swig of wine when he abruptly spit it out. Coughing a little, "Wha..., cough, cough, say that again nephew."

"Cendrin has pledged his full support to the royal faction. It appears he found me an acceptable heir." Prince James said.

"Acceptable my ass! Cendrin, though he has been somewhat supportive, has never fully committed or pledged himself to anyone other than his blasted 'Light'! Pledging his full support means he saw you as far more than 'acceptable' nephew!" Marcus animatedly stated.

Reigning in his emotions, General Marcus continued. "Your father and mother have been trying for years to get the church to publicly show their support for the crown. Sure, High Priest Cendrin has never spoken ill of the royal family, but he has also never praised them either. What did you do to convince him?"

Prince James just shrugged his shoulders.

"Cooper!" General Marcus turned his attention to the jovial knight.

"Yes Sir!" Cooper snapped to attention.

"Care to fill me in on what my nephew did to convince High Priest Cendrin to join the cause?" General Marcus asked in a commanding tone.

"I don't rightly know Sir! They just started talking and somehow at the end of the conversation the High Priest pledged the full support of the Church." Cooper quickly replied.

Hearing Cooper's response General Marcus thought, 'my nephew is a shrewd fox. Either his man is keeping his secrets, or they don't know how he did it. Though I did ask Cooper, he's not exactly the sharpest sword in the arsenal, too many blows to the head from his calvary charges. Perhaps Kira.'

"Sergeant Kira. What do you have to report on this outcome?"

"Nothing Sir." Kira said almost absent-mindedly.

"Nothing?! What do you mean nothing?!" General Marcus asked in exasperation as he thought, 'I know Kira is close to the Church of Light, but she has never refused to answer a question from a superior. And why does she have a big smile on her face all of a sudden?'

"It's ok Kira, tell my uncle whatever you wish, I have nothing to hide from him." Prince James chimed in.

Marcus was unaware that the reason for Kira's broad smile was Prince James had created a mental link with her. She was so surprised and happy she could exchange thoughts with him she immediately replied to General Marcus that she knew nothing.

Prince James told her telepathically, *"It's ok you can tell him. Just keep the fact that the Church's spies work for me now from him... for now. I will eventually tell my uncle, but not until we have learned more."*

"UNDERSTOOD YOUR MAJESTY!" Kira mentally shouted to make sure she was heard.

Wincing inwardly Prince James replied, *"Just talk normally, you do not have to shout."*

"Sorry." She replied telepathically.

"I merely mean there is not much to report General. I have never seen the High Priest act that way. High Priest Cendrin seems to always steer a conversation in a direction he chooses no matter whom he is speaking with. I have never seen him be bested in such a fashion. The prince guided him right back to whatever the prince wanted to discuss. I have never seen that happen General, ever." Kira replied honestly.

After a moment "Hahaha!" Marcus laughed.

After he calmed down General Marcus continued. "It appears nephew that you are so skilled at negotiating that both Cooper here and Kira are unsure of how you achieved it. When I tell my brother, your father, about this I will have to recommend you be our negotiator the next time we have to discuss relations and trade with our foreign neighbors. Hahaha." He said the last part with a mischievous grin on his face.

'I don't like that look. He's up to something. Looks like I'm going to have to put that spy network to use even sooner than I thought.' Prince James internally chuckled.

"Thank you for the food and drink nephew. Your father and I were a bit concerned about Cendrin's visit." Marcus raised his hand, "Yes of course we knew it was coming but to Kira's point Cendrin has a way of guiding a conversation. I can't wait to tell my brother this story. Well done, well done indeed. The nobles won't stand a chance." Marcus stated as he rose from his seat and excused himself.

They all watched General Marcus leave Prince James' suite. They could hear General Marcus saying under his breath, "I don't know how he did it, sir." Chuckling to himself as he imitated Cooper's dumb look on his face as he closed the doors and laughed, "Hahaha!"

"Hey, is he talking about me?" Cooper asked.

"You're fine Cooper, he's just impressed with our Prince." Kira replied at the oblivious man.

"Well, that is completely understandable. Our Prince is a great man, even the Church of Light thinks so!" Cooper replied.

"Dude how many times has this guy taken a lance to the head?" Prince James asked Kira telepathically.

"More than you can even guess. Though he is as kind as a stuffed animal and loyal to a fault. He's just always been oblivious to politics. His motto has always been 'point me in the direction and let me charge ahead." Kira replied telepathically.

*"Welcome to the **Party Link**, Kira."* Sloane said through the link.

Kira was momentarily shocked before saying across the **Party Link**, *"You can hear me Sloane?!"*

"Of course, Kira, the term 'party' implies more than one after all." Sloane answered.

Kira's face seemed to fall as she realized her hopes of getting time to chat privately with Prince James whenever she wished evaporated instantly.

Sloane, who could sense the strong emotion, decided to help their fellow knight. *"Cheer up Kira. As the originator of the Party Link ability, Prince James informed me that we can speak with him privately without the others that join the link hearing the conversation."*

Prince James decided to chime in. *"What Sloane says is correct. As you have to consciously will your thoughts into the Party Link, just focus on only sending the message to me directly instead of the whole chat."*

"LIKE THIS, MY PRINCE?!" Kira practically mentally yelled at Prince James.

Seeing him wince, Kira apologized. *"Sorry sire."*

"It is fine." Prince James replied.

In Party Link Kira asked, *"Wait how did you know what I was feeling Sloane? You are not in the room."*

Prince James answered in what he was thinking of as group chat. *"Strong emotions can sometimes be sent over without you realizing it. Practice masking or 'going dark' in the chat. I do it all the time."*

"He does, it is most annoying when he does it as I cannot sense him or if he is alright." Sloane answered.

"This ability is mine to use as I feel is best and we all require our privacy." Prince James adamantly replied.

"Fair enough, my liege. What are your orders?" Sloane asked.

"Meet up with Cendrin, but as always, use your stealth to make sure you are not seen." Prince James instructed.

"As you command, my liege." Sloane replied before 'going dark' in the Party Link.

"Are you two alright? You have been staring at each other for the last few minutes. Do I need to fetch a healer?" Cooper asked. To him both Prince James and Kira just stopped talking and seemed to have vacant stares in their eyes. At first it did not bother him as he enjoys long moments when off duty that he can just stare and think of nothing. In fact, it is his favorite past time besides jousting and caring for his horse. He had learned though that it was not normal for others to have that look for too long, which is why he spoke up.

"Let me go get the healer, maybe you took a blow to the head during morning exercises. I know I enjoy just staring after such a thing. That and hitting the person back just as hard, if not harder. Where was I? Oh yes, let me get you both a healer!"

Prince James interrupted Cooper's ramblings. "We are fine Cooper. Do not worry yourself, both Kira and I just needed a moment to collect our thoughts."

"Oh, that is completely understandable, your majesty. It is nice to find someone else who likes to stare off into space as I do. I do not feel so alone now." Cooper said with a smile on his face.

Chapter 20 – The Power of Sloane

Sloane made his way out of the prince's wing of the palace. The prince was an enigma to Sloane. When he had informed his prince of the activities of the church, Prince James did not seem surprised or shocked in any way. Any other noble would be stunned, yet Prince James seemed to intuit the reasons for what the church was doing and convinced High Priest Cendrin to bring his spy network under Sloane's command.

Everyone that has met the high priest knew he was shrewd and cunning. The man could steer any conversation in the direction he wanted and many fools who dared to openly go against the man found themselves publicly embarrassed one way or another. Sometimes that embarrassment came at the verbal sparring the high priest would win or later rumors being spread about the noble or merchant. It was this result that first clued Sloane into investigating the Church of Light in the first place.

When Sloane learned how vast the spy network was, he feared it might rival any of the underground organizations. However, the truth was even more unsettling as the church's spy network made the others look like amateurs playing in a local pond of knowledge when the church ruled the ocean of information. Upon learning that the man wisely kept his mouth shut and told no one. Sadly, Sloane became convinced a few of the church's operatives learned he knew something, so they began to leak the truth about Sloane's past.

Sloane was not necessarily ashamed of his past, he had done what he had to as a poor orphan that grew up on the streets. To say his past was bloody and shady would be an understatement. The man had worked hard to overcome such things and eventually be accepted as a royal knight.

He was on the brink of being dishonorably discharged as he heard the talk and concerns of his superiors. Of course, it did not help Sloane's case that he showed only the minimum required respect for some of his superiors, many coming from noble or wealthy merchant families too sheltered from the seedier parts of society. He would not be lectured by such men and women, which only drove him to being removed as a royal knight.

It was sheer luck that Sloane was selected for the mission to retrieve the prince. The kingdom was short on available knight and soldiers with tracking, removing tracks, and monster hunting for long periods in the wilderness. Sloane's past had led him to possess all those needed skills, so his superiors begrudgingly agreed to him joining the mission. The very mission that changed Sloane's perspective and life forever.

The first time he saw Prince James he felt a sense of danger. Everyone else seemed blind to it so Sloane had ignored the feeling until he saw the man's eyes. And a man Prince James was, he may be young, but he seemed to carry a lifetime of knowledge and experience in those eyes.

Sloane, like everyone else, watched the prince carefully. Most seemed focused on learning what type of person Prince James was or could the curry favor with the man. Sure, Sloane watched for some of that, but mostly he noticed the way the man carried himself. There was a sureness to the prince's movements, an aura of authority that you sometimes found with men and women who knew the truth about responsibility and were skilled enough to do the job well.

The first time Sloane met General Marcus, the king, and the queen, they all possessed such an aura. Yet their auras seemed like flickering candles compared to the blazing sun Prince James possessed. Most people did not know Sloane possessed the **Discerning Eye** talent.

Discerning Eye
Description: Grants the ability to see the true threat of a target. Can show you types of auras, threat level, and over time potential weaknesses in combat.

It allowed him to see the threat level, possible alignments, and as he grew in his use it could show him potential weaknesses in his opponents. The talent is how he even survived his younger years in the first place. His **Discerning Eye** was telling Sloane that the prince was the most dangerous being he had ever encountered in his entire lifetime both in comparison to any of the monsters, human and beast, he previously came across.

The first few hours after they retrieved the prince, Sloane was on edge, his muscles were sore from being tense and ready to react at a moment's notice. Then he started to relax as he saw how kind and friendly Prince James was, Sloane began to doubt his senses and shifted to his normal level of readiness. That was until he witnessed the spare between Captain Spears and Prince James.

The fight between the captain and prince was like watching two juggernauts clashing. They kept increasing their speed and intensity of clashing blows. Sloane, like others present, thought it was a real treat to watch a master swordsman fight and at first everyone thought the captain was going easy on the prince based on how smoothly Prince James deflected Captain Spears' attacks. Sloane saw it first; it was clear the prince was the one going easy on the captain. That brought all of Sloane's heightened senses to full alert once again.

It was hard to not eventually relax around the prince over time as they traveled. Prince James also treated Sloane with respect and as another traveling companion rather than the side-eyed looks he would get from others. Sloane found himself liking the young prince even with his **Discerning Eye** screaming caution into his mind.

Then the battle with the undead came. Sloane did his duty and jumped in as ordered to hold the line. He fought valiantly and with precision. Every stroke of his blades Sloane would remove a limb or decapitate an undead head. When he took out one undead it seemed like two more would take its place, but Sloane trusted in his skills and his fellow knights. Many of them may be sheltered from certain aspects of society, but every one of them knew how to fight and hold their own in battle.

The knights and soldiers were holding their own even against overwhelming numbers, then the undead trolls and ogre arrived. It took multiple knights to hold the larger undead brutes at bay putting more pressure on the kingdom's soldiers to pick up the slack. The ogre knocked us aside like we were nothing. Sloane was able to dodge several blows and take out undead that made the mistake of getting too close to Sloane. Yet the undead ogre was remarkably fast for being so big.

When Sloane stepped in to save a soldier from being turned into bloody paste, the ogre's tree trunk club clipped him. He recovered fast enough but once again pushed a fellow knight out of the way and got clipped again, this time sending him prone and dazed. The club was about to be brought down on Sloane's prone form,

"Just great, I die saving a man who treated me like a jerk." Was what Sloane remembered saying as he resigned himself to his fate.

As he watched the club seem to move in slow motion felt an intense heat pass over him as a bright ball of fire struck the undead ogre. The force of the blast pressed Sloane further into the ground as he closed his eyes to shield them from being flash fried. When he opened his eyes, Prince James was there picking up the remains of the ogre's leg and using it to bat away any undead that approached.

Prince James locked eyes on Sloane for a moment, giving him a wink before he knocked undead left and right as he carved a path deeper into their forces. Sloane was not one to ignore second chances in life, especially as he was probably closer to his sixth or seventh chance at this point. Sloane did the only thing he could and got to his feet, helped some of his fellow soldiers up and those that could fight re-joined the battle.

The man had saved his life and the lives of many more that day. It was also when Sloane realized what his **Discerning Eye** was really trying to tell him, if he wanted to survive this world his best bet would be to serve such that man always. He wasn't about to stop listening to his instincts now.

Then Prince James asked him to join his personal guard Sloane jumped at the chance. The prince offered Sloane to become his personal spy master and join his Party Link. Sloane had tried to argue against sharing a mental space with Prince James based on the not so savory things Sloane had done in his life, but the prince had zero hesitation.

"A man's past is a part of him, but it is not the only part. We all have ugly parts of ourselves we try to deny, hide, or ignore, but at some point, we must re-integrate, or those parts will destroy us. I do not fear your past, I require your help in building a better future." Prince James stated as he offered Sloane the Party Link.

Do you wish to join Party Link? Yes, or No?

Sloane never second guessed his choice after hearing Prince James' sincere words. He felt more than heard his words and it is why he would defend this man against the machinations of those in the capital.

Shaking his head to clear it of his thoughts he refocused on his mission. Sloane was to slip into the head priest's chambers inside the Church of Light in the capital. Knowing what he did about their capabilities he knew how to be extra cautious. They were not called the Church of Light for nothing. Many years ago, in a failed heist, Sloane learned several had such an affinity to Light Magic that they could use it to bend the light to hide operatives or create illusions.

'They will not catch me like that again.' Sloane thought as he slipped through the gap in a guard patrol as they passed by as they made their rounds.

As he slipped around another patrol, silently closing the head priest's chamber doors Sloane thought, "This is way too easy."

A light flashed as the door closed.

"You might as well drop your stealth Sloane. I imagine that is you, is it not?" High Priest Cendrin stated.

The high priest was sitting in a high back chair behind an elaborate solid oak desk. The man was writing furiously and did not bother to look up.

"I have multiple wards in this room. You tripped none of them, which is impressive unto itself... which is why I put that light spell on the door when it closes. Normally that is enough to knock out any stealth, your skill and affinity must be exceptional high." Head Priest Cendrin explained, still not bothering to look up.

Sighing, Sloane pulled out one of the chairs in front of the desk and plopped in as he dropped his stealth. "Impressive spell, but yes my affinity is quite high, and I have had some past experiences dealing with the Church of Light."

That statement got the head priest to stop writing and look up. "Oh interesting. It would appear the rumors I have heard might just be true." Cendrin said the last bit with a cold smile on his face.

"Please, your people are the ones that started those rumors. I am sure you already know the nature of my previous involvement with your organization." Sloane answered coldly.

Cendrin's smile dropped yet the priest seemed to subtly relax. "Well, I did not become head priest simply on my good looks. Our prince trusts you enough to put you in charge of his information gathering efforts. For now, that is enough for me."

Waving his hands down to the various papers the head priest was writing. "Do you know what these are?"

Not interested in playing word games with an expert at it, Sloane decided to just cut through the back and forth. "Not a clue, or better yet, let us just get to the point where you just tell me."

Cendrin's eyebrow rose slightly before a more genuine smile appeared on his face. "Fair enough. I can appreciate the directness. Too many in this city talk in circles, I have developed a bad habit of guiding a conversation where I require it."

Sloane gave the head priest a look and gestured with his hand for the man to get on with it.

"Very well. I deserved that." Cendrin stated before gesturing at the papers again. "They are orders to further spread the prophecy and our prince's exploits. These others are instructions to begin to coordinate the information channels through both you and me."

Cendrin poured some wax on a parchment and pushed magic into the document as he pressed his personal seal down on the wax. Once he finished, he passed the letter to Sloane.

"What was that?!" Sloane asked as he felt his own magic get drawn out of him as it connected with the letter.

"It is a magic writ instructing any in the church to follow your word or the prince's as if they were my own. As you will be the keeper of the writ your magic was required to bind the document and yourself." Cendrin explained.

Sloane narrowed his eyes as he replied coldly. "Bind me in what way priest?!"

Cendrin waved away his concerns. "It is nothing so nefarious spymaster. It merely does not allow you to use the document without acting on behalf of our prince or myself. I may trust Prince James' judgment, but I will still help protect him as best I can. What I am turning over to you is the best kept secret of my order."

The tension in the room evaporated as Sloane nodded. "Very well priest. It is a fair precaution. Prince James has instructed me to tell you to he wants a few experts in illusion magic to be present at the ball. I will meet each of them prior."

"That is easy enough to arrange. Inform his majesty it shall be done. Anything else?" Cendrin asked.

"Anything you might have on the necromancer currently residing in our dungeons? I hear a few of your priests have gone to take his confession." Sloane said before leaning back in the chair once again.

"Let me summon my leads and the agents who I have assigned to that task." Cendrin replied.

The head priest tapped on an orb on his desk. A few moments passed before a voice could be heard coming from the orb. "What is it you require your eminence?"

High Priest Cendrin put his hand on the orb and answered. "Summon my leads. I have someone to introduce them to and instructions for them to take."

"It is late in the evening, your eminence." The person on the other side of the orb replied.

Cendrin raised an eyebrow. "And? What of it?"

The voice on the other side quickly replied, "J-just that it will take them extra time to make themselves presentable your eminence. Please forgive any importance... I merely wanted to prepare you for any possible delays."

"That is fine. Convey the level of importance and I'm sure they will hasten their steps." Cendrin replied before cutting off his magic to the orb.

About twenty minutes later several men dressed in priest robes, leathers, or chain mail were standing around the head priest's conference table. They bowed before Cendrin before he waved them to take their seats. Once they were all settled, the head priest began the meeting.

"I am glad you all were able to make it on such short notice. I wanted to introduce all of you to our new spymaster." Head Priest Cendrin stated without any preamble.

"What makes this one so worthy of such a title? He..." One of the men dressed in leathers began to ask before he found both his hands stuck to the table. Two throwing daggers were embedded in the man's leather gloves, one blade in each. The man did not even see Sloane move.

"Ha, ha, ha! Careful Andrew, it looks as if this one has teeth." A large man in chain mail boasted in laughter.

"Indeed. He is clearly capable. Besides you were never going to get the job Andrew." One of the men in priestly robes stated.

The man who sat to the head priest's left slammed his staff on the floor to get everyone's attention. "Enough! You are in front of his eminence!"

A round of apologies could be heard across the table.

"As you can see, Sloane is very capable and has powers you may not be even aware of." Cendrin stated.

Several eyes rose as they recognized the name. Before another round of protests could start Cendrin interjected. "Sloane has been appointed as Prince James' personal spymaster. I have agreed to the prince's request to integrate and combine our efforts."

The boisterous paladin that made fun of the one called Andrew spoke up. "Then you believe the prophecy to be true, your eminence?"

Cendrin nodded. "I do. He was able to steer the conversation in the direction he wanted."

Several eyebrows rose, as they all knew how skilled the head priest was in controlling a conversation.

"Now that is resolved, for now, let us turn our talks on the matter of the necromancer. Andrew, what have you discovered?" Cendrin said.

Andrew had just removed the blades from his gloves. In order to free himself, he had to take his hands out. It took some effort to pull the blades from the table, demonstrating the amount of force Sloane was able to use. The man's face blanched when he heard his name.

"My apologies, your eminence. I have uncovered very little. The man knew nothing of his employer and was paid through an intermediary. I have still not tracked down that broker. I will need more time."

Sloane turned cold eyes on the man named Andrew. "Turn over your contacts. I will take over the investigation from here."

Andrew began to protest. "How dare..."

"Do it Andrew! That is an order!" Head Priest Cendrin cut off the man.

Andrew slumped and just nodded.

Sloane rose from his seat. He bowed his head to Cendrin. "I will take my leave." Turning to the rest of the assembly. "I will meet with each of you individually in due time. His majesty has recalled me, and I must take my leave."

In truth Prince James had been listening in as Sloane shared his senses with his prince. James had picked up the same thing Sloane had.

*"Your **Discerning Eye** is most impressive Sloane. The aura of that Andrew reeks. He is hiding something. Get him alone and find out the truth."* Prince James instructed.

"My thoughts exactly my prince! It shall be done!" Sloane replied through **Party Link**.

Sloane activated his **Stealth** and vanished before everyone in the room, snatching his two blades that Andrew left on the table. He had a job to do and no time like the present, time to find out what he could about Andrew.

Sloane had done his research on Andrew in the middle of his other duties over the last few days. The man was officially a hunter and messenger for the Church of Light but unofficially he was one of their top investigators. Which is why both Prince James and Sloane had a hard time believing the man found nothing about the necromancer.

Prince James had instructed Sloane to not press the issue until after the ball. They both were busy enough learning everything the Church of Light had on the various nobles and influential families of the kingdom. It was an overwhelming amount of intel to absorb. Sloane, who was skilled at parsing information was struggling to keep up and was not surprised to find the prince having no problem assimilating it all. It was one more reason Sloane found to serve the man who saved his life in more than one way.

What Sloane was able to get was a lead on the intermediary that gave the necromancer his assignment. When Prince James shared the image with Sloane, even though the person was hidden, he instantly recognized the ring the man wore. It belonged to a merchant who specialized as an information broker. Many in the underground knew of him and he was known for having flexible morals. In other words, the man was loyal to the highest bidder.

Sloane was on top of the merchant's home preparing to slip in unnoticed.

'I've got to do something. All this information assimilation and no action is driving me nuts and I know it is bothering Prince James, he just hides it better than I do.' Sloane thought before he dropped down right behind a guard.

With a quick choke hold from behind the guard collapsed unconscious. Sloane dragged him behind a bush, setting him down out of sight. The whole exchange took mere moments, and the guard never even had a chance to make a sound. This was one of Sloane's specialties, infiltration.

After subduing and hiding a few more guards, Sloane slipped into the merchant's bedroom. Skulking up to the sleeping man, Sloane unsheathed his dagger and brought it close to the merchant's neck. Using Discerning Eye, Sloane discovered the man had a knife in his hand under his pillow. With agile fingers Sloane relieved the merchant of his dagger and secreted the blade into his sleeve.

Now with the merchant disarmed, Sloane put one hand over the man's mouth and nose and the other hand holding the dagger close to his throat. "Wake up Seville, you pissant. I have questions for you."

Seville the merchant awoke with a startled expression that quickly turned to horror as he felt the cold steel on his throat.

"That's right. Give me any trouble and you won't make it out of here alive. I will slit your throat faster than you can imagine and not lose a wink of sleep over it. Got it?" Sloane threatened.

Seville blinked furiously as his way of agreeing. Sloane removed his hand from Seville's mouth but left the dagger up against the merchant's throat.

"Wh-What do you want? I do not know who you are, but I assure you I will cooperate." Seville croaked out.

“I know you will Seville. You would not dare cross me, now, would you?” Sloane said as he lowered his cowl to show Seville his face.

Seville’s eyes widened in shock and recognition. Of all the people that could invade his home the last person he ever wanted to see again was the very man holding a blade to his throat. He knew without a doubt now that this was no idle threat. “Th-the wolf of the underworld, the Shadow of Death ma-made manifest. Please spare me, I have made a point to never interfere with your interests, I swear it!” Seville sniveled out in fear.

“Ah but that is where you are wrong worm. You are interfering in my business. I am going to remove my blade but do not be a fool and think that you can do anything before I slit your throat. Understood?” Sloane said as he moved back to take a seat on a chair by the bed.

Seville sat up slowly worried one wrong move would end his life this night. “What can I do for the Shadow of Death?”

“You hired a necromancer to ambush the prince and his men. I was present and attacked by the necromancer’s army, which means you hired someone to kill me.” Sloane said coldly as he narrowed his eyes at Seville.

Realization dawned on Seville’s face, and he immediately dropped to his knees and prostrated himself before Sloane. “I-I swear oh great one. I would not have taken the job had I known you would be there. I-I would never be so foolish! Please spare this lowly worm!”

“That depends on a few things. How you answer the next few questions will determine how long you live. Understand?” Sloane stated with a sense of finality in his voice.

“Yes-Yes! I understand! Oh, thank you great one for giving me the chance to earn back my life!” Seville said.

“Who hired you?” Sloane asked.

Seville answered as quickly as he could. “It was Behat from the Feuhari delegation.”

“Did he say why they wanted the prince dead?” Sloane asked his follow up question.

“He said he was working with someone inside the capital, someone who would favor relations with his country. Behat seemed confident and I was promised no one would find out. They had the chief investigator in their employ. If it was discovered, I was to flee to his country if all else failed.” Seville replied.

“Interesting. Do you want to live to see the sunrise?” Sloane asked.

“Yes! Please, I will do anything you command!” Seville exclaimed.

“You are going to find out which investigator was assigned to this. I want it confirmed. Secondly, you work for me now. Anyone comes to you; I want to know about it. Lastly, you take no jobs against the prince or his people.” Sloane explained.

“Oh, thank you! Thank you, great Shadow of Death! I will do as you command!” Seville practically squealed out in relief.

“We will be in touch worm. Do not fail me.” Sloane said.

When Seville finally looked up Sloane was gone as if he was never there. The information merchant said several words of thanks and vowed not to do anything that would anger the horror of the underworld. Anyone who spent any time dealing with the seeder parts of the kingdom has heard of the wolf, more appropriately the Shadow of Death. The myth of a man took control of any underground enterprise he set his mind to and only the foolish and now dead crossed him. He did not know why the man wanted the prince protected but he would not question it, ever!

“I will make sure to pay Behat back for the trouble he has brought to my doorstep. This I vow!” Seville said before collapsing on his bed exhausted from the whole ordeal.

Chapter 21 – Royal Ball

The day of the ball came quickly. Leading up to this event, Prince James met regularly with the King, Queen, and Uncle Marcus as they did their best to bring him up to speed on the various nobles. The subjects of these discussions included what faction they were a part of, some family history, current heads of family, and which ones had children around his age or if they are already enrolled in the Royal Academy. They also discussed key merchants and mage families. It was a lot to cram into such a short amount of time, but everyone was amazed at Prince James's eidetic memory.

There were a few follow up meetings with High Priest Cendrin who would help give additional information on how the Church viewed the various nobles and affluent families. What the King, Queen, and General didn't know was Cendrin and Sloane also used that time to provide some of the more specific secrets their spies had already uncovered. Prince James was extremely grateful to have such valuable information networks in place.

Sloane's investigation into Andrew was slow and cautious. Prince James was not in a rush to get the answers about the necromancer, not yet anyway. Sloane had discovered Behat from the Feuhari delegation who would be present at the ball. Sloane had wanted permission to abduct the man and torture the truth out of him. Prince James had cautioned restraint for now at least. They had enough to worry about trying to learn everything they could from everyone.

The preparation for the ball and the various cram sessions were enough to give the prince a headache, not from difficulty but the feeling that he was behind and was playing catch up. Prince James would be happy when the ball was over. After the ball concluded James would be free to explore the city and, in his mind, officially be able to live his new life. Sadly, he was getting ahead of himself and had to refocus on the ball.

The plan for the ball was to wait until all the major nobles and prominent families arrived. The king and queen would welcome them all and then introduce their son. Prince James was then to arrive with all his personal royal knights wearing his livery. While he waited, Prince James reviewed the highlights of what he knew.

Besides Duke Spears there were two other dukes, Duke Rodchester, and Duke Arcum. Technically Uncle Marcus had the rank of duke when it came to the peerage but most focused on his leadership of the military forces of the kingdom, which in terms of power was of a higher rank. Duke Rodchester and Duke Arcum were the pillars of the Noble faction. They each had increasingly grown frustrated with the Drake family. Both men each saw an opportunity for their family's influence and power to grow. Their biggest problem was agreeing which family would take over should the Royal family "die out".

Sloane had discovered that stalemate could come to a possible resolution. Duke Arcum has a son by the name of Josh who just came of age, and Duke Rodchester has a daughter by the name of Ria, who has come of age. Both will be starting at the Royal Academy, just as Prince James was about to. Josh was said to be an excellent swordsman and fighter with strong body enhancement Magic but average spell casting ability. Whereas Ria Rodchester possessed average skills with a blade but high spell casting ability. Together they would be a force to be reckoned with.

'Man, my isekai senses are tingling. Guessing ole Joshie is going to be a problem at the academy. Best to steer clear of him and Ria. New goal, avoid certain tropes for sure.' Prince James thought.

'The fact that both Dukes had promising heirs helped their faction. As far as the rest of the aristocracy was concerned, I was an unknown. High Priest Cendrin told me he planned to have his priests and the Church of Light in general begin to spread the gist of the prophecy to the masses to give them hope and help rally people to my side. It was rather an ingenious approach, sadly it would not help me much in time for the ball.' Prince James continued his review of what he knew and what to prepare for.

'Several counts and barons had joined either the Traditionalist faction that Duke Spears led or the Noble faction. To recap, the Traditionalist faction consisted of Count Malcum, his wife Countess Francesca, Count Atraities, his wife Countess Priscilla, Baron Whitman, his wife Baroness Rumina, Lady Nightshade, Mira's mother, and the widowed Lady Firebrand. Of course, Duke Spears and his wife Lady Spears have thrown their support fully behind my faction. From what my spies have uncovered, Lady Spears is quite pleased with me. Apparently, me being the cause of her husband and son's reconciliation has earned her support.' Prince James checked off his recap of the Traditional faction.

'Now as for the Noble faction; they have Count Hayes, Count Sylus, Count Syrian, Count Lucious, and Baron Sexton. The most challenging aspect of this faction is they each have standing forces that are part of each other's family's guards and knights. The dukes of course have the larger of the forces. Luckily Uncle Marcus did not ignore his duties of building a strong military that for the most part was loyal to the crown. Sadly, some of these nobles have been able to infiltrate the ranks with their men or influence others. This made them almost impossible to pin down as many merchants and other prominent families would work to secretly support multiple factions as a way to hedge their bets on the future of the kingdom.' Prince James thought of the Noble faction with a frown at how interwoven their faction was throughout the kingdom.

'This is just one of many issues I've learned of over the last several days. As if the infighting faction politics were not enough our kingdom has pressures from outside. The continent held a few larger countries such as The Beast Tribe Alliance, Helios Dominion, Feuhari Dynasty, and the Isles of Terresia to name some of the more prominent. There were other continents and smaller factions and countries but those four countries each held an embassy in the capital and they all would be sending a delegation to attend the ball.' Prince James' mental recap of the outside factions done it was time to focus on their relations.

'The Beast Tribe Alliance eastern expansion was currently being blocked by the Helios Dominion. There were rumors the Beast Tribe Alliance saw our kingdom in a less than favorable light which might lead them to attacking our eastern borders which butted up against their Western front. That is just one of the foreign challenges to deal with. Each country had a sorted past of conflict and disagreements with their fellow neighbors on the continent. With at least one or more representatives present at this ball conflicts may arise during the event. I might've waited until we secured our own internal factions before dealing with others, but my parents insist we show strength to everyone.' Prince James paused then had another random thought.

'Man, when did I accept them as my parents? I haven't been here that long, but everyone has been the most inviting and supportive. Guess I am just accepting my new life and hey they are awesome people. Though I still think it's super weird Gerald looks like me in my older dad years. Something tells me that my guide or their faction had something to do with that. I mean did they bring one of my ancestors here to this world? How does he look like a mix between my dad and myself in my older years? Super weird. Well, not like I can answer that question now, best to keep making decisions with my gut and follow my instincts and emotions.'

"Your majesty, are you alright? I felt a wave of emotions coming from you." Kira asked in Party Link.

"I too sensed your inner rumblings, is there something we can do for you, my prince?" Sloane replied in Party Link.

"No, no. I am fine. Just got a bit overwhelmed as I recapped all the information, I have been studying the last few days." Prince James replied in Party Link.

"That is to be expected of your highness. You have been cramming in information that usually takes others a lifetime to realize. We are here for you just say the word, James." Kira answered.

Prince James had insisted she call him James in their mental link, but she only used when she wanted to sincerely express herself to the man. The last few days have been a rollercoaster of emotions for Kira. She learned more about Sloane and found the man to be utterly loyal to the prince and the kingdom, which in some ways surprised her based on the rumors she had heard. Then there was Prince James, her pronouncement of him being a genius to her squad members she was realizing was an understatement. The prince could intuit problems and devise solutions before she even realized a problem might exist. Kira was by no means unintelligent; she was seen as a gifted healer and was one of the top scorers in her graduating class at the academy, but Prince James made her realize how big a gap true genius was. Rather than dishearten her, she saw and felt how much the man loved and cared for his people, which only strengthened her resolve to stand by him.

Kira had at first been reserved when Sloane and Prince James talked about the espionage aspects Sloane was learning, but she when she realized they were including her in the conversation on purpose, she began to share her opinions on what she knew and what rumors were being spread among the peerage.

"I'll be fine you two. Besides, we have bigger worries than my nervous emotions. I think they are ready to escort us in." Prince James replied via Party Link before closing off his emotions and preparing the best mask of indifference he could put on his face; it was time to meet the court.

The courtier came to bring Prince James and his personal royal knights to the bellman so he could announce them.

"Alright here we go. Remember to be on your best behavior. You represent our Prince, and these nobles are not beneath using underhanded tactics to help tarnish him in some way." LT Simmons told everyone as they started walking.

"Do you think they will really resort to messing with us to make Prince James look bad?" Rita asked.

"They are nobles Rita. You are more familiar with LT Simmons family; they are honorable people far removed from most of the politics of the capital as their lands are towards the border. The Simmons family also were one of the few that remained loyal to the royal faction. You haven't had a chance to interact with most of the other noble families, but you've met some of the nobles who are in the military. They are restricted in their actions when it comes to the military. In that ballroom they will be able to fall back to their expertise." Kira answered.

"Yes, most of them are arrogant and entitled. Got it, avoid nobles." Rita replied.

"Stay close to my mother Lady Nightshade. She has a way with the other nobles." Mira chimed in.

LT Simmons chuckled. "A way with the nobles indeed. Her tongue is quite sharp, no one is foolish enough to get into a verbal quarrel with her. Quiet now, we are about to enter the hall."

"Your majesty are you and your personal royal knights ready? Or do they require more time to prepare." the bellman asked in a condescending tone.

Prince James turned to LT Simmons and the rest of his knights. "Do you guys need more time?"

LT Simmons walked right up to the bellman and put his arm around the man. "Perhaps we do your majesty. We could remain and get to know this bellman even better." LT Simmons said the last part as he squeezed the air out of the man until he passed out.

LT Simmons dropped the bellman. "My apologies your highness, I apparently used too much strength in getting to know our bellman."

Several of the knights chuckled.

Prince James tried to keep the smile off his face. Turning to the courtier who had not left yet. "Go fetch some servants to carry this man to a healer. He has collapsed."

The courtier quickly ran off to get some help carrying the passed-out bellman to a healer.

Once the servants carried the man away, Prince James turned to the second bellman with a big smile. "With that resolved, I believe we are ready to be announced."

As they entered the hall, Prince James was momentarily stunned at the opulence and grandeur of this massive ballroom. At the opposite side of the ballroom was a raised platform with stairs leading to four throne-like chairs where the King, Queen, and Princess sat, with his Uncle Marcus standing behind and to the side of the King.

'I sometimes forget I am a Royal then bam it smacks me in the face, I am loaded! Hahaha.' Prince James thought and internally chuckled.

"Boom, boom, boom" the bellman pounded his massive staff, on a circle near his feet, that caused the sound to reverberate across the ballroom bringing silence to the hall.

'Man, the acoustics of this room is amazing.' Prince James thought.

The bellman spoke towards the staff, and it seemed to project his voice. "IT IS WITH GREAT HONOR I ANNOUNCE THE ARRIVAL OF PRINCE JAMES AND HIS PERSONAL ROYAL KNIGHTS!" The bellman announced.

'Ow! That guy has got a set of pipes on him. I don't even think he needed to use the staff. Note to self, do not stand close to the bellman.' Prince James winced as the bellman yelled near his ear.

Prince James walked to the other side of the ballroom while his personal royal knights followed behind him. Everyone watched as he walked past them. It was clear some looked at him with fascination and others more sizing him up. As he walked up the platform, his personal royal knights took up various positions next to the other personal royal knights around the platform.

When he arrived in front of his family, Prince James greeted them. "Greetings father, mother, sister, uncle."

"Well met son, please take your rightful seat next to me." King Gerald told Prince James.

After taking the seat next to his father, his uncle stood behind both.

His uncle spoke up in a low voice. "Good to see you nephew."

Turning his head to his brother, his uncle spoke quietly again. "Best to make your intentions clear brother."

King Gerald then stood, and the Queen, Prince James, and Princess Aurora also went to stand by the King. General Marcus stood next to Prince James to subtly show his support as well.

King Gerald's voice boomed across the ballroom. "Good people of the Kingdom of Aerouant, esteemed guests from our neighbors across the continent! Many have questioned the queen and I in our decision not to name a successor. Princess Aurora has made it clear on many occasions she does not want the throne. Many pressured us to choose an arranged marriage for our daughter so that person could succeed me."

King Gerald paused before continuing his speech. "It is no secret that the queen and I love each other deeply and I would not deny my daughter the chance to marry one she loves in the future. Others have suggested we name a noble as heir, but our family held out hope for a prophecy given to us many, many, years ago."

King Gerald looked at Queen Sophia, took her hand in his and continued. "When our son was born, he was very frail. The healers told us that there was a high risk of his death before he reached adulthood. Such news would break any parents' hearts but before despair could fully take root the great Seer Rollara, sister to Lady Rollara, Headmaster of the Royal Academy, came to us most urgently."

Making sure he had everyone's attention, the king continued. "She had told us of a prophecy she received. According to Seer Rollara it was the most intense and strongest prophecy she had ever received!" By this time King Gerald was really getting into his speech and the entire ballroom was silent. Many of the nobles had only heard rumors for why the royal family sent their first born away, many felt they were finally about to get answers straight from the royal family.

He continued, "She told us that the only way to save our son was to put him in isolation in a valley far from home and only two caretakers were allowed to guide and protect him. He could receive no visitors until after he came of age. In this isolation his body would have time to heal and very slowly overcome the frailness that threatened to take his life. She was very clear that not even I as king or the queen could visit our only son."

The king paused as if the memory was still painful to recall. "We asked the legendary adventuring team John the Wise and Sarah the Pure to do what we could not. They loved this country and graciously took up this charge. For you see, not only were we told our son would survive, but that he would return stronger and smarter. He would return better than before, he would return as someone who could bring this kingdom through any strife to prosperity, he would return as a man worthy of a throne. You see we did this for both the sake of our son and the future of our great kingdom."

"Seer Rollara took one look at our son and adamantly told us to keep what she shared quiet until such time as our son became of age. So, we have kept this secret only telling few people of this until now." The queen finished for her husband who held her hand tightly.

High Priest Cendrin spoke up almost startling some of the audience. "What King Gerald and Queen Sophia say is true! Even though they kept this secret quiet, this prophecy was also revealed to us in the church. The Light always shines through to the truth! I came to the king and queen and counseled them to follow the prophecy. Their love for both their son and this kingdom shows their dedication to the principles of the Light!"

This pronouncement caught more people off guard than hearing of this prophecy. It was paramount to the Church of Light backing the royal family. Most nobles were shocked by this statement as it clearly showed the Church of Light changing its long-standing neutrality and choosing to back the royal faction.

Then Lady Rollara spoke up. "My sister confided in me on her death bed of this prophecy. She said he would be capable of great feats. I can attest that my sister was right. I had the pleasure of conducting Prince James's Royal Academy entrance exam. He scored the highest marks I've ever seen!"

More murmuring erupted across the crowd. What were they hearing?

King Gerald spoke again, "SILENCE!"

King Gerald had everyone's attention once again. "Now to continue. Let me formally introduce and announce our royal heir to the throne of our great nation. That is right we formally acknowledge my son, PRINCE JAMES and heir to the throne!"

Several people started to clap and speak up again.

"We finally have an heir."

"Finally."

"Wait what does this mean for the other factions?"

It was as if, on que, Duke Spears' voice echoed across the ballroom and everyone turned to him and parted, making a path to the royal family. "I HAVE SOMETHING TO SAY IF YOU WILL PERMIT your Majesty!"

King Gerald nodded in agreement to Duke Spears.

Duke Spears walked towards the platform, heading straight to Prince James.

He talked as he walked. "As was my right as a member of the Royal Academy Board I tested and witnessed Prince James prowess in a fight!"

Once he arrived at the foot of the platform, he withdrew his sword and quickly bent the knee in front of Prince James. "I formally, in front of the church and my peers pledge my loyalty to you Prince James! My life is yours; my people shall stand with you to protect this kingdom from threats both from outside and within. The Traditionalist faction formally pledges their service to you!"

This seemed to shock the nobles even more. Everyone knew Duke Spears was a force to be reckoned with and a strong-willed man who took honor and duty very seriously. To see him pledge himself so fully sent ripples of shock through the crowd once again. Even his own faction who were told ahead of time were still shocked to witness it firsthand.

Prince James spoke with strength in his voice. “Rise Duke Spears. I accept your fealty and acknowledge such a noble and honorable dedication to the protection of this kingdom.”

Prince James turned to his parents. “Father and Mother thank you for your trust in both the Light and in me.”

Prince James then turned to High Priest Cendrin. “High Priest Cendrin, it is good when both the Church of Light and the Royal family can come together for the betterment of the people. It is important that the Church of Light be autonomous from the state so they may focus solely on the salvation of the people. As my father and mother believe this, know that I do as well. I thank you for your continued dedication to the Light and I feel blessed that the Light would grant me such a wonderful family.”

‘Not sure if it was the Light or the Dark but either way, I am grateful.’ Prince James thought.

High Priest Cendrin smiled and gave a slight bow as he thought, ‘This Prince is even better than I could have imagined.’

Prince James turned to Lady Rollara. “Lady Rollora, I am saddened to not be able to meet your sister whose prophecy helped to give me new life. I thank you for all she did and all you continue to do for this kingdom. I look forward to attending the Royal Academy and further benefitting from your wisdom.”

Lady Rollora gave a slight bow as well.

Prince James turned to the crowd. “You have all heard much about a prophecy and what others have witnessed, but to me that cannot be enough. So let me say this, I graciously accept my duty as heir to this kingdom and shall endeavor to show all of you why a United Aerouant shall lead to prosperity across the land. I look forward to meeting all of you and getting to know each of you, and you getting to know me. Now! This is supposed to be a party! So, enough talk and let us enjoy ourselves!”

That last statement earned him some cheers and laughter. It also seemed to break the spell of silence, and everyone began to mingle once again.

The royal family descended the platform and began to mingle as well. Duke Spears spoke up to Prince James as he gestured for the prince to follow him. "Come your majesty, let me introduce you to the other nobles who are now part of your faction."

Chapter 22 – Let the Fun Begin

“It would appear my daughter has chosen wisely.” Lady Nightshade said as she approached her daughter, Sloane, and Rita who were trying to keep relatively close to Prince James without making it too obvious.

“Mother!” Mira exclaimed as quietly as she could.

“What, my dear? I was merely stating a fact. It is clear the young prince is very sharp. To gain both High Priest Cendrin’s and Duke Spears’ public support. To bring one to your side is impressive, to win them both over so completely is unheard of. How ever did he manage it?” Lady Nightshade said.

“He was just being himself; he is the crown prince after all, that seemed more than sufficient.” Mira retorted.

Lady Nightshade chuckled, “Hardly.” Then she introduced her friend Lady Firebrand. “Felora, you remember my daughter Mira.”

Lady Firebrand had just walked up. “Yes of course, Minerva, how could I forget your lovely daughter. How are you, Mira? I heard you made Sergeant of one of our prince’s royal knight squads.”

“I am well. Thank you for asking Lady Firebrand. Yes, I am Sergeant over the Stalker squad, one of three squads that report directly to Prince James. It is an honor to serve one such as his majesty. Let me introduce you to some of my squad mates, Rita and Sloane.” Mira waved over to her squad mates, “Rita and Sloane, this is Lady Firebrand and my mother Lady Nightshade.”

“It is an honor to meet you both.” Sloane said.

“Yes, a true honor Lady Firebrand and Lady Nightshade.” Rita answered rather sheepishly.

“Oh, do not be so shy dearie. Regardless of what my daughter may have told you, we won’t bite.” Lady Nightshade greeted.

“Mother!” Mira exclaimed.

"Oh Minerva, stop teasing your daughter." Lady Firebrand told her friend before turning to Stalker squad. "It is nice to meet you both. Tell me, how is it to serve our young attractive prince?" Lady Firebrand asked Stalker squad.

Sloane excused himself, "My apologies but I must do something for his majesty. Please excuse me ladies."

Sloane disappeared into the crowd before anyone could even respond.

Rita and Mira weren't so lucky and began to blush quickly.

Lady Nightshade came to their aid. "Now who is teasing? Felora."

"My apologies, but you have to admit the prince is quite handsome." Felora stated before commenting on the redness of the squad member's cheeks. "It would appear I've struck a sensitive chord. Very well, let's talk about that pompous fool Duke Arcum."

Lady Nightshade nodded. "He looked rather perplexed at how things unfolded earlier."

"I thought he might burst a blood vessel." Lady Firebrand said while chuckling a little.

Rita was surprised to see noble ladies gossiping in such a manner but decided to keep quiet for fear of getting into trouble. 'I am way out of my depth here.'

Mira leaned over to Rita and spoke softly. "Do not worry my friend. My mother and Lady Firebrand can be trusted. They are few of those in the kingdom that have enough power that they can speak their minds without too much concern."

"My daughter is correct. We brought it up so you would be aware. As one of the prince's personal guards you should make a point to pay attention to the reactions of others. It might clue you in to future threats that require watching." Minerva stated matter-of-factly.

"Wise advice. I thank you, my lady, for your insight." Rita replied sincerely.

Lady Nightshade and Lady Firebrand both nodded to Rita.

Mira spoke up. "You raised me well mother. I noticed two dukes that seemed to look rather displeased at the turn of events."

"Yes, Duke Rochester is a bit more cunning than Arcum but do not underestimate the man, he did not rise to be one of the leaders of the noble faction by title alone." Minerva commented.

"You have your work cut out for you, as does our handsome prince. The noble faction has gained far more power over the last decade. They will make various moves, both of you be ready." Lady Firebrand stated.

Both Rita and Mira nodded in acknowledgement before giving each other a knowing look. They each knew the uphill political battle their liege would have even with his miraculous achievement of gaining public support from Duke Spears and the Church of Light. They would do everything they could to help him succeed.

——- - - -

"My majesty please let me introduce you to Count Malcum, his wife Countess Francesca, Count Atraities, his wife Countess Priscilla, Baron Whitman, his wife Baroness Rumina." Duke Spears said as he waved to each person as he introduced them.

"It is an honor your Majesty." They each repeated as they each gave a slight bow or curtsy.

"It is a pleasure to meet all of you." Prince James said after meeting everyone. Then turning his attention to Lady Spears.

"Saving the best introduction for last, this is my lovely wife, Lady Spears. Though I'm not sure where Lady Nightshade and Lady Firebrand are. Their influence should not be ignored." Duke said.

"I believe I saw them talking to Minerva's daughter dear." Lady Spears replied to her husband before turning to Prince James.

"Ah, of course." Duke Spears nodded to his wife.

Lady Spears turned to Prince James.

"It is a pleasure to meet you, your Majesty. I cannot thank you enough for what you have done for my family. To see my son and husband finally reconciled. It warms my heart to see them aligned, finally!" Lady Spears said gratefully, giving her husband a stern look when saying the last part.

"Yes, well I had to be sure. Our duty to the people cannot be ignored." Duke Spears replied.

Prince James turned to Duke Spears. "I also agree with you duke, our duty to our people must not be forgotten. It is just some of those plans can take many years to come to fruition."

"Well said, well said indeed." Duke Spears replied happily.

Turning back to Lady Spears, Prince James continued. "It is my pleasure that I was able to help your family, Lady Spears. From what I have seen and experienced both men are two of the most honorable men I have ever met." Prince James stated.

"You honor me sir!" Duke Spears said, standing a bit straighter and clearly beaming with appreciation.

"Nonsense. I merely speak the truth." Prince James replied.

It was time for Prince James to demonstrate some of the knowledge he gained and further grow his faction. "Count Malcum, it is my understanding that your county has been dealing with issues with your crops. I'd like to send you some instructions on how to use night soil to help the crops take better hold and grow larger. If you're open to it, I can have one of my men send you the information."

"Really, your majesty? How did you know we were struggling with our crops this season?" Count Malcum asked before muttering to himself, "He has not even been in the capital a month."

"Hahaha, I told you he was worthy. See! He makes a point to take interest in the well-being of our people!" Duke Spears boisterously laughed as he slapped Count Malcum on the back.

Count Malcum knew the duke was sharp and a force to be reckoned with on his own. When the count received Duke Spear's missive instructing his allies to pledge their support to this new unknown prince, to say he was shocked would be an understatement. Now, however, he could see a glimpse of why his duke went all in with his support.

His county held some of the more arid lands in the kingdom. It made feeding his people a challenge and they usually had to import food in to provide what he could make available to help feed his people. If the prince was offering a way to help make his county more fertile, he would be a fool to not at least attempt it.

"Quite right, Duke Spears. You once again prove your keen eye for the truth of things." Count Malcum replied.

Turning to Prince James, Count Malcum bowed his head in deference. "If you do have something that would work, I gladly accept. Thank you, your Majesty for considering my county."

"Of course, Count Malcum. Since my return I have made a point to learn everything I can about our kingdom. I appreciate how welcoming everyone has been. It is the least I can do to help make their lives better." Prince James said.

"Everyone except that fool necro who dared to attack you." Duke Spears practically growled.

"I heard about that. Did they find out who was behind the attack? How did they even know you were returning?" Count Atraities asked.

"Sadly no. It is an unknown. The only thing we do know is that he was hired through an intermediary and for them to even know about my trip to the capital they would've needed to know multiple things. First, some inclination of my parents' intentions to have me return. Second, know the exact route the convoy would take. And perhaps they even had awareness of the prophecy." Prince James answered.

Sloane approached having heard both the question and the prince's answer. "Either way it tells us there are some leaks here in the palace. I wish his majesty would give me permission to interrogate the staff to get answers." Sloane said.

"Ah you will have to excuse Sloane, as one of my personal royal knights they are very dedicated to my safety." Prince James said.

"That is understandable. You may wish to take Sloane up on the offer to find answers. If someone tried once they will try again." Baron Whitman chimed in.

"I would have to agree with Baron Whitman. Do not suffer traitors, my prince." Duke Spears said solemnly.

"Do not worry my friends I have no intention of allowing such things to stand. Plans are underway to get answers. I just will not make loyal people suffer for the acts of some subversives." Prince James replied.

"Hahaha! Now that is the man I serve!" Duke Spears boisterously claimed.

"Your Majesty Duke Arcum and Rodchester are approaching." Sloane telepathically warned.

"What are you going on about Duke Spears?" Duke Arcum asked.

With a big smile on his face that did not reach his eyes Prince James explained what they were just talking about. "We were just discussing the foolish attempt someone made to try and kill me on my return trip home. It failed so utterly as it appeared they underestimated both myself and the royal knights."

"I had not heard of such an attack. Had you Duke Rodchester?" Duke Arcum said.

"No, I had not. You look none worse for it. I doubt it was more than some bandits looking for some coin. Perhaps Young men and old war dogs tend to exaggerate when it comes to retelling of battles. No offense intended Prince James." Duke Rodchester replied.

Duke Spears grabbed the hilt of his sword tightly, clearly not pleased with how dismissive his two peers were acting towards his liege.

Prince James just continued to smile.

"Tell me Duke Rodchester what would you do to the traitors who were responsible for such a blatant attack?" Prince James asked Duke Rodchester.

"Traitors must be executed. Examples must be made to deter future problems from occurring." Duke Rodchester answered matter-of-factly.

Smiling wider as he directed some of his aura in their direction, "I couldn't agree more with you Duke Rodchester. Treachery shall not be allowed. You will find I'm not as tolerant with such things as my father is." Prince James said while looking at both Duke Arcum and Duke Rodchester.

After seeing the two men flinch at the barely veiled threat Prince James decided to change tactics and subjects. "Speaking of dealing with threats swiftly, I hear your family's gryphon riders are some of the key deterrents of those that would foolishly think to invade. Such an amazing and fascinating history. I would welcome the chance to see such majestic creatures and such noble knights in action." Prince James even shifted his body language, so his focus was solely on Duke Rodchester as he spoke.

"You honor my family's legacy Prince James. Perhaps a tour and demonstration can be arranged." Duke Rodchester said with pride.

'Damn this upstart. Why does he give my family such praise? He is making me kind of like him. How annoying, but I cannot show it, I would lose face among everyone watching us. So much for embarrassing this child.' Duke Rodchester begrudgingly thought.

"I would be honored Duke Rodchester. Once I have a moment to settle in and find an attaché, I will have them arrange the visit if that is alright with you." Prince James explained.

"Of course, of course. That is completely understandable, Prince James. I would never turn away the chance to demonstrate the might and pride of my family." Duke Rodchester replied as he thought, 'Perhaps I can spin this to gain further support.'

"If you will excuse me but I must speak with a few people. I look forward to future discussions." Prince James said to Duke Rodchester.

Prince James gave a quick nod to Duke Spears, his wife, and the other nobles gathered around before very purposefully not acknowledging Duke Arcum as he walked away.

"He is turning a nice shade of pink bordering on red. You shunned him well your Majesty." Sloane telepathically said.

"Keep an eye on him. If he didn't have something to do with the attack, he most certainly is up to something. Divide and conquer. One gets an olive branch, the other gets the stick. Plus, I don't like his pompous attitude." Prince James telepathically replied.

"He's a high noble, pompous is in the job description." Sloane telepathically replied.

Prince James just smiled as he made his way to Mira and Rita.

—————

“Good evening, Mira, Rita. Care to introduce me to these lovely angels in front of me? One looks like she could be your sister.” Prince James greeted.

“Oh, you are a charmer aren’t you.” Lady Firebrand said.

“Indeed Felora. And pleasing to the eyes to go along with such eloquent speech.” Lady Nightshade said.

“Mother!” Mira protested.

“Mother? That’s impossible. Did you have her when you were a child?” Prince James asked.

“We are all children until we have kids of our own. It is only then that we truly mature enough to understand our place in the world and find reserves we never knew to fight to keep our family safe. Well, that is if the person is not some self-centered prick.” Lady Nightshade replied.

“Well said.” Prince James replied as he thought, ‘I learned that lesson far too late with my own family.’

“I look forward to the day I can understand that truth for myself. If only I am so lucky in the future to create my own family.” Prince James continued while his thoughts briefly dwelled on his past life and his own children, all of which were now grown. ‘She is not wrong. I thought I knew everything until I had children, then I truly began to understand I knew nothing, yet would gain insight into myself in a way I never thought possible. The world provides no greater mirror I could stare into than my children.’

“It would appear my daughter is a bit flummoxed currently, so let me introduce myself to your Majesty. I am Lady Minerva Nightshade, and this lovely woman is Lady Felora Firebrand.” Lady Nightshade stated as she gave a subtle bow and curtsy.

Prince James took each of their hands and kissed the top of them. “A true pleasure to meet such beautiful and esteemed ladies of the Realm.” Prince James spoke with all sincerity. These two ladies held themselves with grace and femineity. It was hard not to get a nosebleed right then and there.

Lady Firebrand giggled. “He, he, he!” Your majesty is very kind. You make me feel like a young fey girl again.”

“You still look like a young woman to me.” Prince James replied, and he truly meant it. ‘She looks maybe in her early 30s and drop dead gorgeous, they both do. Good to know what Mira will look like when she gets older. My uncle would always advise me to look at a lady’s mother, it gave a glimpse of what your future held if you chose to marry the girl. Still great advice uncle.’ Prince James sent a silent thank you to his uncle for being like another father to him.

That thought caused a pang of pain in the prince’s heart as he missed his family terribly. ‘If he only knew how much I appreciated everything he did for me growing up. Re-focus, do not dwell on what you cannot change right now.’

“Magic my dear prince. Both Felora and I are strong in magic, it both delays our aging quite a bit and rejuvenates us.” Lady Nightshade replied.

‘Good to know there is such a nice perk with magic. Errrr, wait a minute, did Felora say she was fey?! How do I ask about that one?’ Prince James thought.

Deciding he would figure out how to work that into the conversation somehow, Prince James decided at that point to get to know these ladies far more. “Good to know that is one of the benefits of magic. I’m curious, are you both enjoying the ball? It is my first one after all, and I’d like to know how it rates.” Prince James asked.

“Ah of course. I briefly forgot; you hold yourself so well for one who has not been in court before today.” Lady Nightshade said before continuing. “These events are usually quite the same, though today has been far more entertaining. Duke Arcum’s face has either turned red or held a look of shock multiple times, even a few moments where both were plain for all to see. Quite impressive a feat for one who has only begun to swim in these waters.”

“Yes, I had heard you tend to be one of the more informed nobles at court.” Prince James commented.

“Yes, well one just needs to be observant to be well informed. Though I do take my observations a bit farther. Like the fact that your shadow Sloane has been rather quiet most of the event yet you two seem rather in sync.” Lady Nightshade said casually.

“My liege is a master communicator. It makes my job even easier. I would however be remised if I did not comment on how impressive your ‘observations’ tend to be Lady Nightshade. One would be a fool to not realize how invasive those ‘observations’ can be.” Sloane chimed in.

One of Lady Nightshade’s eyebrows rose which was all she gave away as a reaction to Sloane’s comment.

“Sloane! I am not sure what you mean by that comment, but I will remind you that you are speaking to a Lady of the court and my mother! Tred carefully.” Mira said coldly with clear anger in her voice.

Mira preferred more direct approaches and did not like subtlety in conversation even though her stealth, subterfuge, and dagger skills are some of the highest seen in the kingdom thanks to the training from her mother.

Sloane nodded to Mira. “My apologies Lady Nightshade. I meant no disrespect.”

“No, you just wanted me to know that you are well aware how much I keep an eye on what goes on in this kingdom.” Lady Nightshade stated.

Prince James felt it was time to step in at this point. “Being so observant is a critical requirement in not only surviving but thriving in this kingdom.”

“Quite right you are your majesty. It is good to see one so young understanding that truth. We have an obligation to be as well informed as possible and use our own mind to determine what best course of action should come from such knowledge.” Lady Nightshade stated.

“Of that we are completely aligned. Which brings me to my ask Lady Nightshade. Should you be so inclined to share those observations I would appreciate you keeping Mira and Sloane informed. As I am sure you already know, your daughter Mira leads my Stalker squad. Their primary mission, behind watching my back, is information gathering and missions that require a stealthier approach. Anything that can keep my squads protected or give them an edge is always appreciated ladies.” Prince James explained.

“Ha, ha, ha” Lady Firebrand’s laugh was like a pleasing summer breeze. “He has you there Minerva. I say we go all in. It is clear this prince is both good looking and intelligent. A very attractive combination would you not say? He, he, he.”

"Lady Firebrand!" Mira said without realizing it she was getting more and more uncomfortable as they talked about how attractive Prince James is. 'Why am I getting so upset anytime someone compliments Prince James? I mean look at how dreamy his... focus Mira, focus!' Mira tried to refocus her thoughts.

"She is merely speaking the truth daughter. This prince is indeed smart. He ties together your safety to his objectives. Whether that is intentional or not, I cannot ignore the masterful way that has been played. I have done something similar many times in the past. I can support a man..." catching herself, she cleared her throat "I can support the future ruler of our kingdom. Very well Prince James, you have our full support, our resources are at your disposal. Please see to it that my daughter remains as safe as possible." Lady Nightshade stated.

"Mother! I am his personal royal knight, it is my duty to protect him, to lay my life..." Mira was interrupted by Prince James.

"Done. I am rather fond of Mira and the rest of my royal knights. It is my job to protect them as much as it is theirs to protect me. To be clear, I do not treat the lives of those I care about frivolously."

Mira and Rita both turned pink at Prince James's words. 'I am supposed to be protecting him. Why is it I like it so much when he gets protective over me?' Mira thought.

"That is what I like to hear, a royal who cares for their people. I really am fond of you dear Prince James." Lady Firebrand said in a way that made James want to sweep her off her feet.

Shifting his focus, Prince James decided it was time to broach the subject he was curious about. "Your family name, it means masters of fire and other battle magic, correct?" Prince James asked.

"Yes. I am part of the Summer Court fey. Fire is one of the best elements to use to devastate your enemies and bring down destructive power to the battlefield. Your father and uncle were some of my best students. If what Lady Rollara said is true, you will most likely be in my class Prince James." Lady Firebrand explained.

"Come again?" Prince James asked.

"That all depends on you." Lady Firebrand deadpanned.

Prince James immediately picked up on the joke and was trying to figure out a way to bring his thoughts back on track when Lady Firebrand continued. "You did not know I am one of the teachers at the Royal Academy? I am headmistress of magical combat. I teach the top Battle Magic class. Usually, first years aren't included unless they score exceptionally well on their entrance exam. So, if you did as well as Lady Rollara says, I am sure we will be seeing much more of each other soon."

"I look forward to it Lady Firebrand. Now did you say you taught my father and uncle?" Prince James replied.

"Oh yes, your uncle was not as gifted with fire as your father but the two of them were unstoppable on the battlefield. Add in your mother's healing ability keeping their party alive and they set records during their years at the academy."

"Good to know." Prince James said more to himself than anyone else.

Just then a small entourage of pretty and finely dressed girls in their late teens to early twenties approached. At their head was one of the most beautiful girls Prince James had ever seen in this life and his previous one. She had blue hair, wore an elegant blue dress that matched both her blue hair and gorgeous blue eyes. The dress seemed to accentuate her slender but curvy figure.

'Focus, focus James, no nose bleeds, must control body.' Prince James tried to concentrate and remain calm. He had met many beautiful women in both his previous life and this one, and usually he could keep his biological interests in check.

'Her charisma must be exceptionally high as well. I will have to make sure not to rise to the occasion.' Prince James internally chucked at his internal joke which seemed to help him reign in his control.

"Lady Nightshade and Lady Firebrand. It is an honor to meet you." The girls all bowed as they greeted the Ladies.

"Ria Rodchester at your service. This is Leah of house Moore, Nikki of house Orelia, both pledged in service of the Rodchester duchy." Ria finished her introduction of her entourage.

"What has you interrupting our time with my daughter and the crown prince?" Lady Nightshade quipped.

“My apologies. We just wished to introduce ourselves to Lady Firebrand. All three of us scored high in our magical aptitude and will be in Lady Firebrand’s class this year. We figured we would be remised if we did not introduce ourselves during the ball.” Ria answered.

“Sucking up cannot start early enough, is that it?” Lady Nightshade commented.

Mira and Rita quietly chuckled. “He, he, he.”

Ria, Leah, and Nikki all blushed.

“Come now Lady Nightshade, they were just excited to meet their teacher. Had I known Lady Firebrand was my teacher I would’ve made a point to introduce myself too.” Prince James interjected.

Mira went from chuckling to a frown on her face instantly. She did not like Prince James coming to this manipulative harlots’ aid.

The girls used this opportunity to excuse themselves. Ria ignored the help Prince James offered and stuck her nose up at him as she walked away. “If you will excuse us. I believe my father wanted to speak with me.”

Both Leah and Nikki mouthed the words ‘thank you’ to Prince James as they left to catch up with Ria who was most certainly walking away quickly.

“A gentleman coming to the defense of a woman, how honorable. I think my queen would like to meet you some day.” Lady Firebrand stated.

“Do not be fooled, that girl is quite smart. I doubt she only came to introduce herself to Felora. She is as cunning as her father and from what I hear more adept at magic than he is. A dangerous combination.” Lady Nightshade stated.

“But your comment threw her for a loop, which is exactly what you intended Lady Nightshade.” Prince James responded.

“Oh, I like him. He sees right through your ploys and word games Minerva. Not many are so skilled to do so. Yes, I must introduce you to my queen one of these days.” Lady Firebrand giggled.

Lady Nightshade joined her friend in giggling. It was like music to Price James ears. “He, he, he, sharp wits indeed. Oh, I like him too. Perhaps age is just a number.”

"Mother! What has gotten into you!" Mira said in complete shock.

"It's alright Mira. They are both just trying to get under my skin with a little teasing. It is an excellent tactic to disarm someone. Lady Firebrand, you have now mentioned your queen twice. I am confused, I thought you held title here in our kingdom."

"Ah, yes. I can see why you are so confused, my young crown prince. For fey, no matter what kingdom they reside in, they still hold loyalty to the court from which they originate from. When the Summer court was cast out of Avalon and we lost our king and home, we all pledged a binding oath to remain bound to Queen Titania and our lost king."

"Lost king?"

"Oberon. He died. It is a painful racial memory. Worst for Summer fey, we are strong in our emotions and gut feelings. When we feel, we feel deeper than the mortal races. His loss is a scar on the psyche of all our race, those present and passed down to those after, like a curse we cannot remove. We rarely discuss it so please do not ask to ruin my evening." Lady Firebrand said, her previous joyful mood clearly beginning to fade.

"Perish the thought. Perhaps this is a good time for me to attend to the other guests. Ladies thank you for such a welcoming conversation, we must visit each other again. If you'll excuse me." Prince James said before bowing his head slightly.

"We both would welcome that your majesty." Lady Nightshade said while putting her arm around her friend.

Prince James had much to ponder as he made his way towards LT Simmons who seemed very uncomfortable while in conversation with his father and mother.

'It appears I need to learn more about the history of the fey here. I only know of the stories from back home and random warnings I would get from my family about making deals with forest spirits. Are the fey common here? I wonder if one of the libraries has anything on their history. It bares exploring.' Prince James pondered as he made a straight line for LT. Simmons.

Just before arriving at LT Simmons and his parents he sent a telepathic message to Sloane. *"I think Ria is carrying a magical artifact, perhaps one that stimulates or distracts a man. It's the only explanation for my sudden difficulty concentrating. I was not planning for such things. Perhaps a mistake on my part and not one I will be making again. See what you can find out."*

"As you command your highness!" Sloane replied before going to investigate.

Chapter 23 – Family Concerns

Prince James could hear the uncomfortable conversation LT. Simmons was having with his parents. His heart ached for the man.

"We just think it would be good for you to consider letting us arrange a marriage my son. You are not getting any younger and I am only thinking of the Simmons line." Lady Simmons said to her son as Prince James approached the trio.

LT Simmons groaned. "Mother. Please I am leader of the crown prince's personal royal knights. My duty comes first."

"Exactly. Such a prestigious title will only help in the negotiations." Lady Simmons said not relenting.

"Greetings Baron and Lady Simmons. Lieutenant." Prince James greeted in turn.

"Crown Prince James, it is an honor, your Majesty." Baron Simmons said.

"Oh, your Majesty, you honor us with your presence." Lady Simmons said. They both greeted the prince with a slight bow.

"I can't thank you enough for the honor you bestowed upon our family with our son's appointment as the leader of your personal royal knights." Lady Simmons practically fawned over the prince as she rushed to thank him for what he had done for her son.

"Lady Simmons, I assure you that the Lieutenant earned the title and other than the captain there is no one else I'd rather be guarding my back." Prince James answered honestly.

"You do not know how hard it is to advance our family living in one of the more rural baronies." Lady Simmons seemed to swell with pride. It was clear she was very proud of her son and wanted to further her family's name.

"I hope you won't mind but I need your son's help with an important matter." Prince James said.

Hope seemed to blossom in LT Simmons' eyes.

“Of course, your Majesty, we would never interfere with matters of importance.” Lady Simmons said while bowing to Prince James.

Baron Simmons smiled at his son. “Do us proud son.”

“Of course, mother. If you would excuse us, mother and father.” LT Simmons said.

As they walked away LT Simmons spoke so only Prince James could hear. “Thank you, my prince! I owe you a greater debt than you know. I think another minute and my mother would’ve married me off to the first woman she felt had good prospects.”

Prince James chuckled “Your parents mean well but I understand, one should choose their partner.”

“Oh, I know that, but mother can get a bit carried away. What did you need your Majesty?” LT Simmons said.

“Nothing really. I just figured I’d spare you from the badgering. Just remember this when I want to go explore the city. Come let us go introduce ourselves to some of the foreign delegations.” Prince James stated.

LT Simmons and Prince James approached the delegation from the Beast Tribes Alliance. They delegation consisted of three male beastmen and a fourth hidden behind the three large men. All the men were tall, tone and muscular build, each man in light armor under loose-fitting kimonos. They held what looked to be a ceremonial sword at their side. All their outfits seem to be built for combat as well as for formal events.

The largest of the beastmen smiled a wolfish grin as LT. Simmons and Prince James approached. The white-furred man’s kimono was a deep red and purple and looked the most ornate out of the three beastmen.

“Greetings Prince James. The Beast Tribe Alliance greets you. My name is King Hiroshi, and these are my attachés Shirken and Marook.” Hiroshi pointed to the panther beastman, then the bear beastman as he introduced each.

Then he moved to the side and introduced the person they had been blocking before. The beastwoman was the most human looking for the four of them. She had white foxlike ears on the top of her head, her red, purple, and white kimono was by far the most ornate, even more than the beast king's. She exudes grace and charm, every aspect of her being screamed elegance.

Prince James was not the only one to move their attention to this feminine beauty that was before them. Many of the people in the close vicinity stopped talking as they sneaked glances her way.

"And this is my daughter Princess Zenka. She is a kitsune, they are revered among my people as gifts from God to help guide our people." King Hiroshi introduced his daughter with genuine joy in his voice.

'A kitsune! No way! Those tails look so FLUFFY! OK rain in your inner Despicable Me moment. Do not get sidetracked by the gorgeous princess.' Prince James tried his hardest to reign in his excitement at meeting an actual kitsune. He had so many questions but figured it be best not to insult the king and his daughter by asking something they might consider rude.

After reigning himself in he introduced himself. "I am Prince James of the Kingdom of Aerouant. It is a pleasure to meet you King Hiroshi, Princess Zenka, Shirken, and Marook."

The two attachés seemed to be surprised to be greeted. Most would not bother to acknowledge the attachés when foreign royalty was present. I thought that kind of attitude was complete nonsense. Regardless of station or standing, life had meaning and should not be so easily dismissed. Plus, threats can come from anywhere.

From what Sloane and Head Priest Cendrin gathered the Beast Tribe Alliance were a people who believed in duty, responsibility to family and community, and all around the mindset I could admire and respect. Finding out that their king was here in the capital was a bit of a surprise to say the least. They had told me he was here to enroll her into the Royal Academy. Apparently, our academy was the leading institution when it came to magical theory and combat. Seeing his daughter was a kitsune, it made sense he would focus on her magical aptitudes. The more tails a kitsune had the more types of magic she could or had mastered, the lore on the subject was unclear. Some kitsune were seen as mischievous troublemakers and others benevolent forces for good. The way Princess Zenka held herself I had a hard time believing she was a force for the dark but looks could be deceiving.

“I hear you will be enrolling Princess Zenka into the Royal Academy. It will be a pleasure to have you as a fellow attendee.” Prince James stated.

Princess Zenka spoke in a melodic tone and what reminded me of a mix of different Asian accents I could not quite place. “Yes, I must learn to harness and control the magic within me for the betterment of my people. The wise woman Zarusha convinced my father to send me here along with Shirken and Marook who will also be attending.”

“Kitsune must wrestle control of the wild magic within you. This process must begin before you reach a certain age, or it can kill you. I believe I read something to that effect.” Prince James commented.

Princess Zenka’s eyes widened. “Prince James is well informed. We were only told this by Zarusha a few months ago. It appears the rumor of this kingdom’s extensive magical knowledge is well founded.”

‘Never mind I read that in my old life, but no need to tell them that.’ Prince James thought.

Just then my father approached. “Ah Hiroshi, I see you have met my son. Good, Good. Oh, and this must be your lovely daughter Zenka. A pleasure my dear, a pleasure.”

It was clear my father had been drinking a bit by the rosy color on his cheeks.

“Yes, Gerald. Your son seems to have studied much based on his knowledge of my daughter’s condition.” Beast King Hiroshi commented in a gruff voice, not sure if he should be pleased or cautious, I held such knowledge.

“That is to be expected. He was raised by our kingdom’s two most powerful adventurers.” King Gerald stated.

“So that rumor is true as well. Perhaps the young prince would be open to a sparing match some time?” Beast King Hiroshi asked.

“Always with the fighting. I heard you were an expert at rice wines. I happen to have some that we imported, shall we sample and get to know each other, king to king?” King Gerald asked.

Hiroshi’s eyes lit up after hearing they had rice wine. “That is the first sensible thing I have heard you suggest all night. Shirken, Marook, protect my daughter! Any harm comes to her your lives are forfeit." Beast King Hiroshi stated before allowing King Gerald to lead him away.

"Yes, great Beast King!" Marook bowed.

"As you command my liege." Shirken stated as he bowed.

As the two attachés rose from their bows, they stared daggers at Prince James.

Picking up on the change in mood, Prince James decided to change tactics. Seeing Princess Zenka had three tails, he decided to ask one of his burning questions. "If it is not too personal, can I ask what two magics you have begun to manifest?"

Once again, Princess Zenka was surprised by the knowledge Prince James possessed. "Lightning, Wind, and Fire."

"Powerful elements. If you are open to it some time, it would be nice to practice magic with you if you are open to it." Prince James stated. He could see her two guards did not seem happy at that suggestion.

Princess Zenka paused for a moment before answering. "I would welcome a chance to learn from each other. My father is unsure of your kingdom, but I know he welcomes peace, if nothing else to not have enemies at multiple borders."

"You speak of the Helios Dominion?" Prince James asked.

"Yes, though your nation and mine have not always seen eye to eye, and we have fought each other many times, your people still welcome beastkin into your kingdom with open arms. Helios believes we are abominations that should be either killed or enslaved." Princess Zenka practically growled at the thought.

"That is horrible." Prince James said as he grabbed two glasses from a drink tray a waiter passed by with. "Well then here is to our parents getting along and our two kingdoms remaining in peace." He said loudly before quietly adding so only she would hear, "So your people can wipe the floor with those bigots."

Princess Zenka giggled, and it was music to Prince James' ears.

The two of them chatted for a bit about random subjects before Shirken and Marook could tolerate it no longer and recommended the princess retire for the evening.

“It appears we have made my guards uncomfortable and too nervous for what my father might do to them should we continue. I look forward to seeing you at the academy. I know I at least have one friend among all the strangers.” Princess Zenka stated before giving a slight bow and excusing herself.

Prince James replied with a slight head bow and quickly said before she left, “I welcome a new friend as well.”

‘I welcome a new friend. What kind of reply is that? Man, look at the way those tails swish back and forth as she walks... Ok, get mind back on track. I cannot afford a nosebleed at this moment in time.’

Via **Party Link** Prince James told Sloane, *“I was planning on talking at great length with Helios but after hearing that lets make quick introductions with them and head to Terresian delegation before the Feuhari Dynasty.”*

“Leaving Feuhari for last is wise. It will be seen as a minor slight but not one they can press on or speak without sounding petty.” Sloane telepathically replied.

“Besides I want Behat to sweat a bit. We will figure out one way or another why he hired that broker. My gut says there is more going on with this plot than just him, it would be too clean.” Prince James replied via **Party Link**.

“I have been able to discover he has held a few meetings with Duke Rodchester and Duke Arcum’s men. What those meetings entail I have not been able to find out yet my liege.” Sloane replied via **Party Link**.

“Do not worry Sloane. We have only begun to peel the layers on this plot. Something tells me this has been long in the making.” Prince James telepathically replied.

It was plain to see who the Isles delegation was. Their style of dressing was distinct. They wore colorful robes over what would best be described as a cross between steampunk and pirate garb. High leather boots that fanned out towards the top, black in color and meant to be watertight yet usable in any terrain. Tapered pants tucked into the boots. Loose fitting shirts, clearly made to not hinder movement in battle. The robes they wore over covered mesh armored coats, made light for easy movement but able to block a glancing blow from a weapon. The only thing missing from their outfits were their blades.

The Isles of Terrisia delegation consisted of four members, three men and one woman, just as the Beast Tribe Alliance. Prince James found that an odd coincidence as he approached them. All of them were of tan to darker skin, living a life on islands and the sea. From what he learned of the isles they were closer to this planet's equator, meaning the sun's reflection off the water was far more intense than the waters of the north. He recalled those family members that were from southern Italy talking about how they got darker tans from their time in the Mediterranean.

Shaking off that random memory and emotions of loss that came with it, Prince James refocused on the delegation he was now approaching. Where the Beast Tribe Alliance held an aura of strength and power, whereas the Isle delegation screamed skilled fighter and swordsman.

"Greetings your highness. I am Rohan, the burly man to my right is Glenroy, the ugly one to my left is my brother Jaden..."

"I am the best looking one between us and you know it Rohan." Jaden interrupted.

"Ha, ha, ha! Perhaps you are right brother. Perhaps you are right." Rohan chuckled.

Waving to the lady with them, "This is my light and daughter, Kiyana." Rohan introduced.

"It is a pleasure to meet you your Majesty." Kiyana said as she gave a slight bow.

Kiyana's outfit was the most colorful of the delegation, the bright colors a perfect contrast to her darker skin. She was quite attractive, and her eyes held a combination of clear intelligence and deadly cunning.

It was not lost on Prince James that each delegation seemed to bring a daughter or stunning lady with them. He was all too familiar that his mother made her desire to see her son married sooner than later very public. Plus, the fact that history was filled with political alliances sealed with a marriage. It was clear these delegations were thinking of the possible political benefits of such a union.

‘They are not pulling out the stops and Kiyana is quite lovely. Remain focused, nosebleeds are not becoming of a prince.’ James mentally focused.

“It is a pleasure to meet all of you. I hear your people are skilled swordsmen and uncanny sailors. This is the head of my personal royal guard LT Simmons.” Prince James replied.

The men gave a slight nod of acknowledgment to LT Simmons, and he returned the same. It appeared even in another world men still held some of the exact unwritten rules of interaction. A simple sign of respect from one warrior to another.

Kiyana, completely oblivious to the unspoken exchange that had occurred, exclaimed her praises for her family and country. “Oh yes! Both my father and uncle are the greatest sailors our nation has ever seen. My father says my mother was one of the greatest wielders of a blade. Our skills with the sea and the sword are why the fleet is unmatched on the oceans of our world.” Kiyana exclaimed.

It was clear she was proud of her people and her family. It was an admirable thing to respect where you come from regardless of history. Prince James knew that their country was brutal in battle, and several were known for piracy, but that did not detract from the good they did against the various sea monsters and other factions.

“My Kiyana is no slouch either! Her skill with the blade and ability to sail are unmatched for anyone many years her senior.” Rohan stated.

“Oh father. I doubt the prince wishes to hear of such things.” Kiyana replied.

“I find it very interesting in fact. Sailing is not something I have any experience in but that doesn’t mean I cannot appreciate the importance such a skill has on trade and warfare. I would welcome a chance to learn more about your people should you be open to it.” Prince James said as he watched each of them.

It was clear he said the right things based on Jaden’s response. “The prince seems to understand the importance of a strong navy.”

“I agree. Perhaps we can arrange for Kiyana to show you some of our ways. How about it my dear daughter?” Rohan suggested.

"Yes father. I will show him why we are feared on the open waters. Let me know when you'd like to go for a trip, and I will arrange it." Kiyana answered.

"I look forward to it. Now if you'll excuse us. LT Simmons and I must meet some of our other guests. Please enjoy the ball." Prince James said before they headed towards the delegation he really wanted to meet.

'Time to see if I can get some answers.' Prince James thought as a wicked grin flashed on his face before it vanished just as quickly.

Chapter 24 – Well, That Happened

Everyone had returned to the prince's wing to find Prince James and LT Simmons weren't there.

Sergeant Thorn was not concerned as he knew the lieutenant and he would not risk the prince's safety. 'I remember my first ball; I am sure he just found some fun to get into.'

Kira and Mira however were not so calm. They had wanted to start a search of the palace grounds until they turned up. Oddly enough it was Anara and Aeria who calmed them down.

"I bet you it was that bitch from the Rodchester line." Mira exclaimed.

"It was not. I made sure of that after I saw how she was with him." Anara commented before casting an ice shard and holding a wicked smile as she continued. "I followed her and her little click until they left the palace. She seemed flustered after her interaction with the prince but seemed more upset with her missed opportunity to ingratiate herself with Lady Firebrand."

"OK we will unpack why Anara was following Ria later…" Aeria stated.

"What?! I just wanted to make sure she did not have any designs; I mean ill intentions towards our prince." Anara defended.

"Right… So, as I was saying. I am sure the lieutenant is keeping an eye on him. If I recall Sloane was staying close to the prince all night as well. Let them be, we are his guards not nursemaids." Aeria commented.

'Besides the prince could use a chance to let loose and have some fun. Sad it is not with me, but I also would not mind some time with the lieutenant, I just want his hands all over…'

"You have a nosebleed Aeria, wow that is a gusher. Here stop moving around and let me heal you." Kira said while casting her healing spells on her friend.

A few hours later LT Simmons and Prince James burst into the room in discussion, Sloane not far behind them.

"I'd say that didn't exactly go as planned your highness." LT Simmons said as they entered the prince's private suite early in the morning.

"Nonsense." Prince James replied.

"What didn't go quite as planned?" Kira asked as they entered.

"The daughter of the Ambassador from the Feuhari Dynasty practically jumped the prince's bones. We had to sneak the prince out the window and backtrack to this wing." LT Simmons replied.

"What?!" Several of the female members of his personal royal knights said at once.

"I'll kill her. How dare she lay a hand on the prince." Mira said coldly as she drew one of her daggers.

"You can carve her up after I've turned her into an ice statue." Anara said while her staff started to glow blue, and the temperature of the room dropped a few degrees.

LT Simmons and Prince James looked at each other. Simmons whispered, "I am not touching this one."

"Really?! Now you draw the line? They are under your command." Prince James admonished.

"They are your personal royal knights." LT Simmons replied.

Shaking his head, Prince James spoke up. "Calm down. I think she just had too much to drink."

"Well, you did challenge the delegation to a drinking contest your Majesty." LT Simmons said.

Prince James glared at the man he thought was a friend.

LT Simmons just smiled back clearly enjoying messing with him. "What is the phrase you use? Oh right, I'm helping."

"Yea, sure you are. As I was about to say, I read that drinking was a time-honored tradition of building rapport. If you can drink them under the table, it proves your endurance and virility. I was just improving relations with our neighbors." Prince James.

“I bet you were.” Aeria joked.

Both Mira and Anara glared at her to which she just held up her hands.

“Hey, she jumped me the moment her father passed out. It’s not my fault.” Prince James protested.

“She was googly-eying you the whole time, how could you not notice? Also how are you not drunk? I just realized with as much sake as you drank it would knock out a gryphon.” LT Simmons commented.

That only earned the prince more glares.

“Ah that, well technically alcohol is a type of poison. I just kept casting purify poison spell every time I could. Luckily, I can silently cast my spells, so it allows me the ability to be subtle in the use of my magic. Perhaps my focus on cleansing my body and winning over the ambassador had me distracted.” Prince James replied.

“Wait a minute, you can silent cast your spells?!” Kira asked astonished.

“You know, now that you say that I do not recall you saying anything when you cast that fireball spell in the fight against the necromancer.” Mira stated.

‘Ha, it worked. I thought revealing one of my secrets might get them off that train of thought.’

“The moment I could untangle myself I had LT Simmons escort me to the restroom and we snuck out the window. Fortunate for us, we both know body-enhancement magic, otherwise we might’ve broken something with that two-story drop.” The prince commented.

“He was a real gentleman all things considered.” LT Simmons said. That seemed to finally calm the ladies down a bit.

‘Now you say that! Just had to see me sweat, didn’t you. I am going to figure out how to get you back Lex.’ Prince James thought.

“I’ve seen the ambassador’s daughter. She is smoking hot. It would have been hard to say no to that beauty. I mean maybe if one of you ladies had asked but not her. The red hair alone, it’s like liquid fire and her breasts...” Cooper commented, swirling his words a bit as he talked.

It was clear he had been drinking but he didn't get a chance to finish his comments as the girls' rage found an outlet. Mira punched him through the door. Anara shot a few icicles into his rear-end as he went flying. Rita, like lightning, shot a few arrows into his backside as well. While Aeria used her wind magic to keep his momentum going until he crashed in the wall at the far end of the hall.

Aeria wasn't really upset, she just thought it was funny.

Kira got up, "Excuse me your majesty, let me go heal him."

A few moments later you could see flashes of light, each after a slapping sound as Kira was admonishing the man.

"Don't..."

SLAP!

"YOU..."

SLAP

"Know not to..."

SLAP

"Talk that way..."

SLAP

"In mixed company!"

SLAP

Prince James, LT Simmons, and the other men just stared dumbfounded at the girls.

"Geez ladies. LT Simmons would you please go ensure Cooper survives Kira's healing treatment." Prince James said.

"At once." LT Simmons said before heading down the hall.

LT Simmons could be heard saying, "Kira, I don't think you need to keep slapping Cooper to heal him."

"How do you know that. I must make sure the healing takes effect. He is clearly suffering from poison." Kira replied.

SLAP

Shaking his head, Prince James ordered Leonard to go see to Cooper's recovery. "Leonard, make sure Kira's zealous healing doesn't kill one of my knights."

Turning to the remaining members of his personal royal guard, "I'm going to bed. I require a nap for a few hours. I suggest the rest of you try to get some shut eye. Good night." Prince James said the last while looking disappointed at his female protectors before shutting his bedroom door.

Prince James flopped on his bed.

'Geez Mikko was gorgeous. I almost gave in. Sadly, I think the ambassador would look unkindly at me deflowering his daughter while he and his men are passed out on the floor. Thank goodness LT Simmons was there. I think she had some kind of magical item because I was about to...' Prince James thought before his thoughts were interrupted by Sloane.

"My liege, are you still awake?" Sloane said through the **Party Link**.

"What is it Sloane?" Prince James sent telepathically.

"You were correct about the artifact. It was designed to increase the biological drive in a man. The second part would affect the mind but that seemed to have no effect on your highness. Why is that?" Sloane reported.

"I made myself immune to such mental manipulations and intrusions with a Mental Shield. I had not accounted for my biological drives but that too can be controlled." Prince James replied through their **Party Link**.

"Immune? How? Can you teach me?" Sloane asked telepathically.

"Perhaps one day. Give me time. Believe it or not I am still learning a lot. Soul magic is more my specialty over Mind magic though I do have some skill." Prince James telepathically replied.

"Understood my prince. I was able to plant the devices on Behat and do some investigating while they were passed out." Sloane answered.

"Good, we can discuss what you found later. Oh, I forgot to ask you, was Ria using a magic item? It felt like what I encountered while with the Feuhari delegation." Prince James inquired.

"Your highness should know that in my spying on Ria during the ball, I discovered she too had a similar item. I overheard her tell her two friends her father ordered her to use it but she couldn't after you came to their defense with Lady Nightshade. She said it felt wrong and her two friends agreed." Sloane telepathically reported.

"Interesting. Perhaps there is hope for her yet. Her father on the other hand. Here I was worried about Duke Arcum. We might need to move up our timetables for Duke Rodchester. Keep me informed and start putting things in motion." Prince James telepathically replied.

"At once your Majesty!" Sloane telepathically replied.

Before forgetting, Prince James decided to acknowledge everything Sloane did throughout the event. *"And Sloane. Good work tonight."*

"Thank you, your Majesty!" Sloane answered.

Prince James could sense Sloane's satisfaction, both from being so useful to the prince and in his praise. He could tell Sloane didn't get jealous when he praised others or was distracted in the objectives he had to accomplish. It was like the trust Prince James put in appointing him as spymaster and acknowledgement of the man's capabilities breathed new life into Sloane. Even Mira and LT Simmons had taken notice.

'More to consider later. Time to go to my Realm and continue my plans for tomorrow I visit the Dwarves. I also need to give more consideration to finding a head butler and maid. People I can trust who could fill multiple roles for me.' Prince James thought before opening a portal and entering his domain.

Chapter 25 – I Finally Get to Meet Some Dwarves

The next day quickly arrived. Prince James spent most of his time practicing his metallurgy, smelting, and smithing. There was something very soothing in crafting. He found he loved to create and be creative and this was just another outlet for such things.

After his traditional bath which he grew more and more to enjoy, Prince James exited his realm and quickly left his bedroom. He knew he would someday have to deal with the ladies growing yandere behavior but today would be kept to a minimum.

"Good morning, Lieutenant. First and foremost, how is Cooper?" Prince James asked as soon as he saw the Lieutenant.

"He is well your Majesty. Kira really did do a good job healing him, after a fashion." LT Simmons said the last part under his breath, but Prince James still heard him.

"With Cooper resting, I will be accompanying Sergeant Thorn today. I have also arranged for Leonard Phillips to be our resident healer for the day." LT Simmons stated.

"Where are the ladies? Other than Taka I don't see the other female knights." Prince James said.

"I had to discipline the ones who acted last night. Taka went to bed early, so she was not present last night. I have most of the other squads helping with the morning exercises or other such activities." LT Simmons replied.

"Very good lieutenant." Prince James said before turning to the sergeant. "Callus let us get a move on. My father asked that I join them for breakfast this morning before I do anything else so that is what I intend to do." Prince James stated.

After arriving at the royal family's private dining room, Prince James found his mother, father, and uncle already seated. His sister walked in just about the same time he did.

"Good morning, everyone." Prince James said.

"Good morning son." King Gerald said.

"Good morning, dear." Queen Sophia said.

"Good morning brother." Princess Aurora said in a yawn.

"Good morning my favorite nephew." Uncle Marcus said all loud.

"I am your only nephew Uncle." Prince James quipped back while taking his seat.

"Hahaha, quite right you are my boy. Here I thought you'd be nursing a hangover after your visit with the Feuhari ambassador and his men. You father and I made that mistake the first time we met with their delegation." Uncle Marcus laughed.

"No hangover uncle. I find the poison purification spell I know does wonders." Prince James replied.

"Poison purification spell? Hahaha, it appears our son was smarter than you two." Queen Sophia said while laughing at her husband and brother-in-law.

"How was I to know the Feuhari could hold their liquor like a dwarf?!" King Gerald mock replied.

"Biggest headache I ever had. Almost started a war when they asked if I wanted more sake the next day." Uncle Marcus said while chuckling.

Marcus then said giving Prince James a knowing look, "My men tell me Mikko, the ambassador's daughter was asking about you and your availability. She seemed quite enthusiastic to find you."

"What evil, vile woman is after my brother?" Princess Aurora asked, seeming to get upset that someone was daring to chase after her big brother.

"It's fine dear sister. She is merely interested in..." Prince James paused as he looked at his uncle's lifted eyebrows, the expression on his face saying, 'how are you going to explain this one to your innocent little sister?'

"She just wanted a tour of the city. Speaking of which, I would like to go the Military and Smithing quarter. I'd like to work with a master smith to craft a weapon for school. I am supposed to have one before class starts, right?" Prince James finished and tried to change the subject.

His Uncle elbowed him in the ribs and said, "Good deflection."

"Why not take one of the weapons from the royal treasury? It is your birthright son." King Gerald replied.

"I appreciate that father, but I also wish to learn more about crafting and smithing. The best way to do that is learn from the dwarves and master smiths in the quarter." Prince James answered.

"Very well. It is your right to choose your weapon for school. I will arrange for funds to be made available for you." King Gerald replied before going back to his breakfast.

"Thank you, father. Uncle, who would you suggest I visit?" Prince James said.

"Hmmm. Good question." Marcus stroked his beard in thought, "There are several master smiths in the quarter but if it be a sword, you're after, then there is no better smith than Master Smith Galdren. He has made some legendary blades. However, be warned nephew, the old dwarf doesn't care about your status, he only cares about the craft. You will have to entice him to help you on your own, your father or I will not be able to help."

"I understand Uncle. Thank you for the information and advice." Prince James replied before scarfing down his breakfast.

"Breathe dear, you act like you're starving." Queen Sophia said with concern.

Prince James slowed down his eating and answered, "Sorry mother. I'm just excited to get started. May I be excused?"

"Of course. Come give your mom a hug before you go." Queen Sophia said.

It was clear she was still having struggles with her separation anxiety. She would not let Prince James go at first, but she did finally relent when King Gerald spoke up. "Let him go honey. He's not going anywhere. Come we must start our day as well."

Queen Sophia released her bear hug hold on her son, "Very well. I know you are right husband; it is still so hard to not hold him tight for fear of losing him again."

King Gerald took his wife's hand in his. "I know my love, but we have our family back now, we will not let anything change that."

Nodding and squeezing her husband's hand back, Queen Sophia turned to her son. "Be safe in the Smithing quarter dear."

"Yes mother. Thank you." Was all Prince James said before quickly heading towards the exit of the palace. He couldn't wait to get started.

Prince James and the Bulwark squad exited the palace and took a carriage to the Smithing quarter. As they traveled, Prince James decided to strike up a conversation with the sergeant. "Have you heard of Galdren, Sergeant Callus?"

"Of course, your Majesty. His swords are legendary. Your father and Uncle both have one of his blades. He's one of the few Master Smiths who can work with Adamantine, Orichalcum, as well as other super rare metals. It is part of what makes him so sought out." Sergeant Callus answered.

"That is good to know." Prince James commented.

"What I've heard is he will only take a job if there is a chance to work with rare metals or something to challenge him to new heights." Sergeant Callus replied.

They arrived in the Smithing area and decided to exit the carriage a few blocks from Galdren's forge. Prince James wanted to take it all in. The smell of the metal and the forges going mixed with the clanging of hammers to anvils, Prince James loved it. For him, it was like he was witnessing the very act of creation itself as they passed the various smithies and saw the blacksmiths working their trade.

The excitement was clear on the prince's face and his men found it fascinating. Usually the prince was calm, controlled, genuinely warm or kind to those he cared about, but never excited in the way they saw him now.

'Seeing our prince like this, I get a glimpse of how young he truly is. Usually, he is so refined and controlled, he comes off far older and we forget how young he really is.' Sergeant Callus Thorn thought as he observed his liege.

They arrived at Galdren's forge and Prince James took no time to enter.

"Welcome to Galdren's Forge. How can I help you, young sir?" A younger clerk behind the counter greeted them as they walked in.

The first room of the forge was clearly the face of the shop. As they looked around, they could see various weapons on the walls and racks. Some more ornate than others but all looked exceptionally well-crafted.

As he looked closer, Prince James could see subtle quality differences, so he decided to ask, "Are all of these weapons crafted by Galdren or did some of his apprentices do these?"

"Ah, the young sir has a good eye, yes several of these pieces have been made by the Master's apprentices under the Master's watchful eye." The young clerk replied.

"Is young sir looking..." the clerk began before being interrupted by Sergeant Thorn. "If you call him young sir one more time, I might wallop you for disrespect. You are addressing your royal highness Crown Prince James Drake!"

The clerk looked like a combination of shock and horror. It was clear he did not know what to do before his delay led to more fear as he dropped to his knees. "Please your Majesty, please forgive me. I did not know. Had I known..."

Prince James interrupted the young clerk. "It's fine, don't worry. I am not offended. Please get up." Prince James turned to Sergeant Thorn. "Stop scaring the poor man, he is just doing his job."

Noticing a smirk on the sergeant's face and LT Simmons giving Callus an approving nod, Prince James commented, "Here I thought the lieutenant was the one that liked to mess with people. Looks like I will have to keep an eye on you as well."

Turning back to the clerk he continued. "Is Galdren in by chance. I would like to discuss a special job with him."

The clerk jumped to action. "One second, your highness. Let me go get him, I'll be right back." The clerk spoke quickly before disappearing through a curtain in the back of the room.

After the clerk disappeared, Prince James turned to his men. "Do not respond to any perceived disrespect. My Uncle warned me that Galdren does not care about rank or station, only his work. I will not have him throw us out due to such misunderstandings."

"Understood your highness." The squad replied in unison.

It only took a few moments, but they could hear Galdren before he showed up. "Calm down boy! I don't care who he is. I'll get there when I get there. These legs only move so fast. If you do not stop jumping around all nervous, I'll knock ye out so I can have some peace. Maybe get a drink after work, a good stout. It'll calm your nerves and put hair on your chest, so you stop acting like a wee lass!"

Galdren walked out of the back. The dwarf had a long grey beard that went down to his stomach. He was broad-shouldered and covered in muscles from the years of swinging the hammer. He wore a blacksmith's apron with a belt that held many tools, including a rather impressive mithril hammer.

Seeing the prince and his entourage, the dwarf frowned. He hated dealing with nobles, they tended to be self-important and full of themselves and that irked him. "Now what's the point of scaring' my help and makin them interrupt me?!"

Ignoring the frustration in the man's voice Prince James decided to get right to the reason he came. "I am James. I came here because I heard Galdren was the best swordsmith in the entire city."

Seeing the frown on Galdren's face deepen, Prince James quickly continued. "It was not my intention to scare your assistant. My men were a little zealous in their duties, which anyone can appreciate. Seeing how you're here Galdren, I am hoping you can talk business. I'm looking to craft a master blade."

Prince James pointed to the room "This is great work but I'm guessing you keep the really amazing stuff in the back." He said the last bit while staring at Galdren, refusing to back down from their impromptu staring contest.

Finally, Galdren broke the silence. "Hahaha. You got stones boy. I'll give you credit, you gave me your name without any titles even though this one" Galdren pointed to his clerk, "already told me who you are. I could take your comment as talking down about my work, but I am also guessing you realized most of what is upfront was done by my apprentices."

Galdren kept talking as he turned around and walked back through the curtain. "Come in the back. I'll hear ye out but there's not enough room for all yer men, so you figure that out."

"Lieutenant with me. Rest of you stay here."

"Yes, your majesty!" the rest of the squad replied in unison.

As they walked through the curtain, they saw Galdren turn down a corridor and head to what passed as his office and seating area.

"Clearly a busy man." LT Simmons commented.

Prince James and LT Simmons followed Galdren to his office. The office had a large drafting desk and a few stools, a huge chalkboard on one wall, a cabinet filled with various liquors, and a few chairs throughout the room.

Galdren took out a bottle, pulled the cork out with his teeth, spat the cork to the side, and took a long swing. "Ah, good stuff. Now what ye want?"

"I want to work with you to craft a master blade made of Adamantine, Orichalcum, inlaid with Mithril and Elementium. The combination of which to be used as a magical focus, possibly storing some spells or mana." Prince James jumped right to the point.

Both LT Simmons and Galdren looked shocked. They both stared at the prince for a moment.

Then Galdren slapped his knees and let out a good hearty belly laugh. "Hahaha! That's a good one boy! I never even heard of anyone using that combination of metals, some but not all. Mithril sure, Adamantine, maybe, though getting that much is the biggest challenge. Inlaid with Elementium, hell ye can't even get that much! Maybe if yer lucky and extremely wealthy ye can acquire some but then to be able to work all those metals into one weapon! I am not sure if even I have the skill to do it!"

Galdren's eyes seemed to grow distant for a few moments as he stared off lost in thought, "Something like that would be my masterpiece." He then seemed to come back to himself.

"It can't be done boy. Here I thought ye wanted somethin' reasonable."

"If we had the materials? Could I work with you to make it?" Prince James asked.

Galdren shook his head.

'This fool royal, & I thought his father and Uncle were crazy with their weapons.' Galdren thought before answering. "Look kid, I tell you what, you gather several bars of each metal, and not only will I work with you to craft it, but I'll also teach you all my secrets!"

"Do you agree under oath?" Prince James asked.

"Are ye daft boy?! There isn't enough material in the continent let alone the kingdom!"

"That's not what I asked. If I had the materials, would you do as you said under oath?" Prince James asked.

"Look boy, yer starting to annoy me. I'll make it simple; you produce several bars of each metal and I swear under oath that I will help you craft the blade, teach you all my secrets, pledge absolute loyalty to you as my king, and serve the best I am able. Heck and work for you craftin anything you desire! So, say I under oath and bonds of Power!"

The feeling in the air seemed to shift. All three men felt it, as if the Universe or the very powers that be began watching this moment as if something important was about to happen that would change all three men's fate.

That is when Prince James began pulling stuff out of his pocket dimension, making it look as if he was pulling everything from his bag as he slammed the items on the drafting desk.

THUD!

THUD

CHING

CLANG

.....

When Prince James was done, he had placed four stacks of bars. One stack of mithril, one stack of Orichalcum, one stack of Adamantine, and finally one bar of Elementium!

"That meet the requirements of the oath?" Prince James asked with a shit-eating-grin on his face.

Galdren fell off his stool in shock.

LT Simmons too sat there in silence but kept thinking, 'when did he get these? How? There is enough wealth with these bars to fund a rather decent sized army. He must have gotten them from John and Susan. It is the only thing that makes sense.'

"Well, Galdren? Does this meet the requirements of the oath?" Prince James asked still with a huge smile on his face.

'This man is not like his father and Uncle. This man, no, not man, this king, by rights he is my king!' Galdren thought.

"What do you know about dwarven history?" Galdren asked.

"Not much, please enlighten me." Prince James answered.

Letting out a breath Galdren told a story. "Long ago, when the world was new the dwarves fought in a great war. We are told this war spanned the cosmos. Our people fought alongside dragons and angels against the forces of the fae, demons, and all sorts of foul creatures. I will not bore you with the details but when the war was over one of the angels came to us and the dragons. Many of our people were lost in the great conflict. The dragons suffered even greater losses. The angel told us that for our efforts and sacrifices in fighting back the dark we are promised a king. Though it is not clear if the angel was speaking to the dragons or dwarves or both, since that day there has never been a dwarven king, only lords and thanes."

"Fascinating story, I had not heard that before. Is that way the dwarves have no kingdom of their own?"

"Aye. A kingdom needs a king. We have some settlements and great cities in some of the mountains, but it is not the same. Several of my people believe we have wasted enough time on some random promise, but our love of crafting has held our focus. That and drinking. Sure, we are skilled warriors but that is not where our hearts belong. Since that day we have pledged fealty to no king, nor sovereign. Many of us are followers of the light, but our faith has waned over the years in some of our younger generations who think we are fools. I wanted you to understand our history, so you understand the gravity of what I do…my liege." Galdren stated.

Galdren got up off the floor and bent down on one knee and bowed his head. "Yer majesty, you have proven this old dwarf the fool but more importantly ye taught me a lesson, which is very valuable at my age. I give you my oath of Loyalty and oath of Fealty! From this day forth until my last breath, I will serve you your Majesty. Should I die in yer service I shall find a way to return and keep serving. I am a dwarf of his Word. You have fulfilled a lifelong dream to be able to work with such precious metals in such quantities."

"I accept your oath of loyalty and fealty with the same gravity in which it was given. You shall always have a place by my side as long as you remain loyal and will have my protection should you need!" Prince James answered as he clasped wrists with Galdren and helped the dwarf to his feet.

"Now let's talk design and function!" Prince James said while clapping his hands together excitedly.

LT Simmons still sat there stunned as he thought, 'What just happened? Did he just get a dwarf to pledge fealty? What is the king going to do when he finds out?'

Throne Room in the Royal Palace

The soldier bowed before his king and the general of the army, "My King, General."

"Report" General Marcus commanded.

"As ordered, I and a few others watched the crown prince from the shadows while he went to the Military and Smithing quarter."

"And?" General Marcus asked impatiently.

"He went to Galdren's shop as you said he would. I was able to sneak into the back of the shop and listened in to his conversation with Galdren. As you told us he wanted a special sword made. He told the master smith he wanted one made of mithril, orichalcum, Adamantine, and Elementium."

"Adamantine? Orichalcum? Elementium?" King Gerald asked.

"Yes, your majesty." The soldier reported.

"Galdren must've told him such materials are super scarce. He must've laughed him out of his shop." General Marcus said.

"How was my son to know? Brother, if Galdren treated my son with disrespect I want action. Galdren maybe a master smith but he is my only son!" King Gerald exclaimed.

"Calm yourself my brother. I do agree with you. We knew this could be a possible outcome when it came to dealing with that stubborn dwarf. He cares about one thing only, his craft." General Marcus said.

Looking at the nervous soldier who seemed like he wanted to speak up but did not dare interrupt his king or general, Marcus exclaimed, "Out with it man! What happened?"

"As you both said general, Galdren began laughing and told the prince such materials are super rare, and no one has ever attempted such a combination before. But the prince pressed the issue." The soldier answered.

"I bet Galdren didn't like that." General Marcus said.

"No General, he did not. He said if the prince could provide the materials, he would not only work with him to craft the sword but also share with him his smithing secrets." The soldier said with some hesitation before he continued. "He also promised that he would bend the knee and declare the prince his king and serve him from that moment on. He said all of this under an oath. One with such weight to it I could feel the energy in the forge completely shift as the very air felt heavier."

"Could we do it brother? Could we acquire all those metals?" King Gerald asked.

"Mithril and even orichalcum is possible. Getting enough adamantine, however, would be very difficult. That metal is so rare it would cost us a fortune and I am still not sure if we could obtain enough. However, the biggest problem is the Elementium. It typically can only be found in extremely dense areas of energy like very old and powerful dungeons or other planes of existence. Even then there is hardly anything out there available that we could purchase." General Marcus replied thoughtfully.

"Tragic really. The number of powerful spells that could be cast from a sword like that would be unheard of. Not to mention having a Master

Blacksmith of such renown pledged to and working for the royal family." King Gerald said sadly.

"Your majesty and my General." The soldier said meekly, again not wanting to interrupt.

"Finish your report so we can determine our next actions." King Gerald said.

"Out of nowhere the prince began pulling out bars of metal. First several bars of mithril, then several bars of orichalcum. Then a few bars of adamantine, and lastly a bar of Elementium. Needless for me to say, Galdren was shocked, but he stayed true to his word and bent the knee giving his fealty to Crown Prince James."

"What?!" King Gerald said.

"How did he pull that off?" General Marcus said.

King Gerald and General Marcus looked at each other for a moment before they both replied, "John and Susan!"

"It must be! They were top end adventurers for a couple decades. It's possible they amassed that much wealth." King Gerald said excitedly.

"If that's true then my nephew is even smarter than I thought. First Duke Spears, then the High Priest Cendrin, and now a Master Blacksmith who crafts unrivaled blades. You and Sophia may be able to retire sooner than you thought brother!" General Marcus said while clapping the king on the back with a smile on his face.

"You just might be right brother! Though let's see him get through a year or two of the Royal Academy before I had over the crown. I do look forward to when that day comes." King Gerald said in good spirits thinking of the future.

General Marcus turned to the soldier and his squad. "Tell no one of this, understood?"

"Yes General!" They all said in unison.

They dismissed the soldier and his squad before they went to tell Queen Sophia the good news.

Chapter 26 – Sanctuary

Prince James was both exhausted and energized. The last few days and been long and grueling. As far as his men knew, he spent practically all his time at Galdren's forge. The dwarf was a wealth of knowledge and shared that knowledge with Prince James freely.

After Galdren gave his oath of fealty he dismissed his apprentices and closed up shop. Dismissing the apprentices took some effort, especially after he told them he had a special project. Through some pestering from the apprentices, Galdren told them only he would be crafting his masterpiece and showed them the precious metals he was going to be working with. This led to the other dwarves begging to stay when they saw the precious metals. Galdren shocked them with his response.

"I have pledged my oath of fealty to Prince James. It is his decision on if ye be stayin. But I be warnin ya, anyone who isn't willing to pledge their loyalty to such a man should not get a right to work with such metals!"

"You pledged fealty?! A dwarf has not done that to a royal in thousands of years." One of the apprentices said in shock.

"Aye, and I would do it again. This one is shrewd and has a passion for crafting. If he can hold his liquor, he be an honorary dwarf!" Galdren exclaimed.

It was clear to Prince James his charisma was once again at work here. Once he overcame initial doubts and provided the person with something they truly care for, they seem to go from lukewarm to fanboy. He was going to have to watch that effect.

Most of his apprentices were from the younger generation so they did not hold on to the old ways as strictly as Galdren did. If they could witness a masterpiece being crafted, they would do whatever it took to stay. Sure, they hoped to glean some secret technique but more than anything they saw it as being present to watch a moment of history. Besides, they all felt the weight that had settled in the forge, knowing that was due to an oath, all of them believed they would be fools not to remain.

Prince James first asked for a vow of secrecy, but when Prince James produced some additional bars of each of the metals the other apprentices practically drooled. One by one they gave their oaths but instead of oaths of secrecy they too gave oaths of fealty.

"Why?" Prince James had asked.

"Your majesty for a dwarf working with our hands is a part of who we are. For a smith working with rare metals is a dream come true. For a dwarven smith it runs far deeper than that. You've offered us something we could only dream. If you can continue to provide such opportunities more will rally to your banner my king!"

"Let's keep the king stuff quiet, ok? I do not need my father or some uppity noble hearing such words and thinking the wrong thing." Pince James stated.

"As you command my liege." The dwarves said in unison.

"OK I really must get a handle on this high charisma. How do I keep getting put in these situations?" Prince James mumbled to himself.

"Lex, I mean lieutenant. Please ensure no one enters Galdren's forge. I will respect his privacy in regard to his crafting."

Chuckling LT Simmons replied, "Lex is fine your highness. You do seem to gather a following wherever you go. You got to rub off some of that charm when we go drinking." Saying the last part before leaving the forge to carry out the prince's orders.

"He has to be messing with me." Prince James said while shaking his head and re-focusing on the master smith.

"Now watch closely my liege, you are going to love this." Galdren said as he picked up one of the bars of mithril and put it into the forge.

So it went, day after day, Prince James worked with Galdren and his apprentices and began forging his blade. The process was a long and arduous one. It was during the beginning of this process the dwarf confided in Prince James that even his master forge had limitations on what they could do.

"My forge even with pouring all the magic I have into it may not be sufficient to work the Elementium proper. As it is workin with adamantine requires the fire to be as hot as the bowels of a volcano and huge amounts of magic. I have a decent energy pool, as do my apprentices, but still, it will not be enough. Plus, we need more resources."

"Tell me exactly what we need and what we are missing." Prince James had asked.

Galdren informed him of everything down to the minute details like any master smith could. It was then the prince made his decision. With his personal royal knights forced to surround Galdren's forge and not be allowed inside, this had been one of Galdren's conditions to share his secrets, Prince James could do something for the first time since coming into this world.

He gathered Galdren and his apprentices together, erected a soundproof impenetrable barrier. "Now that that is up, we can talk freely. As all of you have already sworn an oath there is no need to be concerned. What I am about to tell you and show you none of my people know, not even my personal royal knights. Perhaps in time I will tell them but not now. Spread not a word of what you are about to witness. Understood?"

All the smiths present nodded their heads emphatically. They appreciated the prince sharing with them something he had not even shown others.

Prince James waved his hand and a giant portal opened before them. "Beyond this portal exists a special Greater demiplane, what I refer to as my Domain, my sanctuary. I have full control over this realm and with my vast knowledge have begun to create many wonders. There are limits to what I can do, as I can only do so much each day, but you will find a few things I think you will appreciate. First, time moves much faster in my domain. Second, you will find mines and a special forge. Lastly, I have workers there who have been gathering the materials we need. Come with me and be the first to enter my home, my sanctuary."

With those words Prince James walked through the portal. Galdren was the first to follow, though the others all followed shortly after.

Prince James deliberately opened the portal with a perfect view of the forge and the mountains in the distance.

Waving his arm out, Prince James proclaimed, "Welcome to Sanctuary!"

The shock was evident. Every single dwarf rushed to the forge as various excited sounds could be heard.

"I've never seen a forge so grand!"

"Look the bellows are powered by magic! Air can be forced through at different speeds with these magic levers!"

"There are different quench tanks with various liquids!"

"How many anvils does this place have?!"

On and on the smiths exclaimed, one excitement after the other.

Galdren came back to Prince James. "Are you sayin we get to work here?!"

"Well yea, that is why I brought you here." Prince James said as though it was as plain to see as the air we breathe.

"It's a blacksmith's dream!" Galdren said excitedly as he did a little dwarven jig.

"Hahaha. You haven't seen the best part. Follow me. Come on, you will be able to return, do not worry." Prince James chuckled as he turned around and beckoned the dwarves to follow. Which they reluctantly agreed to.

"What are those? Hey, are they carrying ore?!" One of the dwarf apprentices asked as he saw one of Prince James' construct workers.

"They are my workers, or CWs for short. Specially created to do a multitude of tasks. I'll show you." Prince James replied as he beckoned them to continue to follow him.

He led them to the storehouse. As they came in view, "See what they have been gathering." Prince James said while waving his arm to the various mounds of ore, minerals, and metal bars.

He had ordered his workers to stop smelting, as he wanted to give the dwarves time in the forge and to surprise them with this. The storehouse was ginormous and there were huge piles of materials, some the size of large hills.

The dwarves fell to their knees in awe!

‘Is that dwarf weeping?! Wait, are those tears in Galdren’s eyes?’ Prince James had thought in surprise. He figured they would be surprised and excited, but this was on a whole other level.

Galdren out of nowhere picked up Prince James in a big bear hug. “Lad I never thought I’d witness such things in my whole life! This place is wonder after wonder! I am your man always my King!”

“Need to breathe Galdren...” Prince James said getting Galdren to release him.

“Sorry, sire. I just am so overwhelmed.” Galdren said as he wiped a tear from his eye.

“I am glad you all like it my friend.” Prince James said before trying to catch the other dwarves’ attention.

Prince James gave a mental command but said the words out loud for the dwarves’ benefit, “Pick up and drag them out of the storehouse. We have work to do.”

Turning to Galdren and the other smiths as they walked back to the forge, “Hahaha! Hopefully now all of you are beginning to grasp the fringe benefits of your oath of fealty. All joking aside, you should now understand why I have kept this place so secret. Far too many would go to war or do everything they could to strip this place bare of the resources within.”

All the dwarves bobbed their heads adamantly.

“I’ll take this secret to my grave your Majesty.” One apprentice said.

Another asked, “Your majesty, can we please stay here?”

After the question came out of the dwarf’s mouth all the others quickly requested the same thing.

“Yes, please your Majesty!”

“I’ll do anything, please sire!”

“I do not even need a bed; I will sleep on the floor of the forge!”

“Calm down ye fools! I share your sentiments but use yer noggins! What would happen if I and all of you just disappeared from the capital? What about our other customers, would we not draw suspicion? Would this not do the very thing our king is asking us not to do? We must do everything we can to guard this secret and protect this place!" Galdren rallied his men.

The sad realization hit the dwarves as they realized they would have to leave a place that was like heaven on earth for them.

'Traveling between dimensions/planes held with it some serious risk. It was like breathing air for me, but I could not risk my new vassals. One I had actual dwarves that worked for me now, there is no way I'm going to let something bad happen to them. The question is how to solve this problem?' Prince James pondered.

Then the outline of plan was starting to come together. 'You gotta love when a plan comes together! Ha, ha, ha.' Prince James internally laughed at his internal monologue.

"For now, this is what we are going to do. Every day I will come to your forge Galdren. I will erect a barrier and then open a portal here. We will spend a few days here, rest when needed and return as if nothing is any different." Prince James explained.

Snaping his fingers as he recalled one benefit, he knew the dwarves would love. "Oh, that's right I need to show you all the baths, anyway back to the plan. After we have spent time here, we will return to your forge, rest for the evening, and then repeat the process each morning. It's not perfect and the time dilation can be disorienting so I apologize in advance. This will give us all time to work together, enjoy this place, and give me time to develop some longer-term options for us."

"Understood yer majesty!" Galdren and the other dwarves said.

So, it went for several days straight. The dwarves enjoyed the baths and several of them were shocked to find furnished rooms with beds.

"The bed felt like I was sleeping on a cloud, so I decided to sleep on the floor. Got to keep myself grounded!" One dwarf proclaimed.

"Non-sense! I heard ya snoring like a newborn babe on that bed."

"Yea! You kept some of us up ya daft fool, I was about to make ya eat yer pillow just to get some peace and quiet!"

Everyone was in good spirits and full of mirth and having fun teasing each other.

Each evening they would lock up Galdren's forge and go their separate ways. Prince James relished the time crafting and working with the dwarves, but he knew he had to come up with a more permanent solution.

His personal royal knights were rather surprised each morning by how zealous the dwarves were to see him. In the knights' eyes it looked like every morning the dwarves' devotion to their prince grew by leaps and bounds. They had no clue that for the dwarves they spent days with the prince side by side. In a few days to others, weeks had passed for the prince and the dwarves.

"Your Majesty, not to sound rude but how have you won over these dwarves so fully? I saw one grab his hammer when he thought the royal messenger wasn't showing you enough deference! I've never seen dwarves act like that." Kira asked as she escorted the prince back to the castle.

"Like with everyone Kira, you just need to understand them and get to know what is important to them. Show them how they matter. But most importantly genuinely mean it. Blacksmiths work with their hands, they put in backbreaking effort, pouring their blood, sweat, and tears in what they do. Dwarves take that to a whole other level. To them there is no purer judge of a man than what he creates. I truly enjoy my time with them, so much so, I find myself a bit sad each evening."

'Never would I have thought the prince would enjoy such hard work, him sweating as he bangs that giant hammer... wait what? When did we get back to the castle?' Kira daydreamed before realizing her escort mission had ended.

Prince James woke up the next morning. A week had passed in real time and the first day at the Royal Academy was fast approaching. He needed to meet with his father and Uncle before bringing his plan to fruition. Plus, he still wanted to set aside time to go visit the library here in the capital.

Having added Galdren to **Party Link**, but the best way he could describe it was like having a separate channel in his mind, he sent a message to the master smith. *"Good morning Galdren. I think I'm ready to implement a solution. For now, you can have your apprentices rotate. To the rest of the world, they will see you as having grown more reclusive and not available to* *meet with others. At least that will be the cover story. In reality, this will allow you to move to my domain and run the forge there. Does this work for you?"*

"Would that work for me?! Does a dwarf like mead? You're talking about allowing me to live in paradise! You would really allow me to live in your domain?" Galdren quickly replied.

"Are you not my most loyal vassal?" Prince James asked.

"I'd give ye me life ten times over. If I had any children, I'd be givin ya my first born as proof of my commitment to ye! I am with ye always my king!" Galdren practically projected both his thoughts and heartfelt sentiments to the man who keeps showing him wonder after wonder.

"Do you think other dwarves would want to join you?" Prince James asked as he internally chuckled at Galdren's responses.

"Ye must be jokin yer majesty! If the other dwarves found out there would be a mass exodus from this city for a chance to live in paradise!" Galdren exclaimed.

"Well, I was truly curious. Though we must be careful with what we call it. People cannot know it is another plane of existence, not until we have more controls in place. From now on, I shall refer to my domain officially as Sanctuary and ask that you and your people do the same." Prince James stated.

"That is easy enough to do my king. And to answer your question, if yer serious about the possibility of others joining, let me be yer emissary. I'm part of the crafting guilds. I'll be subtle and feel potential prospects out. If ye could find a way to get me and my men to and from Sanctuary, we could start to rally the dwarven people. It's been a long time since we had anything tangible to rally behind." Galdren said emphatically.

"I have some ideas. Begin your talks and we shall discuss later." Prince James responded before ending the mental dialogue.

Chapter 27 – Making New Friends

Prince James wasted no time and left his bedroom, heading to the private dining hall for breakfast. When he arrived, as expected, he found his father and mother talking and his uncle of course stuffing his face full of bacon.

His Uncle seeing him, smiled and said, "A meal without bacon is not a meal I wish to break my fast with!"

"Good morning family." Prince James greeted.

"My son finally finds time to break away from that awful forge." Queen Sophia said clearly not thrilled with the lack of time she had seen me over the last several days.

"My apologies mother but my zeal has gotten the better of me." Prince James replied as he gave his mother a hug before taking his seat at the table.

This simple act made his mother smile once again and Prince James knew he made the right call.

"Well apparently that zeal has rubbed off on the dwarves as I heard all Galdren's apprentices have pledged their fealty to you too. Impressive feat nephew!" Uncle Marcus said in-between mouthfuls of bacon.

Prince James quickly grabbed a pile of bacon before his uncle could eat it all. The look on his uncle's face when Prince James took the bacon was one of mock betrayal.

"What? I better get some before you eat it all." Prince James teased.

"Hahaha! He's got you there, brother!"

"I don't know what you're talking about my king." Uncle Marcus said before popping more bacon in his mouth.

Prince James marveled at how good the bacon tasted in this world. It had just the right amount of crisp crunch and he was convinced they glazed it with honey or some other kind of deliciousness. Coming out of his momentary revelry of such great food, he decided to broach the subject he knew he needed to.

“Speaking about Galdren, father. As you know he and his men have pledged themselves to me. Moreover, Galdren wishes to speak on my behalf with the other dwarves and smiths to form a new merchant conglomerate. If Galdren can pull it off, the royal family and our army would have priority over higher quality arms. We could begin to better outfit our forces and bring economic pressures on the other factions. What do you think?”

Marcus spat out a piece of bacon. Looked upset and heartbroken that he did such a thing, then regained his memory of what caused him to do such a horrible thing. “Are you saying Galdren can convince the dwarves and key crafters to join our cause?”

Smiling at his uncle Prince James replied. “That is exactly what I’m saying Uncle. We could begin to outfit the army and if nothing else use it as bargaining chips in the future with the other factions.”

“Ha, ha, ha! Son, you make me more and more proud every day. You truly do think about this kingdom and look out for our family. Whatever you need from us just say the word.” King Gerald said.

Prince James continued. “Thank you, father. Right now, while Galdren is in the process of doing his recruiting I thought it would be a good idea for me to do some recruiting of my own. I would like to hire a personal butler that can act as my seneschal. He will also double as an interface between me and the smiths. I would also like to hire a maid to carry out other duties as I require. Whomever I hire I will make take a magically binding oath to ensure no treachery and they see to my wishes.”

“That would be wise, especially with you starting at the academy soon. It would ensure the conglomerate can still be guided while you are busy.” Uncle Marcus commented.

‘Now is the time to push for what I really want.’ Prince James thought before putting his thoughts into words. “But I will recruit them on my own, I have someone in mind for each position. I know exactly the people John and Susan would want for me.”

‘Never mind the fact that that does not have anything to do with my request, but they don’t need to know that.’ Prince James internally smiled. “Is this acceptable father and mother?”

“Of course, son. We trust your judgment.” King Gerald replied.

“Anyone spoken highly of by John and Susan would be most trustworthy.” Queen Sophia said.

“Thank you. If you’ll excuse me, I have much to arrange.” Prince James said as he got up, taking his plate of bacon with him.

Uncle Marcus looked crestfallen watching Prince James walk away with a pile of bacon on his plate.

After breakfast Prince James immediately headed to Galdren’s forge with his squad in tow. The bacon was quickly scarfed down and the plate left with one of the staff just before exiting the palace.

Aeria was one of his guards today and complained to Prince James about how bored she was of late as he locked himself away in Galdren’s forge. “Your highness can we please be allowed in to watch you work? We cannot exactly protect you if we cannot see you. Besides it is sooo boring just standing around. I should at least be able to look at you work your muscles; I mean observe what you are doing.”

“As I have said many times, this is part of the agreement with Galdren. Stop asking. There has been no issue and there is not likely for one to start while you have the place surrounded.” Prince James answered.

Seeing Galdren they immediately grasped forearms. “Good to see you Galdren.”

“It is my honor to see you again my king.” Galdren greeted.

“Come there is much to discuss and even more to do.” Prince James said after entering Galdren’s forge and erecting a barrier.

Once they were all in his domain. The prince excused himself, “I will be very busy for the next several hours. I have been saving up for the last several days and keeping some of the wonders of this place in reserve. Please see to it that I am not disturbed.”

"As you command my king." Galdren nodded before turning to his people. "You heard his majesty, get to work and if I catch wind of anyone thinking of bothering our king you will be getting my hammer... to the face... then to yer family jewels."

Several men did the automatic response when such a threat was issued, they crossed their legs and emphatically made it clear they had something urgent to get done.

Chuckling Prince James left the smiths and went to a special area in the bowels of his keep. Once there he started the process of creating intelligent life. He had been saving up his Omniverse Points or OPs to use on this very thing.

Prince James wasn't completely honest with his parents. The 'people he was going to hire' to be his personal butler/seneschal/attaché and the person he was going to hire for his maid were going to be beings he created. This was key in the plans Prince James had discussed with Galdren. They needed someone who could help fare his people back and forth using Galdren's forge as a hub to avoid suspicion. Then he needed someone who could be seen but dismissed as 'help' and of little concern. Both positions would back each other up and each fill their roles perfectly in secret yet in plain sight.

Creation magic was calling to him as he gathered the points he wanted to expend. Deciding to start with his butler first, Prince James thought long and hard about who to create, some key personalities came to mind. 'I want someone powerful and honorable, like Seb, loyal and attentive like Al, sharp of mind and wit like Owen and Puck, and lastly caring like Mr. Belvedere.'

Once he had a clear picture in his mind Prince James became laser focused. He shut out everything else, there was only the act of Creation.

'The most faithful and loving creature I can think of is a canine, a wolf, wait, A WEREWOLF! I shall mix this werewolf with the capabilities of a dragon, for I have no greater connection or think of no other being so clearly. This being has a bite that when chosen has a chance to turn a creature into a werewolf loyal to his pack. He shall have a warrior mage's capabilities but a merchant's attention to detail, and as his pack master, I shall give him my drive to protect those I care about. The ability to shapeshift into humanoids, a wolf, werewolf, and of course a dragon! He must be able to hide his aura and power, or his very presence will overwhelm most mortals. As a protector he must have some limited healing and telepathic communication, along with some dimension and spatial magic to ensure he can move our people and resources where needed. Yes, I can feel it! Almost there!' Prince James finished his detailed thoughts with one final requirement he liked to call the **Loyalty to their Supreme Being effect**.

Loyalty to their Supreme Being effect: *You will forever see the one who created you as a Supreme Being. They are your creator and as such deserve your undying loyalty and respect. This effect is written into the very mind, body, and soul of the creation and as such cannot be interfered with or subverted.*

With a final flash of light and creation magic the dragon in humanoid form took its final shape. The eyes blinked and then the humanoid werewolf-dragon hybrid kneeled. "Oh, great one, I am forever yours to command! Thank you for creating me master!"

"I NAME YOU GODFREY HIRAETH! This name shall symbolize the good I wish you to do and both the longing for what I miss from my old life. You shall be one who does what is needed for others!"

After naming Godfrey Prince James felt a wave of exhaustion hit him. After constantly practicing his mental and physical exercises pushing his limits, he had learned how to not lose control even through exhaustion. However, this act seemed to have strong spiritual undercurrents he could not quite place just yet.

Regaining control of his senses, he looked down at his creation in his humanoid form. Godfrey was staring up at his creator in awe, complete devotion clear in his eyes.

"Rise my creation!" Prince James instructed.

"Yes master." Godfrey said with reverence.

Prince James felt another wave of exhaustion and began to waver. Godfrey waved his had casting earth magic to create a temporary throne. He guided Prince James into his seat. "Please great one, you are clearly tired. Had I known thy creation would have done this to you, I would have figured out a way to warn you. Please forgive my failing!"

"Stop spouting nonsense Godfrey. I knew this would be a possibility. Doing something new has inherent risks. Would you rather I not have created you to help me?" Prince James admonished.

Godfrey whimpered and wined a bit as he realized how foolish he was being. "Please forgive my foolishness. I am honored to be created by you and will endeavor to do my best to serve you in any way I can."

"Relax Godfrey. We will have plenty of time to get to know each other. I just need a few more moments of recovery before I try again." Prince James said as he was still catching his breath.

After a few moments, Prince James felt right as rain and decided to finish what he came down here for. He began to gather the creation magic once more thinking about the perfect maid.

'She would be like Mary Poppins in ingenuity and grace. Speed of a cheetah. She must be my shield against outside magic, yet our connection should allow my magic to flow as a conduit. Let me give her the ability to reflect magical attacks. Her link to me will allow me to speak with her no matter where we are or how we are separated! Let her be a holy terror to anyone who challenges us. What type of base model can I think to use... Of course, a tarrasque!!! In her true form she will be unstoppable. She will have the ability to change her size and shape so she can take the form of a diminutive maid. She too will need to mask her aura and power, or she might make those around her piss themselves in fear. Yet with all of this she will be kind and attentive, concerned for the well-being of my followers. Some magic and healing to help. Cooking knowledge from home would be the perfect touch. And lastly, I cannot forget about the **Loyalty to their Supreme Being effect**.'

With that final thought the tiny woman took form before Prince James and Godfrey's eyes. She too got on her knees and bowed her head to the ground. "Command me oh Supreme Being! Thank you for giving me life so that I may serve!"

"I NAME YOU TINA TARRASQUE! This name will symbolize you as a follower yet bringer of great change to this world! Help as you can and be a terror as you must! You shall forever stand by my side and aid me in what is to come!" Prince James spoke the words and felt the power rush out of him.

This time Prince James was planning on the wave of exhaustion and just let himself sit back into the chair.

"You may rise Tina. You and Godfrey shall be my left and right hands. Now give me a few moments to rest." Prince James said as he further slumped into the stone throne.

"Supreme one, what can I do to help you feel better. I know..." Tina summoned a glass of water out of nowhere. "Here, drink this. It is magical water from one of the streams in Sanctuary." Tina said the last as she helped Prince James drink the glass's contents.

Prince James found himself surprised that the water did help him feel better. "How did you know that would help me, Tina?"

"Sanctuary is intrinsically linked to you Supreme One. What comes from it will heal and empower you greater than anyone else who comes here. As Godfrey and I are linked to you, we can sense your needs. Your wonderful mind must have known you would need us to have this ability to better be of service." Tina explained.

"Interesting. My subconscious mind must've helped the creation magic fill in the gaps based on my intent. I would say that is very handy. Just be mindful I may have emotional moments, make a point to ask before you do anything too extreme."

"Understood Supreme One." Godfrey said.

"As you command Supreme One." Tina replied.

Feeling much better after the moment of rest and drinking the magical water, Prince James rose from his makeshift throne. Waving his hand, he made the stone throne dissolve back into the ground.

With a telepathic thought Prince James commanded Godfrey and Tina to follow him to the forge. "Come Godfrey Hiraeth and Tina Tarrasque, there is much for us to accomplish."

Once they left the underground part of the castle fortress they headed to the dwarves. 'Why are we walking in my domain? I did give him the ability to teleport.' Prince James thought.

"Godfrey. Tina."

"Yes, Supreme One!" Godfrey replied.

"What is your command Supreme One?" Tina answered.

"Ah, that could be awkward. Don't call me that, or at least not when others are within earshot. Call me your Majesty or Master if you must." Prince James said to them both.

"Your will be done master!" Godfrey replied.

"Yes Master!" Tina quickly bowed.

"I gave you both the ability to teleport and to be able to follow or find me anywhere. Do you sense it?"

“Yes Master, I can sense you. It is the most centering feeling. I feel very comforted knowing I shall always be able to sense you. It will make it quite useful in serving you Master.” Godfrey replied and Prince James felt contentment across their bond.

“I too sense you Master! The feeling gives me great peace.” Tina shared her feelings of contentment as well.

“Yes...well... the point I was making is I want you both to follow me by teleporting where I do. Understand?” Prince James shifted the conversation back to why he had asked Godfrey and Tina about the bond in the first place.

“Completely understood Master!” Godfrey quickly replied.

Tina nodded. “Lead the way, Master.”

‘Geez, this master stuff. It is better than hearing Supreme One or Great One all the time but come on, must they say it with every sentence. Oh well, not like it is the worst thing to happen.’ Prince James internally lamented.

“Good. Follow.” Prince James said before immediately teleporting to Galdren and the other dwarves.

Once they both arrived, Prince James introduced Godfrey to Galdren and the other dwarves.

“Hi Galdren!” Prince James said right next to Galdren just as Godfrey and Tina appeared right next to him making the poor dwarf jump multiple times.

“By the great maker! Are ye trying to make my beard even whiter?!” Galdren exclaimed.

After he caught his breath, Galdren continued. “Alright I think my heart and family jewels are back where they should be. Who might these two be my king?”

Prince James took that as his que to introduce his new creations. “Everyone this is Godfrey Hiraeth and Tina! They shall be my eyes and ears. My voice in all matters when I am not present. I have given Godfrey the ability to come and go between my domain and be able to bring others with him. As far as the outside world will know he is my personal butler and attaché. Tina possesses some similar abilities but will primarily serve as my personal maid and help coordinate our business dealings behind the scenes when a softer touch is needed."

"Greetings vassals of my master!" Godfrey said.

"It is a pleasure to meet those who see the glory of our master." Tina greeted.

The dwarves seemed to go pale all of a sudden as though a delayed reaction hit them.

Sadly, Godfrey had not yet learned to hide his aura and was exuding his raw power. Being mortals and not used to being in such a powerful being's presence, the dwarves were having a hard time, a really, really hard time. All of them were shaking in utter terror, several dropped to their knees, one dwarf even wet himself.

Seeing all of this happen in a matter of a few seconds Prince James shook his head and scolded Godfrey, "Hide your aura immediately. These men are not used to such things!"

Godfrey immediately did as he was told. The pressure instantly vanished from the dwarves, and they all seemed to visibly relax.

Godfrey got on his hands and knees, "Forgive me oh supreme being! I failed your first task. Please punish me!"

"For heaven's sake, calm down Godfrey! Other than scaring our allies and making that dwarf over there piss himself, no permanent harm done. Go explore the domain and practice restraint. Learn as I had to on applying as little effort or strength to your actions. Now go!"

"Yes Master!" Godfrey said before disappearing right in front of the dwarves' eyes.

Looking at Tina, Prince James noticed she did not forget to shield her aura. "Why did you not have the same problem Godfrey did?"

"You made me to be unseen, it is instinctual to hide my aura with ease. Godfrey you made to be your face and in some ways as your first creation possesses more raw power." Tina answered.

“Makes sense.” Prince James said as he helped Galdren to his feet, like several other dwarves they had collapsed from the sheer presence of Godfrey.

Seeing the glazed look in Galdren’s eyes clear up, Prince James continued. “Give him some time. He will be ready soon. I did make him rather intelligent, but he is still getting used to his power.”

“Y-you...m-made...h-him?” Galdren stuttered out.

“Yes, of course, I made them both using Creation magic. How else could I ensure we had people who could follow my orders to the letter and understand the intentions behind them. For that matter, have someone to bring everyone back and forth to Sanctuary.” Prince James answered offhandedly.

One dwarf asked, “Are ye a god?”

“I don’t like that term. I may be a creator, I’m just not THE creator. I am still sorting out who I must thank for my gifts. Regardless, free will means I choose what to do with them.” Prince James answered before clapping his hands together.

CLAP!

“Now why don’t you help your fallen comrade; he seems to have both passed out and soiled himself. Please help get him to the baths and extend my apologies for scaring the literal shit out of him.”

All the dwarves were looking at Prince James in new wonder. All of them were counting their blessings for pledging fealty to such a man that could create such wonder.

“Guys!” Prince James snapped his fingers in front of them.

SNAP!

“I feel bad and he’s really starting to smell pretty bad.” Holding his nose, Prince James continued “Geez! What did that guy eat?! I’m going to go... be somewhere else. Galdren come find me when you’re ready to talk.”

Without another word Prince James turned around and walked away, still holding his nose closed, Tina right behind him.

That seemed to snap everyone out of it, and they too realized the smell. "Mountain troll dung! What did Caleb eat?! Do as our king commanded and get that numbskull cleaned up! Our king needs me!" Galdren ordered as he thought, 'even if he doesn't need me right now, anywhere is better than here right now. Caleb might seriously have something wrong with him with a smell like that!'

Chapter 28 – Let's See How This Will Work

A few destroyed trees later, Godfrey had sufficient control over his strength that he was confident to return to his supreme being. His master had imparted some of his own memories to help Godfrey understand the current situation and what was expected of him. To Godfrey, having personal memories from his creator was like treasured gifts. He felt blessed and far luckier than other beings, Godfrey knew his purpose. Most inferior beings spent their whole lives trying to figure out their purpose, but Godfrey knew it clearly. Godfrey would do everything he could to make his creator's life easier and fulfill his wishes!

Godfrey could sense exactly where his master was, it was like a compass that always pointed in Prince James's direction. Once again, he felt profoundly blessed to have such knowledge for it would help him better see to his master's needs. He found his Master near the grove talking with the inferior dwarf.

'Didn't master call him Galdren, yes that was it.' Godfrey thought before weaving the magic around him and vanishing from his spot to appear right next to Prince James in supplication.

"EEK! Oh, it is Godfrey." Galdren said as he held his chest catching his breath.

"Good you've returned Godfrey and I see you have masked your aura, very good!" Prince James replied deciding to ignore the fact the Godfrey managed to scare the crap out of Galdren again.

'At least his aura is contained. Baby steps.' Prince James thought.

"Your praise honors me master!" Godfrey said while bowing his head.

"I'm going to have to teach you a few things. To start with I don't expect such deference, especially when we are in the outside world. Understood?" Prince James said as he looked at both Godfrey and Tina.

"As you command master." Tina answered.

“I will do my best master, though it will be quite difficult.” Godfrey replied.

Shaking his head Prince James replied, “Very well, do your best. Now that you are here let’s discuss Galdren’s plans to recruit more dwarves and blacksmiths.”

They talked in length about Galdren’s plans. Galdren was quite confident he could convince the other dwarves in the quarter to join up. First, Galdren was well known and very respected both in the Dwarven community and with the other blacksmiths. Second, Galdren was adamant that for the dwarves, and in his opinion, any ‘true smith’ would consider this place paradise.

Of course, Godfrey wholeheartedly agreed, his master created this place after all. To Godfrey any place his master created would be paradise.

Prince James, however, was not as convinced. “For those you decide to bring here, they must take a binding oath of silence to only speak of what they have seen to others who have taken the oath or who have already given their oath of fealty.”

“I do not think that will be a problem my…” Galdren started to reply but was interrupted by Prince James raising his hand.

“Let me finish my friend. Before they take the oath of fealty, they are to think they are merely stepping through a portal that took them to a distant land. The story that will be allowed to get out is that one my caretakers had instructed me on how to come to the place they found on their many journeys. It is isolated by mountains, as you can clearly see.” Prince James waved his hand towards the mountains that surrounded them.

“That is easy enough to convey my king.” Galdren replied.

“As long as they do not stay long, they will not be able to tell this is a completely different reality. I shall not have this place become widely known. However, if somehow word does get out, they will be focused on finding the location on the continent to no avail.”

“Fair and wise precautions my king.” Galdren said.

“The binding oath you taught me prevents them from sharing the knowledge. If they start to, they get a headache and pass out, waking up having lost their memories of this place and what they were told." Godfrey said.

"That is correct Godfrey. Ask your question." Prince James replied instinctively knowing Godfrey wanted to ask something.

"Why not kill them? The oath could be modified to kill them instead." Godfrey commented.

Prince James explained his reasoning, "Waste of resources and more importantly waste of life. There will always be fools, no matter what the world. If we killed every fool, we would remove a potential threat, but we also are depriving them of a chance to learn. When there are actual punishments for poor actions and bad decisions there are chances for growth and learning. A chance to go from a young fool to a wise person. I will give the people of my kingdom that chance. Make sense?"

"Completely! Thank you for taking your precious time to explain your logic to this naive servant." Godfrey apologized.

"Stop that. Naive just means you have yet to learn or know. You cannot learn if you do not ask questions. I created you with both a curious and critical thinking mind, always be willing to use what I gave you."

"Thank you, Master! I will strive to do so!" Godfrey said excitedly that his creator did not see his lack of knowledge as negative but instead gave him a path forward.

"And what of you Tina? What are your thoughts in the matter?" Prince James asked.

"They cross you or try to harm you, I kill them, quietly, and leaving no trace of course my master." Tina replied matter-of-factly.

Galdren audibly gulped. "Ye remind me of my brother's ex-wife, she did not take to kindly to betrayal."

"I did not know you had a brother Galdren." Prince James replied.

"Used to." Galdren said before busting up laughing at his own joke. "Ha, ha, ha! I almost had ya there my king!"

"Good one." Prince James chuckled before turning to Tina. "I was asking if you understood my stance on not wasting life."

"I understand master and I will do my best. Please know that anyone who crosses you I see as less than deserving of life." Tina answered.

"I completely agree with that statement master." Godfrey chimed in.

Sighing, Prince James replied. "Fine, just try to keep the killing to a minimum."

Godfrey and Tina looked at each other before Godfrey said, "Understood master. We will at least try."

Shaking his head and deciding to drop the issue, Prince James decided to get back at Galdren for his minor prank.

"Galdren did you see the special section of private baths I setup?" Prince James asked.

"No, my king. I have not had a chance, been a bit focused on the forge." Galdren replied.

"Well then let me show you before we leave." Prince James said as he guided Galdren back into the keep in a part he had sectioned off for himself.

When they entered the private bathing room Galdren was shocked. There was a large shallow pool with heat coming off it and a small waterfall to the side with a few smaller tubs for mineral baths, and an area to shower.

"This is very impressive my king. How do you control all these fancy tubs?" Galdren said.

"Do nothing." Prince James said telepathically to Godfrey and Tina.

"I am glad you asked, follow me." Prince James led Galdren to a wall with a few levers.

"You can control the various pools and temperatures with those levers. Go ahead and give it a try." Prince James instructed.

"Why thank ye my king. Don't mind if I do." Galdren said as he walked up to the wall.

"Go ahead and pull the lever." Prince James instructed.

Galdren pulled one of the levers and steam started to rise off one of the pools. "Very impressive."

Seeing what one lever did, Galdren pulled one of the other levers. As he did so a trap door opened up underneath Prince James causing him to immediately fall through the trap door.

"WRONG LEVERRRR!" Prince James called as he fell.

Galdren's face took on a look of shock and horror as he ran to the trap door but saw only darkness down below.

"What have you done to our master? I should kill you for what you have done!" Godfrey roared.

"How was I supposed to know?! Who builds a trap door right in the middle next to other levers?! I canna believe I killed my own king!" Galdren said fear stricken.

Prince James flew out of the trap tunnel. "Gotcha! That is what you get for trying to mess with me!"

Godfrey smiled at the dwarf and Tina chuckled.

"Yer alive?! Wait you can fly?!! Galdren jumped and embraced Prince James. "Oh, yer alive. I am so happy I did not kill my own king by accident. I am not even mad at ye for messin with me, especially if we can pull that prank on a few people I know!"

Prince James laughed. "Ha, ha, ha! That has got to be the most fun I have had in a long while. You got a deal Galdren!"

Prince James continued. "With future shenanigans decided, I would say it's time for us to return. Godfrey and Tina need to be introduced to my knights first and then my family."

"While yer doin that. I'll start recruitin" Galdren said.

Taking one last look at what he affectionately considered his happy place, Galdren stepped through the portal.

'No better time than the present' Galdren thought before exiting his shop to start his recruiting efforts.

Prince James exited the shop and called over his knights. "Kira, Aeria, Anara, and Rita. Let me introduce Godfrey Hiraeth, my new personal butler and attaché. He has already given me his oath of fealty and service."

To their surprise, they saw a well-dressed man in formal butler attire. He was tall, with short grey hair and a very neatly trimmed gray beard. The man didn't have a speck of dust or dirt on him. Next to him was a petite woman in a maid outfit. Her outfit too was immaculate. Yet if they did not stare at her she seemed to almost blend into the background.

"Where did they come from?" Rita asked concerned as she had not seen a single person enter Galdren's shop.

"They were in there with us. Besides they both have teleporting abilities. Show them."

Godfrey nodded to Prince James then disappeared only to reappear behind Rita and tap her on her shoulder.

Rita let out a very unladylike scream. "Ahhhh!!! Please do not do that!"

"My apologies Ms. Rita. I'll endeavor to 'not do that again' as you put it." Godfrey apologized.

Rita patted her chest in the hopes of calming her racing heart.

"Now that you're done scaring poor Rita let's go introduce you to the rest of my knights."

Godfrey slightly bowed. "Yes Master."

"What about her? Can she teleport?" Anara asked.

Tina nodded her head in Anara's direction. "My skill is not as advanced as Godfrey's, but I am able to be of use to Prince James."

Everyone seemed to take Tina at her statement and did not press. Her ability to blend in meant if they did not focus on her, they naturally focused on Godfrey.

"Tina, remind me to introduce you to Sloane. Your natural talent to blending in I think will be of great service to our growing spy network." Prince James mentally relayed.

"Of course, Supreme One. I will help in whatever way is needed." Tina sent back telepathically.

On the trip back to the royal palace Godfrey was peppered with questions.

"Where did you learn that teleportation skill?" Aeria asked.

"When did you arrive in the city?" Rita asked.

"Do you know any other magic beyond your teleportation skill?" Anara asked.

"Be careful in how you answer these questions Godfrey. I do not want us to get into a habit of outright lying to my people." Prince James telepathically warned.

"As you command Master!" Godfrey replied.

"Let me see if I can answer your questions in the order asked. My teleportation skill was a gift from birth. I arrived in the city just today. Yes, I do possess some other magical knowledge, but I only share such things as my employer, now Master dictates."

Anara and the other girls looked at Prince James pleadingly, their expressions clear, they wanted to know more.

"No, I have asked Godfrey to keep his talents mostly hidden. I want some of his capabilities a mystery for now." Prince James replied.

"Awe, no fair!" Anara pouted. Which quite surprised everyone as she was usually so cold and collected. They had noticed that her icy exterior seemed to melt when she was around Prince James. The other girls in Tempest squad knew why, but Prince James just figured that was how Anara was as she had not seen her any different around him.

Prince James patted Anara's head and ruffled her hair a bit. "Don't pout, you'll understand later, ok?"

Anara and the other girls all froze at the prince's action.

"Master why did they all stop at your sign of affection to Anara? Are they going to attack? Should I kill them before they strike?" Godfrey asked telepathically.

"Hmmm. I guess they consider it affection. I did it out of reflex. Oh wait, did I just fall into another anime troupe? Ah well, nothing to do but move on." Prince James telepathically replied.

‘I wonder if I pout if master will give me a head pat?’ Tina thought to herself as she observed the situation.

“Come on ladies, we have much to do.” Prince James said while he and Godfrey kept walking. That seemed to snap them out of it as they all rejoined the duo, albeit much quieter as if they were deep in thought.

‘What does this mean? Does the Prince like me?’ Anara thought.

‘Maybe I should be more inquisitive. Perhaps then I might grab his attention.’ Kira thought.

‘Man, Anara is so lucky!’ Aeria mentally lamented.

Rita was focused on her orders. ‘I must report this to Mira. She ordered me to report anytime the prince had any physical contact with anyone. Is this what she meant? She is focused on poisons and subterfuge. Hmm, she must be worried they might use that opportunity to harm the prince. I don’t think Anara would hurt him though. She seems to really care for him like the rest of us do. Oh well orders are orders.’

As the prince has been busy over the last several days holed up in Galdren’s forge, most of his personal royal knights were able to catch up on sleep. This allowed all of them to be present and awake when they returned to his wing and gather them up in his private conference room. After introducing Godfrey and Tina to the rest of his knights, he ordered food be delivered for everyone so they could all enjoy a meal together in his wing of the palace.

Godfrey and Tina were assigned the other room right next to the prince’s bedroom, the other being taken by LT Simmons. This particular room was reserved for a head butler and provided a side door into the prince’s bedroom so it would allow them easier access to Prince James without disturbing anyone else. James had a second bed brought in to accommodate Godfrey and Tina sharing a room.

They were all sitting down eating and Prince James noticed Mira seemed agitated.

“You ok Mira?”

“Yes, your highness. Do not concern yourself with it.” Mira replied as calmly she could manage.

“Very well.” Prince James replied while thinking, ‘She is totally giving off yandere vibes. This has got to be from the head pat with Anara, unless I’m missing something. Add it to the list of things to resolve later.’

“Godfrey and Tina, tomorrow go introduce yourselves to High Priest Cendrin. Sloane, go with them. I want you both to be connected to the network of spies for different reasons. Sloane you will continue to be my Spymaster. I want Godfrey to learn things that might affect the market and trade. Tina, I want you to work closely with Sloane and help him where you can. It will be invaluable to the new conglomerate I am having Galdren create.” Prince James explained.

“Conglomerate?” Cooper asked.

“Yes, Galdren will be the public face to the merchants, artisans, and traders that will join the organization. We will profit from it and have access to some of the best craftsmen in the kingdom.”

“Oh, I just didn’t know what conglomerate meant.” Cooper said.

“Hahaha! Never change Cooper!” Prince James laughed.

“No really I don’t know what conglomerate means.” Cooper said in a low voice.

Turning to the knight Prince James answered his question. “Think of it as a giant business that has a bunch of smaller businesses under it.”

“Oh, like how a duke has multiple counts and barons under him.” Cooper answered as he felt he understood the concept.

“Very good Cooper.” Aeria patted his shoulder.

This caused Cooper to beam with a big smile on his face.

Prince James refocused on Godfrey and continued, “After your meeting with Cendrin, see Galdren to get an update. Inform me when he has others for me to meet. Any questions?”

“No Master. I understand.” Godfrey replied.

Telepathically he sent a message, *“When do we return to your domain Master?”*

Prince James replied through the separate **Party Link** channel he had with Godfrey and Tina. *"Tonight, after we retire for the evening. Teleport to Galdren and bring him and anyone else. I will be modifying the fortress to ensure they have proper permanent living conditions. Tina, I want you to remain here and ensure no one tries to sneak into your room or mine while we are gone. I worry that some of my people are getting a bit curious, but it is not yet time to bring them in."*

"Understood master." Tina replied.

"As you command master." Godfrey answered.

That resolved Prince James decided to set some other plans in motion as well. "Lieutenant, I will be starting at the Royal Academy in a few days. My understanding is there are strict rules on guards and servants allowed on Academy grounds. Thoughts?"

"Yes, even royals are only allowed one servant or guard. This fact has been a bit of a point of contention among your personal royal knights." LT Simmons replied.

"I figured the palace is so close to the Royal Academy, I would just return each evening." Prince James said.

"Though several nobles stay in the dorms, it is not unheard of for a high noble to stay at an estate off grounds. We will have at least one squad added to the guard rotations at the entrances to the Royal Academy, we may not be able to enter but we can still provide some level of protection." LT Simmons explained.

"That is a reasonable precaution." Prince James commented.

"With your return each evening that will help alleviate some of our concerns, but all of the sergeants do not think one guard is sufficient to ensure your protection your Majesty." LT Simmons finally expressed his people's concerns.

"Well then, we might as well address this now. I plan to have Godfrey at my side. When he is not available, I will have Tina at my side, or we can rotate a guard in. I'll leave it to you on the rotation as Godfrey will be required to handle various assignments and coordination with Galdren and Tina will be working closely with Sloane." Prince James said.

"Hmmm. Not ideal but fair and understandable. I'll work out the details with the sergeants." LT Simmons replied.

"Before I start at the Royal Academy, I would like to see more of the city. Especially, I would like to take a trip to the library. I do love to read and would like to make a day of it." Prince James stated.

"That can easily be arranged. The last word I received from Captain Spears, other than assisting from time to time during our morning exercises there are no other pressing matters. Give the word and we can arrange whatever you require your majesty." LT Simmons explained.

"Perhaps tomorrow or in a day or two." Prince James said as he stood from his chair.

"Understood your majesty." LT Simmons acknowledged.

"Well then, I am going to call it a night. Have a good night, everyone." Prince James said before walking to his bedroom.

"If you will all excuse me. I too should get some rest so I may better serve the Master in the morning." Godfrey said before he retired to his room.

"Yes, morning comes quickly. If you will all excuse me." Tina said before she too left the conference room.

"I like her, she seems nice." Cooper stated to no one in particular.

"Godfrey is strong. He hides his strength, but it is there in how he carries himself." Taka Anella chimed in.

"Yes, well, I think we can all see it is clear his majesty trusts them. The rumor is they had John and Susan's confidence which explains why Prince James holds them in his confidence." LT Simmons observed.

"Then we should strive harder to gain his trust. I saw how the dwarves at Galdren's Forge were towards Prince James. In such a short time they seemed to revere him, and I can tell you that in my conversations with High Priest Cendrin the Church of Light is throwing their full support as well." Kira shared.

"Lady Firebrand wants to tutor the prince privately. Mother said both her and Lady Firebrand were impressed with how he comported himself during the ball. I am to work with our house's contacts to help grow our information network." Mira relayed.

Prince James' personal guards talked amongst themselves for several hours before retiring for the evening, enjoying the rare case where they were all awake and in the same room together.

Once in the room, Godfrey teleported to Galdren.

"Ahhhh!" Galdren let out a yelp, startled, as Godfrey teleported right in front of him.

"Oh...it's just you Godfrey." Galdren said after catching his breath.

"My apologies Sir Galdren. Master sent me to retrieve you. Are you ready for me to take you to Sanctuary? Is there anyone else we must retrieve prior?" Godfrey asked.

"Yes, there are a few very interested. One dwarf we absolutely must show up like ye just did. The ole bastard deserves a good fright. He, he, he." Galdren chuckled thinking of the expression on his old friend's face when they just show up out of nowhere.

— - - -

James finished modifying the rooms for Galdren and his people. He added more comfortable beds, modern day plumbing and personal bathrooms for each room using magic. After making the necessary modifications, James headed to what he was starting to consider his crafting area.

Once there he created some additional buildings. First a lumber mill, then a few additional workshops for other craftsmen. Just as he was finishing the final building and walked out, he was greeted by a shout from a scared dwarf as his vassals were falling on the floor, holding their sides laughing.

"Ahhhh! Galdren, you bastard! You had him do that on purpose!" One red-faced dwarf exclaimed.

"Ha, ha, ha! That's what ye get Dunham for tryin to mess with my ale, never mess with a man's ale, ye ole white bearded bastard!" Galdren said laughing.

There were a few new dwarves, a well-dressed elf, and a few older humans. Galdren seeing his liege straightened up, wiping a tear from his eye. Still doing what he can to calm his laughter so he could do proper introductions.

"He, he, he. My apologies for the disturbance to you, my king. I was just messin' with an ole friend. Let me make introductions."

Galdren pointed to the red-faced, white-bearded dwarf. "This is Dunham. He is a fellow smith and specializes in armor."

Turning to the elf, "This Neaman. He is a master tailor and enchanter."

Turning to the older humans, "Anduin and Marcia. They are master jewel-cutters and jewelers."

Turning to the gnome, "This is Pierre. He is a master alchemist."

Finally turning to the large well-built human who looked like he had to have some other race mixed in, "This is Luigi. He's the best lumberjack and carpenter in the city."

Turning to the crowd, "Let me introduce you to my king and ruler of this place we affectionately call Sanctuary. This is Prince James Drake!" Galdren said proudly.

"Welcome to Sanctuary. It is a pleasure to meet all of you. As I trust Godfrey and Galdren explained, as part of your oath of silence everything here you will all take to your graves. Once you get a chance to see everything you will better understand why. Enjoy the tour."

Turning to Godfrey and Galdren, "Godfrey and Galdren, please show everyone around. After everyone has had a chance to see what Sanctuary has to offer, figure out who will bend the knee and who will be going home. If they do decide to bend the knee, bring them to me if they decide to pledge themselves to our cause."

As you command my king." Galdren replied.

"Yes, master." Godfrey bowed.

"Oh, and Galdren I do give you permission to show them my private bathing area. Godfrey can help you with that." Prince James stated.

Both Galdren and Godfrey smiled and nodded their heads.

Prince James turned and addressed everyone. “Again, enjoy this once in a lifetime tour.”

One of the neat tricks James had learned while exploring the capabilities of his demiplane was how to remotely view what was going on anywhere within his realm.

‘Scrying is pretty cool.’ Prince James thought as he scried the visitors.

Prince James internally laughed at the various expressions that would occur over the newcomers’ faces, it was priceless. Deep down James figured most would join their team and give their oath. As he watched, Galdren and Godfrey replicated the prank Prince James had played on the dwarf. The utter shock and horror made James laugh and laugh.

‘Ah, thank you Emperor’s New Groove for such a great idea!’ Prince James thought as he continued to laugh.

Sure enough, after the tour, Godfrey and Galdren brought every single person before James.

One by one, they bent the knee and gladly gave their oath of fealty. Some couldn’t wait and practically got on both knees and crawled before James in their excitement to pledge fealty. To most craftsmen what Sanctuary offered was a dream come true and they were not about to pass on the chance to have access to not only the precious resources but the extravagant living conditions.

After all the oaths were given and the question of fealty was resolved, James left the coordination to Godfrey and Galdren.

‘My two OG’s can handle this. There must be a joke in there somewhere. Ah well, back to other matters.’ Prince James thought as he entered his private quarters in the fortress.

Chapter 29 – Logistics

"I'm open to additional suggestions to address the problem." James said to Godfrey and Galdren. They were discussing the issue of relocation of the craftsmen. Practically all the people who had given their oath of fealty wanted to move their families and relocate to Sanctuary.

"I canna seem to see a way around it my king. People will take notice of so many dis'a'pearin." Galdren said.

"I am more than happy to transport everyone back and forth every day." Godfrey replied.

"No. That'a won't work. Most of us don't even want to work in our ole shoppes after we get the chance to work with what's here. This be a dream come true. It's like dangling the best mead in front of a man and then tellin him he can't have it. This place calls to our hearts and souls." Galdren replied.

"That I can understand master smith. This place feels more like home than any other." Godfrey agreed.

"Don't get me wrong my king. We will do as you command even if it leaves an ache in my heart." Galdren continued.

James waved off Galdren's concerns. "No Galdren. I'll not deny my new charges their hearts desire for the wonders I've created here. I built this place for more than myself. We just need to be smart about this."

A thought started to form in James's mind. "Hmmm. How many of the shops next to your forge would be abandoned?"

Galdren stroked his beard in thought. "Well let me think.... If all the smiths we recruited moved, that'd be three shoppes to the left of my store and five to the right. Keep in mind some of those are tanners and military stock leather workers as the hoity-toity nobles can't stand the smell near where they shop so the only area they are allowed is in the military quarter."

"What about the craftsmen and artisans in the other quarters. Any of them have shops near each other?"

“Of course, my king! Several have been neighbors for generations. The biggest grouping would be about seven shoppes towards the border between the Artisan and Trade quarters.” Galdren replied.

“That’s actually perfect.” Prince James stated.

“How so, my king?” Galdren asked.

“What if we demolition the shops and build a transport hub and open market? Oath place would become an actual transport hub where we build a teleportation pad keyed to those that have magically given the oath of fealty. You could teleport goods from here to the hub and transport them via carts to the rest of the city or kingdom for that matter.” James said.

“Master, why not just teleport goods rather than use carts?” Godfrey asked.

“In time Godfrey. We first should get people used to this concept. People will realize we are using spatial magic to teleport things across a very long distance. We need them to understand that concept first. Plus, we must deal with some corrupt nobles beforehand anyway. This will begin to change trade as we know it. Heck we could probably find a few traders and merchants interested in joining up or at the very least take advantage of the benefits this could bring.”

“As always you think of everything!” Godfrey said once again impressed by how ingenious his creator is.

“No Godfrey. I do what I can but never stop questioning or looking at things from multiple angles and perspectives. This is how we come up with even better plans. I appreciate your praise of my gifts, but if I believe in what I was taught, I was made in my creator’s image, so I shift my thanks to THE creator in helping me be able to create now. A bit complicated perhaps but it helps me remain centered and not get too full of myself and what I can do.” James answered.

“I acknowledge your humility master and understand your disregard of pride. You made it clear in my creation that pride cometh before the fall. Regardless, it is most impressive what you consider Master.” Godfrey replied.

“I follow my gut; it guides me well. Now, shifting focus back to the subject at hand. What do you think Galdren, could it work?” James asked.

“It be bold and ambitious, I like it! Hahaha!” Galdren laughed thinking of the fools who turned him down when he tried to recruit them to his king’s cause. ‘Those idiots are gonna be beggin or be bitter. Either way I am gonna enjoy the looks on their daft faces!’

“Talk to everyone Galdren and get all the shoppes in the conglomerate’s name as soon as possible. We will do this in phases starting with an overhaul of your old forge to lay the foundation of the giant teleportation circle. After that, we begin tearing down the adjacent buildings to build larger warehouses and the transportation hub. Those buildings will need magical locks and security measures to keep our goods safe from unwanted visitors.” James laid out the initial part of his plan.

Turning to Godfrey James said, “Thinking we can do this without keeping it a secret will be impossible without some additional help. Go find Sloane and bring them here. It’s time to start bringing some of my personal royal knights into the fold.”

“As you command master.” Godfrey said before instantly teleporting away.

Galdren took that as his que to get started and left to go talk to his people. This prompted James to take a seat in the new throne Godfrey and Galdren created for him in the keep. It was gaudy and huge, but they were both so proud when they showed him that he didn’t have the heart to not use it.

It took about 5 minutes before Godfrey returned with a very confused Sloane in tow. ‘Man with the time dilation that’s extremely fast.’ Prince James thought.

“Five minutes Godfrey?” James asked.

Misinterpreting the question Godfrey replied, “Sorry I took so long Master. I put a tracking spell on Sloane so I could find him at a moment’s notice, but I did not account for the time dilation effects. Please forgive me Master, I deserve to be punished!”

Sighing and shaking his head James said “Sigh. No Godfrey I am impressed you are thinking ahead. Remember to maintain your composure in front of others. You are my honorable butler and attaché.”

"Understood master. It may take me time to adapt as every fiber in my being wants to serve you and the thought of failure feels unbearable." Godfrey replied.

"Do what you can." Prince James stated in resignation.

Turning his attention to Sloane who was still recovering from the abrupt location change. "Sloane, welcome to Sanctuary. There is much I must tell you and before this day is out, I will require more of you. Let me know when you've collected your wits, and I will begin."

Sloane shook his head and took a few moments to regain his center of gravity. "I am ready now, my liege. I was not expecting such a change in scenery. What is this place?"

Prince James smiled. "Come, let me show you around and share with you what I have been up to."

It took some time to bring Sloane up to speed on everything. The spymaster had their suspicions Prince James was keeping secrets. However, when he received the tour of Sanctuary, Sloane finally began to realize how big those secrets were.

When Sloane realized he was the first of Prince James's personal royal knights to be brought to this place, it gave Sloane a sense of pride and even greater appreciation of his liege. Sloane didn't even have to be asked before reaffirming a magical oath of fealty and silence, he once again bent the knee and gave an even deeper oath to make it clear where his loyalties lie.

"Thank you, my friend, for your recommitment. We have much to accomplish, it is why I want you to work closely with Tina. She can help bring you here when needed. Her teleportation powers are limited in comparison to Godfrey, but you will still find her ability to bring you here invaluable. Come, let me take you to my new council chambers." Prince James explained.

"Council?" Sloane asked in confusion.

Smiling, James replied, "You'll see."

James modified the throne room in the keep adding some additional chairs along the sides starting right below the stairs up to the throne itself. He would've preferred a separate council chamber with a central round table, but this concession was given for now until more join the ranks. Once Sloane, Godfrey, and Galdren sat in a few of those chairs James continued the conversation. “Now that Sloane is here and up speed, let me share my concept with you.”

“Here I thought I was up to speed, and I thought I had secrets.” Sloane grumbled.

Concept my king?” Galdren asked.

“Yes. I want to form an advisory council for Sanctuary and to see to my interests on the continent. They would see to matters in Sanctuary and help to run the conglomerate. Oh, and they would coordinate with my spymaster on all intelligence matters, whether it be of a competitor or a rival faction.” Prince James explained.

“Ambitious, but to be expected from my king.” Galdren commented.

“Having the merchants and craftsmen you bring in as additional eyes and ears is smart. Many of them already work with my contacts, so this will work out nicely.” Sloane stated.

Galdren raised a bushy eyebrow at Sloane. “That be sounding like you have your hands in the syndicate’s pockets.”

“I am the syndicate.” Sloane stated flatly.

“WHAT?!” Galdren said in shock before turning to Prince James. “My king, did you know about this?!”

“Know about what? That Sloane was the enigmatic unknown ruler of the city’s underground? The one some call the Shadow?” Prince James asked, taking a pause for effect before continuing. “Of course. Why do you think he is my spymaster.”

Galdren had risen from his seat in surprise before collapsing back into his seat.

“I do not understand the significance of this matter.” Godfrey stated.

“Aye, you would not know. There are rumors of the horrible things the Shadow did to become the most feared person in the city... heck he made the syndicate. Before it was just a bunch of street gangs, bandits, and random thugs. Some shoppes and traders paid for protection here and there. Now, everyone knows the syndicate gets its cut. Those of us in the Military quarter are not as affected, which is probably why it is now referred to as the smithing and military quarter, but the truth is many of us moved our shoppes there after certain mysterious fires took place over a decade ago." Galdren said the last part staring daggers at Sloane.

"Yes... the fire was regrettable. Failed negotiations I am afraid. I can assure you heads did roll." Sloane once again replied matter-of-factly.

"What?! Are ye daft man?! Why would heads rolling make me feel any better?!" Galdren said flabbergasted.

"Heads rolling would make me feel better. Good job Sloane." Godfrey replied.

"What?! How in the... Why would that make you feel better?!" Galdren said in confusion.

"It is rather simple; they are lesser beings and as such..." Godfrey began to say before being cut off by Prince James.

"That is enough! All of you!"

'Man, my emotions are way more in control since coming to this world.' Once he had their full attention Prince James took a deep breath and continued in a more controlled tone. "Galdren, we have all done thing in our past we are not proud of."

"Why would making heads roll not be something to be proud of?" Godfrey asked in confusion.

Sighing, Prince James looked at Godfrey. "We will get to that later." Turning back to Galdren, "Sloane told me everything when I made him one of my royal knights. He came to me in private and shared his history with me and his current position he held. No one ever fully accepted him among the military and the royal knights, but they could not dismiss his skills."

Sloane spoke up. "Prince James was the first to accept me. He looked into my dark soul and told me that I was still capable of good. He saw the worst of me and said I still held something worth redeeming. You do not know what that meant to street rat like me. Who could accept or love the monster I saw myself as, I..." Sloane said, clearly getting choked up as he talked.

Prince James had moved next to Sloane and put his hand on his shoulder sending a wave of acceptance and understanding through their **Party Link**.

"The hardest thing we must accept is the ugly parts of ourselves. No one is a harsher judge of us than our own mind. We have free will but make choices that can have lasting affects to how we see the person we are inside." Prince James said with a clear understanding and pain in his voice.

Galdren thought in surprise, 'How can one so young have felt so much pain? I can hear it in his voice.'

"I know too many this does not mean anything and no one respectable knows this but as part of taking over and creating the syndicate, Sloane removed the rather twisted practices that existed in the city. Things like child trafficking and brutal torture of innocents." Prince James stated.

"No matter how bad your situation growing up, you have no excuse to brutally rape and kill children. Such individuals deserve slow and painful deaths." Sloane growled as he recalled some of the horrors he witnessed growing up.

"And that is why you are a good man Sloane. You see it is a fine line between darkness and light. A good man is not one who is incapable of terrible things, that is a weak man, not a good one. No, a man who is capable of violence and terrible things but tempers that, those are the people I want by my side and those are the ones that shall inherit this world." Prince James spoke those words with a level of conviction that radiated out from him.

Everyone present knew that that statement was core to who Prince James was and it gave Galdren a new perspective.

"I not be sayin I understand everythin, but I also know I have made my own mistakes in life or done things I not be proud of. Prince James is right, if you were the one who stopped such atrocities then I would be honored to stand beside ya in battle, and make no mistake, I think a fight is unavoidable the way my king keeps shattering the status quo." Galdren said as he stuck his hand out to Sloane.

Sloane grasped the wrists of the surly and stalwart dwarf.

Galdren smiled, "Now that you are part of the council, how about we celebrate with a drink?"

Chuckling Prince James decided to get them back on the topic he wanted to discuss, security.

"Later Galdren, you and Sloane can get plastered later."

"Plastered? Why would we do that. I be talking about drinkin!" Galdren replied in confusion.

'Damn idioms!' Prince James thought before replying. "It is an expression meaning getting completed fall down drunk!"

"Oh... Why did you not just say that?" Galdren answered before shrugging his shoulders. "I keep forgetting my king was raised in isolation, some weird terms are to be expected I guess." Galdren said the last part more to himself but loud enough for everyone to hear.

Steering the subject once again back to what he wanted. "Yes, now that has been resolved... Let's discuss security and whom if any we bring into this secret from the rest of my personal royal knights."

Chapter 30 – Difficult Conversations

“Security will be difficult but not impossible. I can personally attest to the effectiveness of your barrier spell in keeping people out but it’s not foolproof. The barrier only lasts so long and must be brought down any time materials and people need to move in and out. Your idea to use earth Magic for a good part of the construction is a great idea your Majesty but in doing so will reveal part of your capabilities to the world. We need alternatives to that happening.” Sloane gave their honest feedback on what was discussed so far.

Prince James had shared his plan of creating a handful of teleportation circles that could help them bring goods and materials from Sanctuary to the capital. They had discussed using his barrier spell and other security measures they could take in both the construction projects and ongoing security.

“Some of the craftsmen we’ve hired have an affinity to earth. It’s hard not to being a dwarf. They could help, all-be-it not much.” Galdren chimed in.

“Use illusion magic to make it look like workers are manually building everything while getting help periodically from the crafters attuned to earth. That way it will appear the reason the final buildings look like they were completely created by magic was just smart craftsmen using their talent to make it look that way. We could even erect an obfuscation shield around the site to both obscure what is happening inside and confuse any magical monitoring devices.” Godfrey offered.

“If we got some of the lads to help and look like they go to a construction site every day it would help sell the illusion. I think most of the dwarves in the capital would come to show their support.” Galdren chimed in, liking the idea.

“It could work. We use the excuse the barrier is in place to protect the outside public from any noise or dust from the construction and the workers from being interrupted.” Sloane added.

"Sounds like we have a plan. Well done, Godfrey, I am so glad you are adept with magic. That will serve us well in the coming days." Prince James praised his personal butler.

Turning back to the others, Prince James asked his next question. "What about my question regarding my personal royal knights?"

Sloane hadn't forgotten when Prince James first asked that question, but rather was delaying the answer. 'The longer they don't know the longer I am the only one in the inner circle.' Sloane thought, but with a mental sigh knew he had to do what was right.

'This man has accepted me for who I am, with all my flaws, above any rumors or nonsense spread about my motivations and behavior. I must share my liege with the world, only then am I truly giving back.' Sloane thought before he gave his answer. "It is a tough question to answer your Majesty. In truth I believe all are loyal to the crown and the kingdom. I have investigated each of your personal royal knights to be sure of that."

Sighing, Sloane continued. "The issue is this place is yours and yours alone. It does not belong to the kingdom or your parents, and I do not know which of your knights might take offense to that statement."

James knew Sloane's sentiments. Sloane served James, not the crown or the kingdom, James, and James alone. Before James came along, Sloane served in a loose sense, but after meeting and being so completely accepted by Prince James, Sloane finally witnessed true loyalty and as such is giving it in return. Since then, the man had no other loyalty than to Prince James. Knowing this, he did not want to just ignore the concern Sloane expressed.

While Prince James began to ponder, Galdren immediately agreed with Sloane's statement. "Here, here! I agree with Sloane! We can't risk some uptight noble knight thinking the kingdom has rights to this place."

Of course, Galdren felt the same way as Sloane. James was doing more for his people, his friends, and own personal life goals than anyone from the kingdom has ever attempted. It was a big reason why the dwarves of the kingdom rarely went into the military or fought for the kingdom unless their families' lives were on the line.

"Of course, I agree with both of your sentiments. This place was my Master's creation which means it is precious to me and must be protected.

We can all agree No One will Ever Take this Place from Us! If they try, I will rip them apart, gorge on their entrails, and ...." Godfrey began before realizing he was losing control at the thought of someone daring to betray his master.

Regaining his composure, Godfrey continued. "However, that is not the issue at hand. The real question is which knights can we trust to keep this secret and not betray Master out of some other misguided duty?" Godfrey chimed in.

'I am impressed with Godfrey. He thinks critically and remains laser focused on my needs. I couldn't ask for better. I even appreciate the zero to murderhobo mentality when it comes to my interests, it lets me know he has my back always.' James thought before sending a silent prayer of gratitude for the gifts he possessed.

James voiced his appreciation to Godfrey. "Thank you, Godfrey, for keeping us focused on the real question. Make no mistake Sloane and Galdren, I appreciate your sentiments and loyalty. This endeavor is the start of a strong foundation from which we will begin to help all our people prosper. We cannot do such an endeavor alone and I will not consider my family enemies until they act as such."

Turning to Sloane again, Prince James pressed the issue with some force behind his words. "You have spent the most time with the knights, both before my arrival, and as part of investigating each of them. Who can we trust with this big a secret? I have my thoughts but am asking for your input."

Sloane seemed to deflate a little realizing in their zeal to protect Prince James they aren't helping as they should. "Forgive me your Majesty for my impertinence."

With a softer and kind voice James replied, "There is nothing to forgive. Please continue."

Hearing their liege say please almost broke Sloane's heart. 'No royal or noble I have ever heard of has ever used the word please but here my liege is asking me for my help. I can't ignore such a plea.'

"Of course, your Majesty. Putting my personal feelings aside, there are a few that stand out the most. Before answering let me say, I would also consider recruiting a few specific nobles for the conglomerate, not for this secret, but to keep them close enough they won't find this out and they will help keep others away. It will take some finesse, but it would allow us to test out their loyalty before bringing them into our confidence." Sloane said.

"I have been thinking the same thing Sloane, so thank you for the suggestion. We can discuss it after the knights." James replied.

Giving a bow of his head and recognizing his liege was keeping him on task, Sloane gave his advice. "Of course your Majesty. In short, each knight is loyal to the crown and the kingdom, with several loyal to the noble family they come from. Rita is probably the most likely top choice. She is the most likely to see through any subterfuge with her uncanny sight. Kira would be my second choice. She is a strong follower of the Light, it's at the core of who she is. The fact that High Priest Cendrin has put the full support of the Church of Light behind you makes it easier for her to not feel conflicted. This also may be a good point to bring up including Cendrin in joining the council."

Prince James interrupted him. "That was already part of my plan. He will help us in more ways than one when the time comes. He has already pledged to help spread my influence amongst the people. Now back to it Sloane."

Sloane nodded and continued. "Lastly, Anara and Aeria are frankly both obsessed with you. I thought I would never see anything Anara was focused on other than her magical studies but her obsession with you makes her interest in magic look like a random hobby. However, if you do decide to bring in Aeria, I recommend at some point bringing in Simmons and Mira. Simmons will have family loyalties as will Mira, but if you can win over her mother... then there is no family conflict, AND Lady Nightshade is very close with Lady Firebrand."

James was still trying to wrap his head around Sloane's comment about Anara's infatuation. "What?! What do you mean obsession? Sure, I figured she had a thing for me but not to the extent you are speaking about." James exclaimed.

"Oh yes, your Majesty. I have caught her saving napkins you've used as random keepsakes. Aeria isn't much better, there are a few times I found her coming out of your quarters when you aren't there looking extremely flushed." Sloane replied.

"I wondered why I kept smelling Aeria's scent in my room." James said offhandedly.

"Though the one that is probably the most obsessed with you is Mira." Sloane continued.

"Mira?" James asked, though he mentally told himself, 'Yea that fits with the yandere vibe I get from her. Aeria, I think is just a horn dog.'

"Yes. I've caught Mira several times trying to figure out how to sneak through the wards you place on your room when you go to bed. I would say all three of those lovesick ladies would keep your secret. Mira is loyal to her family but since the ball I think she has made up her mind about her feelings towards you your Majesty. Though I still recommend speaking with Lady Nightshade first."

"That does not exactly fill me with warm fuzzies." James said.

"Warm fuzzies sire?" Sloane asked confused by the phrase.

"Yes. It just means good and comfortable." Prince James replied, having gotten used to explaining his idioms.

"Ah, warm fuzzies, good one your Majesty." Sloane replied with a light chuckle.

"Back to my point. You're telling me that several of my personal royal knights are lovesick and obsessed with me. I hope I in no way led them on." James continued.

"You do not have to lead anyone on, your majesty. You are you, that is all that is needed." Sloane said while gesturing her hands. "I mean just look at you, then add the way you are so caring yet carry an unwavering aura of strength. It's hard not to be."

Dumbstruck for a split second before shaking his head. "Regardless. Romantic emotions can be fickle and lead to misunderstandings, which in turn can be dangerous."

"Ignorin' a woman's heart is dangerous lad." Galdren chimed in for the first time since Sloane gave his assessment. "Doin' nothin' is still doin' somethin', don't forget that lad. Women need love and want respect; men need respect and want love. That is a fundamental truth about life. Never forget that my king."

"Wise words my friend. I will not ignore them, Galdren. Very well, perhaps it is time I stopped acting like an ignorant blind fool when it comes to relationships. I will speak to them or address each of them in my own way."

Prince James remembered something Sloane said earlier and decided to ask about it. "You mentioned Lady Nightshade but rather than what she can bring to the table you seem focused on Lady Firebrand, why?"

"One simple fact. She is part of the Fae Summer Court and has the ear of Queen Titania herself. At some point the fae will get wind of this place, it is better you have an ally that can speak on your behalf." Sloane answered.

"Very well, you give me much to ponder." Prince James said before turning towards Sloane. "If you think these individuals are the ones, we should start with I'll heed your council. We will have to address Simmons and Thorn eventually, but we can start with the Tempest and Stalker squads. Let's put plans into action."

Turning to Galdren, Prince James continued. "Galdren, begin the steps to consolidate assets within the conglomerate and let the rest of the team know what is being asked of them."

Finally turning to look at Godfrey and Sloane at the same time, Prince James gave his final instructions. "Godfrey, go and help begin our elaborate illusions. Sloane, dig deeper with Simmons and Thorn. I don't want to wait too long before bringing them in. As for me, it's time to face my fears and talk to Mira and the others."

"Good luck with that one lad. I do not envy ya. Let me know if you want some armor. I can make ye some strong shielding for your vital areas and family jewels." Galdren offered.

"I just might take you up on that. A man can never be too prepared." Prince James replied earnestly.

After discussing some minor details, they concluded their impromptu council meeting. Prince James decided to return to the kingdom. 'Barrier active over my body, Check. OK let's do this.'

Reappearing back in his room, James didn't waste any time on his part of the plan. Opening his bedroom doors, he saw Mira and Rita were on guard. He decided to start with Mira.

"Mira." James said in a commanding tone.

Mira snapped to attention. "Yes Prince James? What is it you require of me?"

"It's time we had a discussion in private. Please join me at my small sitting desk in my room." James ordered.

"Yo-you-your room?!" Mira exclaimed in shock.

'Is he? No, he would not do such a thing, he is too respectful.' Rita thought as she watched the byplay.

"Yes, my room. Do not deny you've tried to figure how to get past my wards while I sleep. It's time we had a discussion and not one for everyone else to hear." James said while moving to the side and sweeping his hand towards the room in a come in gesture.

Mira looked horrified. 'How did he find out? Was I sloppy in my attempts? Wait... Sloane! If Sloane cost me this assignment, I'll skin them alive!' Mira thought as she walked in a defeated manner into James's room before he shut the doors.

James immediately put up his wards which included sound canceling effects so no one could listen in. He took his seat by the chair at his desk and motioned for Mira to take the other chair.

"Please sit Mira, and don't look so defeated. I am not firing you, so get that out of your head. Also do not worry about me making any advances. I respect you too much to bring in to question your honor as a lady."

A series of emotions crossed over Mira's face. First, she looked relieved at the fact she wasn't about to be fired, but then disappointed Prince James wasn't planning on making any advances on her.

James continued after she sat down. "As much as I've tried to ignore the way some of the female knights and royal magicians act around me at times, I was reminded no action is still action. I have been simply trying to adapt to my new life and..." James stopped as he realized he was trying to explain away behavior or inaction and frankly he knew that never works.

Sighing, Prince James decided to just be genuine and focus on what he really thought. He would share his completely unfiltered feelings. "Sigh... Mira, I think you are one of the most beautiful and amazing warriors I've ever met."

Mira had a look of complete shock on her face, she never expected those words to come out of the prince's mouth.

Seeing her facial expression, James continued. "It is clear your family is shrewd and smart; your mother is a clear example of that. Coming here I did not know whom I could trust, in many ways I still don't fully trust anyone, but I know you're an honorable woman. Hopefully the fact that I chose you as a Sergeant of my personal royal knights demonstrates I have some level of trust with you."

Mira finally spoke almost still in shock. "You-you think I am beautiful?"

Shaking his head and internally chuckling. 'Of course, that's what she focuses on.'

"You didn't hear a word after that did you?" Prince James said before sighing. "Mira a blind man could see your beauty. To be blunt, I thought you and a few of the others might be too distracting for me."

"Others." Mira said clenching her fists as she was reminded of competition.

"Yes, others Mira. I am not going to lie to you when it comes to such things. I find more than just you attractive. That is being honest and nor does it diminish your beauty in any way. Each of you I see something special. As hard and perhaps empty as those words may sound, there is no benefit to comparing yourself to another. We should all only comparing ourselves to our past and future selves."

Pausing to catch his breath before Prince James continued. "I am attracted to you Mira, but I refused to say or do anything about it as I felt wrong. You are one of my personal royal knights, as such I must lead and I need you to have my back, I would feel like I am taking advantage of our dynamic and that bothers me greatly."

“And now? Why are we having this conversation if you feel it is wrong?” Mira asked.

“Because what I said was all about me, it is not being fair to you or taking your thoughts and feelings into account so here we are, discussing.”

“But if I want more than just ‘discussing’, would you consider it?” Mira asked.

Sighing, “I’d be a fool not to.” Taking her hand in his James continued. “You know my parents are not the norm, especially for royalty. I am expected to have multiple wives whenever that time comes and most likely at least some of them if not all of them will be for political benefit.”

“I am a noble of this kingdom Prince James. I know better than most the price some of us must pay for our people.” Mira commented.

Nodding, Prince James spoke the next words from his heart. “I will not rush love, nor will I ignore it. I like you Mira, your sharp wit and fierce attitude that shines through even in your fighting. I also cannot ignore the others, several of them are your friends and you know that.”

James took a breath and continued. “So, I propose an alternative. First let me confide in you some of my most guarded secrets as a sign of faith and trust. More importantly, this will serve as a first step in growing a bond of trust between us. I will then talk with a few of the others and entrust them with some of my secrets. We must all be able to trust each other more than anything if any hope for something more is going to blossom. We start there. Give me time to get my bearings in this kingdom and step into my role as crown prince. I also have much to learn at the royal academy. During this time, we will grow our trust and our friendship as I grow my trust and friendship with the others. We must be honest and respectful of each other as we proceed to see what develops. Can you accept that?”

Mira took his words to heart. He came to her instead of making her force the issue with him, she respected him for that. He also was being honest and transparent with her about others, she didn’t like it, but she respected it. Lastly, he was willing to share some of his secrets, and she knew he had secrets, everyone did, he was too multifaceted not to. The problem was all of this just made her feelings for him deepen further. Deep down she knew he was right though, so she shared her thoughts and feelings.

"You are right James. Yes, I am speaking to you as a woman who is talking to a man she respects. We cannot ignore these things. I also agree with you that we will need trust between us most of all if we expect anything sustainable to blossom from this."

Mira then got down on her knees in supplication. "Now I speak to you as a loyal royal knight speaking to her Crown Prince. I will give you my oath of silence and oath of fealty for I would be lying to myself and my king if I denied where my true loyalties lie."

"Thank you, Mira. I appreciate..." Prince James began before he was cut off as Mira leapt from her position and kissed him. She knew she had to do it now before her nerves fled.

The kiss was like magic. She felt intense warmth spread throughout her body at what started as a chased peck on the lips turned into a full-on passionate kiss. They both broke for air, gasping.

Breathing deeply Mira said, "Where...did you learn to kiss?! That...was...amazing!"

"You're...telling...me!" James replied.

After a few more deep breaths to calm his racing heart, James pulled Mira in and softly said, "Hold on real tight and don't let go." Before transporting them to Sanctuary.

Slightly disoriented after arriving, Mira held on to James for a few moments. James grabbed her hand and gestured to the world around them. "Welcome to Sanctuary. Let me show you around."

Mira looked on in wonder as she took in everything around her. They stood on a precipice that was part of a giant castle which she realized was more like a massive fortress. Far off in the distance they were surrounded by mountains in all directions. She saw rivers and massive trees, stones, grassy plains.

After the wonder of all her surroundings changing so suddenly, Mira started to pick up on more of the details. She noticed the buildings and the... 'Wait are those people?! What are they doing?!' Mira thought.

Noticing where her eyes were, James led her by her hand. "Come let me introduce you to everyone."

Now that James had Mira’s fealty and made his decision to share several of his secrets with her, he was now excited to do that very thing. He led her down to the growing town below them.

Chapter 31 – Recruiting

After bringing her down into the hustle and bustle, James had to leave Mira there as Godfrey had an important report to deliver that was time sensitive.

"Welcome Lady Mira to Sanctuary. It is good to find you among us. Please accept my apologies but I must take some of my master's time on an urgent matter." Godfrey stated.

Mira just stood there lost in thought and had not even really noticed Godfrey's statement or when Prince James left.

'How is all of this possible?' Mira kept asking herself over and over as she saw one wonder after another. Her mind finally stopped the repeating cycle of confused questions once she saw Sloane.

"Sloane! Of course, you are here!" Mira said bitterly.

"Hello Sergeant!" Sloane said jovially, completely ignoring the clear frustration in Mira's voice.

"Pretty amazing..." Sloane waved around indicating their surroundings, "all of this could change so much for so many."

Seeing all the dwarves and craftsmen bustling about, Mira said softly, "So this is what they have been doing."

"Indeed Sergeant. I am still wrapping my head around all of this and I have had several days to comprehend it all." Sloane stated.

"Of course, you've known for several days." Mira said bitterly.

Sloane started to laugh, "Hahaha. It's been several days because of the time dilation effect in this place; besides I am our liege's spymaster."

"Time dilation effect?" Mira said confusedly.

"Ha, ha, ha, yes, the time in this place moves much, much faster than normal. Several days have passed here and it's only been a few hours back home." Sloane explained.

Sloane continued, “You know Sergeant that I advised his majesty to recruit Rita first. In fact, to be honest, you weren’t even my second or third recommendation.”

Mira looked like she was about to attack Sloane, yet Sloane kept talking. “Yet you were the first one he chose to bring here. Sure, he had to bring me, I am his spymaster, it’s my job to know secrets. Yet he was adamant you be the first.”

It was like a switch, all Mira’s anger and jealousy just melted away. “Really? He wanted to tell me first?” Mira said as a big smile spread across her face.

‘Geez this girl has got it bad.’ Sloane thought before deciding it be best to go find James and Godfrey.

“How ye holdin’ up lass?” Galdren asked Mira.

She had not even noticed the dwarf had approached her. It was this question that brought Mira back out of her internal musings. “Huh? What was that? Wait where did Sloane go?” Mira asked the last question, looking around and realizing the spymaster was gone.

Chuckling Galdren replied. “Aye lass we all get dumbstruck from the pure awe of what this place holds. Sloane went to go find his majesty. Lot to prepare for. Most of the people can’t wait to move here.” Galdren waved towards all the people moving around busy with one task or another.

“You think the other knights will support him and what he’s doing here?” Galdren decided to jump right to the question in his mind that mattered most. He needed to know if his people had to protect their king from fools.

“His majesty told me those he planned to approach next. I know those ladies well. Knowing what is in their hearts, I believe every single one will pledge fealty. You see giving such an oath doesn’t violate our existing ones. Prince James is the heir to the throne after all, serving him serves the future of our kingdom.” Mira answered honestly.

“You know lass it be easy to do somethin when the stars align, and everyone be in agreement. It be much harder to do somethin when we don’t all agree. What is being done now is both the right thing and the honorable thing. But lass, you see what be here…” Galdren waves is arm acknowledging everything going on. “The treasures in this place are many. Greed be a powerful motivator that can turn people together or against each other. Where do ye stand when the others end up on the other side?" Galdren spoke bluntly in the hope Mira truly considered her oath and what could come to pass one day.

Mira did not expect such deep political thoughts from Galdren. All her previous interactions showed him to be a shrewd businessman but all he seemed to truly care about was smithing.

'Perhaps I misjudged him too quickly. Mother would like this dwarf.' Mira thought.

She decided to speak her true thoughts. "From the moment I met this man he has defied expectations. He has been kind yet quick and decisive. He sacrifices for others and thinks both in the present and the future. I trust him as my liege and with my heart. I will stand by him always for if the kingdom goes the opposite way of our Crown Prince and his consistent actions, then by all accounts, the kingdom is making the wrong choice."

That was good enough for Galdren. He shook her hand and left, heading back to his true love, smithing. Of course, James had been remotely watching the exchange while talking to Godfrey and Sloane. James was getting quite good at multitasking.

"How do you wish us to proceed Master?" Godfrey asked.

"Move the craftsmen and their families here. Begin the demolition after that. Several of them can donate their people to help with the demolition even though I know you don't require it Godfrey. People are going to get suspicious about where these people have gone so it is best, they can see some of them helping both the demolition and building process."

"As you command Master." Godfrey bowed and left.

"You chose well your Majesty." Sloane said.

Prince James nodded. "Mira was the right call. I'm going to grab Rita in a few and bring her here next. She was on duty with Mira and will get suspicious otherwise. Eventually I will have to address Leonard but that will be after Kira and her squad."

"Can I ask why you chose her despite my recommendations your highness?" Sloane asked.

“We cannot deny or ignore people’s nature. Many nations fail because they ignore the fact that you can only distract or suppress one’s nature for so long. I want my people to think, to thrive, to make informed choices. Mira was one of the first to take up the mantle of my personal knight. I had somehow earned her loyalty from the very beginning. It was only right she be the first to receive mutual loyalty. Now enough of conversion, it is time for action. Over the next few hours kingdom side, I will be bringing Kira and team here. They have the duty next and will wonder where Mira and Rita have gone.”

Without another word they left to retrieve Mira and continue their mini recruitment effort.

——————

Convincing Rita to join their cause and give her oath was remarkably easy. Rita was a soldier and seeing her commanding officer and friend already agree helped. In addition, since Rita arrived in the capital, she never met a noble, or royal for that matter, like Prince James. He had saved her life, got her promoted to royal knight, and every action, though he seemed to rely on his gut, still was made with clear purpose. She gladly gave her oath.

James could not decide who was more shocked, Mira or Rita. Where Mira was shocked, she still held a sense of control which he assumed had to do with her noble upbringing. Rita on the other hand was all over the place, and her head seemed to be on a swivel with how much it kept changing directions. For Rita, Sanctuary was true to its name, and she longed to explore every inch of the place.

To Prince James the responses he was receiving so far from those he brought here warmed his heart. People were in awe with something he had created. James laid bare a part of himself to all he showed this place to. This created a feeling of true vulnerability for James. Yet the people he brought here were in awe and accepted this place, so to James they were in a sense accepting him. This fact drove his resolve more than anything prior. James now knew he wanted to be a part of the world he was now in and leverage this place to make his new home better for all those interested in building a better future.

James, Mira, and Rita had just returned from Sanctuary after James shared some of his plans with his two knights. They appeared in Prince James’ private suite just before Kira and the rest of Tempest squad arrived for their shift and relieved Mira and Rita. Opening his bedroom doors he saw Kira, Anara, and Aeria walking into the private suite.

"Ah, perfect timing." Prince James commented.

Seeing Mira and Rita coming out of Prince James's bedroom Kira immediately spoke up. "Mira! Rita! What are you doing coming out of the Crown Prince's bedroom?!"

"What were you three up to? Something torrid perhaps?" Aeria asked teasingly.

"The same thing the three of you will be doing. Get in here and shut the doors." Prince James commanded.

Kira and Anara turned bright red from embarrassment while Aeria had the biggest smile on her face. "Absolutely my prince!" Aeria said before using wind magic to rush to the bedroom doors.

"Hurry up you two slowpokes, I got a prince to satisfy!" Aeria said before using wind magic to pick up Kira and Anara, fly them into the bedroom, and dropping her two squad mates on Prince James's bed. With a final gust of wind, Aeria shut the bedroom doors closed.

James raised his hands up in a stop motion. "Wait a minute, that is not what I meant. I only wanted us to speak in privacy."

"Oh, it'll be plenty private my prince. I erected a wind barrier to ensure no sounds are heard from this room." Aeria said excitedly.

'Wow this chick is excited! I better real this in quick.'

"Look you little airhead, if you don't knock this off right now, I'll bury my blade into one of your tits to see if it'll pop!" Mira growled out.

Aeria quickly covered her chest with her hands. "You wouldn't!"

"Try me." Mira said with a deadly smile.

"That's enough Mira. We talked about this jealousy nonsense. They are your sisters in arms." Prince James commanded.

Aeria seemed to perk up at Prince James's words but deflated a moment later as he continued to speak. "Though I do appreciate you getting things back on track. I did not ask you into my bedroom for anything of a sexual nature. I merely wished to talk where no one can hear."

James saw that Kira had gotten off the bed, but Anara was still trying to untangle herself from the bed sheets. He walked over and picked her up in a Princess carry.

"Yip!" Anara squealed in embarrassment and excitement before James set her down on her feet. "Thank you, your Majesty." Anara said after composing herself and adjusting her robes.

"Not a problem." Prince James said.

'Why does he keep doing that with her?' Several of the girls thought to themselves.

"Now back to why I asked to speak to you in such an intimate and private setting. As I told Mira and Rita, I am new here and still getting comfortable with trusting people and figuring out who I can trust."

"Your Highness, I hope you know you can trust any of us here or for that matter any of your other personal royal knights." Kira said.

Putting up his hands he continued. "Kira I would not have selected those I did as my personal royal knights if I did not trust them to some degree. However, I am a man of many secrets. Surely, you all have realized that by now."

James could see the agreement in their eyes, so James continued. "I would be a fool to trust blindly, far too many want to use me in some way or if they do not want to use me for their goals, they would rather see me dead."

Sighing, he continued. "Now I asked you three here because I've decided to confide some of my secrets to you, but I will require some additional oaths beforehand. However, before I get to that it's time, we got some things out in the open."

"Things, your Highness?" Kira asked.

"Yes. It is clear to see that you ladies have feelings towards me. Some like Aeria are extremely over the top about it, plus she is just a big flirt." Prince James stated before Aeria replied.

"Hey! I resemble that remark."

Shaking his head, Prince James continued. “As I told Mira, I may have tried to ignore such feelings as I sorted out my own feelings being new to this place. I hope all of you know the last thing I wanted was to misstep and end up hurting someone I cared about, as I do care for all of you. So, I will tell each of you I ask for your patience and understanding.”

Of course, Aeria was the first to respond. “We aren’t going anywhere my prince. I for one appreciate the sentiments and attempts to air all this out in the open. Also, know that I’m not asking for any kind of long-term commitment.” She said the last part and winked at him.

“Thank you Aeria for the acknowledgment. Bringing us back to the topic. If all of you can accept my request for patience, I would like to take the next step in building trust. I require your oath of silence, but I will not turn away any oaths of fealty. To be clear, an oath of silence is the only thing I require for us to continue.”

Aeria practically glided to James before kneeling before him and giving both her oath of silence and oath of fealty. Surprisingly to James, Anara was next to bend the knee, giving her oath of silence and of fealty. Before Anara finished Kira bent the knee and gave both oaths after Anara finished.

“I accept your oaths with the same gravity upon which they were given.” Prince James said seriously before clapping his hands together and smiling. “Now that that is over, it is time to show you some magical wonders.”

“Magical wonders?” Anara’s ears seemed to perk up.

“Yes, now I would ask everyone to move in real close and hold on tight.” Prince James said.

Aeria wasted no time pushing herself into Prince James. “Is this close enough my prince?” Aeria asked.

‘How are those things so buoyant?’ Anara thought as her and Kira moved in as well. Before she could think of anything else they teleported away.

When they appeared at their destination all the ladies grabbed on to Prince James to steady themselves from the initial disorientation.

“Don’t worry it will pass. Welcome to Sanctuary! Let me show it’s wonders.” Prince James said as he waved his arm across the landscape.

Godfrey, who knew where Prince James would appear when he returned, was standing by and interjected. “If you would like Master, I can give them the tour. I believe Sloane and Galdren have much to report.”

“Very well Godfrey, please show them around and come find me in the baths.” James instructed.

“Baths? I don’t remember getting a tour of any baths.” Mira stated.

“That is because I was saving it for when we had more time. I think you’ll love them.” James said before teleporting away to Galdren and Sloane.

They all just stared for a moment at the spot where Prince James was just at.

“How does he do that?” Kira said in wonder.

Godfrey decided to snap them out of their revelry by giving them a loud cough. “HMM, HMM! Right this way ladies. I think you will find this place quite enjoyable.” Godfrey said before guiding them along the ‘tour’ as his Master called it.

——————

“What do you have to report?” James asked once he arrived in the throne room where Galdren and Sloane waited.

A bit startled at Prince James’ sudden appearance, they jumped.

“Oey, I almost lost me lunch!” Galdren exclaimed.

Sloane had his hand on his blade before dropping his hand. “That is very unnerving and will take some time to get used to.”

Realizing their liege asked them a question Galdren answered first. “Much my king. All the families are settled in already. This time dial effect is very handy.”

Prince James decided to ignore Galdren’s mispronouncing of the time dilation. “And what of their agreement to help with the facade of construction?”

“Each family has pledged several members to help with construction. With all the manpower they have offered we could construct many a structure, even without your magic, my king.” Galdren replied.

“Excellent. Good job Galdren.” Prince James said before turning his attention to his spymaster. “Sloane what about your concerns about security?”

“Several dwarves have come forward and offered to be part of a guard rotation detail for each area of the realm. They were adamant about helping protect their new home...and to use their words ‘keep the greedy no good intruding bastards away.’” Sloane reported.

“A guard rotation is a great idea. Let’s coordinate an armory to kit out our guards and soldiers when they are on duty. I want my people armed. An armed society is a far safer and more protected one.” James stated.

“It will be done your Majesty. We are ready to begin the construction phase of this plan. With the dwarves providing additional guard details we could begin immediately, just give the word.” Sloane said.

“Do it. Godfrey should be almost done with the tour. I will have Mira and Kira coordinate a royal knight presence at the site as well.” James said before leaving and heading to the baths.

Chapter 32 – Mistress of the Baths

When James arrived at the baths, he saw several dwarves both male and female at the baths. James had built separate baths for men and women plus several private baths. In fact, his main quarters in Sanctuary had separate private luxury baths he could use without being disturbed. However, he felt it best to join these to help the ladies acclimatize to them.

As Godfrey returned with the ladies, James greeted them. “Welcome back. What did you think of the tour?”

“It was wonderful. The materials you possess could fuel so many magical rituals and items.” Anara said in wonder.

“Yes, well the last part of the tour just might be the best part. These baths are separated for men and women. I....” James was interrupted by a nice Dwarven girl. “Excuse me your Majesty.”

“Yes?” James asked.

“If you don’t mind. I can show these ladies around the baths. Our people have gotten most comfortable with the amenities you have created for us.”

“What’s your name miss?” James asked.

“Dolores, your majesty. I have been assigned the role as Mistress of the Baths. If you would allow me, it is my job to tend to the ladies that come here and help show them all that you have created your Majesty.”

“Nice to meet you, Dolores. Your offer is most kind and greatly appreciated.” James said to Dolores.

Turning back to the ladies. “Please follow Dolores and enjoy. Seriously take some time to relax and take a breather. I’ll be with Godfrey and some of the other guys in the baths assigned for the men.” James said before turning around and walking with Godfrey towards where the male dwarves were entering.

“Come ladies. Let Ole Dolores show you around the place.” Dolores beckoned.

————

"This is heaven." Kira said as she melted into the mineral bath.

"Yes, it's great for yer skin lass. It took us a bit of time to figure all these different baths out. At first, we couldn't understand why his majesty built all these different types of baths. Now we just thank the light he did. I use this place every day. My skin has never felt so good! No wonder he be wantin to keep this place a secret. I don't think even the nobles have it this good." Dolores said.

"No, I think not, at least not every day. It is a luxury not even nobles can afford every day. My mother and her friends would kill for such luxuries." Mira stated.

"The Magic to make such things. It boggles the mind. I would spend an eternity with him." Anara stated.

The girls all looked at Anara with raised brows. Seeing all the girls staring at her, it then dawned on Anara what she said. Waving her hands about, "I meant to study and learn these magics. I didn't mean it that way!" Anara said while thinking 'Though of anyone to spend eternity with I would choose him.'

"More reason to protect his secrets." Rita chimed in.

Rita had already made up her mind about her prince.

"Indeed. Our prince and his secrets must be protected. Far too many would use such things for nefarious purposes." Kira said.

"Please stop talking...I... am... enjoying...bath." Aeria barely blurted out before seemingly falling asleep.

"I think the heat is making the air in her head rise." Mira teased.

"Ha, ha, ha. I liked that one Mira." Anara chuckled. Anara's friends noticed that either the prince, these baths, or both were melting Anara's cold exterior.

"Ha, ha, ha. Good one." Rita chuckled.

The ladies enjoyed the remainder of their baths, each falling into deep reflection on both their current feelings and best next steps.

After their bath, Dolores escorted the ladies to a grand banquet hall where many craftsmen and their families sat and shared meals together.

"Where are you taking us Dolores?" Kira asked.

"In Sanctuary, the families do what they can to eat as a community. It forces the more passionate among us to take time out of their day to come together and spend precious moments together. For dwarves, it is also an excuse to drink." Dolores replied, chuckling, as she led them to their seats.

Prince James, Godfrey, Galdren, and a few others sat at the head table. Six empty place settings were set up at the head table. Dolores sat Mira, Kira, Anara, Aeria, and Rita down before taking her place at the sixth empty place setting.

The men rose to their feet and greeted the ladies.

"Welcome ladies." The men said in unison.

"Did you enjoy the baths?" James asked.

"Oh yes they were absolutely divine." Kira said with fond memory.

"Once again you impress and go above and beyond." Mira said.

"They were quite lovely." Anara replied.

"I have never experienced such a thing." Rita replied.

"Most relaxing my prince." Aeria said.

Galdren and several other dwarves nearby seemed to frown at Aeria's words.

"Did I say something wrong master Galdren?" Aeria asked upon noticing his frown.

"No lass, not really. It is just here in this place; we don't like addressing his majesty as prince. In the Kingdom of Aerouant, he may be the crown prince but here he is our king and master liege. It just seems wrong to only address him as a prince when standing in all of this." Galdren said the last part waving his arms to signify the whole room and subsequent realm they were in.

“That is a fair point master Galdren. I will be mindful while in this place.” Aeria replied.

The others around the table nodded their heads in agreement and raised their mugs. “To his majesty! May the light continue to shine through his actions!”

The others in the dining hall echoed this toast once they heard it being said.

“To his majesty! May the light continue to shine through his actions!” The whole hall cheered.

“Interesting toast.” Kira commented.

“Aye lass. His majesty has told all of us to praise God and not him, sayin that’s where his gifts come from. We honor him in this way while thanking the Light for giving us such a man.” Dolores chimed in.

‘At least that is where I hope my gifts come from, cause if the Dark had some hand in bringing me here, I worry what that might mean.’ Prince James pondered before speaking up. “I am sitting right here you know. Let us discuss other topics please.”

“Aye! Stormstout tell the table what ye were sayin to some of us earlier!” Galdren said before taking a big swig of his giant goblet.

‘Seriously how big is that tankard?’ James thought as he saw Galdren down even more mead.

“I was just saying how the mines are yielding some nice stones and gems. We have a pretty nice stockpile of em and our miners are finding more each day.” Stormstout explained.

“Marcia and I have started to cut several of them. Many will work as mana stones and other gems for the crafting of magical items. I’ve have never seen such abundance. So many possibilities.” Anduin said in clear excitement.

“Quite right Anduin! I have used several mana stones in some initial enchanting tests. Never would I dream of the ability to test and experiment with enchanting materials. Such costs would make such things prohibitive!” Neaman said, also clearly excitedly.

"Good! Keep it up everyone! We are building a future here for our families and for our kingdom. Keep looking for good talent and work with Godfrey and Sloane to get them vetted. Together anything is possible!" James said as he raised his tankard.

"Here, here!" Several at the table said in unison.

"As I'm sure you've already been told, we will be building a teleportation circle to act as a transport hub. After that we will be building an open market. Security is of the utmost priority, and I want the Stalker and Tempest squads to have routine patrols and guard shifts until these are built. Understood?" James said.

"Yes Sir!" Mira and Kira said in unison.

"Now as you have already been told, time works faster here. With this in mind, we will be resting here before returning to the kingdom." Prince James instructed before turning to his butler. "Godfrey."

"Yes Master!" Godfrey replied before explaining the sleeping arrangements for his personal guard while in Sanctuary.

"As we have tried to account for all of you, there are a few shared rooms in the interim until private quarters can be established later. Mira and Rita will share a room and Kira, Anara, and Aeria will share the other. Both rooms are close to the Master's suite in size, so you should be most comfortable. Once we are done eating, I can show you all to your rooms so you can retire for the evening." Godfrey explained.

—————

The rest of the evening was rather uneventful. The girls asked the conglomerate several questions and the mood remained rather light as laughter could be heard throughout the great hall. Everyone ate and drank their fill before deciding to call it a night. True to his word, Godfrey showed all of them around.

The only commotion that occurred that night was when Aeria tried to sneak out of her room. Anara had frozen the locks and doors shut to 'prevent intruders from entering', but the truth was she knew her friend would not pass up the attempt to sneak into the prince's room.

‘She is so bold. If only I had the Gaul to discard proper etiquette.’ Anara thought while outwardly scolding her longtime friend. “Have you no shame?!”

“Not really, now unfreeze my hand, it is going numb!” Aeria replied.

The next morning, they enjoyed breakfast with the rest of the conglomerate. Galdren and the other members had recruited some farmers and herbalists to help create a series of farms and herb gardens in a section of the cleared plains by one of the rivers. Apparently, the land was rich in nutrients and the farm animals and crops multiplied and grew quickly.

“Thank you for another wonderful meal. Everything was delicious.” James said to Dolores.

“Thank ye, yer Majesty. I have always enjoyed helping with the culinary arts.” Dolores replied with a smile on her face.

“Yes, it is truly amazing what everyone has been able to create here. This meal was delicious.” Kira said.

“Aye lass, yer cookin’ be a treasure for all who get the pleasure to sample it!” Galdren exclaimed.

Dolores blushed at Galdren’s words.

‘Wait… are they an item?!’ James thought before he decided to file that away for later.

After some head nods and words of agreement at how good the cooking was, the craftsmen got up and headed off to start their work for the day.

James stood as well, turning to his knights. “It is time we head back. There is much to coordinate in the kingdom. If any of you wish to return to Sanctuary, please coordinate with your sergeant and Godfrey. Mira and Kira, I expect you two to work out something that is fair and still ensure the construction sites are protected.”

“Understood your Majesty.” Kira and Mira said in unison.

“Also, Galdren told me they plan to establish a guard for here and our construction sites to ensure proper security. Make sure to coordinate with him as needed. You know the risk if anyone found out what we are doing before we are ready.” Prince James stated.

The whole table nodded in agreement.

After they returned to the Kingdom of Aerouant, James decided it was time to have a conversation with his family. Once that was completed, he would finish preparations for starting at the Royal Academy and make a trip to the library.

Exiting his room several minutes before LT Simmons and Sergeant Thorn started their shift, Mira, Kira, and the rest of Tempest squad said their farewells. They felt well rested and knew they had much to do so they made their leave from the suite. LT Simmons was just exiting his room as he saw them all leaving the suite.

"Where are they off to so early?" LT Simmons asked out loud more to himself than Prince James.

Tina exited her room, having already filled Prince James in on her, according to her, very boring evening.

"Good morning your majesty." Tina bowed.

"Good morning, Tina." Prince James said out loud before telepathically letting her know his thoughts. *"I want you to help protect the construction site and coordinate with Sloane. If anyone if caught poking around, interrogate them if you feel it is more than idle curiosity."*

"Understood, Supreme One." Tina replied through their **Party Link**.

Sergeant Callus Thorn, Cooper, Taka, and Muro all arrived a moment later to start their shift, several yawning as they walked into the reception room for the suite.

"Good morning your majesty!" Sergeant Thorn said as he bowed.

The rest of Bulwark squad gave similar greetings.

"Good morning gentlemen and Ms. Anella. LT Simmons I will be attending breakfast with my family and discussing some business. Lieutenant, as you can see..." Prince James said waving towards the doors. "I have ordered Sergeants Nightshade and Lighthope to coordinate guard duty of the construction site down in the Smithing & Military quarter."

LT Simmons looked confused. "Construction site, your Majesty?"

"Yes, construction site. I have convinced Galdren and several other craftsmen to form a conglomerate and establish a transportation hub in the quarter. As I am a majority investor in this new conglomerate, I have a vested interest in its success. Security and magical warding are required, something the Nightstalker and Tempest squads specialize in. I expect you to resolve any scheduling issues as I will be starting the Royal Academy soon and will not be allowed the current level of guards and protection. Understood Lieutenant?"

LT Simmons did not completely understand and was a bit confused. 'When did this happen? Has he been planning this? Why didn't he tell me? Have I lost his majesty's confidence?'

"Lieutenant..." Prince James called to him to bring him out of his internal thinking. "Lieutenant!"

"Yes, your majesty! My apologies, your Majesty. I still am waking up." LT Simmons replied.

Turning to Callus Thorn. "Sergeant, can I call you Callus? I may like to give Simmons grief by calling him Lieutenant all the time but as you have already seen I prefer to be a bit more informal when it is just us."

Sergeant Callus Thorn bowed again to Prince James, "Your majesty honors me. Who am I to say no to such a request!"

"Calm down Callus, you do not need to be so uptight. That is fine when instructing the troops, but it is far too early in the morning for such formalities."

In a bit more relaxed demeanor Callus Thorn replied, "Understood your majesty. It will take some time for us to get used to how you prefer things. Captain Spears is far more formal when it comes to the knights, so I have tried to be mindful if how I and the squad present themselves in public. However, I have been known to enjoy a good game of cards if his majesty is ever interested."

That last statement surprised him. Prince James was not expecting Callus to be a gambling man. "I might just take you up on that one of these days."

"I would not recommend it. The sergeant is rather good. He has cleaned out a few officers and parted several knights from their coin." Simmons commented.

“I’ll keep that in mind. Now, come, I am hungry and have much to discuss with my family.” Prince James said before exiting the suite and heading to the royal family’s private dining room.

Tina, LT Simmons, and the Bulwark squad followed behind Prince James.

LT Simmons did not fail to notice how quickly the prince changed subjects away from the construction site to something else. ‘I know he has secrets, we all do, but it is clear the prince does not completely trust me. I will have to work harder to further gain his trust.’

After they arrived at the royal private dining room, LT Simmons and Bulwark squad took up guard stations outside to give the royal family their privacy.

Prince James was the first to arrive at the royal family’s private dinner room. Arriving earlier than normal, the servants were not yet ready to serve breakfast. He took his seat, and several servants began rushing to bring out food and drinks.

“Stop.” Prince James said while holding up his hand to catch their attention. “I am rather early this morning. Do not rush on my account. Please go about your normal schedule. I am in no hurry. Also, if Tina can be of assistance this morning, please have her do so.”

Tina took up a standing position behind Prince James. “Yes, whatever I can do to help.”

The head butler bowed and said, “That is too kind of you Prince James. Let us at least bring you some juices while we finish preparing the rest of the food. I do appreciate the offer of assistance, but we should be fine your highness.”

“That is fine. Seriously the one maid looked like she had a heart attack seeing me arrive early and not having food ready. Please convey my apologies for making them worry.”

“Of course. If you will excuse me, my prince, I will convey your kind words. I know they will appreciate it.” The head butler said before ducking back into the kitchen.

“Geez. I’ll never get used to that. I’m not some spoiled rich kid who will throw a tantrum.” Prince James telepathically told Tina as he shook his head.

"They do not know that Supreme One. Besides it is only right that they serve you. They are lesser beings after all." Tina telepathically replied.

"Oh, don't you start that nonsense. I appreciate your devotion Tina, I really do. However, it is important you and Godfrey understand that these people have merit and worth. Life has value and I will not just treat people who cannot do what we can as lesser beings." Prince James replied via their **Party Link**.

Tina frowned. *"I did not mean to displease you Supreme One. You created Godfrey and I; we cherish you for bringing us into existence and giving us clear purpose. Understand that to us, those not created by you will not hold the same weight as something you created."*

"I do not..." Prince James began to reply but Tina quickly continued. *"Please let me finish Supreme One."*

"Go on." Prince James replied.

"Thank you Supreme One. Godfrey and I have spoken at great length telepathically. We both can see how much you value people. Give us time to shift our thinking, it is hard to not see or categorize those around us by degrees of importance. With that said, we can tell these beings matter to you and will do everything we can to be mindful of this. Please accept that you made us to be fierce in our defense of you and that is where this thought process comes from." Tina explained.

"It was not my intention..." Prince James began before sighing. *"Perhaps subconsciously it was when I envisioned you loyal to me above all else. I created you and therefore hold some responsibility to how you are and the ways in which you develop and grow. I will consider your words and take them to heart Tina. Thank you for explaining your feelings."*

"You are most gracious Supreme One." Tina bowed as she replied.

James didn't have to wait long for others to arrive. Just as Prince James and Tina finished their telepathic conversation, King Gerald and Queen Sophia walked in holding hands. General Marcus entered a few minutes after James finished greeting his parents and giving his mother a good morning hug.

They greeted Tina, wishing her good morning as well. Prince James had sent Godfrey and Tina to introduce themselves to his family while he was busy bringing some of his knights up to speed. According to Godfrey and Tina, his family seemed to think they had some connection to John and Susan. As such, they accepted them readily.

“Up early this morning nephew. Perhaps some of that early riser can rub off onto my niece.” Uncle Marcus said chuckling.

“Yes, Aurora has never been an early riser, even as a baby.” Queen Sophia said.

“What has you up so early Son?” King Gerald asked as the servants finished bringing out all the food.

Chapter 33 – Making Plans with Family

"I have some things I wanted to discuss with father and mother." Pausing for a moment for effect before James continued "And even old Uncle Marcus." James said with a big smile looking at his uncle.

"Hey who you calling old? Don't make me jump over this table and eat all your bacon!" Uncle Marcus said with an even bigger grin as he ate a mouthful of bacon.

In mock shock, covering his plate, Prince James replied. "I never! That is a low blow Uncle!"

They both stared at each other for a minute, neither one moving. Then they both let out a good laugh "ha, ha, ha, ha" which made Gerald and Sophia smile and join in the laughter.

"Ah having my son back brings new life into these walls." Sophia commented.

They finished eating, both Marcus and James mock rushing to eat all their bacon to ensure the other did not pull anything.

"Ha, ha, ha. So, son what is it you wanted to discuss?" Gerald asked.

"If you will allow me father." James said before erecting a soundproof ward around the table.

Gerald raised an eyebrow. "A soundproof ward?"

"Yes father."

"Where did you learn that?" Marcus asked.

"I have learned many things Uncle."

"My baby always impresses." Sophia said.

"Well go on son. It must be important with this kind of precaution." Gerald stated.

"First, I am glad you all approve of Godfrey and Tina. I was concerned you might not accept them, so thank you for that." Prince James stated.

"Of course, son. They seem very capable attachés and servants." Gerald said.

Nodding Prince James brought up what he really wanted to discuss. "As you are already aware, I have recruited Galdren. Yes, I know of your spies."

Not missing a beat Marcus started to proudly boast. "Ha, ha, ha! He is a Drake for sure brother! Sharp as a dragon's talons!"

"Indeed. Right, you are brother." Gerald answered.

"In all fairness to your father and Uncle. I was the one who insisted on the spies, son. I wanted to know that my son was safe and protected. That was easier to have spies and a few royal knights keep an eye out." Sophia chimed in.

Prince James gave a nod to his mother. "I understand mother. Let me be quick and get to the point. I have convinced Galdren, along with several other craftsmen and artisans to form a conglomerate. I am the majority holder of the company, but for now Galdren and eventually a board or council will be the public face. This conglomerate will provide rare goods and needed services to the kingdom. With priority given to the Royal family and the army."

Marcus was stroking his beard while listening.

Gerald was the first to speak up. "First let me say impressive son. I will hold my other questions for later and just ask, why?"

"I am not blind father. The Noble factions are not to be trusted and we have much to do if we hope to turn around perceptions of our family and rebuild our power base." James replied.

Sophia took Gerald's hand. "Look Gerald, our son is looking out for us."

Gerald squeezed his wife's hand as he answered her. "Yes dear. It is clear that John and Susan trained him well in politics, the importance of family, and it seems business."

Prince James smiled. "As you have already gathered, I have access to a secret location that contains rare resources and materials. That is a big part of what has won over Galdren, and the others. Their gaining access to work with such materials helped to seal the deal. To that end the conglomerate has purchased several shops in the Smithing & Military quarter. After that we will be purchasing several stores in the Trade quarter. These shops are being torn down."

"Torn down?! To what end?!" Marcus asked.

"I figured the quarter is the perfect place for storage and a transport hub." James answered.

"Transport hub?" Marcus asked.

"Yes. It will contain a large and very secure teleportation circle. This is how we will transport goods from a distant location I own to the capital. Our best craftsmen and artisans will get access to rarer materials, and we gain a way to grow our economy. All while gaining the people's loyalty and being able to make things difficult for the nobles that try to work against us."

"I take that back; our son is a genius!" Sophia said as she looked like she wanted to bolt out of her chair and give me another bear hug.

Gerald held his wife's hand tightly, helping to give her the strength to maintain her cool. "Indeed honey. It appears our son has been planning several steps ahead for our family." Gerald said to his wife before turning to his son and asking, "What do you need from us, son?"

"There are multiple reasons for building the transport hub in the Smithing & Military quarter. First that is where several of the smiths shoppes are located together making it easier to demolish and rebuild. Secondly and more importantly it will be near the military barracks and warehouses. This will allow the military to patrol the quarter and help provide security for this future endeavor as the conglomerate will become the primary provider of military gear and weapons."

Continuing to stroke his beard Marcus gave his opinion. "Shrewd planning nephew. The nobles will be less likely to interfere or be able to easily poke around with the military patrols occurring and the barracks being so close. Now, I do mean less likely. Once this gets out, these vultures will swoop in as much as they can get away with."

Prince James nodded as he continued. “And that leads me to a few other points. The conglomerate will be setting up separate markets in each of the other quarters. This keeps foot traffic in those quarters and reduces the need to come to the soon-to-be-renamed ‘military and transportation’ quarter. In addition, I have asked my Nightstalker and Tempest squads to provide additional security and warding during the construction.”

“Our involvement will become known at that time. Once the nobles get wind of your personal guard protecting the site, it will be impossible to pretend the royal family is not involved.” Marcus said.

“I am counting on it. Remember part of this plan is to rebuild the power base of our family. We want them to know who is really pulling the strings, we just don’t want them to know right away. Galdren and Godfrey assure me they can have most of the construction done in a few weeks at the most. The conglomerate is bringing all their resources to bare to get everything up and running as quickly as possible.” Prince James explained.

“Most impressive. You have whatever support you require, son. What do you think brother?” Gerald said.

“It is a well thought out plan. I will instruct several of my officers to begin routine exercises and patrols in the military quarter. It will be a good enough excuse to put the added training Prince James shared to good use.” Marcus answered.

“Good. If that is all, let us adjourn and if you could please take down this soundproof barrier before your sister accidentally walks into it half awake.” Gerald said.

Chuckling Prince James took down the barrier. “Thank you, my family. If you’ll excuse me, I would like to visit the city library and do some exploring.” James rose and left the room.

“The nobles won’t like this once they find out brother.” Marcus said.

“I agree. Which is why we must be united and show our full support.” Gerald said.

“Of course, brother. I will see to it my officers know what’s good for them and keep them inline.” Marcus answered.

“I worry for our boy.” Sophia said as she held her husband’s hand.

"As do I dear." Gerald replied.

Out of nowhere the room filled with murderous intent radiating off Sophia. "If they try to hurt my boy, I'll kill them all!"

"We all agree Sophia, no one hurts our family!" Gerald and Marcus said together.

Then like a light switch flipped off, the murderous intent was gone, and she leaned on Gerald as he embraced her in a hug.

——————

"Speak your mind, Lieutenant." James said.

Prince James could tell LT Simmons seemed to be in deep thought ever since they returned from breakfast with his family. James pulled him aside into his conference room so they could speak privately.

"I do not know what to say your Majesty. It is clear you and the royal family have your secrets if the soundproof barrier was any indication as it kept all the guards and servants from overhearing." LT Simmons said.

"We all have secrets Lieutenant. What is the real issue you are concerned with?" James inquired.

"I am concerned I have done something to reduce your trust in me but for the life of me I cannot think what it could be." LT Simmons answered honestly.

Shaking his head James took a seat, instructed LT Simmons to do the same, and erected a soundproof barrier.

Sighing, James made his decision, and shared his honest thoughts. "Sigh, you have done nothing wrong Lexington, can I call you Lex?"

"Of course, Sir, you do me much honor." Simmons answered as his mood began to improve with James' simple gesture of friendship.

"Listen Lex, I am still getting used to all of this. You know I am new to this city and am cautious about who I trust and to what degree." James stated.

"It is very clear your Majesty tends to keep things very close to the breastplate." Simmons replied.

“You are one of the first people I met Lex. You have always seemed a straightforward man, especially for a noble. I respect that.” James said.

Simmons smiled. “Thank you, Sir.”

Waving him off James continued. “Sigh, something is wrong, and it has been bugging me for a while now. The nobles have too much power and many have forgotten their duty to the people. That is not unheard of in the history of other nations. I have gathered the sense that someone or something is pulling the strings behind the scenes. Very few people should’ve known the route we were to take back to the capital and from my study of trade routes and a few maps of the kingdom there were a few options to get us here. Yet someone knew the exact route.”

Simmons’ mood instantly changed, and he began to protest. “Are you insinuating...”

James immediately waved his hand and interrupted LT Simmons. “Oh please, do you think I would’ve chosen you to be the leader of my personal royal knights if I suspected such things. No, my statement is to first make you aware of my suspicions. Secondly, it is to begin to bring you into my confidence. I plan to shake things up in this kingdom, in some ways perhaps this whole world will be affected by the ripples of change. We need allies to grow our faction, but it is clear not everyone currently in the royal faction is a true ally. Sloane is helping to get to the bottom of this, but it is time you help in this subterfuge.”

Simmons expressed his concern. “How? I don’t even know what I am looking for?”

“Do not worry about that. Leave that to the Nightstalker squad. No, you are going to help recruit allies. We start with your father.” James explained.

Simmons’ eyebrows shot up. “My father?! Why my father?!”

“It is simple. Your family is relatively removed from the politics of the capital. More importantly, being a noble of a relatively remote land allows us to go relatively unnoticed away from most prying eyes. You will head home...” pulling out a sealed letter and handing it the Simmons, “and deliver this to him personally. We are going to set up a trading hub in his territory. At least that is the public excuse for the traffic and need for routine visits and inspections.”

“Trade hub, hmmm. You are hoping to draw them out by distracting them with this.” Simmons said it as more of a statement rather than a question.

“That is correct, well in part correct. My gut says war is coming. I expect a few battles here and there before whatever is really going on shows their faces. Hopefully we can direct those battles to happen when and where we want. This is part of that effort to draw our foes out. There is much more to go over, but I will discuss those things with you at a later time.” Prince James explained.

“When do you want me to leave?” Simmons asked.

“Immediately. Take Rita, she could use the leave to visit her family. I also have given her special instructions once you get there. I’d also like you to take Cooper with you.” Prince James answered.

“Rita makes sense with her perception and marksman skills. But Cooper? The man is an idiot when it comes to subterfuge. He has zero understanding of sarcasm. The man is not even fun to tease as he does not even get the fact that someone is messing with him.” Simmons groaned.

“Exactly. Everyone knows Cooper doesn’t get sarcasm or subterfuge, he’s too honorable and straightforward a knight. That and I think he’s been hit one too many times in the head. The point is he is an excellent rider and if he goes there is less suspicion of anything else beyond helping establish a trade hub for the new conglomerate being backed by the Royal family.” James explained his reasoning.

“Understood. Leave it to me your Majesty.” Simmons answered.

“James. When we are in private, please call me James.” James said as he clasped wrists and dropped the barrier.

‘Time to finish my preparations for the Royal Academy and visit the library. Gotta go back, back, back to school again!’ Singing that last line in his head and internally chuckling to himself at the Grease 2 reference. Maybe he was a little unhinged, but he wouldn’t have it any other way.

———-

Cooper Cavaliere

“Cooper, Rita, you both will accompany me on an important mission for our prince. I must hand-deliver this letter to my father and gain his support for a new trading hub in his barony. We ride out within the hour. Do whatever you need to prepare for the trip.” LT Simmons informed them.

Cooper snapped to attention, “Yes Sir! It is an honor to be selected for this mission Sir. I love to ride and being able to ride while serving my prince is a great honor.”

Rita put her hand over her mouth and started to giggle a little. ‘This guy has to know what he is saying, right?’

“Something funny Rita?” LT Simmons asked.

“Sir I think she is just overcome with joy at being able to serve his majesty. Isn’t that right honorable Rita?” Cooper said.

Holding back a giggle, “Y-Yes that’s it, Cooper. How astute you are cutting right to the heart of it.” Rita replied. ‘Wait is he actually posing.’

Cooper stood a little straighter and put his fists on his hips. “Quite right Ms. Rita, come let us prepare for our journey. I shall show you the best riding secrets for a long ride so one does not get chafed.”

Giggling Rita replied, “One… One would not want to get chafed while riding. Ha, ha, ha.”

“Quite right you are! Come let us prepare.” Cooper said while leading Rita out of the room.

LT Simmons put his hand on his head and internally groaned. “This is going to be a long journey. I am convinced more than ever that I have somehow earned punishment for some unknown offense.”

Chapter 34 – The Row

With LT Simmons and part of Bulwark squad out on assignment, Prince James felt it was the perfect time to make his way over to the city library.

'Finally, I get to read some new books and see what the place looks like on the inside.'

Stalker and Tempest squads were busy, and with Lex leaving for his family's barony that left the remainder of Bulwark squad responsible for the prince's protection. James thought they would be the perfect squad to take to the city library. Minus Cooper, the squad tended to be quiet and reserved, just what you need in a library. Sure, they would most likely be bored out of their minds, but the point is they will be quiet. James chuckled at the thought.

"Callus, it is far time I visit the city library. Let's head there now. I doubt many are up this early, but you never know." Prince James stated.

"As you command, your Majesty." Callus replied.

Prince James dawned a hooded cloak to help hide his features. After doing so, he looked back at his knights. Callus had withdrawn a cloak as well and was in the middle of putting his on. Taka was also attempting to put on a large cloak clearly made from some giant animal or monster. Lastly, was Muro who did not even bother with a cloak. The knight was a mountain of a man. Muro made Taka, who was rather tall, seem like a tiny lady.

'It must cost a fortune to kit him out in his armor.' Prince James considered.

"Well at least one of us is going to stand out. He, he, he. This should be interesting." Prince James chuckled.

Not too concerned with being spotted, James figured if he was noticed, he would just deal with it.

They left the palace on foot, taking a roundabout way to get there. As they walked through the Military quarter, Prince James passed by the main construction site on their way through the quarter. Using his True Sight ability, he was able to see through the obfuscation glamour Godfrey was using and glance at the progress so far. Based on what he saw they perhaps had another two to three days left to finish the overall building.

'They are moving faster than even I planned. Godfrey must be working nonstop. Hmmm, I will have to talk to him about not pushing himself and the workers too hard. As much as I wanted to watch the progress of one of my critical plans, that was not the purpose of this outing.' Prince James thought as they passed by.

After the Military quarter they moved through the Trade quarter. James had decided to avoid the Noble and Artisan quarters. He did not want to tempt fate and run across some snooty noble that might set him off.

'The ball was bad enough in dealing with some of the pompous fools with their overinflated egos. I'd rather reduce how much I involve myself there until our power base has grown enough where I can approach them from a position of strength. Perception of position and power seems to be everything to them.' Prince James contemplated as they entered the Trade quarter.

The quarter was bustling with activity, even this early in the morning. Several miners and laborers were making their way towards the outer gates so they could start their day mining or farming. Many could not afford to live on one of the farms or the owner simply did not have enough space to house all their workers.

As they moved through the barely awake workers, one accidentally bumped into Prince James.

"Hey, watch where Yer going pipsqueak! Do not make me put you in Yer place!" The miner threatened.

Faster than the miner could track Muro was in between the prince and the miner. "Where do you think his place might be?" Muro asked as he released some of his aura.

The pressure from the aura brought the miner and several of his friends to their knees. The miner's face went ashen white. "F-for-forgive me. I-I meant nothin' by it. I am just tired, is all. I was not paying attention to where I was going! It was my fault! It will never happen again, I swear!"

One of his miner buddies spoke up. "Yea, he bumps into people all the time. He did not mean anything by it!"

Prince James put his hand on Muro's arm. "Thank you, Muro. I think you can retract your aura now."

A moment later Muro's oppressive aura vanished and the miner and those around him felt palpable relief.

Prince James stepped around Muro. "I understand what it means to be tired from an early morning rise. A word or caution, be careful who you threaten as anyone can walk through this city."

"I-I-I will. Thank you for your leniency, Milord." The miner whimpered out.

"Be safe in the mines. I hear it is dangerous work, so be careful." Was the last thing the miner heard from the cloaked man before they walked around the miner and continued along their journey.

The miner's best friend came running up to him and helped him to his feet. "You got lucky! I keep telling you that temper and mouth of yours is gonna get you in trouble!"

In a daze the miner replied, "I think you might be right. I nearly pissed myself when that behemoth showed up."

Prince James internally chuckled. He remembered what it was like to get up and work a long shift from sunup to sundown. It drains a man on a whole other level if one is not careful. 'I will have to look into working conditions in the mines when I get a chance.'

As the prince and his guards moved through the Trade quarter, they saw several shoppes begin to open and various vendors who could not afford a building begin setting up their street stalls for the day. There was a clear economic distinction as they moved through the quarter. Most of the stalls were set up closer to the main gate leading out of the city, of those stalls, the ones closest to the gate were food related.

While the nicer buildings were closer to the Artisan quarter, Prince James had noticed an offshoot of streets that seemed more worn down. Curious, Prince James asked his question to Sergeant Thorn.

"Callus, what is that area? I do not recall seeing when I arrived in the city."

"To be expected Sire." Callus answered, using a less formal reply to not draw further attention to them. "That area is unofficially called 'The Row'.

Though it encompasses many streets, it is the most dangerous part of the city. Mind you, it is not only the poorest part, but the area the Syndicate holds the most sway."

"Syndicate? I have heard of them before." Prince James mentioned. Sloane had revealed it all when it came to the underground organization, but he was curious what the knight knew and thought of such a group and place.

"There rise to power was rather impressive for a bunch of criminals. They are scum, but they do keep the gambling dens relatively organized."

'Of course, Callus would be a gambler. No wonder he likes to play cards so much.' Prince James thought.

Not aware of his prince's musings, Callus continued. "I begrudgingly must agree with some of my peers that they are far more organized than the gangs of old, but it is well known that they have their hands in practically every illegal enterprise in the country. Their leader, the Shadow, is known for being a brutal cutthroat and was the main reason the organization exists today."

"Shadow? What is known about this Shadow?" Prince James asked, genuinely curious what the royal knights might know.

"If you want to know about the Syndicate and their mysterious leader you should ask Sloane. He has been known to associate with the underbelly of the city." Callus said with a bit of an edge to his voice.

"I am asking you Callus. I have already heard about the negative perceptions people have regarding Sloane." Prince James said with a similar edge to his words.

"My apologies, Sire. I have mixed feelings about Sloane. In some ways I do think he gets a bad rep, but I have seen with my own eyes that he frequents the less than reputable establishments." Callus explained.

"And why were you there, Callus? You enjoy gambling and perhaps your fellow knight does too." Prince James emphasized the words fellow knight to remind Callus Sloane was still one of the team.

Callus winced a bit. "I do agree with you, Sire. The problem I have seen is that he seems to be on friendly terms with the people who run said establishments. These people are not the kind to have friends who are not somehow involved in the seeder aspects of their organization."

"Noted, but I also believe we have gotten off topic. Back to the Syndicate. What can you tell me?" Prince James reiterated.

"What I can tell you is how things were before the Syndicate rose to power. Before that organization showed up, the underbelly of the city was divided amongst several gangs, street thugs and thieves the lot of them. The gangs kept for the most part to the trade quarter which houses a good part of the city population. From my understanding there were some higher end gangs that were known to also run in parts of the Artisan quarter as well." Callus explained.

"Interesting. Go on." Prince James commented.

"Yes. Well as I was saying, I was much younger back then and was only a fresh soldier in the army at the time. Every now and then the army would get called in if the gangs attacked an influential trader or noble; otherwise, the gangs had the run of the streets in the Trade quarter. We would do what we could but most of the time the gangs would scatter like rats and vanish. We were not equipped to hunt them down or really incentivized to root them out."

"Why is that?" Prince James asked.

"Simple. Money and resources. Most of the army was not trained in man hunts, let alone urban tracking. Most who are skilled in such things are out in the kingdom protecting our borders. We would arrest who we could, but it was minimal. As such, the Row and the neighborhoods around it were dangerous places for our citizens. Deaths were not uncommon, but you cannot extort a dead person, so for the most part the gangs would beat up and even rape those they wanted. The nobles did not care as they stayed away from the Row, and the nobles have always held an attitude of ignoring something if it does not affect them."

"Of course. No surprise there, but I cannot believe my family would stand for such things." Prince James commented.

"Your family can only do so much, but when I was a younger lad your grandfather led a force of royal knights, and purged much of the city and towns of any criminals they could find. The rumor I heard was they were returning from war and your grandfather witnessed a thug assault a baker's wife and no one around would get involved. He could not believe his own citizens would act in such a way. Your grandfather interceded and had the man whipped and flayed in the town square. I am not sure what town, but after that your grandfather spent multiple years going from every town and city bringing capital judgments to the worst he found." Callus explained.

"Good for grandfather. Criminals will not stop if there are no severe consequences for their crimes." Prince James replied.

Prince James heard a version of this story from Sloane. 'Though what I heard from him was that my grandfather and his knights saved Sloane's life. He was an orphan street kid and had a run in with some of the more brutal gang members. The sicko liked to beat kids and do things a child should never have done to them. According to Sloane my grandfather killed the bastard when he beheld the scene. It was a pivotal moment for Sloane that changed his life forever. My grandfather had told Sloane he was brave in trying to help the other kids. In addition, he told the young Sloane boy that he would be welcomed into his royal knights and gave him a royal insignia. Per Sloane, my grandfather honored that promise many years later. I believe it was the only reason the man was allowed to join the knights.'

How much Prince James would've liked to meet his grandfather. The man seemed honorable and a man of action, much like his own grandfathers from his old life. They were the bedrock, along with his uncles that helped to forge him into the man he was today. Sure, his mother and aunts were key as well, it does take a village after all, but there is something about a boy and his grandfather that is a special bond.

Shaking his head, Prince James refocused on Callus and his explanation.

"After your grandfather's purge, the worst criminals were either dead, imprisoned, fled the kingdom, or took up banditry on the outskirts. Our kingdom had a golden age of peace and prosperity. Sure, we had wars that popped up, but the people inside our kingdom were happier than they had been in a long while."

"So, what happened?" Prince James asked genuinely curious at how the gangs reasserted themselves after being broken so thoroughly.

"What else, time and bad politics. As the years passed people forgot what it was like. Several nobles increased their taxes while at the same time advocating for prison reform. They argued that the criminals had served their time and should therefore be released. Those prisons held in such territories released many of their prisoners to save money. Once they were released, most, if not all, went back to what they knew. Many learned new ways to be cruel while in prison. At first the effects across the kingdom started off slow, but it eventually became worse than it was before."

"What of my grandfather?" Prince James inquired.

"I do not know all the details, but what I do know is that he, your father, and uncle were busy dealing with wars to protect the kingdom from outside invaders. It was the perfect opportunity for criminals to take advantage of the distraction."

"So, that's when the Shadow that came along?" Prince James asked.

"Yes, though I do not know the details. No one will talk about how he took over, only that he did, and anyone was foolish enough to cross him ended up dead. To corroborate that sentiment, we found several brutally butchered bodies during what we think was his rise to power." Callus answered.

"Interesting. You have given me much to ponder." Prince James said before realizing they had arrived at the library. They had traversed through most of the Trade quarter as Callus had explained some of the history about crime in the kingdom.

Not realizing that most people tended to steer clear of Muro and Taka allowing them to move rather quickly through the quarter.

Prince James was a bit lost in his thoughts as he entered the city library. 'I will have to ask for a more detailed accounting from Sloane as I am hearing rather large holes in timetables and motivations.'

Chapter 35 – Reading Rainbow

The first thing Prince James thought as he looked around the inside of the city library was 'impressive'. There were multiple floors with winding staircases and wall to wall shelves filled with books.

"I have died and gone to Heaven." Prince James blurted out without thinking.

"Well dearie. You are not in Heaven, but it is rather nice isn't it." A soft older feminine voice said to his right.

"EEKK! I mean ahhh, yea ahhh!" Prince James squealed at first before using a much deeper voice.

'I did not just scream like a little girl, not at all! Wait, how did she sneak up on me? Was I just distracted by the ambiance and majesty of this place?' Prince James thought.

"Now dearie, control your volume while you are in the library. People are reading and studying. Do not be rude." The older feminine voice said to his right.

Turning to look at the woman that had startled him, he saw before him a rather diminutive woman. She was barely five feet tall and looked to be in her 80s or 90s. She had grey hair tied in a tight bun that helped to show off her pointy ears. Her face held laugh lines and there was clear Intelligence and mischief in her eyes. She wore a white robe with reds and browns accenting the stitching.

"I am Silvin, but everyone calls me Silvie. I am the head librarian here. What can I do for you, your Majesty?" Silvie said.

"You know who I am?" Prince James inquired.

"Of course, dearie. First it is hard to not recognize Muro and Taka there..." Silvie leaned in close and whispered, "They stick out like a sore thumb."

"Fair point." Prince James replied before turning to his Sergeant and the two massive knights.

Callus took that as his cue. "Muro, Taka, go stand guard at the entrance outside. The library is heavily warded, so we should be safe within these walls, but just in case having you stationed outside can give us any warning of approaching danger."

"As you command sergeant." Mako saluted.

"Yes Sir." Taka replied.

"Hopefully that will be less of a distraction for those within these walls." Callus said to Silvie.

"Yes, thank you dearie."

After the two knights left, Prince James gave his undivided attention to Silvie.

"Plus, I was at your introductory ball." Silvie continued.

"I do not recall seeing you." Prince James stated with some confusion.

"I doubt you would dearie. I pride myself on being rather quiet and stealthy. Such skills come in great use in working in a library." Silvie explained.

"Hmmm, I guess you'd be right there. I can see the benefits of such skills." Prince James commented.

"Now dearie, what can I do for you?" Silvie asked.

"I finally have a chance to explore so I wanted to come see this place. Plus, I love to read and who doesn't like a good story. Is it possible to check out any of these books?" Prince James said.

Silvie cocked her head to the side. "Of course, you can review any book you want, but something tells me that is not what you mean."

"No, I was asking is it possible to leave with any of these books and return them later?" Prince James asked.

"No, I am afraid that is not something we typically do here. You can request private viewings but those must be scheduled in advance and depending on the books it must be cleared by myself. Usually someone from the library would be present to ensure proper care of the books the whole time. There is also a fee for doing so." Silvie explained.

"Interesting." Prince James replied before looking around at all the shelves filled with books. "I am surprised with how many books are here. It is most impressive for a city library."

"Well, we do have a symbiotic relationship with the Royal Academy." Silvie answered.

"Symbiotic relationship?" James queried.

"Oh yes! All the students come here to study. We work very closely with the Royal Academy to ensure we provide an environment for studying and learning. In return, the library receives a portion of the tuition and funding from the crown. The Royal Academy staff also share parts of their private collections of books to help their students and in turn, they help others in the city too." Silvie explained.

Prince James thought. 'I was surprised to learn that the literacy rate is rather high for the capital. Most children are taught basic letters at a young age. For most it stops there but depending on the trade they take up or their social status, they learn far more.'

"Wow. Most impressive! With that in mind, any recommendations on what to read?" Prince James said.

"Of course. What would you like to learn more about?" Silvie asked.

Prince James knew he needed to understand more of this world's history. "I am rather fascinated with history. Any good books you recommend I start with?"

Silvie's eyes sparkled for a moment. "Follow me."

After her statement she turned on her heels and headed back deeper into the library.

Prince James looked at Callus. His sergeant just shrugged his shoulders. The two men quickly caught up to the diminutive woman who seems rather spry for someone who looked to be a hundred years old.

Silvie led them to a room with a large desk and a few shelves and locked cases. On the desk were several open books. "This is one of our private study rooms. This room in particular is only used by the faculty and royal scholars. It has some restricted books that are quite old." Silvie explained.

"Why are they restricted?" Prince James asked as he took one of the seats across from her.

Silvie got up out of the chair as she pulled out a key from a chain around her neck. "Simple answer is knowledge is power. With that said, several of these books are thousands of years old. They must be handled with care and without context of the writing at the time, many of these books would not be understood."

Silvie opened one of the cases and withdrew a rather large tome and gently placed it on the desk before closing and locking the case back up.

'How is she able to carry that huge thing? She can't weigh much of anything.' Prince James thought as he watched her.

Finally catching back up with what she was saying, Prince James asked a follow up question. "Context?"

"Ah yes dearie, good that you caught that. The events of the time were so well known that many of the books left gaping holes in their subjects as everyone at the time had lived through it. The brain fills in gaps if you do not pay attention." Silvie responded.

"Makes sense. What does that tome tell us?" Prince James asked.

"After enough cross-referencing it tells of the great war for reality itself." Silvie answered.

Seeing Prince James' raised eyebrow, Silvie continued. "What do you know of the origins of the Light and the Dark?"

"Only that the forces of Light and Dark have been battling each other since the beginning of time."

"That is for the most part true, dearie. What you are leaving out is that long ago there was a great war and ever since the Light won the outcome of that war, every other conflict has been a skirmish in comparison." Silvie explained.

"Oh, I do recall reading something about that." Prince James said as he thought, 'This sounds like what I remember learning in Sunday School. Could there be some correlation? This is a whole other world and reality as far as I understand it. Hmmm, this will require more investigation.'

Seeing the prince in deep thought, Silvie paused before steering him back to the subject at hand. "What do you know of the courts of fae?"

"Only that there are two main courts, Summer and Winter." Prince James answered, a little confused in the change of subject.

"Yes, that is true, but do you know what distinguishes each court?" Silvie asked.

"Not really." Prince James answered.

"The fae of the Winter Court are calculating and as cold as their season. Summer fae are full of passion and tend to favor the elements of fire and earth." Callus commented.

Both Prince James and Silvie looked at the sergeant.

"What? That is how it was always described to me." Callus stated.

Silvie raised her hand a gave a 'so so' gesture. "Not too far off. Winter focuses on the mind, battle, and cold hard facts. Typically, they use water, wind, and, at times, darkness elements. As they use logic primarily, many categorize them as cold and calculating. Summer, however, is about passion and life. Their common elements are fire, earth, and some nature magic thrown in there for good measure. In a nutshell, Winter focuses on the mind, and Summer focuses on the heart or soul, depending on one's perspective."

"Those can be diametrically opposed elements and viewpoints." Prince James commented.

"Right, you are dearie. For thousands of years Summer and Winter have not exactly gotten along, but their rivalry runs deeper than opposing elements." Silvie stated.

"Runs deeper? How so?" Prince James asked.

"Winter blames Summer for the outcome of the ancient war, and Summer blames Winter for not doing their part." Silvie stated.

Prince James raised his hand. "Their part? Outcome of the war? I'm confused. Can you back up and start from the beginning?"

“Well, the beginning is too much to cover but I will give you more background. The ancient war between the Light and the Dark first started between angels and demons. Their battles were brutal, and it was only a matter of time before some of the older races chose sides.” Silvie paused as she opened the tome to a page showing angels and demons fighting.

Silvie turned the page, it showed demons approaching what Prince James assumed were Summer and Winter fae along with what looked to be genies. “Winter refused to get involved. The Winter Queen saw little reason in risk her people in the conflict. She was logical, perhaps the Winter Queen calculated the odds and realized the demons would not win. No one knows for sure except the Winter Queen herself, but what we do know is she ordered her court to abstain from the war.”

“I doubt either side was a fan of that.” Prince James commented.

“Indeed. Even though the demons were filled with rage, they were smart. They realized the demons needed to play to their strengths and decided to focus on beings with strong passions and emotions. Rather than approach the Summer Queen, the demons recruited some of the djinn children, those who were young and arrogant who thought they knew better than the older generation. The demons played on their egos and convinced them they deserved better than their lot in life. When the djinn joined the fray, the war started to shift in the demons’ favor. Having such success with the younger djinn, the demons did not approach the Summer Queen, and instead began to appeal to the younger Summer fae and their passions. Soon the court decided to throw their lot in with the Dark.”

“Summer joined the Dark?!” Prince James asked in surprise. He always envisioned Summer as being lighthearted and would’ve expected them to join the Light.

Silvie raised her hand. “Not all of Summer joined but several of us did.”

“Us?!”

“Yes dearie, I am half Summer fae, unlike Lady Firebrand who is full fae. What I can tell you is that it was our greatest regret.”

“But how did they win them over?! Which ones abstained?” Prince James asked.

“Please dearie. You must know that it is easy to manipulate emotions and convince someone to abandon what is good for them because you have stirred their heart to such an extent. To answer your other question, the oldest of the Summer fae most attuned to life and nature abstained. They could not go against their court, but they were wise enough to see the folly of what their people were doing.” Silvie answered.

“That is true about using people’s emotions to manipulate them. At least some of Summer did not get involved.” Prince James answered. He felt genuine sadness for some reason hearing that Summer sided with the Dark. ‘Why am I feeling so sad from this story? Maybe because I know it won’t end well?’

“The universe was young, we, like the djinn, were a bit full of ourselves. Our king argued against such actions but as the young think they know better than the old, they could not be swayed from their choices.” Silvie continued.

“Your King?” Prince James perked up. This was the first time he ever heard of a fae king.

“Yes, Oberon. He was king of the Summer and Winter Courts, along with the djinn. He loved to hunt, create new things, and to craft. Oberon was the greatest of us. Many of the other races respected him for his skills and his fairness. He taught the elves to hunt and live within the forests. The dwarves learned much from Oberon when their fledgling race came to be during this dark time. He taught them to work the earth and how to mine and forge. I think the dwarves more than even the elves would spend as much time as they could learning from Oberon.” Silvie explained.

“Is that why the dwarves love to craft so much?” Prince James asked.

“Yes, Oberon helped them find purpose and a love for creation. It was that love that led the dwarves to join the Light in the war. The elves forever split, some joining the Light and others the Dark.” Silvie continued.

“How did Oberon handle that? Dwarves on one side. Summer fae and djinn on the other. Elves split between both.” Prince James asked.

“The Winter Queen implored him to not join the fight, that any side he chose would forever upset the other. Oberon heeded Winter’s advice and abstained. It is rumored that it broke his heart to do so.” Silvie said with what sounded like sadness in her voice.

“I can imagine. It is the worst when families fight.” Prince James commented as he recalled his own children when they would disagree on something.

“Yes dearie. But the war turned to Light’s favor when the dragons joined the angels. They have always been guardians and guides, well at least they used to be. I am getting off track, where was I? Oh yes. Shortly after the dragons threw their full might in with the Light, the Dark fell, and when I say fell, they fell hard.”

“I remember reading something about that in a history book at the cottage.” Prince James commented as he recalled what he read.

“The demons and some of the other members of the Dark were banished but the others that sided with them had to pay a terrible price. The queen of the djinn begged for leniency. Her pleas fell on deaf ears. The angels wanted to strike down the djinn and the fae both.”

“All the fae?” Prince James asked.

“Yes dearie. The angels did not take kindly to Winter and some in the Summer court abstaining. They wanted to remove fae from existence. When the things seemed the bleakest, our king came to our rescue.” Silvie answered.

“How so?” Prince James asked in rapt attention.

“I am getting to that dearie. Oberon offered his life in place of his people.” Silvie said as she started to get choked up. “Can you imagine it? Loving your people so much that you would pay their price. This time the plea was heard, and Oberon was struck down.” Silvie said as a tear fell from her cheek.

Prince James pulled out a handkerchief and handed it to her. Silvie took it and dabbed her tears. “T-thank you dearie. I still have a hard time with this. So much changed for so many with that one act. Those djinns were bound in service, their power to never be used for selfish purposes again. Their queen shackled and forever bound. Summer was cast out of Avalon, to live among the races we had betrayed.”

“What about Winter?” James asked.

“For their lack of action, their penance has been to fight and hold the line against the Dark and those who seek to invade our reality. The Light can be poetic at times. The Winter Queen buried her grief in war, and to this day she has never forgiven Summer for the loss of her love. What the Winter Queen does not know is that Queen Tatiana has never forgiven herself either." Silvie explained, clear sorrow in her voice.

"How sad. So much suffering from the wrong choices, but that is the way of life." Prince James commented.

"Yes, but even in tragedy something good can come of it. An angel came to the Summer Court to deliver a message. God was impressed by Oberon's sacrifice. Such a selfless act was to be rewarded. Oberon was to be reborn." Silvie said with renewed hope in her voice.

"Reborn? Did it happen?" Prince James asked with clear anticipation in his voice.

"We were told it would happen but not when. The angel said that if it was too soon then the sacrifice would have little meaning." Silvie explained.

"But has it not been thousands of years? If it was to happen, you would think it would've happened already." Prince James inquired.

Silvie chuckled a bit. "I think that is the point."

"Huh?" Callus asked in confusion.

"If you knew exactly when something would happen, do you really learn what it means to have faith? The Light will always give you a path to redemption even when the Dark lies to you that such a thing is impossible. There have been a few potential hopefuls over the past several thousands of years." Silvie explained.

"Really? What happened to them?" Callus asked the question before Prince James could.

"They have either been brought before one of the queens. The outcome has always been the same. Summer in her fury kills the candidate for daring to get her hope up. Winter is far crueler; she sends them to the front line of the fight with little to no support to be torn apart by things that dwell outside our reality. Neither are a fate I would wish on anyone." Silvie solemnly stated.

“You have given me much to think about. Thank you for sharing such an important story. If you will excuse me Silvie but I have other matters, I must attend to. Hopefully I can return at another time, and you can tell me more about this world’s history.” Prince James said as he stood and bowed before leaving.

“Sire, why did you want to leave so abruptly?” Callus asked once they exited the private viewing room.

“I don’t exactly know. I just felt like someone had walked over my grave. Not sure you noticed how intensely Silvie was staring at me. It felt like she was looking for something. Either way, felt it was time to leave.” Prince James said as he walked quickly towards the library exit.

Godfrey and Tina both reached out to Prince James via **Party Link**.

“Master are you alright?” Godfrey asked.

“We both sensed your unease, Supreme One.” Tina explained.

“I am fine, do not concern yourself. It was nothing. Let me speak with Sloane. I have questions for him.” James answered.

“Understood Master, we will not dare to bother you further.” Godfrey replied.

Prince James shook his head as he reached out via Party Link. *“Sloane.”*

“Yes, your Majesty?” Sloane replied telepathically.

Prince James got right to what he wanted Sloane to work on. *“Find out what you can about the head librarian.”*

“Silvie?” Sloane replied in confusion.

“Yes, you know her?” Prince James asked.

“Let me tell you of the story of when I arrived in the capital...” Sloane began before Prince James interrupted as he exited the library.

“Hold that thought.” Prince James interrupted.

Prince James’ brain finally caught up to what seemed off. “Callus, where is Taka and Maruko?”

"I do not know Sire. They should be here guarding the doors. It is not like them to abandon their post." Callus replied as he looked around for some signs of the two knights.

SWISH!

Prince James immediately dodged back, barely avoiding an arrow to the face.

"We want him alive you fool." A cloaked figure said to another cloaked figure wielding a long bow.

"Eh, I should still get points if he dies." The cloaked figure with the long bow replied.

Both men, along with a third cloaked figure walked out of the alley between two buildings across the street from the library.

"This is not some game you fool, quit your weird speech. Why I got paired with you I do not know." The first cloaked figure said as he threw a few vials.

"Stand back your highness!" Callus said as he stepped in front of the prince and slashed at the vials with his drawn sword.

The vials shattered when his blade connected. Instantly the contents of the shattered vials spread like a fog that surrounded Sergeant Callus and Prince James.

Callus started to cough. "Cough, it is dousing powder! Cough, it closes off your energy pathways and... and can, cause... you... to... pass... out." Callus barely said the last part before collapsing into unconsciousness.

THUD

TING, TING

Sergeant Thorn's body collapsed to the street and his sword skidded across part of the street.

Prince James took a deep breath just before the powdery mist hit him. 'Great, no magic, they must've done their homework. Luckily, I have **Enhanced Breath Control**. That should give me a few minutes of oxygen to deal with these jerks.'

Enhanced Breath Control

<u>Description</u>: Increases length user can hold their breath. Allows user to supplement Stamina for oxygen to keep the body going until Stamina runs out. Stamina consumption increases over time.

Prince James unsheathed his sword and charged the two cloaked figures.

“He’s got guts, I’ll give him that.” The first cloaked figure said.

The other cloaked figure not carrying a bow drew a short sword and charged the prince.

“Yea but not that smart.” The cloaked archer said as they began to rapidly fire arrows at the prince.

James dodged each arrow with a quick bend of his body or twist of his blade causing an arrow to veer off.

The cloaked figure with a short sword met the prince with a quick slash to his face.

Prince James quickly parried the blow while bending his body to dodge another arrow directed at his heart.

James did not wait for another arrow and backhanded the cloaked figure he was fighting causing the person to stagger. Moving with lightning speed Prince James buried his backup dagger in the cloaked figure’s chest, killing them instantly.

Sensing more arrows on their way, James let go of the dagger and adjusted his position, so the now dead cloaked figure took the arrows instead. Unfortunately, this caused the prince to lose his dagger as the body dropped to the floor.

“Why is this fool not going down?!” The cloaked archer exclaimed as he picked up his pace and began to back up.

The second cloaked figure withdrew two blades, one a shortsword, the other a long dagger. “It matters not, he cannot use his magic! Keep up the pressure and I will take him down!”

The cloaked figure’s blades began to glow a sickly green that gave James a feeling of wrongness.

‘That can’t be good.’ James thought as the swordsman darted to the side and then slashed at James.

On instinct James cast a wind spell called **Repulse**. The wind smacked the cloaked swordsman completely off guard and right in the face. The figure flew back in the air, flipping end over end until they slammed into a nearby building wall.

Repulse
<u>Description</u>: *Wind magic attack, blunted with a focus on quick intense burst of air to push back the target. Minimal to no bludgeoning damage. Spell can be channeled for sustained effect.*

‘Maybe the magic dampening effect hasn’t started yet?’ Prince James thought as he realized his magic should not be working.

“I thought you said he wouldn’t be able to use his magic?!” The cloaked archer called out as they continued to back up as James ran at them.

The cloaked swordsman shook their head, trying to remove the dazed effect they felt. As they stood, they replied, “He should not be able to! Once dousing powder touches the skin it is unavoidable. If one breathes it in, they knock out rather quickly.” The cloaked swordsman pointed to the unconscious sergeant.

“Well, I don’t really care about your fancy powder! Get over here and help me with this psycho!” The cloaked archer said right before they had to quickly dodge a slash from Prince James.

“You want to see psycho?! I can show you psycho!” James roared as he slashed again, this time kicking the archer right after the cloaked figure dodged.

The cloaked swordsman arrived just in time to parry a follow-up blow from Prince James, saving the archer’s life.

“Get up you fool!” The cloaked swordsman called out to his companion as he performed a follow up slash causing Prince James to quickly dodge and back up.

The swordsman was fast and strong, easily keeping up with James’ attacks.

The cloaked archer slowly got to his feet. “The kid hits like a Mac truck! Give me a minute.”

Those words caught James off guard, allowing the swordsman to get in a good slash to James’ right arm. Worse, James felt like something was attacking him from within.

“It matters not. That poison will cripple him soon enough!” The swordsman said with vicious glee as they increased their attacks.

The archer pulled a dagger of their own and charged into the fight.

‘Well, I don’t know what is going on, but I better apply as much strength and speed as I can before whatever they cut me with takes effect.’ Prince James thought in a panic.

Prince James began to apply more of his power to his swings, moving faster and faster, hitting harder and harder, allowing him to keep up with both attackers.

“I thought you said you poisoned him!” The once cloaked archer said in exasperation.

“I did!” The cloaked swordsman said a bit out of breath as they were struggling more and more trying to time keeping up with the prince’s attacks.

James moved in with a feint and caught the out of breath swordsman with a sharp knee kick knocking him back.

CRACK!

“AHHH! The bastard cracked my ribs!” The cloaked swordsman exclaimed in pain.

“Told you he hits like a Mac Truck!” The second cloaked figure said.

“I do not know what you say half the time you fool. I have no idea what a ‘Mac truck’ is.” The swordsman wheezed out.

The swordsman being slower prevented them from interceding when James punched the cloaked archer lifting him in the air before James turned to slash hard at the follow up attack from the swordsman.

Using the momentum from the blow to roll back to where the downed archer was, the cloaked swordsman winced as he came back to his feet. "AH! It is time we left... Now!"

The cloaked swordsman dropped another vial and smoke filled the alley they were fighting in.

With a quick use of **Repulse,** the wind cleared the smoke in the alley. The two cloaked figures were gone along with the body of the third. As Prince James scanned the area just in case, he saw Muro and Taka sleeping in a heap in the corner further into the alley.

"My liege, are you alright? You went quiet." Sloane said telepathically.

"Master! I sensed your unease increase, what has happened?!" Tina asked.

"I am fine. Though my guards may need some medical attention. I am healing my wounds now."

"Wounds?!" Godfrey and Tina both exclaimed before the two of them and Sloane appeared right next to Prince James.

Apparently, Godfrey was with Sloane and Tina discussing plans for Sanctuary when Prince James contacted Sloane. At first, they thought nothing of Prince James' abrupt cut off the conversation as he had just been talking about a librarian and he said not to worry. Figuring James was just frazzled about the conversation, so they dismissed the uneasy feelings they were receiving from their master.

Rather than explaining what happened, Prince James decided to try something different and sent the last few moments of the fight through **Party Link**.

"That is most convenient way of sharing information Supreme One." Tina said.

"Pick up my guards and make sure they are ok. They were hit with something they called dousing powder." Prince James ordered.

"Dousing powder!" Sloane exclaimed.

"Yes, that is what they said." James answered.

"Then how were you able to still use magic?!" Sloane asked.

"Guess it didn't hit me."

"The images you shared; it looked like you were hit. Dousing powder is one of the most dangerous compounds to anyone who uses magic. The only beings I know who are immune are beings with fully developed magical cores like dragons, elder fae, or archimages at the pinnacle of their power."

'Well, I am a dragon. I might have to tell Sloane that at some point but let's hold off on that now.' James thought as he realized why the powder had no effect on him. Then another realization hit. "You mean I could've used more magic?! I would've wiped the floor with them. Good to know next time. Luckily both Godfrey and Tina have magical cores.'

Prince James changed subjects. "Let's sort that out later. Sloane go with Godfrey in taking my knights back to the palace."

"But my liege, you should not remain here. Especially after you were just attacked!" Sloane protested.

"Fine. You investigate the area, and I will go back with Godfrey and Tina." James answered.

That seemed to placate Sloane as he bowed. "Thank you, my liege."

Poof!

James, Godfrey, and Tina teleported back to Prince James's wing in the palace.

"Why did you acquiesce so easily Master?" Tina asked.

Telepathically he said, "I wanted the three of us to talk. I believe one of my attackers was from my world!"

Epilogue

Back in the City Library

"What do you think Silvie?" Lady Firebrand said as she walked out of the shadow in the private viewing room.

"It is possible. I can see what it is you sensed, but it is as if something is hidden." Silvie replied.

"Yes, perhaps his soul is waiting for something. One thing is for sure, Queen Tatiana will want to meet him." Lady Firebrand stated.

"Delay it as long as you can my lady. If he is not the one, she will surlily strike him down. The kingdom would go to war with the Summer court over it." Silvie commented.

"Perhaps. I will delay as much as I can, but it is clear he loves to create and craft as he did. My spies tell me the dwarves are quite taken with him too. These signs cannot be ignored." Lady Firebrand explained.

"Yes, but my **Soul Sight** says something is missing, it is hard to explain. It could be as I said his soul is waiting for something or it could be he is not the one." Silvie pleaded. She liked what she saw of the prince so far and worried what would happen should Queen Tatiana strike him down.

"As I said, I will delay it as best I can, but I am not the only Summer fae in the kingdom. It is only a matter of time before our queen hears of him and will demand an audience." Lady Firebrand replied.

Trying a different tactic, Silvie asked. "What of Winter? She is not exactly the forgiving type and will not be pleased if Summer gets her hands on him."

"My loyalty is to Summer. Winter is not my concern." Lady Firebrand stated.

"You know it is more complicated than that. All the signs point to the Dark being on the move. What if he is part of their plans?" Silvie said.

"Summer would not fall for Dark's machinations twice. If he is part of their plans, I will strike him down myself!" Lady Firebrand adamantly replied.

“Fair enough, my lady. I will take care of the testing of this.” Silvie held up Prince James’ handkerchief. “If it proves positive...”

Lady Firebrand interrupted, “Then I will have no choice but to take him to Queen Tatiana myself. Do not rush your test. If his soul is waiting for something, we should help him discover it first.”

Silvie nodded in agreement. “I cannot put my finger on it, perhaps he needs a catalyst to bring it out.”

“War is coming, it is only a matter of time. Nothing has proven a greater catalyst than fighting for one’s life and the lives of others.” Lady Firebrand stated before exiting the room.

Lady Firebrand too liked the prince, in fact she really was fond of him, but her duty to her court had to come first. The only thing that would trump that would be the promise she made to the angel when he delivered the message their Oberon would one day be reborn. She gave her oath that should the Dark use a false Oberon she would strike him down. It was her commitment and thanks for the Light one day giving them back their king, the one she could never deny.

Shaking off her conflicting thoughts. “That is a worry for another day. I must prepare for the new school year. Perhaps I can use my class to help find this catalyst Silvie speaks of.”

Arcum Estate

The Heavily armored solider went flying into the wall.

CRASH!

“Well done my son! Well done!” Duke Arcum exclaimed after his son Josh defeated yet another skilled warrior.

After removing his helmet, Josh ran his gloved fingers through his hair. “It was nothing father. Though you must find better opponents for me to face, or I will not improve.”

“Yes, yes. The man you just beat was one of the better defenders in the kingdom.” Duke Arcum commented.

“Ha, he was nothing!” Josh Arcum roared with power from the anger still flowing through his veins. “I want a shot at that good for nothing joke of a prince!”

“Ha, ha, ha! Yes, my son, soon enough. While you are at the academy you will have plenty of opportunities to spar against the young prince, and accidents do tend to happen. Ha, ha, ha!” Duke Arcum chuckled.

“The whole ball I could not even get close to Ria! That weakling monopolized her time and then she left shortly after!” Josh said as he picked up the unconscious warrior and threw him across the room into another wall.

“Yes, even that pompous Duke Rodchester was not himself during the ball. Though he is no fool, he knows his only path to power is in our faction! Do not worry son, Ria shall be yours. Your union with Ria will forever solidify our noble future!” Duke Arcum commented.

“Do not worry father, I spoke with several of the noble heirs, they will come to our side even if their parents do not!” Josh had a cruel smile on his face.

“Yes, perhaps some of those parents just might need to retire sooner than later. We are too close to success to tolerate any interference now.” Duke Arcum shared his son’s cruel smile.

As the defender slowly got to his feet, “You two are mad! You did not pay me enough to betray my oath to the Adventurers’ guild!”

Faster than the defender could track, Josh closed the distance.

SHWEEN

Without a second thought, Josh separated the head of the defender, the wet thumping sound is all that was heard as the head rolled away.

THUNK, THUNK, THUNK

“Well done my son!” Duke Arcum said as he clapped his son on the shoulder before turning to the servant in the corner. “Clean this mess up! My son defended himself against the defender who could not take losing to my son’s skills. Is that not, right?”

"Y-y-yes, your grace! Right away, your grace!" The sniveling servant said before rushing out of the room to get help to remove the body and clean up the mess.

"Yet another clean kill! You are honing your killer instinct well my son. Keep that up when you are at the academy. Fear is the most useful way of ruling. They will flock to your banner, and we will use the younger generation to get rid of anyone from the current generation who disagrees with our plans. He, he, he! Come let us eat, you have to keep up your strength!" Duke Arcum chuckled as he and his son exited the training hall as several scared servants entered with buckets and mops.

Some Unknown Location

Several hooded individuals in dark robes sat around a table reviewing reports from recent events. One of the hooded figures dropped his fist on the table in frustration.

SLAM!

"That pompous upstart! We should have never put our faith in that two-bit necromancer!" The cloaked figure that slammed his fist on the table exclaimed.

A different figure commented. "Surely the arrogant prince can be used to our advantage."

"Yes! He is young and full of emotions. Such a thing is easy to prey on and manipulate." A third one stated.

"Agreed, the necromancer was a test. It is clear he is a capable fighter. Which is what we require. When war comes to the continent, he will facilitate much death." A fourth cloaked figure chimed in.

The second cloaked figure asked. "What of our efforts in Helios?"

"They are fully under our control now." This statement seemed to calm the first cloaked figure down as he smiled at the thought of how easily they were able to manipulate those zealots.

"Zealots are even easier to manipulate than upstart princes." The fourth cloaked figure stated.

"Yes, they have been conquering lands left and right." Another cloaked figure chimed in.

"True, it does not matter how we get there only that suffering is felt across the land. Only then can the gateways be opened." The final cloaked figure sitting at the head of the table finally spoke up.

"Yes! Then we will be gods among men!" The first cloaked figure exclaimed in excitement.

"All in good time. All in good time. Inform the spider god to move forward with the next phase of our plan." The cloaked figure at the head of the table ordered.

"Do we really have to deal with her? We cannot trust her." The second cloaked figure commented.

"No, we do not have to trust her to get what we want out of her. She has her own machinations, but that still serves our purposes just fine." The cloaked figure at the head of the table answered.

"Understood." The second cloaked figure replied.

"Do not forget we are part of a larger effort to destabilize and open rifts everywhere we can. One way or another, we will have our prize." The cloaked figure at the head of the table stated.

End of I Got Isekai'd as A Dragon Book 1 – Am I In an Anime

Characters

Character	Description
Prince James (MC)	Smart, quick to action. Does plan but mostly follows his gut and heart. Transported to another world. Not sure if the Light or the Dark brought him as he was too busy moving forward with his new life.
King Gerald Drake	Father to Prince James and Aurora. King of the Kingdom of Aerouant (word for dragon). Talented warrior and battle mage. Expertise in Fire and Earth magic.
Queen Sophia	Mother to Prince James and Aurora. Queen of the Kingdom of Aerouant. Talented healer and water mage
Princess Lily Aurora Drake	Named after Queen Titania's daughter Aurora. Due to this, everyone calls her Aurora instead of Lily. Younger sister to Prince James. Princess to the Kingdom of Aerouant. Still being tutored and learning magic. Loves her brother dearly.
John & Susan	Famous adventurers who retired to raise Prince James. Among the few people who knew the prophecy regarding Prince James. Their memories and knowledge have been transferred to Prince James. Both known for their unmatched skills in magic and combat.
Reginald 'Reggie' Spears	Captain of the Kingdom of Aerouant's Royal Knights. Son to Duke Spears. Famous for getting faster and stronger as a battle continues.
Marcus Drake (General of the Army)	Younger brother to King Gerald. Duke and General of Kingdom of Aerouant's army. Talented warrior and battle mage. Stronger with Earth than Fire.
High Priest Cendrin	Leader of the Church of Light (the main religion in the Kingdom of Aerouant). Smart and shrewd man. True believer in prophecy.

Duke Rupert Spears	Duke of the Kingdom of Aerouant. Leader of the Traditionalist Noble Faction. Sits on the board for the Royal Academy.
Royal Court Magician & Headmaster Lady Rollara	Leader of the Royal Court Magicians. Greatest healer of the kingdom. Also, the Headmaster for the Royal Academy. Personal tutor for Princess Aurora. Sister to Lady Lara the prophetess, the person who had the vision regarding Prince James.
Lady Lara (Seer & Prophetess)	Older sister to Lady Rollara. Most talented prophetess the kingdom had ever seen. Died shortly after telling the King, Queen, and Lady Rollara the prophecy regarding Prince James.
Mrs. Teege the Seamstress	Short older human tailor. Kind and matronly. Very particular about style and traditions when it comes to how one dresses. Best seamstress in the capital.
Royal Knight Daria	Daria is a human royal knight who specializes in body enhancement magic and magical shields. Personal bodyguard to Princess Aurora
Illyrian (Archery Instructor)	Elf male. Skilled archer who works closely with the Royal Knights. Instructor at the Royal Academy. Conducted the archery test as part of Prince James' Royal Academy private entrance exam
Saffron (Alchemy Instructor)	Gnome male. Instructor at the Royal Academy. Conducted the alchemy test as part of Prince James' Royal Academy private entrance exam
Krag (Blacksmithing Instructor)	Dwarf male. Instructor at the Royal Academy. Conducted the crafting test as part of Prince James' Royal Academy private entrance exam
Sir Lexington Arthur Simmons (LT. Simmons)	LT. Simmons in the royal knight ranks. He is the leader of Prince James' personal royal knights and magicians. Comes from a barony on the outskirts of the kingdom. Excellent melee fighter. Strong in body enhancement magic.

Mira Nightshade	Sharp and quick-witted. Excellent small blades master. Possesses sone stealth and interrogation skills. Daughter to Lady Minerva Nightshade. Sergeant in the royal guard. One of Prince James' personal guards. Leader of the Stalker Squad. Gives James a bit 'Yandere' vibes.
Sloane (The Shadow)	Highest skilled rogue in the royal guard. Known to associate with all people, including ones associated with illegal activities, this has led to many in the royal guard not trusting him. Part of Prince James' Stalker Squad. Acts as Prince James' spymaster. Is secretly, the one known as 'The Shadow', leader of the underground crime organization called the Syndicate.
Leonard Phillips	Jack of all skills ability holder. Member of the royal guard. Part of Stalker Squad. Is average in ALL skills including healing magic, making him Prince James' perfect utility resource. Used to be looked down on due to his average skills until Prince James helped people realize how useful he could be.
Rita	Was part of the Kingdom's army as a scout and archer. Became one of Prince James' royal bodyguards. Part of both Stalker Squad and Tempest Squad. Possesses multiple skills and magic related to archery, scouting, and wilderness survival. Best archer in the kingdom.
Kira Lighthope	Healer and devout believer of the Church of Light. Sergeant in the royal guard. Leads Prince James' royal court magician Tempest Squad. Went to the Royal Academy with Anara Rane and Aeria Chemos, her fellow squad mates.

Anara Rane the frost battle mage	Royal Court Magician. One of the strongest battle mages in the kingdom. Very cold and calculating due to latent winter fey heritage. Specializes in water and ice magic, earning her the moniker the Frost Battle Mage. Member of the Tempest Squad. Went to the Royal Academy with Kira Lighthope and Aeria Chemos.
Aeria Chemos wind mage	Royal Court Magician. One of the strongest wind and support mages in the kingdom. Care-free, flirty attitude. Member of the Tempest Squad. Went to the Royal Academy with Kira Lighthope and Anara Rane.
Sergeant Callus Thorn	Sergeant in the Royal Guards. Leader of Prince James' Bulwark Squad. Strong in body enhancement magic. Excellent tank and melee fighter. Once of the trainers of the royal guard due to his 'drill-sergeant' nature. Stickler for rules and protocols. Rose up through the ranks of the army first giving him many war stories of the trenches.
Cooper Cavaliere	Royal Guard. Member of the Bulwark Squad. Comes from a long line of mounted-combat warriors. Not the 'sharpest tool in the shed' and tends to take things at face value. Does not understand sarcasm at all. Loyal and kind, believes in chivalry.
Taka Anella (female knight)	Royal Guard. Member of the Bulwark Squad. Strong in body enhancement magic and tanking skills. Tall and muscular. Quiet but observant. Very dedicated to honing her combat skills to be of service to the kingdom.
Muro (tank)	Part giant. Member of the Bulwark Squad. Very large and tall with natural resistance to melee damage. Possesses body enhancement magic and is known as the best defender in the royal guard. Has the nickname of 'Gentle Giant'.

Lady Minerva Nightshade	Mother to Mira Nightshade. Member of the Traditionalist faction. Sharp wit and cunning mind. Her family has one of the best information networks in the kingdom. Excellent knowledge of poisons and subterfuge. Has winter fey heritage many generations in the past. Friend to Lady Felora Firebrand even though she is Summer fey.
Lady Spears	Wife to Duke Spears and mother of Captain Spears. Warm and kind. Cannot stand the rift between her husband and son. Excellent skills in navigating the various noble factions in the kingdom. Uses those skills to help her son and husband.
Lady Felora Firebrand	Summer Fey. Holds nobility title in both the Kingdom of Aerouant and the fey Summer Court. Strong Fire mage and magic instructor for the Royal Academy. Pretends to be uninterested in politics and only interested in magic. In truth she is cunning and is one of Queen Titania's key agents.
Head Librarian Silvie	Half-Summer fey. Intelligent and has a strong thirst for knowledge. Honorable and loyal to the fey Summer court. Friend to Lady Felora Firebrand.
Duke Rodchester	Leader of the Rodchester duchy. One of the leaders of the Noble faction. Father to Ria Rodchester. Family known for gryphon riders and a key part of the kingdom's air superiority.
Ria Rodchester	Daughter and heir to Duke Rodchester. Talented mage. Starting the Royal Academy same year as Prince James.
Leah of House Moore	Retainer and friend to Ria Rodchester. Friend to Nikki Orelia. The House Moore are part of the Rodchester faction.
Nikki of House Orelia	Retainer and friend to Ria Rodchester. Friend of Leah Moore. The House Orelia are a loyal part of the Rodchester faction.

Duke Arcum	Leader of the Arcum duchy. One of the leaders of the Noble faction. Father to Josh Arcum. The family is known for their strong soldiers and sailors. Some of the wealthier port cities of the kingdom are in the Arcum duchy.
Josh Arcum	Son and heir to Duke Arcum. Cruel and sadistic. Cares only for power and wealth. Skilled warrior and swordsman. Strong in body enhancement magic. Not as strong in other magics.
Galdren	World renown master Dwarven blacksmith and blade maker. One of the leaders of the kingdom's blacksmiths. Loyal to Prince James. Boisterous and full of life. Loves alcohol and his craft.
Godfrey Hiraeth	Humanoid werewolf/dragon hybrid created to be Prince James' personal butler and attaché. Master in space and gravity magic. Loyal and worships his creator, Prince James. Dotes on his master yet stoic and proper around others. Intelligent and imparted with all the knowledge on local customs and protocols.
Tina Tarrasque	Humanoid tarrasque/dragon hybrid created to be Prince James' personal maid and seneschal. Made to be a living siege weapon in large scale battles. Cunning, cold, fiercely loyal and protective of her creator, Prince James. Master in small blades combat. High stealth skills with the ability to blend into the background.
Dunham	Dwarf craftsman friend of Galdren who specializes in armor. Holds a friendly rivalry with Galdren. World renown master blacksmith specializing in armor.
Neaman	Elf master tailor and enchanter. Seen as a master in his craft. Sought out by nobles and the wealthy. Has no interest in politics, only the purity of his work.

Anduin and Marcia	Elderly humans, master jewel-cutters and jewelers.
Pierre	Gnome master alchemist. Lover, not a fighter.
Dolores	Dwarf helper at the ladies' baths in the realm Prince James created known as Sanctuary. Strong-willed, kind, and nurturing. Excellent cook and leads the cooks living in Sanctuary.
Stormstout	Dwarf Master Miner and geomancer. Runs one of the most prosperous mining companies in the kingdom.
King Hiroshi	King of the Beast Tribe Alliance, one of the larger countries on the continent. Cunning ruler and warrior. Strong believer in honor and the code of a beast warrior. Father to Princess Zenka. Despises the Helios Dominion due to their slavery practices.
Princess Zenka	Kitsune beastkin. Princess and heir to the Beast Tribe Alliance. Her birth was seen as a good omen. Beast tribes revere and honor kitsune, seeing them as wise guides. Strong in lightning magic.
Attachés Shirken & Marook	Attachés and personal bodyguards to King Hiroshi and Princess Zenka. Strong warriors who follow a strict code.
Wise woman Zarusha	Personal advisor to King Hiroshi and mentor to Princess Zenka. Revered as the greatest wise woman the beast tribes have seen in several generations.
Pirate King Rohan	Pirate King of the Isles of Terresia. Greatest sailor of his people. Screwed, cunning, and full of life. Cares for his people and dotes on his daughter and heir Kiyana. Excellent swordsman.
Jaden	Brother to Pirate King Rohan. Dotes on his niece Kiyana. Likes to tease his brother. Not as skilled sailor as his brother but a fierce and brutal melee fighter.
Glenroy	Part of the Isles of Terresia delegation to the Kingdom of Aerouant. Personal

	bodyguard to Pirate King Rohan and Princess Kiyana.
Kiyana (Rohan's daughter)	Daughter and heir to Pirate King Rohan. Excellent sailor and swordsman. Smart, cunning, excellent negotiator and loves her people and the sea.
Behat from Feuhari delegation	Feuhari Ambassador to the Kingdom of Aerouant. Cunning and opportunistic. Tends to play multiple angles for personal gain. Father to Mikko.
Mikko (Daughter to the ambassador)	Daughter to the Feuhari Ambassador. Passionate, spoiled, and very interested in Prince James. Doted on by her father.

Afterword

I wanted to thank you fellow Travelers for reading my second book. This creation is a labor of love. I started writing out of love for fantasy and science fiction but that has grown into a joy of finding ways to remind all of us that we matter and are here for a reason. Hopefully you will continue this journey with me. I Got Isekai'd as A Dragon series is part of a larger universe called the Omniverse. The universe I am creating will span several stories and take us all on a journey of adventure and discovery.

I also wanted to take this time to thank my family and friends who have been supportive through the good and rough times. My family came here with nothing, they talked funny and prayed differently than others, but they came together and helped each other rise. Their stories have inspired me to create and pursue my own calling.

"We are not meant to live this life alone. We are more alike than different; we just have to look past the surface." That fundamental truth has always stuck with me and is a part of my writing. My hope is you will enjoy these stories and find something in them that speaks to you.

If you like these words or enjoy these stories, please leave a positive five-star review, it does make all the difference.

About the Author

ItalianDragon has a love for all things creative from art to fantasy, science fiction, and anime. Writing with a belief we are all more similar than different and just have to look for the similarities. Coming from an immigrant family who taught him the importance of self-accountability, critical thinking, and looking out for one another. You are bound to find such relatable reminders in his writing. ItalianDragon enjoys including cultural, popular, and nerd references to add to the humor and fun easter eggs we can all relate to.

Please click the link to follow the author on Amazon.
https://www.amazon.com/author/italiandragon

Groups

If you enjoyed this book, please check out www.amazon.com/litrpg to find other books in the LitRPG genre.

I am also thankful for the different groups out there such as LitRPG, LitRPG Books and LitRPG & Gamelit readers, Gamelit Society, and Progression Fiction Addicts. The authors and community within these groups have been very welcoming, inspirational, and supportive. If you like role playing games or similar type video game mechanics, I highly encourage you to come check us out.

www.ingramcontent.com/pod-product-compliance
Lightning Source LLC
LaVergne TN
LVHW010633110826
845149LV00014B/2836

9798990741324